A LEGITIMATE BUSINESSMAN

DALE M. NELSON

Severn River
PUBLISHING

Severn River Publishing
www.SevernRiverPublishing.com

ISBN: 978-1-64875-165-3 (Paperback)
ISBN: 978-1-64875-166-0 (Hardback)

ALSO BY DALE M. NELSON

The Gentleman Jack Burdette Series

A Legitimate Businessman

The School of Turin

Once a Thief

Proper Villains

The Bad Shepherd

Never miss a new release!

Sign up to receive exclusive updates from author Dale M. Nelson.

SevernRiverPublishing.com/Dale-M-Nelson

As a thank you for signing up, you'll receive a free copy of *The Robber,* a Gentleman Jack Burdette short story.

1

They crouched in the dark, waiting for the signal.

Once they were inside, they had five minutes to clear the place out. After that, the risk of exposure was too high.

Jack looked at his watch again. Ten minutes until go time.

It had been three hours in a room with no light, breathing hot, stale air that was filled with the dust they'd kicked up. Waiting was the hardest part of any job; it sapped the nerves and played with the mind. Idle hands might be the devil's playground, but a nervous mind could be absolute hell. And that was when you could see.

"Hit the light," Jack said.

Gaston Broussard carried an LED camping lantern in his backpack. He set it on the ground and activated it, filling part of the room with a ghostly white glow. It wasn't much, but they could see the wall, and that was all they needed. In planning, they talked about bringing extra lights, extra batteries so they weren't sitting in the dark for so long, but Jack overruled it. The more gear you bring in, the more you have to bring out, the less room you have for the take. And they already had a concrete saw to contend with.

The light illuminated the third member of the crew, Enzo Bachetti. Enzo slid the black tactical backpack off his shoulders and set it on the ground next to him. He unzipped it and removed a pair of kneepads, which he slid on. Enzo was a safecracker. His pack contained a variety of tools he was unlikely to actually need.

Gaston's responsibility was the breach. He'd saw through the cinder blocks and clear the path for them. Gaston had a demolition background, had served as a sapper in the French Foreign Legion, and his post-military career included a lot of extracurricular work dismantling alarm systems. They wouldn't have to worry about that tonight, however. A shop this small would not have seismic detectors, motion sensors, or even proximity alarms on the inside. Gaston had originally proposed using an expansive grout, which would take the wall down very effectively, but that required drilling holes in the wall and time. That meant they'd have had to drill during the day, when the jewelry store, their target, was open. And it could take up to twenty-four hours for the wall to be demolished. Since they couldn't control that timetable, Jack said it had to be the saw.

Their face, a half-Italian, half-German former model named Gabrielle Eberspach, rented the space they now occupied under the guise that she was opening a business. Jack didn't even know how much Gabrielle agreed to "pay" monthly; all that mattered was she talked the guy into a five-thousand-euro deposit to prorate the first month. The landlord had been paying a lot more attention to her legs than he did the contract he was signing. Gabrielle rented this space under a well-crafted false identity, which would stand up to the kind of background check her landlord was likely to run. Gabrielle said she was opening one of those trendy pastry and espresso shops. It just happened to share an interior wall with the downtown location of one of Spain's leading jewelry store chains. The absence of security on that bit of shared masonry would give the team precious extra time inside and significantly reduce their risk of exposure.

In addition to renting the space, Gabrielle's job was recon and intelligence gathering. It never ceased to amaze Jack how much people would tell a beautiful woman that was simply paying attention to them. Gabrielle was never around when the job actually started, and they went to great lengths to make sure she was never seen with the rest of the crew in public. By now, she was probably in Madrid.

Jack checked his watch again. "Two minutes," he said.

Gaston looked over the concrete saw one last time. That was the largest piece of equipment. Gaston purchased it with a ghosted credit card in France. He'd unpackaged it earlier that day and tested it, but otherwise it hadn't been used. Gaston had only handled it wearing gloves but had wiped it down after use. He'd wipe it down again with alcohol wipes when they were finished with it. It was the only thing they'd be leaving behind.

Jack opened his disposable phone and texted the only number that was programmed into it. It was a little difficult to manipulate the buttons wearing the latex gloves they all had, but he'd practiced that too. The phones would be used for this one purpose and then destroyed. All other team communication happened on separate phones. Jack typed the number 2 and sent it. The response came immediately.

K.

They heard a distant pop outside, louder than a gunshot but quieter than thunder. Then another, followed by two more. Jack sighed with relief. If you counted on the Spaniards for anything, and it was best not to make a habit of it, it was to be on time for a party. Fireworks exploded outside, announcing the start of the Falles Fiesta. The Fiesta was a five-day celebration commemorating St. Joseph, full of light, wine, and sound. Lots of sound. Fireworks, music, and sangria-fueled revelry would blanket the streets for the rest of the night. Somebody would have to be sitting in the back room of the boutique to hear them coming through.

Gaston pulled the starter on the concrete saw, and it sputtered to life. After an initial growl, the saw dropped in pitch to a throaty chuckle, like the bartender at a biker bar.

Jack texted an *X*.

Outside, Ozren Stolar would be reading it in their Fiat Doblò.

He looked over at Enzo, who had donned a small head-lamp so that he could view his work without obstruction. Enzo was at the very edge of the ring of light cast by the lantern, but once he had his gear on, Enzo slid the backpack back on and stepped back to the other side of the one-time storeroom so that he wasn't hit by debris from the saw.

Gaston continued with the saw, cutting the masonry lines on the wall around the thicker cinder blocks in a strange, three-dimensional facsimile of Tetris. Once he reached the lowest line of blocks, Gaston traced a line roughly three feet wide and then pulled the saw back up. Masonry dust hung thick in the air. Gaston completed his work, cutting the top part of their portal by holding the saw just above shoulder height with its blade horizontal. With the roughly square-shaped outline cut, Gaston used the saw to cut the portal into three smaller segments so that it could be pushed in more easily. The Frenchman powered down the saw and set it aside. He and Jack then placed their gloved hands on the uppermost segment and pushed. The sound of stone scraping against stone was quickly followed by a loud crash as the first segment fell against the floor on the far side of the hole. They followed with the second and third segments, pulling the latter into their room rather than pushing it into the connecting room in the jewelry store.

Jack checked his watch again—nine minutes down. They all wore diving watches that, along with any clothes they wore, would get an acid bath when this was all done.

Motes of masonry dust hung in the air. Gaston coughed once, despite the mask.

"Let's go," Jack said.

Jack stepped over the remnants of the wall, careful not to trip. Reginald, who'd set the job up, was able to get them blueprints of the building, so Jack knew they were in a hallway that led to the front showroom in one direction, bathrooms, a break room, and an emergency exit. The building was located in the heart of Valencia, overlooking the Plaça D'Alfons él Magnánimo. Jack had to hand it to the Spanish—they weren't lacking for titles. He activated his penlight and followed the hallway to the right, heading toward the front of the building. The door at the end was locked. Jack produced a set of picks sheathed in a small ballistic nylon pouch. Jack could open simple locks in the dark and regularly practiced working blindfolded. This was a simple one, and he was through in about thirty seconds.

The crew stepped into the boutique. The storefront faced the street but was lined with a series of display cases that had a solid panel backing them. This was for security as much as it was to enhance the visibility of the display. It deterred amateur thieves who might otherwise be inclined to try to enter via a brick through the window; it also meant that no one outside could see in or see the crew with their penlights moving throughout the store. The display cases were red herrings that professionals learned to avoid. Storefront displays were alarmed and almost always contained flashy costume pieces that were worth nothing, meant to draw potential customers in and dupe amateur thieves. The valuable pieces of finished jewelry and the watches would be locked in secured drawers beneath the interior display cases. Sometimes these drawers were alarmed as well, but typically only in the flagship stores found in major cities. Most smaller stores didn't have an in-depth security strategy beyond locking cases or placing the most valuable items in safes.

Jack and Gaston would take the front room and fanned out to their preplanned sides. Enzo moved immediately to the back room where the safe would be. "Five minutes starts now," Jack said quietly. Jack set his picks on the glass countertop and set to work. Much like the door, the lock here was not complicated. It was enough to deter an amateur, which was what it was designed for. Jack was through quickly and pulled the drawer out. He'd worn a tactical backpack as well and had placed it on the countertop, opened flat so that he could easily put things in it. Jack systematically emptied the contents of each of the drawers on his side, which were jewelry pieces like rings, pendants, and earrings. Jack placed the contents into small velvet pouches, which he then set in the backpack. When he was finished with the first case, he moved on to the second.

Jack had nearly finished emptying the contents of the second drawer into the velvet-lined pouch when his phone vibrated. Jack set his tools down, uttering a hushed curse. Jack opened the phone, finding a text message of a single letter—*P*. Jack swore under his breath. That meant Ozren spotted a pedestrian near the van.

Jack went to the next drawer, moving a little quicker than before.

He looked up from his case, seeing only the wraith-like outline of Gaston working the other side of the room. Display cases ringed the outside wall of the boutique's main room, with two larger ones in the center. Jack moved from the third case to the fourth. Jack shined the penlight into the drawer he'd just opened. Watches. Watches were easier to fence because they didn't have to be broken down for their components like the jewelry pieces did. You just had to be mindful of serial numbers.

Jack looked down at his phone after he'd cleared that case, but there wasn't another update from Ozren. "Enzo, how are we doing on the safe?" Though the safecracker was in the other room, Jack knew the look that would be on his face, the lemon-suck expression he always gave when questioned about his progress.

"I'm already through," he shot back in a harsh, clipped whisper that made Jack smirk. "There are two more safes back here," Enzo said.

"What?"

"Come see."

Jack trotted to the interior door that separated the showroom from the back office. Enzo was kneeling in front of the first safe. He looked like he was almost through emptying the contents into the backpack. "These look new," he said.

"That would explain why Reginald didn't know about it," Jack said. "How fast can you get in?"

Enzo shrugged. "It's no problem. I need an extra three minutes, tops."

Jack looked at his watch. The glowing dials showed they were getting close on time. Jack ran the odds in his head. Most of the festival was happening elsewhere in town, and he didn't think that there would be even a casual police presence here. The risk was minimal, and the contents of the other two safes might double their take for the night.

"Do it," Jack said. Without another word, Enzo picked up his drill and set to work on the second safe.

Nothing new from Ozren. What the hell was he doing, and what was going on with the walker?

Jack returned to the main room and continued working the cases.

He carefully but quickly transferred the contents to his backpack and moved over to the last case. One of the reasons they'd chosen this particular store was that they were a licensed dealer for Rolex, Omega and Breitling, among others. Jack placed them in one of the velvet bags and placed them in his backpack. He picked up the pack, still opened flat, and moved it over to the last case.

"I'm done here," Gaston said softly.

"Okay. I'm just finishing up. Go help Enzo with that last safe."

Jack finished his work in another ninety seconds, secured the contents of the pack and slid it onto his shoulders. He walked to the back room where he found Enzo and Gaston emptying the contents of the last safe into their transit bags. There were a few trays of loose stones, larger and more valuable finished pieces, and stacks of euros. Jack shined his light across the small room and saw a jeweler's workstation and tools. Looked like they were set up to do some minor repair work or even change out the settings on some of their pieces. That would explain why there were loose stones in the safe.

This was a good haul. A very good haul.

He still hadn't heard anything back from Ozren.

Enzo leaned back, and Jack heard the safecracker's knees pop. He gingerly set the last black velvet bag into his backpack and then removed his headlamp, placing it in the bag. He closed it and stood.

"Let's go," Jack said, and they moved out, back through the main room.

They'd left the LED lamp in the room they entered from to guide their escape. Once they'd climbed over the demolished wall, Gaston powered the lamp down and put it in his pack. They flashed penlights across the floor to make sure that they didn't leave anything behind besides the concrete saw. Some of the remnants of the building's prior owners still haunted the place—half-filled cardboard boxes, a random poster, a trampled flyer, a stack of to-go cups still in their plastic wrappers. Jack was last out of the store and closed the door behind him. He walked across the small garage and tossed his bag into the back of the idling Doblò in the alley.

He'd just finished pulling the slatted garage door down when he saw the body. The form was slumped over in the alley across from the van. Jack wouldn't have seen it...him—he hoped it was still a *him*—but for the red glow of the brake lights. He took a tentative step toward the body when Ozren must have spotted him in the side mirror.

"Jack, for fuck's sake, let's go!"

Jack spun his head around and shot his driver a hard glare. "What the hell is that?"

"It's fine. He's just a drunk."

Jack walked up to the side of the van. "It's not fine, Ozren. What the hell happened?" he said through the open driver's window, jabbing the air between himself and the body with his finger.

"He's just some guy that was out walking around and started hanging out in the plaza," the driver motioned with his hand, "fucking around with his phone. He wouldn't leave, and then he saw the van. I thought he was going to get suspicious, so I knocked him out."

"Jesus Christ, Ozren," was all Jack said. He couldn't read

the Serb's expression in the instrument panel's reflected half-light. His eyes were little more than black pits.

Jack disappeared from the side and went to check on the man. He was still wearing his gloves, so Jack chanced touching him. He lifted the man's chin and moved his head to the side. His eye was dark and already swelling shut; the man's nose was caved in and blood was flowing out of it, but not gushing. He'd been beaten, swiftly and badly. There were ways to subdue a person and not leave a mark, and there were ways to do it through sheer force. Jack believed Ozren knew both and willingly chose the latter. The man groaned painfully. He was still alive and was starting to come around. Jack stood and ran back to the van, closing the door behind him. "Go!"

Ozren put the Doblò into drive and pulled right into the connecting alley that led to Calle de la Universidad, gradually making his way west.

"I don't see what the big deal is," Ozren said. "He could identify us."

"No," Jack told him in a cold voice, "he couldn't. The guy was a drunk at a festival. He wouldn't think twice about a van on the street, and even if he'd noticed us coming out of the garage, so what? But the big deal, Ozren, is that the police aren't going to launch a manhunt for a jewelry store robbery, but they sure as hell would for one that was linked to a murder. You're lucky he's alive," Jack said.

"Then it is as you say. 'No harm, no foul.'"

2

Their safe house was a four-bedroom flat with barred windows in the town of Puçol, about twenty minutes outside Valencia. They'd driven most of that way in silence, a combination of coming down from the thrill of the job and the taut air between Jack and Ozren. Everyone grabbed a fast couple hours of rest but were up with the dawn. Gaston made coffee.

The plan was to split up now. Jack and Enzo would drive the take to their contact, who would tell his boss that it was good. The price and the quantity was agreed upon in advance, so all the contact was doing was varying that they'd come away with what they said they did. Of course, they'd gotten more than that and the Turk would be pleased. The Turk would pay them, transferring the funds to an offshore bank. No cash would ever change hands.

As soon as they'd entered the safe house, Jack and Enzo transferred their spoils to hardshell Pelican cases with false bottoms. Beneath that panel, there was a compartment that ran the length of the case along both sides of the hinge. The compartment was padded with thick packing foam and, between the two cases, had enough room for all of the jewels, watches and cash from the store. Once that was packed, Jack replaced the panel. He then placed photography equipment on top of it, which would serve as a decoy for all but the most intrusive security examination. Camera equipment was a perfect foil because it was relatively common, expensive, and fragile. Most border guards or port security wouldn't want to touch it for fear of damaging it and having to deal with the fallout. Though the compartment was lead lined, since it only ran the length of the hinge, the black spot on an X-ray would just look like part of the case's hardened design.

"Okay, we're all set here," Jack said. "Good work, everyone." Jack and Gaston shook hands. "See you soon, pal."

"I hope not," Gaston said with a laugh. "I'm going to Nice for a while."

There were a few more words exchanged, but Jack said nothing to Ozren. He was done with the Serb and wanted nothing more to do with him. He was a dangerous liability, and Reginald was going to get an earful about this.

Disposing of the car was Gaston's responsibility. Typically, that's something that would be left to the driver, but Jack didn't trust Ozren to do it. They never touched the car, never took their gloves off while they were in it, but it was still a chance he wasn't taking.

Gaston departed. He'd change the plates to a fresh pair and drive to Madrid, where he'd leave the Fiat in the airport parking lot. Jack and Enzo were driving a BMW 335i that his European fixer procured. It was a stolen car but clean and with fresh plates as well.

"I'm going with you," Ozren said.

"No, you're not," Jack told him and turned to leave.

Ozren put a hand on Jack's shoulder.

"Enzo, go load up the car," Jack said, tossing his friend the keys, and turned back around. Ozren was taller than Jack by several inches and was physically imposing. A former soldier in the Serbian army, Ozren was still in excellent shape. He had a darker complexion, seeming to have a permanent tan, dark eyes, and a short haircut. "Get your hand off me," Jack said through gritted teeth. "What do you think you're doing?" Jack asked.

"I'm going with you to meet the fence. I want my money now."

"Reginald explained how this worked when you signed on. I make the exchange, alone, and we get paid. Reginald will transfer your money to you in a couple of days."

"Enzo is going with you." Ozren waved a hand at the door.

"Yeah, well, I trust Enzo." Jack turned again, and Ozren pulled up his shirt, revealing the handle of a pistol tucked into his waistband.

Now Jack was on dangerous ground, because he was unarmed.

Jack didn't like guns and didn't like working with them. He wasn't a stickup man and believed if you needed a gun to pull a heist, you were an amateur. He also didn't want anyone to get hurt, not his crew, not civilians, not anyone. Ozren knew those rules before he signed on. Reginald was supposed to have told him, but Jack sure as hell did.

Jack felt his heart rate spike.

Ozren was a thief, supposedly had been one of the Pink Panthers. He could probably figure out a place to sell this stuff, though it would be for considerably less than what they would be getting. Would he really murder Jack and Enzo for, what, four hundred thousand?

It had been done for less in this business.

This was why Jack only worked with people he knew.

"Ozren, you'll get your take in two or three days. You're not going with us. Our contact doesn't know you. He knows me.

Enzo won't be there either. He'll be at a bar around the corner, having a beer. Trust is how this works. They have spotters. If they see me coming with someone else, they'll just leave. They won't know you're not a cop, and they'll just go. We'll have two boxes full of watches and jewelry that we can't sell. Is that what you want?"

"Don't tell me what I want," Ozren said in his heavily accented English.

Repeating the question back was what slow thinkers did to stall for time in the moment.

Ozren's hand went to his waistband. Jack sucked in a breath without even realizing it.

"You fucking better not screw me, or I will find you," Ozren growled, his accent thickly lacing his words, and dropped his shirt back over the gun.

Jack backed away from him slowly and said, "Trust is how this works." When he was to the door, Jack turned and exited the house, hands shaking.

They said goodbye to Gaston, got in the BMW and made fast miles to the motorway. He needed to text Gabrielle and let her know the job was successful. He'd forgotten to do it on the way out of Valencia because he was too preoccupied with Ozren.

Jack and Enzo drove mostly in silence. He was still furious.

Jack took the CV-13, which ran north along the coast, and they watched the sun climb over the Mediterranean. There were wispy, broken clouds over the sea, and it looked like God tore some paper and left it floating. Eventually, they stopped for breakfast and some more coffee. By then, Jack had mostly calmed down. He called Gabrielle and let her know it was a success, she did great, and they would have her cut shortly. She thanked him, and he hung up. By the time Jack and Enzo reached Barcelona, it was midmorning. They navigated their way through the city to the Barceloneta neighborhood.

Barceloneta was a beachfront district. It was loud, dirty, and filled with tourists, and there was no better place in the city to make an exchange. By now, the sun was blazing high above them and the Med was practically glowing. Barceloneta was just north of the port, and the industrial area quickly gave way to waterfront hotels and condominiums of cream-colored stucco and burnt-orange Mediterranean roofs. It was warm, and the city already swelled with tourists from the colder parts of Europe.

Jack pulled into Barceloneta's Estación de Francia train station parking lot. The station was enormous and looked like two arcing airplane hangars built side by side. The parking lot ran alongside the station and had a long line of tall, leafy trees on the far side. Jack parked the BMW beneath one of the trees and called their contact, Asil. Jack and Enzo each grabbed their travel bags and left the Pelican cases in the trunk. Jack locked the car, and they headed inside the terminal. They found Asil in the atrium, seated at a high-top table outside a coffee shop.

Jack walked over to Asil, who nodded at him nonchalantly, like it took just enough effort to pull off. Jack set the BMW keys on the table. "It's a black 335i, farthest row near the trees."

"Have a safe trip," Asil said. He scooped up the keys in one swift move and put them in his pocket. Jack nodded and met Enzo.

"What time is your train?" Jack asked.

"I've got about thirty minutes," he said.

Jack nodded. "Sounds good. Talk soon," Jack said and shook his hand. Jack had a flight to Frankfurt in about four hours. Enzo wished him safe travels and complimented him on the job. Jack smiled in response and went outside to find a cab.

———————

Ozren Stolar watched the entire scene unfold behind the screen of a local newspaper he'd picked up. He'd changed clothes on the road and was wearing a ball cap to provide a little cover, but he turned slightly as Jack walked past him. Burdette didn't notice. So much for Enzo being in a bar around a corner, and Ozren wondered what else Jack was lying to him about. Like the cut.

"Trust is how this works," Ozren mumbled in his native tongue.

3

"Would you like another, Mr. Fischer?"

Jack looked from his Kindle to his Omega Speedmaster. They had another forty-five minutes or so before landing at SFO. "I thought you'd never ask." The flight attendant smiled and departed, returning with a glass of the '09 G.D. Vajra Barbera d'Alba, replacing the empty one on his tray.

"Thank you, Ann," he said. She smiled.

The flight attendant was a warm but tired woman, mid-forties with a tall and lithe figure that she apparently worked very hard to maintain. She was attractive, though not without the evidence of hard-earned miles around her eyes. She had no obvious signs of attachment beyond the United wings on her blouse and an American flag pin. Ann wore her blond hair in a bun that had gradually been unraveling despite her best efforts on the long flight from Frankfurt. Somewhere over the Midwest, she'd given up and accepted the inevitable. "When are we going to see some of your wines on board, Mr. Fischer?" As she spoke, Ann lowered herself into that yoga chair-squat pose that only flight attendants could pull off in heels, resting her arm on Jack's armrest for balance.

Jack smiled. "Soon, I hope. We're talking with a company that services some of the airlines and a few cruise ship companies. We name all of our wines after birds, so it seems like a perfect fit for you." Jack flashed a charming smile.

Ann smiled. "Well, I'll have to come by your winery the next time I have a layover in San Francisco."

"We'd love to have you. Here." Jack reached for the bag he had stashed in the small cubby in his first-class suite. After a few seconds of casual searching, he removed a card case. Jack opened the case and handed Ann his card. "Give me a call any time you want to drop by. I'll make sure we take good care of you."

"I will," she said with a long smile. "Enjoy your wine." She slid her arm from his armrest and tapped the base of his wineglass with her index finger. The blue fingernail polish matched her uniform. "And let me know if I can get you anything else."

Jack smiled up at her as she stood and went to see to the other passengers in first class. Jack pushed back into his seat and stretched his legs in front of him before taking another sip from his glass. What he'd told Ann wasn't quite true. They were nowhere near landing an account with a distributor that handled the airlines. Kingfisher was only in a few restaurants in Napa, fewer in San Francisco, and none of the ones that mattered. In fact, Jack hadn't heard from the distributor in about two weeks, and they were supposed to have had another meeting before Jack went to Europe. He made a note to go over to their offices when he got home. Another thing to add to the never-ending list of things demanding his attention. This was something that he should have Megan handle for him, but no, Jack needed to do this himself. He needed to own the negotiations. He drank again and tried to push those thoughts from his head. He wasn't ready for the Frank Fischer problems yet.

There was still much to sort out from the Valencia job.

Their take was about nine hundred thousand dollars, very good for a jewelry store. Because the store was in a fashion center, the jewelers sold heavier and flashier products to cater to their high-end clientele. They had a bigger inventory of expensive items thanks to the festival. Their fence—a Turkish gang that Jack had worked with often—bought the pieces and the watches at forty-five cents on the dollar. That was above standard but one of the benefits of working with a fence you knew. Most fences wouldn't go higher than thirty with people they didn't know.

The Turks bought the finished jewelry mostly for the stones. They would break the pieces down so they could resell them on the gray market in Europe and the Middle East. The gold was either sold in bulk to be melted down or discarded, depending on the quantity and current market rate. A lot of otherwise reputable jewelry makers bought gray market stones because they could get them so much cheaper than they could from the conglomerates or the wholesalers. The watches would go for a little more because those could be sold as is. Jack had put this crew together over the last five years so that he could work with highly skilled people but also people he could trust. Gaston had been with him about five years, Gabrielle two, but Enzo and Jack went back almost twenty. They'd been running on crews together since their mid-twenties.

The Turks paid Jack four hundred five thousand. Reginald LeGrande, Jack's fixer, would get five percent of that for setting up the job, fronting the money, and hiring the crew. The remainder was split evenly five ways, around eighty-five thousand to each member of the crew, including Jack, who never took more than anyone else. Double-crosses happened when people got greedy or felt they didn't get their share. When law enforcement agencies infiltrated burglary rings, it was almost always through a crew member who felt they weren't getting what they deserved. Either they started doing sloppy work on the side, or worse, they volunteered information out of spite. Jack avoided this by giving everyone an equal stake in the job. Over time, he built up a reputation. There was nothing egalitarian about it, and it forced him to take more jobs, but it also reduced his exposure to law enforcement.

The other way Jack avoided law enforcement was being extremely selective about whom he worked with.

While Reginald believed that setting the crew was his responsibility, Jack also had a strict rule about vetting people he worked with and would only work with people he knew and trusted. Ozren was an exception. They'd worked together on and off over the last year; Jack had agreed to try him out on a couple jobs the year before and didn't like him. He was volatile, unnecessarily debated parts of the plan, and always thought he should take a larger role in the job. This was the last straw, and Jack wouldn't work with Ozren again. If Reginald wanted to believe that he was in charge of the team, fine, *he* could sort out the situation with that lunatic Serb. Jack would find another driver. Their usual wheel was a Welshman named Bart, who was a semi-pro rally racer when he wasn't idling in front of jewelry stores. Bart had to pass on the Valencia job because he was in Austria doing a hill climb, and they'd needed Ozren to fill in.

Jack hated violence and didn't tolerate it with his crews. It was one thing to steal from a company that paid insurance to be protected, but Ozren had beaten that guy to within an inch of his life. He was no threat, and Ozren had done it without hesitation or remorse. He was practiced in violence. If Reginald wanted to use the guy on other jobs, fine. It was better for Jack that the Serb continued to get work. There was nothing more volatile than a thief with an ax to grind. Jack just didn't want Ozren on his crew.

Jack took another sip and held the glass in front of him, absently studying it. He watched the red liquid shift its position in the glass, slowly climbing up one side as the 777 banked. The pilot announced they had begun their final descent into SFO. Jack drank again, savoring the Barbera. Most people hated air travel, particularly international, but Jack enjoyed the solitude. Most of the time when he was on an aircraft, Jack was transitioning between his life as Jack Burdette and his life as Frank Fischer. He came to appreciate the few hours of isolation and sanctuary where the dividing lines between those lives were clear and easily parsed. There was a kind of peace and freedom in that transition between lives, even though he was trapped on a plane with a fixed destination.

Jack felt a subtle shift in how his body pressed against the seat. He finished his wine and set it on the tray built into his chair. Then he removed the cognac-colored leather travel wallet he kept his Frank Fischer passport in. He rehearsed the conversations he was likely to have clearing customs. Business or pleasure? *Business, but I try to have a good time. I was visiting some Italian winemakers in a similar climate. I'm thinking of planting Sangiovese in my plot and wanted some advice.* At which point the customs official would stamp Jack's passport, wholly uninterested in his viticulture plans.

Jack maintained several forged passports that Reginald crafted for him. Those were usually disposed of after the job.

On occasion, he would travel under the Frank Fischer passport, which was legally acquired (more or less) through the State Department. On the occasions where he needed the cover of a trip, he used the Frank Fischer passport, which saved him the trouble and expense of having to burn one of the ones Reginald forged.

Jack cleared customs with no problem, other than the time, and made his way to the long-term parking. Jack exited the parking garage at SFO and accelerated onto the 101, keeping the pedal down but not quite buried as he quickly stepped through the gears, tapping the paddles to upshift. The air was damp and in the lower sixties, but he rolled down his window anyway, enjoying the rush of fresh air on his face after spending the better part of a day on an airplane. Jack thumbed the voice command and instructed his car to play Thelonious Monk's "Alone in San Francisco." Just Monk and a piano. He'd once heard this record described as the best album in any genre. There was incredible symmetry in the spaces between the notes and the sound of the car, a jet-black Audi RS 7, as he stepped through the gears and glided onto I-380 already cresting seventy-five. This would take him over the Golden Gate and home to Sonoma.

The RS 7 was an excellent car and certainly scratched Jack's driving itch, but it was more about maintaining an image. Frank Fischer made his fortune in tech, and while most of those guys bought Ferraris and Astons as soon as they cashed their first check, Jack knew it would send the wrong signal to roll up to Kingfisher in a three-hundred-thousand-dollar car when they were barely making payroll. But, Fischer was known for being a little flashy, so the Audi was a decent compromise. It was a fastback exemplar of Teutonic engineering, clocking in at five hundred and twenty-five horsepower and an eye-blink zero-to-sixty rating that casually reminded the driver not all "launches" were reserved for rocket pads and aircraft carriers. It handled nimbly on the twisting switch-backs descending from Jack's house and positively roared when he finally opened it up on the highway. With that, Jack's concerns, at least for the moment, melted away.

The car's style was understated with sleek lines from the long nose, a gentle curve over the front wheels, and cockpit and fastback that was long enough for a wide-body aircraft on final approach. Simply put, it didn't look like one was driving around in a hundred-and-ten-thousand-dollar car. Then again, that was also part of the design. The Audi's perfor-mance was similar to a Porsche or lower-end Aston Martin, but those were statement cars. Which was not to say that the Audi was not, just that its statement was a more controlled, measured form of ostentatiousness.

Jack didn't particularly love being a thief, but it was the only life he'd ever known. He did, however, enjoy the lifestyle that being a thief allowed him to afford. When he'd first gotten started in the trade, driving for bank robbers, he was just running away. He'd met Reginald then, and Reginald had taught him things—safes, alarm systems, setups, how to put a crew together, and how to keep them focused. Later on, Jack realized he didn't like stealing from people but had no problem lifting goods from stores that were going to get paid back by massive insurance companies that charged usurious rates to protect against just this sort of thing. The way he saw it, they were getting their money's worth.

The idea for the winery came on one of the innumerable flights between Europe and America. Jack always flew first class internationally. You got all the booze you wanted, the food didn't come out of a microwave, and the stews were so much kinder than they were to those jerks in coach. Plus, they had fresh magazines and newspapers. Jack decided he wanted to look the part, so he asked for a *Wall Street Journal* and read an article about Silicon Valley entrepreneurs who were cashing out of the tech industry and buying wineries. He got an idea.

Jack had fallen in love with wine a few years before and had built a small collection at each of the safe houses he maintained. Jack didn't wade casually into hobbies. When he found something that sparked him, he wore it like a second skin. For a time, it was rebuilding and racing cars. He'd started his career as a wheelman, and in a matter of speaking, it was cars that got him into this life to begin with, so it was only natural that he'd sink his money into them. Plus, flipping exotic cars was a good enough way to launder money, though it didn't scale well. The problem was that the joy in driving came from driving them fast, and that tended to draw unwanted attention, so eventually, Jack found his way to wine. As with the cars before it, investing in a business was a way to legitimize the income he made from stealing jewels and get his hands on liquid cash. Not to mention, most wineries were in the kinds of places he wanted to be anyway.

Jack created the Frank Fischer backstory, bought the IDs to back it up, and spread money in the right places to bolster his story when people followed up.

And then Frank Fischer bought a winery.

Jack assumed that running a winery was like any other operation, and that was something he knew well. He bought the winery from a guy who wanted out of the game. Apparently, this guy was either nearly broke or was just tired of shooting money out of a cannon. But Jack kept most of that guy's staff on hand to show him the ropes and keep the place running. His first big hire was a winemaker named Fitz Cristoforo. He was a trendy asshole who Jack disliked immediately and immensely—tattoos on his fingers, retro glasses that had been around too long to still be ironic, and T-shirts that were a size too small. Cristoforo didn't want to be a winemaker as much as he wanted to be the head of his own personality cult. He didn't talk about wine as much as he talked about "vision." Cristoforo was as insufferable as he was irritating, and any semblance of humility had been wrung out of his psyche long ago. But another skill that Jack had developed in all these years running crews of hardened criminals was that he knew how to deal effectively with people he didn't like. Jack recognized that Cristoforo was a true talent and was someone he could learn from. Hiring a high-profile, rising-star winemaker was the kind of ballsy move that would get Kingfisher the early exposure they needed.

Their major schism came when Cristoforo declared they needed to announce their winery with a bold move, and instead of using the winery's venerable cab vines to produce "just another Cabernet," they would make a huge Bordeaux blend. Jack loved the idea and had actually been spending some of his "off season" in France talking with any local winemaker that would give him time. Acting on the suggestion of one of these Frenchmen he'd met with, Jack ripped out significant tracts of his vineyard's Cabernet Sauvignon vines and replaced them with Carmenére because "true meritage uses Carmenére." Cristoforo erupted over the intrusion into his "process" and the temerity of this neophyte owner. Most of the staff sided with the winemaker, arguing that even if Jack insisted that they use Carmenére in the wine, they could source it from another vineyard rather than ripping out fruit that was still perfectly good. Even Hugh Coughlin, Jack's attorney and business advisor, cautioned against the move.

Jack was insistent and refused to relent. It would be about

three years before the new Carmenére vines would yield any usable fruit, so they had to source those grapes anyway. Cristoforo selected the fruit they would use and set to creating his meritage. When Cristoforo bottled his "vision," he called it "Ceremony" and demanded they charge three-fifty a bottle for it. This time, Jack relented in a concessionary gesture to ease the tension around his Carmenére decision. The trades lit them up for it, even though the wine wouldn't be available for another two years. No one wanted a three-hundred-and-fifty-dollar meritage from a winery that hadn't made its bones yet. The kindest reviews said they were hubristic.

Cristoforo got wind that the reviews were coming and took off before they hit, going to a boutique operation in Napa, the other side of the winemaking world, that gave him full control of the operation. Later on, when a reporter asked Cristoforo why he left, Fitz flipped the story and said that Fischer wanted to charge outrageous rates for his unproven wines, that Cristoforo advised against it, but Fischer wouldn't listen. Cristoforo actually said that Fischer was going to sink that winery because he didn't know what he was doing and that Fitz didn't want to go down with him.

The reporter called Jack for comment, and listening to Hugh's counsel this time, Jack kept the feud out of the papers, saying only that he and the winemaker couldn't share the same vision and decided it was best to part ways. When asked about the pricing debate, Jack only said that Cristoforo's account was "interesting" and "curious" but left it at that. To this day, Jack and Cristoforo couldn't be in the same room together. Cristoforo bottled his updated "vision" the following year but ran into some bad luck. There was an accident in the warehouse just before they released it. One of the storage racks collapsed and dumped nearly the entire run on the concrete, shattering most of the bottles. They still couldn't figure out how that happened.

Jack replaced Cristoforo with a winemaker Coughlin knew well. Megan McKinney had been through the Mondavi School at UC Davis and had a master's degree in viticulture. She also had a fiery temper and didn't take shit from anyone, least of all Jack. She was attractive, volatile, and wickedly funny. She also had a gut instinct about grapes that was practically preternatural. Their relationship was equally volatile, charismatic, and turbulent, but there was a genuine creative spark between them. When they weren't bickering, they really did make great wine together. Their first effort was to salvage Cristoforo's meritage, which they called "Peregrine" and sold for around fifty dollars a bottle. That year, each of the bottles had the statement on the label that "a wine that doesn't stand on ceremony."

Jack looked down to his phone, opened it, and thumbed an encryption app called Cover Me. He and Reginald had been using this for a few years to send secure texts and phone calls. Jack keyed the button on the steering wheel and asked the car to dial Robert McCray.

A gravelly voice answered on the third beep.

"Charles Hogan, how are you?" he said behind a sardonic laugh.

"Pretty good, actually."

"Sleep on the plane?"

"Not much. It was a morning flight."

"You're the only one I know who doesn't get exhausted coming in this direction. So, how'd it go?"

"It was a breeze, Reg. Man, I got to hand it to you. Using the festival as a cover was brilliant."

"You wait until the fireworks to start the saw?"

Jack could hear in the old thief's voice that he was borderline giddy. He really missed this. Jack ran it down for him. He described Gabrielle renting out the space next to the jewelry store, the team's prep work leading up to the job, and even the smallest details of the day-before logistics. Finally, Jack talked through the job itself as if they were football coaches watching game film. This was ritual now, a tradition. Jack called Reginald after every job and debriefed him. Reginald would ask questions but was rarely critical. Of course, there was rarely a move Jack made to be critical of. Still, Jack knew that these discussions made him better. It also filled a void for LeGrande, who could no longer safely work. If Reginald were arrested again, he'd go away forever. Eventually, Jack steered the conversation around to the Serb.

"Ozren has got to go. He almost killed that guy, Reg. And for what? It was just someone that had too much to drink and was looking for a spot to sit down. He'd never even remember seeing the van, but he's for sure going to remember getting his ass kicked."

"Jack," Reginald said at length. "You don't know that."

"The hell I don't," he snapped. "I could smell the wine on his breath when I checked him. The worst thing about Ozren, Reg, is that it was too easy for him. He's got practice in that sort of thing. It's second nature to him."

"Okay, okay," Reginald said, and Jack could practically see him trying to pat the air on his end of the line. "I'll talk to him."

"No. I'm not working with him again. I don't want that kind of risk. People aren't going to remember some boutique job two weeks after it happens, but if we leave a body behind they sure as shit will. Never again. Just put Bart back on my crew and we'll be fine."

"Well, that's going to be a bit of a problem."

"Why's that?"

"He rolled his car at a race this weekend. Totaled it and broke his leg in a couple places. I don't know how bad it is yet, but he's not driving for a while. Maybe ever."

Bart was a good wheel, and Jack would miss him if what Reginald said was true. They'd only truly needed Bart's skills once, that time they did the hotel collection in Barcelona, but Jack saw the driver put a Fiat on two wheels going around a corner and lost the cops in traffic. That earned him unending loyalty from Jack, who was a good driver in his own right.

"I'll find someone else, and I'll make sure that Ozren stays occupied." That was good. The last thing they needed was an out-of-work thief with a grudge. "Now, can we put this to bed? How'd we do?"

Jack forced a smile, knowing that was the kind of thing you could hear. "Four hundred and five thousand. We did good, Reg. Real good. You'll get your cut in a couple of days." The net was four-oh-five, but the actual haul was around nine hundred thousand.

Reginald chuckled. It sounded like a wet hammer hitting gravel. "Too bad you couldn't have gotten that Hermès shop down the street."

"Reginald," Jack said at length. If LeGrande had a criticism of Jack, it was that he was too cautious. Which he admittedly was. It was one of the reasons he'd never been caught. Jack believed in increments. He only took moderately sized scores, the kinds of jobs people would forget about in time. He simply did more of them. The biggest mistake most thieves made was they tried to make themselves rich with one job. Yes, Niccoló Bartolo took the Antwerp Diamond Centre for a hundred million dollars, but the world only knew about that because he was in jail with a story to sell.

Reginald had been busted once and served four out of ten years, but that was enough. Between the legal fees and the fines, he was cleaned out, and when they let him out on good behavior, he not only was hard broke but had a stern warning from the State of California—no more strikes. Reginald took that to heart after a fashion and moved to fixing jobs instead of actually doing them. Jack took that lesson as well and knew that he wasn't going to ever take that "one last job" that inevitably landed thieves in jail. Jack used Reginald's experience—particularly since he'd advised Reginald not to take that job—to be the foundation of his career. Jack distilled it down to three simple principles: never steal out of necessity, never take a score large enough for somebody to notice, and never steal from somebody that has the will or the means to get it back.

"Listen, why don't you pop down for a couple of days? We'll take the boat out and celebrate."

"I'd like that. It's been too long."

Kingfisher Wines sat on the eastern edge of Sonoma County's Alexander Valley atop a low hill that caught sun most of the day. Late afternoon light cast a gold and orange glow on the property. Jack turned off CA-128 and onto the black oak-lined drive that led to the winery. There was a single indigo sign beside the road displaying the likeness of two of the namesake birds in silver sitting on a branch, facing away with their wings spread wide about to take flight. The words *Kingfisher Wines* were written in simple script beneath them.

Jack slowly guided his Audi up the long drive while two cars passed him in the other direction. It was about closing time for the tasting room. Jack's arm rested in the open window, and he lifted his hand in a wave as they passed. The road banked to the right, and the asphalt gracefully transitioned into the dirt and gravel parking lot. He loved the sound of the crunch beneath the tires. Jack had also wanted to maintain something of the rustic feel of the place—the restored hacienda, the barns, and yes, even the gravel parking lot. He wanted a place that reflected the wines they made: not without flaws but at the same time welcoming.

He parked in the customer lot instead of pulling all the way around and left his things in the car. Jack wore a robin's egg blue Oxford shirt, dark jeans, a blue Canali blazer that he was now carrying in the crook of his left arm, and tan boots. There was a cluster of men in dusty jeans and T-shirts near the barn behind the tasting room, and they waved when they saw him. One detached from the group and jogged over to Jack.

"Hey, chief," he said affably as he approached, a broad smile underneath a bushy salt-and-pepper mustache.

"Hey, Link," Jack returned and shook hands. "How was the game last night? Sorry I missed it."

Lincoln's son Rodrigo was a little league pitcher, and the winery sponsored the team. Jack and Lincoln would sometimes break off work early and go catch games if they were playing close by and if they could sneak out without Megan seeing.

"He pitched a no-hitter," Lincoln said, beaming. Lincoln was the son of migrant farmers who had gotten their citizenship with Lincoln's birth on US soil. They felt like it was a kind of emancipation and named their son accordingly. Link grew up around grapes and knew them in a way you couldn't get from books. "It's been hot while you were gone, but the grapes are fine."

"Good," Jack said, nodding.

"Cutworms are back. I'll be out there with a flashlight tonight if I have to."

Jack smiled and let out a short laugh. "Megan and I are going to check out that new plot in the morning, around ten. I'd like you to go too, if you can get away. I want your opinion on the vines. I don't think this property is going to be on the market long."

"Okay, sure thing."

Jack learned through Hugh Coughlin that a twenty-five-acre plot of nearly legendary old-vine Cabernet was coming on the market in the next few weeks. It was a part of a historic vineyard that was being broken up and sold piecemeal by the warring children of one of Sonoma's founding fathers. This particular plot was called Sine Metu, which either meant "without fear" or "original sin," depending on the translation one used. The owners were asking nine million for the plot, which Jack would have to stake from his personal holdings. They'd tried to get a loan, but the winery was already so heavily leveraged they couldn't take out any more. While extremely risky, it was also an excellent opportunity to legitimize a substantial portion of his income. Jack wasn't convinced that he was going to do it yet. He wanted to get an eye on it and, more importantly, get Megan and Link's opinions. The asking price was most of what remained of Jack's liquid assets in his Vanuatu account, and it would be several years before they saw a return on the investment, but everyone was urging him that it was a very smart, strategic investment.

Jack and Lincoln continued their conversation as they approached the winery's main building. They stopped at the door, now shadowed in the inky blue of the approaching evening. Link said he needed to check a few things before he broke for the night. He slapped Jack on the back with a dusty hand, welcomed him home once more, and jogged back to the barn.

Jack entered the restored hacienda that served as their

tasting room and headquarters. The building was a long mission-style of yellow stucco with a terra-cotta roof. Three large raised skylights broke the roof's silhouette. The rest of the building was wreathed by palms, with large clusters of desert plants at the corners and sides. The tasting room occupied most of the first floor. There was a second story that was about a quarter the length of the first floor that afforded a three-hundred-sixty-degree view of the grounds and vineyards. Jack's office was there. He opened the door to the tasting room and entered.

The staff was busy preparing to close, sweeping, cleaning glasses, and taking inventory. The tasting room manager, Steve, stood behind the counter with a clipboard, running through the checklist of things his team needed to get done. Steve was a retired Air Force officer that had discovered a love for wine during a posting to Italy and decided that after twenty years of military life, the perfect existence was a quiet and happy one in the heart of wine country. He didn't talk much about his service, and Jack didn't press. He knew the value of privacy better than anyone. Steve had picked up the trade-appropriate, though entirely unrelated, nickname "Corky" during his service. He had explained once that nearly everyone in the Air Force officer corps earned one, usually for doing something stupid or as an embarrassing twist on their given name. Corky never shared how he'd earned his but assured Jack it was a good story.

"Welcome back, boss," Steve called out when he saw Jack enter the tasting room, sounding genuinely excited to see him. "How was the trip?" Steve still had the traces of a Southern accent, the kind of foundational speech patterns that would never go away regardless of how long he'd been away from his birthplace.

"Meg keep you guys out of trouble?"

"Inasmuch as she does," he said. Corky once told Jack that in the South, it wasn't so much how the words were actually spoken as how those words were approached.

Jack nodded. "Really good. Italy is good for the soul, as you know. Nice to be home, though." He meant it. The winery made him happy. It was the only time in his life he'd felt like he'd had a home. Jack thought of himself as Frank Fischer. Frank Fischer's imagined history became his own real history. Fischer's failures, his triumphs, his lonely existence in the tech world until buying and restoring this old winery, the path that led him here—all that Jack wished was his own and tried every day to make it so. That his "other" life as Gentleman Jack Burdette was some abstract conglomeration of criminal acts that Jack did his best to push to the back of his mind.

Jack looked around the counter. "What's open?"

"Got some Osprey left."

Jack nodded, and Steve poured him a glass of their Cabernet. A brief smile cracked Jack's lips as the dark garnet wine crashed into the glass and spilled lightly up the side. Steve reserved a quarter glass for himself and poured one, as he usually did, when closing up the tasting room. The stubby ex-Airman with a perpetual smile held his glass up and said, "*Salud*," before going back to work cleaning up the bar.

Jack took his glass and walked through the tasting room to the stairwell that led to the second floor. Evening light flooded the large square office that sported windows on three sides. The windows were open, and a soft breeze blew in, gently rustling some of the loose papers on his desk. Megan occasionally used his office, especially when he was traveling, and she usually forgot to close the windows when she was done. Megan McKinney was also the Chief Operating Officer of Kingfisher Wines, though she'd just as likely take his head off as thank him if he referred to her as such, particularly in mixed company. She said titles were for people who didn't have dirt on their shoes.

Jack stood for a few minutes, sipping his wine and looking out over the northern stretch of vineyard, now drenched in the yellow-orange glow of evening that was quickly turning to dark. He turned back to his desk and the three weeks' worth of decisions that were waiting for him on it. Jack set his wineglass down on the desk and picked up the first stack of papers, most of which appeared to be invoices. In addition to the paperwork, there would be another couple hundred emails at least.

The money he'd made in Europe would help.

At this point, Jack needed everything he could get just to keep them afloat. The winery wasn't profitable yet, and he couldn't take on outside investors for obvious reasons, so any infusion of cash came from his personal reserves or from jobs. Jack hid their situation from the staff as best he could. Jack didn't want people worrying about whether or not they were going to get paid. They would, even if that meant taking on more side jobs than he was comfortable doing.

Someone told Jack once that running a winery was not about making money so much as it was about not losing it. And that was when everything was on an honest footing. In 2008, and after much insistence by Hugh Coughlin, Jack hired an accountant to manage Kingfisher's books. Jack interviewed several candidates that Hugh presented but eventually decided to go with an outsider. Hugh didn't know Paul Sharpe, but his résumé was great and he wasn't asking too much. The guy had a similar story to Frank Fischer's. After so many years in big business, he wanted a hand at creating something, and he thought wine was a nice way to make a living.

Hiring an accountant was a dangerous, though calculated, risk. The entire purpose behind Kingfisher Wines was to legitimize Jack's jewelry theft income, and that wouldn't work if the winery folded. Jack knew that he had neither the time nor the expertise to manage the winery's finances, so he eventually agreed to hire someone to do so. Jack also knew that if he refused to, particularly with his offshore banking, it would raise too many questions about why.

Before bringing Sharpe on board, Jack launched into Frank Fischer's libertarian rant about denying a government that he didn't agree with their taxation by offshoring his money as a form of political protest. Sharpe took him on his word, or, at least, he didn't seem to care where Jack stashed his money if some amount of capital could infuse the winery when necessary. But they got along well, and Jack appreciated Sharpe's business savvy. Not long after hiring him, Jack made Sharpe his CFO.

Sharpe pushed hard for the Sine Metu acquisition, arguing they could sell much of that harvest at a high premium now as well as supplement their own Cabernet production to make up for what Jack ripped out what he replaced and replanted with the Carmenére. Selling those well-known and highly regarded Sine Metu fruit to select other wineries would allow them to recoup the initial invest-ment faster and get back to profitability.

In fact, that's exactly what Megan and Sharpe were arguing about when they entered Jack's office.

"Finally," Sharpe said, indicating Jack with an outstretched arm. "Someone that will listen to reason."

"It's not about being reasonable, Paul, it's about being rational. It's going to take five years before the cab we put in to replace that Carmenére is going to be ready to harvest. That costs money and not a little. You should know that."

"I know the numbers, Megan," Sharpe said in a wounded tone that set Megan back a bit. "We can afford this," he said in a softer voice. "I think it means we have to push off some of the capital expenditures we've been planning, but I think that's manageable. Guys, there's To Kalon, and then there's this. It's not even on the market yet, but we've got an inside track, and if we lead with a strong offer, we'll get it. We'll make our money back in a few years."

To Kalon was one of the most storied vineyards in Napa history and had produced legendary wines. The Sine Metu vineyard was considered to be a very close second.

Sharpe's estimation on how quickly they'd recoup the investment was optimistic at best, which wasn't a position that an accountant normally took. Jack read Sharpe's business plan for the Sine Metu acreage while he was in Europe. Sharpe concluded that the idea was fiscally sound, and he strongly advised they move now. The plot wasn't on the market yet, but because the sellers were old friends of Coughlin's, they'd agreed to give Kingfisher an early opportunity to buy if they agreed to the full asking price. Sharpe argued that if they waited until it actually was on the market, they'd be subject to a bidding war and likely would get outmaneuvered by one of the conglomerate-backed wineries that had more capital at their disposal. Sine Metu was a legendary plot of Cabernet in Napa Valley, and the fruit from that would make wines that were world class. To say nothing of the price they'd command for selling what they didn't use.

"I know how good the fruit is. Jesus, I've had it. That's not really the point, though. The point is that's *all* of our money. And it's not even our money. It's Frank's."

That was another source of contention between Megan and Jack. Jack would never try for a small business loan. While it was true, in this instance, that they were too heavily leveraged to get one, Jack also didn't want to owe anything to a bank. If the time ever came that he had to cut and run, debt held by someone else wouldn't help him. But, of course, he wouldn't tell his people the real reason why. So it became just another of Frank Fischer's proclivities that occasionally bothered some and drove Megan up an actual wall.

"It is my money," Jack said. "And I understand the risk that we're taking with it, but I also feel like it's an investment worth considering. Paul, you're overselling a little to say that we can make the investment back in a couple of years just by selling off the fruit. But we can do a combination of that and make some truly exceptional cabs. Not only that, it raises the overall value of the winery." In the back of Jack's mind, he was thinking about Cristoforo's wine and the reviewers' accusation of hubris. He wondered if this would be taken in the same light. "I've got some thinking to do."

"I'll let them know we'll have a decision in—"

"Paul, I haven't made my mind up," Jack said in a hard tone. "Megan is completely right that it's a lot of money and it's a lot of *my* money. I need to think through recouping it. I will let you know what we're going to do, and you'll have no contact—with anyone—until that happens. Are we clear?"

Sharpe left after telling Jack he understood and offering a ham-fisted apology for appearing too aggressive.

Megan hung back.

Jack assured her he wouldn't do anything rash and that whatever he decided, it'd be with the best interests of the winery in mind.

"That's fine," Megan deadpanned. "I just didn't want to walk out with Paul."

They'd had plans to have dinner tonight, but Megan suggested they push it a day or two, saying she could tell he had a lot on his mind. Megan left him to his thoughts.

Jack refilled his glass from downstairs and watched the land grow dark through his window. Jack thought of how leveraged he'd be after making the Sine Metu purchase. Almost his entire savings was in this winery, and while the additional income from the jobs he worked was steady, it amounted to about two to three hundred thousand a year. It'd be a long time before he made back the ten million if something went wrong.

4

Jack decided to cut a ten-million-dollar check.

He knew it was risky, emptying out most of his remaining assets, but he wasn't going to be stealing jewels forever. There would come a time when he needed to transition into civilian life. If it weren't for the winery, he'd have enough now to live comfortably for the rest of his life. But living comfortably wasn't something Jack was interested in. The winery gave him purpose; he was creating something for the first time in his life. It was a good feeling. Megan disagreed with the purchase, though it was mostly because they drew so much on Frank Fischer's personal assets to make investments in the winery and slightly because she disagreed with Paul on most things. She wouldn't admit it, but Jack knew that she couldn't wait to get her hands on those grapes, some of the most storied fruit the Napa Valley had ever produced. She was dying to see what she could do with it. This was also a tremendous opportunity to legitimize his remaining money. The way real estate was appreciating here, he could sell this in five to ten years and almost double his money.

But there was a lot to do in order to make the acquisition.

He had to move the money from the various offshore shell corporations that he used to hide his money to the accounts that he used for Frank Fischer's money. Frank Fischer's money was kept in a separate offshore corporate account. From there, Jack organized the complicated process of purchasing the tract. Because the vineyard was acquired by a corporation that Frank Fischer's other corporate entity owned, Hugh Coughlin had to draw up an agreement for him to sign that granted Kingfisher exclusive usage rights to that tract. Hugh Coughlin then coordinated the actual purchase. There was so much to do on top of what he and Megan already had to manage, and Jack insisted on being part of everything. It meant a lot of very long days.

Jack didn't notice that Reginald had been trying to get in touch with him for several days. When he wasn't working, Jack kept his "Jack Burdette phone" locked in a safe at the house. In the first few weeks after a job, he might go days or weeks before he checked it. Reginald would know this and was usually patient with him. It wasn't always like that, but as the winery drew more and more of his time and attention, Jack went longer and longer between checking in. He'd only powered that phone on that day because he wanted to let Reginald know he'd be ready for something in a month or two. Now that the Sine Metu acquisition was in play, Jack wanted to try to get one more job in before harvest. It would be very hard to come up with an excuse good enough to explain why he needed to be away from the winery for a week or two, especially now, but for the right job, it might be worth it. Jack wouldn't be happy until his liquid assets were back in the seven figures.

Then, with everything else going on, the seal on their Cabernet tank blew the previous morning. They'd saved most of the wine, but they'd still lost close to twenty percent of it.

That was the story of Kingfisher. Everything was held together with baling wire and duct tape. It worked...until it didn't.

So when he finally got to return Reginald's calls and the old fixer told Jack he'd be in San Francisco the next day, it was an unwelcome distraction. Jack missed his old friend, and they did need to talk, but now was not the time. Jack could tell him that he wanted to try to get one job in over the summer with a text. There was too much to do, and he felt like he'd already been absent from the winery far too much lately. Even though Reginald was just asking for an afternoon, Jack didn't feel like he should pull himself away. But Jack relented, deciding that he probably should take an afternoon off. Jack made up a story that he was going to meet some restaurant sommeliers. Hearing this, Megan quizzed him on the tasting notes of the wines he would allegedly be taking down to sample. He decided that he would need to cold-call a few of them and leave a few bottles. If he was going to burn an afternoon meeting with Reginald, he might as well get something out of it.

"Meet me at the Embarcadero," Reginald had said, "around two, two thirty." Then Reginald added, "Hog Island. I feel like oysters."

Jack's initial warming to the distraction collapsed in on itself. Oysters meant work. Reginald had this weird, old habit of always pitching a job over oysters. Something in the way his small mind defined irony. But Jack couldn't handle another distraction right now. As it was, he wouldn't be sleeping until the Sine Metu purchase was done, on top of every other demand on his attention. Sometimes, he wished he could just tell Reginald about the winery so that he'd understand why Jack had to be selective not only about the jobs but also about the timing.

Jack loaded a case of wine into the Audi for the restaurant stops he'd now have to make and headed to San Francisco.

Jack arrived at the Ferry Building on the Embarcadero thirty minutes early, found the restaurant, and grabbed a couple of chairs outside. The sky was gloomy, holding that dirty-water coloring that resembled third-world laundry and felt basement damp. The Ferry Building struck Jack as out of place against the city skyline. The sprawling blue-and-white Beaux Arts–style complex sharply contrasted with the towering glass-and-steel modernism of the Financial District, like some confused god with no sense of aesthetic had placed it there and then forgotten about it. The building itself was an anachronism, and maybe that's what Reginald liked about it. It was a building out of time. Jack sat facing the Bay Bridge so that he could see Reginald approach. The air was soup thick with the pungent reek of sea lion, fish, and saltwater, and Jack honestly didn't know how people could eat outside. Jack ordered a beer, wishing for something stronger, and waited. Cold, damp air seeped into his bones.

Reginald LeGrande strode up to the Ferry Building at two thirty-two. LeGrande, now in his late fifties, had a once-muscular build that came more from work and less from the gym and was slowly fading with time. His thick blond hair was silver-streaked, tarnished like some long-forgotten heirloom. It came to rest just above the top of his shoulders as though it had somehow became exhausted and simply stopped. Behind the large aviator sunglasses were watery blue eyes that tended to squint, even when he was indoors, and had the furtive side-to-side dash of one used to constantly checking the corners.

Reginald wore a camel-colored mohair sport coat over jeans and cowboy boots.

Jack stood, and his mood lightened immediately as he shook his friend's thick hand, his financial troubles and the weather forgotten. Reginald always set Jack at ease. But it was also the better than twenty years that had passed between them, an old friendship that was earned the way rewarding things were, in the hardest of ways.

Reginald said, "Thanks for the oranges," as he shook Jack's hand. "You know Valencias are my favorite kind." He'd gotten his cut. They sat, and Reginald peered over the top of his sunglasses to focus on the menu the way people who had poor eyesight and either didn't know or refused to admit it did. He eventually settled on the same ale Jack was drinking. "You look like something's bothering you," he said.

"I—" Jack began and then trailed off, unsure of how to begin, how to talk around the problem.

Reginald picked up on it immediately and held up a hand. "It's okay. I don't need to know."

The old thief was the closest thing that Jack had to family, but even he didn't know about the winery or the identity Jack had built. It wasn't that Jack wanted to keep anything from Reginald. There were times that Jack felt true guilt at the deception. Perhaps *deception* wasn't the right word; it was more like *avoidance*. Still, Jack kept this life separate from anyone who knew him as a thief, as Jack Burdette. He needed that security, even if that meant keeping it from his oldest friend, of all people. When Jack was finally ready to retire, to become Frank Fischer for good, he would tell Reginald. Jack just wasn't sure that he'd tell him all of it. That was something he wrestled with a lot. You can't partially disappear.

It was also possible that Reginald would understand. He was a man who understood the value of a second chance, and a way out.

Reginald had settled in Long Beach when he left prison. Long Beach had a workman's vibe that suited Reginald's personality, thriving in the criminal underground. Most importantly, he was unknown to the local cops. Jack had spent some time there, making a point of popping down a few times a year so they could commiserate in the privacy of LeGrande's boat. Reginald respected Jack's privacy, so he never pushed too far into that other life. He knew Jack did something outside of their work, he just didn't know what. That was the thing about this life, you learned to appreciate secrets.

The waitress came by and took their order. Reginald ordered a large plate of oysters for the table. The conversation stayed in social territory. They never discussed business in public. Reginald went through a quiet rundown of current events—who was now in jail and who'd gotten out, who was working, and who wasn't. They had talk-arounds for nearly everything, patterns of speech and phrases that formed innocuous-sounding ciphers they'd built over decades in the trade. Jack often wondered if it was the same way with spies.

The server returned and asked if they wanted anything else. She was young, had purple hair streaked with red, and too much ink for such a small frame. She sported a kanji tattoo on each finger that Jack doubted represented anything deeper than "Eastern stuff is mysterious."

Jack considered his friend sitting across from him and smiled. "We'll take another round."

"Two more, got it. Same?"

Jack nodded.

"What are we drinking, anyway?" Reginald asked. "I never thought to ask."

Reginald had looked a little surprised that Jack ordered another round, given how he'd tried to rush them through. Jack felt bad about treating Reginald that way. He was one of the only true friends Jack had.

"It's called Back in Black. It's a black IPA from a local brewery called 21st Amendment."

Reginald held up his glass, considering the last swallow's worth of beer. He squinted and pursed his lips the way De Niro did when he needed to look serious. Reginald killed the last of it, and the waitress showed up with a pair of fresh beers. She grabbed the empties and Reginald's oyster plate and then disappeared back inside.

"It's good to see you, Reg," Jack said, holding his beer up for Reginald to tap it. "I'm sorry it's not more often."

"Me too, kid."

They finished their food and the beers.

After settling with the restaurant, they made their way through the terminal building to the Embarcadero and walked down the wide concrete way with the gray-green Pacific on their left. The pair walked slowly down the path along the water, watching as a ferry departed the terminal for Treasure Island. When they were finally clear of tourists, Reginald asked, "So, what do you know about Ari Ben Hassar?" There was a devilish glint in the old thief's eye, a throwback to what Hollywood thought was a mad scientist in the forties.

"Israeli diamond magnate," Jack said. "Started out with a mining company in Africa and discovered diamonds. Built that into a global empire. He controls his entire supply chain, all the way through to jewelry production. Has his own jewelry stores in Israel and Europe. Though I think he sells a good bit of the unfinished diamonds off wholesale as well. He's got a reputation for being ruthless. Way I hear it, there's a short list of people in this world you don't fuck with, and he's on it."

"Very good," Reginald said. "This summer, Hassar is holding an invite-only exhibition of his top-grade stones at Cannes. The collection he's bringing is rumored to be worth upwards of eighty-five million dollars."

Jack's mouth hung like it had a rusty hinge that no one

thought to fix. His pulse quickened, the way it did when Reginald revealed the potential take of any score. Jack's mind immediately went to the possibilities—the things he could do with that kind of money. His back-of-the-napkin calculations put that around ten million, assuming a four-person crew and forty-five cents on the dollar from a fence, plus Reginald's cut.

Jack slowed his pace and stopped, turning to face the water. He placed both hands on the concrete railing and looked out over gray San Francisco Bay. If the quality of the stones was as high as Reginald was talking about, Jack might be able to talk the Turks up to fifty-five cents on the dollar. That would pay for the Sine Metu plot as well as refill his coffers quite a bit from what he'd been pouring into Kingfisher over the years.

The winery was only good as a money laundering operation when money was actually coming out of it.

But those thoughts quickly dashed as the cold hand of reality slid its inky arm around Jack's shoulders. Jack thought of his rules.

"The security around that would have to be intense."

"Not as much as you might think."

"What? That's insane. With that kind of money involved, that place is going to be locked down like a missile silo."

"Oh," Reginald opened, a giddy lilt in his otherwise rock-and-pebble voice. "They'll have security guards, but they'll be little better than rent-a-cops. Remember French law. Private security guards can't be armed." That was true—one of the most ridiculous things Jack had ever discovered in his career, given the amount of liquid cash that flowed through that part of France.

"The exhibition is at the Carlton InterContinental Hotel. My source tells me all the salons are on the ground floor, and some of them are even accessible from the street. There will most likely be additional security in the lobby and around the access points, but this is one of the most exclusive hotels in Europe, and they're not going to make it look like an occupying army is sitting there. But really, even if you were spotted, it would just be a race to see who could call the police the fastest. And by then, you're really on your way out."

Jack studied his friend's face for a moment, holding his response. Reginald's face was a roadmap of hard years, a threadbare patchwork of liver spots, freckles, and lines that made his skin look like a poorly folded map.

"You're missing a key thing, Reginald."

"What's that?"

"Most of the security is going to be hotel staff or rent-a-cops, I'm with you there. The ones in the exhibition, though? Those are going to be Hassar's guys."

"So what?"

"So, Hassar is going to have people he trusts around the actual stones. He's Israeli. Those are probably ex-Mossad or Israeli Special Forces. Those aren't the kind who worry about things like jurisdiction or national borders or whether the French will let them keep their guns. I'm not going to start this off with a manhunt, especially with the kind of people who aren't likely to let go. Forget that."

"Come on, Jack. You don't know that."

"Reginald, do you know anything about this guy?" Jack only called Reginald by his name when he really needed to make a point. Jack stopped walking and turned to face his friend.

"Of course I do."

"Hassar isn't just ruthless by Western standards. He won't just collect his insurance check and forget this ever happened. Hassar is going to send people—his people—to recover his property. There's a reason nobody ever steals from this guy."

"Jack, you're being paranoid."

"You're goddamn right I am. But, okay, let's set the guards-who-are-probably-hit-men thing aside for a moment," Jack said. "It's too easy." Reginald's expression immediately soured from excitement to that of someone who'd just drank curdled milk by mistake. "There's no way a take worth that much is just sitting out in the open like it's in a petting zoo. It's going to be in display cases that will be alarmed, and the Cannes police, who *will* be armed, will be on standby and are probably being paid to be responsive. If they aren't on site, they won't be far off it. At night, the collection isn't going to be stored in the hotel safe. They're most likely going to take it to a private vault, which means armored cars and a police escort."

This was something that Reginald should have caught immediately. All those green zeroes obscuring his vision, maybe?

Reginald's expression softened. He placed a hand on his protégé's shoulder. "Don't overthink this, Jack. Forget the armored car. This isn't *Heat*. Focus on the daytime. Let's say they're in the display cases all day and that those cases are alarmed. Even if you don't have an alarm guy to deactivate them and you have to just go smash and grab, that's a couple minutes before the police are on scene. That's a tight window, I won't lie to you, but you can do this."

Could he?

This was a job that was orders of magnitude bigger than anything he'd ever contemplated, let alone attempted. More than that, there was a tissue-thin window to execute the job and get away, unless there was some way to kill the alarm and prevent the hotel staff from contacting the police, which would be difficult—impossible—given that this had to be a daylight job.

Jack doubted the police response would be as long as five

minutes. The Europeans didn't operate on the same level as the FBI, but they weren't exactly the third world, either.

Working in Europe was easy for the simple reason that it was Europe—several medium-sized, first-world countries tightly packed on a single continent with open borders and a penchant for high-end consumer goods. It was a criminal paradise. But Cannes, Jewel of the Riviera, was pushed to the southeast corner of France. It couldn't be any farther from a border—four, five hours by car. The kind of people Hassar was likely to have as his security detail, as Jack pointed out, wouldn't be overly concerned with that border anyway.

"Jack, I never said this would be easy, but I know you can pull it off, and when you do, we're set. Think about that for a second. We won't need to work anymore, either of us. We can just sit on my boat and fish all day or buy race cars or whatever the hell we want."

Jack held up both his hands and squeezed his eyes shut for a second. "What do you *really* know about Ari Hassar?"

Reginald shrugged. "He's eccentric, flashy. He digs being a mogul and wants everyone to know just how big he is."

"The only kind of person who would put that much money on display knows that no one is stupid enough to fuck with him."

"Jack, if we take this job, we don't ever have to work again."

"That's certainly true, though not in the way you think, I suspect." He held up a hand before Reginald could issue the protest Jack knew was coming. "Remember our conversation after Valencia about Ozren? How I said that after a few days everyone forgets about a jewelry store job but the insurance company? This is the other side of that coin. I don't want to take a job so large people are going to be talking about it for the next ten years. The police won't just let this go and write it off. Nor will the insurance company, who will certainly continue the hunt with their own private investigators long after the police have stopped. These aren't the type of people to just let eighty-five million dollars walk out the door. To say nothing of what Hassar's people would do."

"Jack," Reginald said flatly in his rocky, sonorous voice. "I have someone on the inside of Hassar's organization. That's where this came from. I paid a lot of money to get connected to him. He's confirmed the security and can make some other arrangements on my behalf."

"Who is it?"

"No way," Reginald said.

"Oh, so you want me to go do this job and you won't tell me where the intel on it is coming from? You want me to consider doing this, that's part of the deal."

"I shelled out a lot of coin for this," Reginald said, as though that were explanation enough. "But no, I'm not telling you where it came from. That's part of his deal, and I'm going to honor it."

That was a bullshit answer. Reginald was holding back on him because Jack was asking questions and poking holes.

"And I suppose he gets some of the take as well? How much?"

"Twenty percent."

"Off the top? Forget that."

Just then, a man in a suit walked past them, a little too close for Jack's liking. He held up two fingers to pause Reginald in the midst of buttressing his argument.

"What?" Jack said when the man passed.

"It's eighty-five million."

Jack held his hands up to cut off the conversation. "I don't like this, and I also don't like how aggressive you're being in pushing it on me. It sounds too risky. There are a lot of good reasons why I don't take jobs like this, and this one seems to hit all of them. Not only would we have Europol after us, it's an immediate INTERPOL Red Notice, which goes out to nearly every law enforcement agency in the civilized world. And that's to say nothing about what Hassar himself would do. I can hide from a lot of people, but I'm not about mess with a bunch of ex-Mossad guys. Hunting people in hiding is literally what they do." Jack looked off to the blue-gray rolling ocean. "We've got a really good formula, and it has worked out for us. We're making good, steady money, and we're not on anyone's radar. Let's keep it that way."

Reginald said in a low voice, "You have a lot more years to be conservative, Jack. I don't."

"Reg," Jack started, but dropped it. Jack had worked constantly while Reginald was behind bars, and when he got out early thanks to a lenient parole board, Jack staked him a couple hundred thousand dollars to buy that nice house he lived in at the Naples Island Marina. Moving from San Quentin to a home overlooking the Pacific Ocean should have been a good enough trade for anyone.

Jack looked around them again to make sure no one was within earshot before he replied. "Ari Hassar is not someone I want to get in a ring with. If a guy like that doesn't scare you, maybe you've been at this too long." Jack breathed once and tried to calm himself.

"The Jack Burdette that I know wouldn't back away from a job like this no matter who owned the take." LeGrande's voice was snide and sour, baiting.

Jack's mouth opened as the retort formed and died in his throat, leaving a look on his face that was a poorly shaken cocktail of disbelief and incredulity. The Jack Burdette *he* knew? Never in the history of their relationship had Jack proposed something so reckless, and certainly not after Reginald's stint in prison, which had been a serious wake-up call for them both. Reginald started to say something else, but Jack held up a hand and cut him off. The Jack Burdette he knew had never tried for a score this large and wouldn't.

"I'm leaving now, and I'm not talking about this again. It's too risky, and I'm not willing to take the chance that I'd end up in a French prison or at the bottom of the Med. You pushing me is really starting to piss me off. I've got enough on my plate as it is. I couldn't focus on this even if I was interested." Reginald's jaw dropped to issue a protest, but Jack held up a hand and pushed the words back into LeGrande's mouth by force of will. "I'll talk to you when I'm ready to work again."

Jack left Reginald standing in the gray of the Embarcadero. The ex-thief called after him a few times. The first one, Jack dismissed with a gesture, and the rest he simply ignored. Jack had left his other phone in the glove box when he'd met Reginald. It was easier for him to maintain separation between his two lives. He powered up the car and then his phone, quickly scanning messages to see if there was anything important. Megan and Hugh had both texted him several times, asking where he was and why he wasn't picking up his phone. The phone started vibrating as the voicemails registered. Ignoring them, Jack called Megan.

"Meg, what's going on?"

"Where the hell have you been," she half shouted.

"What's wrong?"

"You have to get back here right now. Hugh just called. The money is gone, Frank, it's all gone."

"What money?"

"The ten million. The money Paul was supposed to buy the plot with."

"What? Where the fuck is Paul?"

In a flat voice, Megan said, "He's gone too."

5

Special Agent Katrina Danzig was spending a rare morning in her office. *Office* was being charitable; it was a cube in a cube farm in the FBI building on the southern tip of Manhattan. But Danzig didn't care about the digs so much since she barely spent any time here. Much of the mission of the Bureau's Gem and Jewelry Program was educating industry on the current trends in jewelry theft and international trafficking. Helping them understand the changing landscape so that they would, hopefully, keep pace with their security practices. Equally important was for the jewelry manufacturers and the wholesalers to understand their supply chains. The number of precious gems that had, at one time in their lives, touched criminal hands was staggering. Danzig spent countless hours on the road speaking at trade associations, conventions, corporate retreats, and other events educating industry on the state of play.

While it was important, it was also a sideshow.

Danzig's other full-time job was as a member of the countertrafficking task force. She was the Bureau's rep on a multi-agency, multi-national working group of law enforce-

ment agencies in the US and Europe that was working tirelessly to roll back the tide of jewelry theft and underground
trading of precious gems. The crimes happened almost
exclusively in Europe, but given America's position as the
world's leading consumer of jewelry, the Bureau had a vested
interest in this effort. More than that was what stolen gems
were used for.

Stones were the world's one untraceable currency.

Gemstones had no serial numbers, and their provenance
was impossible to prove. For these reasons, they were one of
the favored ways of transacting business in the dark
economies of the world. Terrorist networks and transnational
criminal organizations frequently relied on gems to conduct
their business. Since 9/11, the FBI was almost singularly
focused on counterterrorism, and a considerable amount of
that was identifying and combating the networks terrorists
used to fund themselves. There was a massive illegal emerald
trade coming out of Afghanistan that helped fund al-Qaeda
and the Taliban, rubies in south Asia, and—as the world was
well aware of—conflict diamonds in Africa.

Danzig joined the Bureau after 9/11 and with a desire to
punch back.

She was in her last year at Columbia earning an MBA and
was looking at a career in international finance when the
towers fell. A few months later, one of her school friends
contacted her. He was a year ahead and had been recruited by
the FBI. He said the Bureau was looking for people with back-
grounds in international finance to help them unravel terrorist
funding networks. Was she interested? Absolutely. Danzig
became an expert in illicit banking, and her squad's work
played a large role in the US government pressuring the Swiss
and other global financial centers to change their policy of not
taking sides in the war on terror. Or at least not getting in

America's way after the FBI revealed the rivers of dark money flowing through their banking systems.

Then she got into jewels.

Danzig's membership on the task force was a continuation of the work she did while posted as a legal attaché, or LEGAT in Bureau parlance, to the Hague. There she worked with INTER-POL, Europol, and the national law enforcement agencies of most countries in western Europe. That job was so much diplomacy, which, arguably, was not Danzig's strongest suit. While terrorism had been a huge problem in Europe in the eighties, with much of that fomented by the Soviet Union or by extremist groups from the Middle East, terrorism had shifted away from much of continental Europe in recent years. Danzig, and others, believed this was intentional as terror organizations realized that they needed bases of operations from which to strike their enemies in the UK and America. So, the task force's focus was predominantly on the criminal aspect of the problem. They pursued gem and jewel thieves with the hope of using any arrests they made to uncover the networks criminals used to distribute their stolen goods.

She missed those days.

That had been a great assignment, the best in her FBI career.

Danzig had gotten to participate in investigations, even a few raids, across Europe. Of course, as an American law enforcement officer, Danzig was strictly an advisor. She couldn't make any arrests unless there was an American involved, and there usually wasn't.

Well, that's not entirely true.

There was one.

During her time at the Hague they'd gotten intel on a very successful crew that had taken down dozens of scores across the continent. The thing was, they were always small. They were jewelry stores at hotels, at resorts, or in Europe's innumerable wealthy tourist destinations. This group was fast, efficient, and uncharacteristically savvy. They never went for big scores. Danzig counted at least four times when they'd executed a flawless job at a jewelry store, netting a few hundred thousand when a much bigger target was maybe a few miles away. The intel they had was that it was an American who led this crew.

Contrast that with the Pink Panthers, who wore elaborate disguises and made heist-film getaways on boats and in fast cars. Many on the task force first thought it was the Panthers pulling these other jobs, just a smarter cell, but Danzig and a few of her counterparts weren't convinced. It just didn't match their profile. The Pink Panthers came from the ruin of Yugoslavia, with the majority of them having served in the special forces of those armies. They applied the skills they learned in asymmetric warfare against the West to thievery and were exceptional at it. But they were also brash. They wanted the West to know it was them, how good they were and how powerless their law enforcement was to stop them. No, this crew was different. They were subtle, they were smart, and they were anything but brash.

Danzig's desk phone rang, taking her attention away from the trip report she was typing on her computer. She lifted the receiver and tapped her extension. "Gem and Jewelry, this is Danzig."

"Hello, Katrina," the voice on the other end said in Italian-accented English. Her face broke into a smile as soon as she heard it.

"Gio," she said. Giovanni Castro was an inspector in the Guardia di Finanza, Italy's economic police. She'd met Castro when she was first posted to the Hague and joined the task force. Castro had been—and still was—serving a tour with INTERPOL.

"How are you? Are you adjusting to life back in the States?"

"Sort of. I miss Europe, and I forgot how fat Americans are," Danzig said. "The new job is good, but it's a little more administration than I was expecting. I miss chasing bad guys."

"Well, then I won't bore you with what *I'm* up to," he said. "Other than Dutch beer is too heavy. I've got a lead from an informant of mine, and I think it might be our friend."

Danzig shifted the phone to her left hand so her right was free to grab a yellow legal pad and a pen from the other side of her desk, grateful for anything to take her away from the monotony of a trip report. "I'm all ears," she said, excitement rising in her voice.

"Our friend" meant the American. She'd been after this guy for years, for as long as she'd been on the task force. He was a ghost, or a chameleon, pick your metaphor—Danzig had them all in her file. According to their sources' accounting, which were disparate and widely varied, this American was either a master of disguise or had the ability to just up and vanish after a job was done. No law enforcement agency in Europe had any idea how he moved the goods he and his crew stole. They also couldn't get anyone inside his organization to flip, not that they'd been able to identify anyone on the crew either.

"This is coming from an informant. He's a source that I'm pretty confident in." Man or woman, Castro referred to all of his sources in the masculine until their identity was revealed. Some police opted for the more generic "they," but Castro said he always found that awkward. "There was a theft in Valencia about a week ago during the Falles Fiesta. They ripped off a jewelry boutique for just under a million, jewelry, watches, cash, and some loose stones the shop had for setting. We think they rented a vacant office next to the store, because that's how they got in. Came in at night, knocked the wall down using the fireworks as cover for the sound."

"Smart," Danzig said.

"Yeah. The landlord said he doesn't remember what the person looked like who rented the space, just that it was a woman. Local police think he's not cooperating because he's embarrassed."

"You don't think he was in on it?"

"No, I spoke with them and read the interview notes. My source tells me it was Gentleman Jack."

Even though she already knew this was who they were talking about, Danzig's pulse jumped a moment at the mention, but then her mood settled into a strange malaise after a few moments. "Gentleman Jack" was the American thief, most certainly an alias and something of a legend among law enforcement agencies in Europe. He'd never been arrested or fingerprinted to anyone's knowledge, and there were no photographs of him anywhere. If he *had* ever been arrested, then it was under another alias and with a very, very good forged identity. What stupefied and stymied the various law enforcement agencies hunting him over the years was that there was zero consistency in what he looked like, what he sounded like, and what his nationality was. The only thing that most people agreed on was that he was very good, very clever, and the only risks he took were highly calculated.

Danzig first learned about Gentleman Jack from Castro. Burdette was an American criminal operating abroad, so she'd taken a special interest in him. Arresting an American citizen was one of the few things she could do during her time in Europe. She also viewed it as her professional responsibility. It didn't look good for the Bureau that one of the most infamous thieves in Europe was an American. Danzig's interest had turned into a quiet obsession over the years.

What frustrated her most was the lack of consistency in the reporting. In fact, the only thing that they agreed on was that Gentleman Jack was most certainly American (some reports had him as Canadian, but Danzig discounted those), and that was based solely on accent, which could be faked. They couldn't get anyone that worked with him to flip, and he only worked with people that he knew and trusted, so no law enforcement agency could get an undercover into his crew. The word was, the reason they called him Gentleman Jack was that everyone on his crew got an equal share of the payout, even him. He treated his crew well, didn't put them at unnecessary risk (for the occupation), and as a result, they were fiercely loyal.

"Jack Burdette" was almost certainly an alias. None of the matches that she got in the social security database for that name even remotely fit the profile. They had a handful of AKAs, but it appeared the same one was never used twice.

"How close is your source?" Danzig asked.

"He was on the job," Castro said.

Danzig didn't ask follow-up questions because she knew Castro wouldn't share anything else until he was ready. She knew the reasons why and respected them. About fifteen years before, Castro was an undercover officer with the Italian state police in Turin. At the time, they were bent like a U-turn and held secrets like a wet bag held water. Not only was his operation disclosed by people on the take, but Castro's identity as well. After that, he transferred to the Guardia di Finanza and took a transfer to Rome, because it just wasn't safe for him in the state police.

Bent cops didn't trust someone that couldn't be bought.

"This is huge, Gio," she said.

The problem was, now the clock on Burdette reset. He only did two or three jobs a year and always several months apart. Let the heat die down from the last one before going after something else. The times immediately following a job, it was like he dissolved.

"Your CI give you anything else?" She heard Castro inhale and then let out a long breath. Giovanni was still a heavy smoker. That meant he was outside calling her on his mobile.

"He doesn't know when the next job is. But he can give us the names of everyone on the crew."

Danzig copied them down. She knew that Giovanni had already run them through INTERPOL and Europol criminal databases, but the Bureau had its own resources. Castro said he didn't have anything else to pass on, but he'd follow up in a couple days to see how she was getting along with those names.

Danzig thanked him, said she'd be in touch, and hung up.

Because Burdette's tradecraft was so good, many in the law enforcement community thought that he had either police or even intelligence training. Danzig knew that wasn't true, though. Despite all of the varied theories about Burdette she'd heard over the years, Danzig could discount almost all of them, and everything she heard she vetted with Castro before entering it into the file she kept on him. She also had enough information about what Burdette looked like and where he came from that she could dismiss about half of the leads they got that attributed nearly every unsolved theft in Europe to him.

Castro knew Jack Burdette personally.

6

It took Reginald the entire flight from San Francisco to Long Beach to get control of his emotions enough that he could think about what to do next.

The fucking *nerve*.

Who did Jack think he was, turning down this job?

This wasn't even a job. This was...this was a legacy. This was the kind of thing that legends were born from. They pulled this off and they wouldn't need to work again. Nor would Reginald need some of the less desirable contingency plans he had set in place. To say nothing of what it cost Reginald to get the information on this job. Almost two hundred grand, but it had been worth it. Reginald had been at this game a long time and knew there was no such thing as a perfect job, but this was as close as they came. On the surface, he understood why Jack was afraid of Ari Hassar, and certainly the man had a reputation for swift and brutal vengeance. There were rumors about what he did to some people who tried to rip him off in Africa, and Jack's warning about his former Mossad security wasn't unfounded.

But Hassar was also a man with a lot to lose. He wasn't

going to risk his entire empire coming after them. Besides, that collection would be insured, and Hassar wouldn't be out anything but pride. The media coverage and worldwide exposure he was going to get would probably drive his sales up a clean ten percent this year. If anything, they were doing Hassar a favor.

When Reginald arrived back in Long Beach, he drove home to Naples Island but skipped his house, opting instead for the marina and his boat, a Chris Craft Corsair 36. He opened the boat's small galley and pulled out a bottle of scotch and a tumbler, reclined on the long leather bench, and forced himself to relax. Reginald's small community built on one of the three islands in Long Beach's Alamitos Bay. It was an exclusive development that had its own marina. Reginald had made a lot of money off his partnership with Jack over the years. That was much of the reason he had a three-story townhouse overlooking the ocean and a boat in the marina, but Reginald trained and ran other thieves. Burdette wasn't the only pony in Reginald's stable; he was just the fastest.

Reginald reclined on the bench and felt the gentle movement of the boat on the water. The Corsair was a masterpiece of nautical craftsmanship. The hull was painted navy with an ivory-colored top and cockpit. Teak accents flowed aft from the bow and streaked across each side, splitting the ivory in two. This motif played out again in the open-air cabin with ivory-colored leather benches framed by tan accents above a teak floor. Reginald purchased this with his cut of Jack's earning last year. This was an escape plan as much as it was a luxury. Reginald maintained a dive apartment a few miles from here that his lazy parole officer never double-checked, but his real residence was the three-story Mediterranean home here on the island and, when he wasn't in the townhouse, here on the boat. Reginald could be in

Mexico within a few hours if he ever needed to run. *And in style*, he mused. That was one thing Reginald picked up from his protégé.

Jack had only disappointed him twice before. This was not a feeling Reginald was used to.

The first was in '95, during Jack's first time on a crew. Before then, he'd just been a driver, but Reginald thought he was ready and he brought him along. It was an armored car depot in downtown Los Angeles. Inside job, disgruntled employee about to get fired and looking to put together his own retirement plan. They'd disarmed the guards inside, but Jack didn't think to check one of the guards for an ankle piece. The guard got one of the crew before they realized what happened, then it all fell apart. Reginald and Jack got away, but not before someone on their crew got ideas and got greedy. When it was all said and done, they had bodies to hide, and Reginald sent Jack to Italy for a couple of years while the heat died down. Reginald wanted Jack to work with his old partner, an Italian thief named Vito Verrazano.

The second time was a few years after that. Reginald wanted Jack in on a jewelry emporium in Beverly Hills. Jack told him no, that he wasn't working in the States anymore. Apparently he'd gotten a taste for Europe when he was over there and decided not to shit where he slept. The advice might have been good or it might have been wrong, but Reginald was convinced that if he'd had Jack on that crew they'd have gotten away with it. He knew from Vito that Jack had been a quick study and, over his two years there, became one of the best thieves he'd ever seen.

Reginald closed his eyes and felt the supple up-and-down motion of the boat floating in its berth. Seagulls squawked overhead. He'd come a long way since his stint at San Quentin after that Beverly Hills job. He'd gotten ten years for that, though his lawyer was able to shave a few off and good behavior took care of the rest.

This third time, this third disappointment...was going to sting. *But the lessons we truly learn are the ones that are the toughest to deliver.*

Reginald still loved him like a son.

That's why what he had to do next was so hard.

Even family had to have a dose of tough love on occasion.

Reginald learned the value of contingency planning when he'd gone to prison the first time. He hadn't had an escape route, and it cost him. He vowed never to put himself in that position again. He was going to get the outcome that he wanted here, and it didn't matter who or what he had to trample to do it. Reginald didn't care that Jack wanted another life. That was fine. Reginald had one. They were all entitled to it. Hell, he'd christened his boat *Second Chances*. Reginald's issue was that Jack was walking away from an opportunity to make themselves both rich beyond their wildest expectations and, more importantly, a chance to walk away from this life, walk away from risk for good. They wouldn't *have* to steal anymore. Gentleman Jack Burdette wasn't the only thief Reginald knew; he was just the best. And Reginald wanted this for him, wanted him to go out on top. It would be the exclamation point to the careers they had and one glorious "fuck you" to the one-mistake system that kept people like them from ever getting to have the picket fence. So, if Jack wasn't going to do this, Reginald would have to find someone that would. Honestly, based on the intel he had, this was going to be easy enough that Reginald himself could probably do it, ten years out of the game.

Wistful, Reginald drained his glass, got up, and poured another. He arched his back and stretched. No matter how short the flight, coach seats always did a number on him, and it wouldn't do for his PO to learn that he was buying first-class tickets on what that clown thought Reginald was making a year. Golden sunlight played across the ocean in the waters beyond the marina as the sky above started to slowly darken. Reginald sat back down, resting his legs on the bench.

He thought about the times he and Jack had, turning that scared kid on the run into a proper thief. He thought about the wild times, the crazy jobs they pulled and the handful of times they spent the entire wad living like big shots. Guess that's what gave Jack the taste for the life he had now. Maybe Reginald was to blame for this somehow. At some point, Jack decided that he had something to lose and got conservative. He made up those stupid rules of his.

But Jack didn't have a prison sentence hanging over him.

Reginald was tired. He was tired of having to check in with this idiot parole officer. He was tired of planning jobs and recruiting crews. He was tired of the risk, of wondering if he was going to wake up to a flashlight in the face, no-knock warrant, and the rest of his life behind bars. He was tired of wondering if the thirty minutes he needed to get to the boat and go would be enough.

And Reginald was tired of dealing with prima donna thieves.

Jack told him time and again: never steal out of hunger, never take a score large enough that someone would notice, and never steal from someone with the will to get it back.

Reginald was of an age where he should be thinking about retirement, whatever his vocation was. He wanted to enjoy his life, on his own, without waiting for the other shoe to drop. Yes, he probably had enough squirreled away here and there in places that the government didn't know about and couldn't find that he could live out the rest of his life without having to worry. But that also felt a lot like playing defense. Reginald had been doing that for far too long.

Well, even the most reluctant would come around given sufficient motivation. Reginald was sad it had to come to this, he truly was, but Jack had enough years left to make it up. Reginald did not.

Resolute, he toasted the air and drained his glass.

If Gentleman Jack Burdette wasn't going to play along, then Reginald would just have to give him a push.

7

"I understand what you're saying," Jack said in a tight voice that was like a dam on the verge of breaking, "but I don't think you appreciate the situation." He was fighting a losing battle against maintaining his composure and keeping his voice down. The warm summer air, fragrant with bloom, floated easily through the open windows. It was a busy afternoon, and the parking lot was almost full of customers' cars. The odds of someone hearing his conversation on their way into or out of the building was pretty good.

"Mr. Fischer, I can assure you we're doing everything we can, but you have to be patient. These things take time."

Jack's temper flared and boiled over before he even had a thought to control it. "Take time," he thundered into the phone. "Take time? Paul Sharpe found a way to steal ten million dollars from my business, and you're lecturing me on patience."

"Mr. Fischer," the state's investigator tried to break in, but Jack was having none of it.

"While you're sitting on your hands, my winery is hemorrhaging money. I don't even know how I'm going to make fucking payroll this week, let alone how I'm going to pay people to harvest my goddamned grapes in two months, and you want me to be patient? I'm going to lose my business."

"Mr. Fischer, if you'd—"

"No, I will not calm down. I don't care about your backlog, and I sure as shit am not interested in you telling me *again* that you understand why I'm angry. Someone stole from me, and you don't seem to be the slightest bit interested in doing a goddamn thing about it."

"Allegedly."

"What?" Jack stammered, finally breaking out of his torrent of invective.

"Allegedly stole from you. This investigation is still ongoing."

The words were so incomprehensible he was actually stupefied into silence. The silence did not, however, last very long. "Allegedly. Allegedly? Okay, you're the investigator, you tell me. My accountant somehow pulls a wire transfer for ten million dollars into an account he had set up that I knew nothing about and then disappears, and you're actually lecturing me on the presumption of guilt? You have to be out of your f—" The word died on his lips as Jack saw Megan standing in the doorway, arms folded impatiently and looking cross. He really hoped she was just here to tell him that the seal broke on the number two tank again and not that a tasting room full of people heard him screaming at a state's investigator like a madman.

Jack quieted and tried to calm himself, to lower his skyrocketing pulse. There was nothing but silence on the other end of the phone, not even static, and he hoped the man hadn't hung up. After several beats, Jack said, "I'm sorry,

Mister..." He paused, searching for the name. "Schoenberg, was it?"

"That's right," the man said, oddly without irritation. He must've been used to getting yelled at.

"I'm obviously upset, and I hope you can appreciate why." Jack's tone was in no way conciliatory.

"I can, Mr. Fischer, but I need to impress upon you that these things take time. We are very sensitive to the fact that a crime has been committed, and my office *will* investigate it, we will find out who is responsible, and we will hold them accountable. But Mr. Fischer, you have to respect that we have a responsibility to the people who were wronged before you to close those cases out and to the system at..."

The man continued talking, but Jack wasn't listening. The last thing he needed right now was another lecture on what he now came to refer to acidly as "the process." Every time he'd talked to the state's investigator's office, it was the same thing. He was trying to impress upon them that not only had Sharpe cleaned out the winery's coffers but also much of Jack's personal holdings. So not only was the winery broke, but Jack, personally, was in a lot of trouble. While the wheels of justice wound their inexorable way around, Jack was faced with the very real fear that his business wasn't going to survive the summer. That didn't seem to conjure up any emotion or any reinvigorated sense of purpose among the drones in the investigator's office who were trying to caution him that it would be years before he got any of that money back. Jack recognized the irony of the situation and couldn't help but think it was some kind of horrible, cosmic prank.

"Mr. Fischer?"

"Yes, sorry, what did you say?"

"I was saying, Mr. Fischer, that we understand your situation and was trying to reassure you that we're giving the matter our fullest attention."

Jack's train of thought started going afield again at the introduction of more drone-speak, so he simply cut the conversation off. He'd gotten what he wanted, which was confirmation that the State of California was, at present, doing jack shit.

He ended the call and cast his eyes down, his head suddenly feeling like it weighed just too much to keep up.

Jack exhaled hard, the perfect expression of a long and terrible day. It had been almost a month since Sharpe stole the Sine Metu funds, and Jack felt that none of the law enforcement or governmental agencies involved were any closer to finding him than when he'd first reported the crime. Jack had even hired a private investigator when he'd gotten impatient with the glacial pace of progress by law enforcement. The detective had yet to turn up anything tangible, and some part of Jack believed it was probably a waste of money, but Jack believed it was important that the staff saw him take action. Jack also had no faith in law enforcement and wasn't going to rely on them as his only option.

He walked over to one of the two Manhattan chairs he kept in his office and sat, first grabbing a pair of plastic water bottles out of the small fridge inset in his bookshelf. He handed one to Megan, who accepted it silently. He cracked the top and drank deep. Megan unscrewed the cap off her bottle but instead of sitting, leaned against the bookcase, extending one of her long legs out in front of her to stretch it. As she bent over, two long strands of curly, reddish-blond hair on either side of her head broke free from the half-assed ponytail and fell, bouncing in midair.

"Sorry," he said, after he'd collapsed into the chair.

"What good does yelling at them do?"

"Makes me feel better," he said, though it didn't and they both knew it. Jack whispered another soft curse for his own benefit but said nothing else.

"I heard you in the tasting room," she said ruefully. "I just told that nice couple from Nebraska that you had Tourette's." A wry smile cracked the stern countenance, and Jack knew she wasn't entirely angry with him. Megan had originally toed the "trust the process" line, but her faith in the system was quickly eroding. She was just better at hiding it during business hours than Jack was.

Megan took a drink from her water bottle and then gave Jack a soft, sad smile. But even with the pain, frustration, and anguish they both rightly felt now, light found its way into her eyes. There was a trace band of red from the sun that ran along the ridges of her cheeks and made the freckles pop out like stars in the daytime. Seeing that, seeing *her* just the way she was lowered Jack's temperature to a moderately angry simmer. Megan wore a navy blue polo with the Kingfisher logo on it and jeans; hair auburn hair was in its usual ponytail. She'd spent the day inside mostly, either helping out in the tasting room to make up for a staff shortage or overseeing repairs to all of their other storage tanks. It was a preventative measure and hard lesson learned after the previous month's spillage. Despite having been inside most of the day, there was a pink line and burst of freckles across her cheeks. She was in her late thirties, but the freckles and the perpetual light in her eyes made her look much younger.

"Well, thanks for cheering me up," Jack said sardonically.

"Luckily," she said, smirking, "no one else heard you. The tasting room is full."

Jack couldn't see how it would matter. He had been in a very dark place since Sharpe's disappearance, and not even Megan had been able to draw him out of it.

Embezzlement was surprisingly common in the wine industry, but rarely in amounts like this. Usually, it was a mid-level employee with access to the books. Winemaking was a strange business, and very few made it rich. Sometimes, it defied logic. Operating a winery required the owner to be a farmer, a craftsperson, a chemist (some might argue alchemist), a marketer, and sometimes a visionary. Wineries, even the smallest ones, required a tremendous amount of operating capital, and even if they didn't turn a huge profit, and very few of them did, a lot of money flowed through it. Everything not directly related to growing grapes and making wine tended to be done on a shoestring. It was very common for multimillion dollar operations to be accounted by hand or on a spreadsheet.

And people were far too trusting.

In Jack's experience, most of the people in this business believed that everyone in it was good-hearted. Winemakers were farmers and artists, they were collegial and friendly, and generally, their businesses reflected that. If they were cynical, and many were, it was about issues like land development or water rights or about the conglomerates buying up and taking over the business, edging the independents out. Most winemakers rarely, if ever, considered an insider threat.

But Jack knew better and should have seen this coming.

They filed charges with the Sonoma County Sheriff's Office as soon as they'd realized what Sharpe had done. The sheriff redirected them to the California Highway Patrol. CHP had absorbed the California State Police in the nineties and had assumed their responsibility with it, which included investigating financial crimes against local businesses. Coughlin had calls in to the FBI, but he wasn't optimistic and told Jack not to get his hopes up about them getting involved. Secretly, Jack was relieved. The last thing he wanted was the FBI digging into the life and times of Frank Fischer.

Jack studied Megan's profile. Afternoon sun lit her from the side. She stretched the other leg, and Jack knew she was stalling. Reading people was an invaluable skill for a thief, perhaps even more important than being good at stealing things. You needed to be able to read a potential crew member and guess whether they'd crack, whether they were nervous because they were nervous or because they were hiding something. You needed to be able to guess who was going to sell you out because they were a double-dealing asshole or because they were police. You also needed to be able to guess whether or not the Hungarian gangster you were selling your loot to was just going to shoot you and save himself the three hundred thousand he was supposed to shell out.

The first step to reading someone was learning their tells.

Megan's was stalling before raising a difficult subject. She'd give him a stage pause, a dramatic look out the window, or fuss with an object for a breath or two. Jack let this play out a few seconds. He had to be careful about calling her on it. When she didn't initiate her end of the conversation, Jack knew it must've been something serious.

"What is it you really wanted to talk to me about, Meg?"

She chewed on her lower lip for a moment before saying, "I was just wondering if you'd heard from Hugh yet."

Jack knew why she didn't want to ask—they both knew the news wouldn't be good. If Jack avoided vocalizing it, that seemed to make it less real. Instead of just closing his eyes, he pressed the lids together with as much force as he could muster until it actually caused a dull ache around his eyes, as if to exorcise some unspoken pain by creating a different kind. The reason Meg was asking about Coughlin was that the lawyer had a meeting with the Sonoma County District Attorney's Office today to discuss their case. Even though the actual investigation was handled by the State of California, Hugh thought that he might be able to get some traction by going to the DA's office with whom he'd originally filed the complaint.

"I did," Jack said finally and slowly.

"I suppose if the news was good, you'd have led off with it," Megan replied.

Jack nodded and just grunted out a sour "mm-hm." After another half minute or so, he said, "It's the same line that the state investigator gave me. The DA's office and the CHP are looking into it, but they have a full caseload, so they expect this to take some time." Jack rolled his hand in the "as-you-do" gesture. "Which was why I called the state's Bureau of Investigation."

"How much time?"

Jack shrugged. "Months. Hugh called our congressman, both senators, and the governor's office this morning, for all the good that'll do."

"That's insane, actually insane," Megan half shouted, throwing her hands wide. "How hard can it be to find a pudgy accountant with ten million dollars?"

"This is California," Jack replied evenly. "Everyone has ten million dollars."

Jack could tell that the joke didn't land by Megan's folding her arms across her chest. The "Frank, I'm serious," seemed an unnecessary punctuation mark.

"They've issued a warrant, but embezzlement doesn't exactly get them up for a manhunt. Even when they find him, the DA's office said it'd probably be a year before we go to trial. If he's convicted, it's very likely we won't get everything back. What we do get back, it'll probably take years to collect."

"That's ridiculous," Megan thundered, before launching into an acidic and comprehensive tirade of California's criminal justice system.

Jack held up a hand, which did nothing to calm her down. By the third "Meg," Jack had gotten her attention. "I said all of that, in pretty much the same tone, to Hugh, and he said that *he* said all of that to the DA."

"In pretty much the same tone," Megan said, with a knowing but mirthless smile on her face. "I suppose it's not getting us bumped to the top of the list, is it?"

Jack answered by shaking his head slowly, sadly. "I've hired a private investigator to find Sharpe. If CHP can't do their job, I'll hand Paul to them on a fucking dinner plate. That son of a bitch stole from me." He said this mostly to himself, but when Jack looked back up at Megan and caught her reaction, he realized that he'd broken character. This was not the kind of thing Frank Fischer would say. Jack attempted to cover for it, saying, "I'm sorry, I'm just angry. This is why I don't trust the government. If the legal system isn't there to protect average citizens, let alone a small business, what good is it?" That *was* the kind of thing Frank Fischer would say.

Megan nodded in notional agreement.

Frank Fischer justified the offshoring of his money as a libertarian protest against the federal government, which he believed was no longer accountable to the people it served. Frank Fischer believed the government didn't use his tax money ethically, and so the only way he could protest that was to deny the government that taxation. The logic drove Coughlin positively insane every time they had the argument, which was often enough, but it worked and was a supremely effective backstop to the Frank Fischer legend.

"Look, for now we have to sit tight and play it their way, as much as it pains me to do it. Maybe if we can show CHP where Sharpe is, we can expedite the trial phase or at least get him arrested. How that stupid shit could just up and disappear is beyond me. For now, we need to focus on harvest and how we're going to pay for the extra labor."

Jack watched the gears in Megan's head begin to turn. They were a lot alike, particularly with the way they handled problems. They were people of action, neither one able to impotently stand on the sidelines and wait for the next action to play out. They needed to *do* something, even if that thing wouldn't bring them any closer to their goal. So Jack focused her on the upcoming grape harvest, which, depending on the weather, was between a month and six weeks out.

"Do we have enough money to pay for it?"

Jack shrugged. He honestly didn't know. Jack was good with numbers and certainly had developed a level of proficiency in moving dark money around, but this was *finance*. In his trade, he dealt in absolutes. A job paid this much, the percentage to the fence was that much, the take some other amount. While he was very intelligent, Jack's formal education ended when he was seventeen. He was naturally intuitive and a very quick study, and he spent much of his spare time or travel time learning, but finance eluded him. As a supposed former software engineer with a computer science degree, people rightly assumed that he was good with figures and were surprised to find out he wasn't. He'd always respond with something like, "I hate adding. That's why I programmed the computer to do it for me."

"We don't have much," he told her. Jack rubbed his temples with his left hand. "I've been pouring over our books for weeks, and I can't really make heads or tails of what we've got. Sharpe covered his tracks pretty well. I know from our weekly meetings that we're bringing in about twenty-five thousand a month, but monthly expenses are about sixty or seven thousand. At least it was all my money and we don't have any creditors to answer to." Jack closed his eyes. "Sharpe basically cleaned us out. Hugh is going to bring in a forensic accountant, but it looks like it wasn't just the Sine Metu money he took. He's been skimming for years." Not only that, they needed to hire someone to figure out what their books should actually read. Sharpe did such an effective job redirecting money and covering his own tracks, it was exceedingly difficult for an average person to figure out what money was where.

"That son of a bitch."

"For what it's worth, that actually helps us in court because we can show that the ten million wasn't just a spur-of-the-moment thing. Hugh says by establishing a pattern, we'll be able to show that this was premeditated." It was a nice sentiment, Jack knew, but hollow words. Because Sharpe's embezzlement had gone on likely since he started, it was no wonder that Kingfisher was operating at a loss. Coughlin figured that Sharpe was skimming systematically to prove that he could while waiting for an opportunity to take a much larger amount.

Jack knew that he was to blame for this. He agreed to bring Sharpe in and hadn't insisted on tighter controls. Jack knew that he'd bought into the conviviality of the industry and thought everyone in the wine business was basically good at heart. Ironically, Coughlin used the statistic about embezzlement to convince Jack they needed to bring in someone to guard against just such a thing. But sentiment didn't make payroll or keep the lights on. The immediate problem was that they had very little operating capital. "I'm going to have to move more money over—just to keep us floating, but I don't know how much more of that I can stand to do. The only alternative is to try and get us a bridge loan, but even Hugh doesn't know if that's possible given how deep we're in."

They'd had this conversation so many times over the last five weeks that Jack knew exactly what Megan was going to say next, so he asked instead, "What choice do I have?" Jack had a few assets left here and there, but the ten million he'd staked for the Sine Metu buy represented the bulk of his remaining wealth.

"We could sell a stake of the business to an investor," Megan offered.

Jack's blood froze just hearing the words. He tried to deflect, saying, "I doubt we're profitable enough to even make that attractive. Besides, with the embezzlement hanging over us, I think most people would see it as being more trouble than it's worth." Not to mention, the last thing he needed was more scrutiny. Jack wasn't interested in partners that had a vote, even in the best of times.

Megan was silent for a time, and Jack went through a mental list of his accounts.

Not only was the winery broke, but Jack was dangerously close to it as well. Jack had a couple of stash accounts, but those were supposed to be for him to make an escape—in case of emergency, break glass. He wouldn't touch any of those, and anyway, none of that money was readily accessible by design. There wasn't enough in any of his accounts that he could float the winery for long, though he might be able to make it through the harvest. Jack's house was worth about two million. He could sell that and use that money to float them.

Each of those options left him with basically nothing.

Jack's mind had arrived at the answer some time ago, though he'd been trying to deny it.

He needed to *work*.

Reginald was his oldest friend, and Jack knew he deserved better than a pier-side shouting match on the Embarcadero. Jack had rarely turned a job down, and the few times he had, Reginald quickly saw the reasons why and agreed. This was different, and Jack couldn't understand why. Sure, it wasn't just a lot of money, it was a goddamned fortune, but even Reginald should have been able to see past those numbers to understand the risks Jack would've had to take.

LeGrande had called him one time after Jack left him standing on the pier. It was the next day, after what Reginald assumed would be time for cooler heads. But he just reissued the same arguments more logically and less passionately, which struck Jack as a bit odd. The conversation ended roughly the same way.

They hadn't spoken since.

Enzo actually called him not long after, and he asked Jack what he was thinking, why was he passing. Jack gave him all the reasons that he gave Reginald, including a short course on why Ari Hassar was one of the most dangerous people in this business and the last guy they wanted to cross. Enzo said he understood and respected Jack's position. They'd talk soon and hadn't since.

Jack rolled that eighty-five million dollar number around in his head for a while.

It was still bad for all the reasons that he told Reginald originally, but Jack's position on risk versus reward was a thousand miles from where it was when Reginald first pitched him. He'd almost wished they'd found out Sharpe ripped them off sooner so that he could've skipped the bullshit and just gotten started.

Reginald told him originally that the exhibition was set for the end of July. That was a little over a week away. Gaston, Enzo, and Gabrielle tended only to work with him, so they should be available. They were good and Jack trusted them. If anyone could pull this job together in a week, they could. He wouldn't try to bring a driver in on such short notice. Jack had come up a wheel and could handle that part, plus he had a guy in Europe who worked fast and could get them clean vehicles. The question was if Reginald would set his pride aside? Jack sure as hell hoped he would. Not even Reginald was *that* stubborn.

Jack sighed and corrected himself. Actually, Reginald was.

Jack flicked his eyes up to Megan. "I think I know what we need to do," he said hesitantly.

He studied her face for a long moment before continuing. There was a smudge of dirt on her left cheek. Megan had told him once that this winery was her second chance too. She'd never told him exactly what she meant, though he knew that she'd been married once and that it ended very badly. He also knew that she'd been part owner in a winery that had gone under several years ago and that she'd lost nearly everything.

Jack needed to save this as much for himself as he did for her.

"I'm part owner in a technology consulting company that's based in Switzerland," he said with a long breath. "I can sell off my stake. That and some other investments I can divest should be able to raise the money we need."

Her entire upper body tensed. "Jack, no."

Jack put a reassuring hand on her shoulder. Despite everything, he felt the same electric surge whenever he touched her. Megan's face softened slightly, but she was clearly wearing her concerns.

"Really, it's okay. I've been thinking about it anyway. I'm

not that involved in the business anymore, but because of how much I own, I have to attend board meetings and shit like that." He faked a laugh, and a flash of guilt shot through his stomach. Jack hated lying to her. Somehow, he bifurcated Frank Fischer in his mind so that when he said he'd need to go over and manage the sale of his pretend company, it eased the sting of the lie. "I'll need to go over there to manage the sale in person. Shouldn't be more than a week or two at the most. Can you handle things here?"

Megan nodded and softly said she could. Then she added, "Are you sure you don't want me to go with you?" Megan gently placed a hand on his forearm. There was a softness in her voice that he hadn't heard in a while. "Look, I know it's not the best time. But we're obviously not getting anywhere with the police, so..." Her voice trailed off.

For a hot moment, Jack actually considered how he'd make that work. What he wanted right now was for them to have forty-eight uninterrupted hours in a place without phone calls, cops, lawyers, and reporters. He wanted a glass of wine, a sunset, and Megan McKinney. He realized, too, how stressful this had been on her. Beyond dealing with the embezzlement and subsequent fallout, keeping their employees calm and reassuring them that the winery wasn't going under (and most of the time believing it), Megan had to manage the day-to-day operations...and manage Jack. Jack wanted to be involved in everything, believed he had to be, despite the trust he had in Megan and others. As a result, he micromanaged and didn't always make the best decisions. Megan was burned out from the pressure she was under and probably looked at a couple days in Europe as a fast getaway, anything to take her mind off of what was happening here.

"Meg, I need you here. Someone has to keep a lid on

things. The team needs you. Besides, how would it look if we were both off with everything that's going on?"

A look of hurt and confusion flashed across her face.

Jack's heart sank into his stomach as soon as he saw it. "Shit. I...that's not what I wanted to say. I'm sorry. I want nothing more than for you to go with me. If it was any other time, I'd take you to the Riviera on the way back, but not now. You have to be here to lead the team. They need to see that everything is going to be okay."

Megan stared back at him for a long, silent moment and then nodded.

"You're right. I'm sorry. It's just been hard."

Jack closed the distance and put his arms around her. "I know it has. In a lot of ways, you're bearing the brunt of this."

Megan squeezed back and then took a couple steps toward the door. "Frank," she said. "We can't keep asking you to do this."

"Do what?"

"Every time the winery gets in trouble, you pump more of your own money into it. At some point..."

But he knew what she really meant. At some point, their employees were going to start thinking that the reason he kept the winery afloat with his own money was because he didn't know how to run it. Jack knew their team loved working there, loved Kingfisher, but how much longer were people going to put up with it if they didn't believe in their owner?

Jack walked over to her and paused. Then he placed both arms on her shoulders. "Meg, you're right. Someday I might overextend myself to save this place. But not today. Paul stole from us, and I will not allow this place to just go away because of him. What the hell good is my money to me or anyone if I can't use it to protect something we love?"

Twenty minutes later, Jack was standing on his deck with

the phone Reginald gave him. Minutes rolled away as he stood and stared across the undulating gold and green valley spilling out beneath his home. In his mind, Jack tried to convince himself that he was simply steeling himself for the difficult conversation he was about to have, but his heart knew it was nothing so noble as that. Jack hadn't spoken to Reginald since he'd turned the Carlton job down, shooting myriad holes in the logic and plausibility of the affair. Now, it seemed, it was his one good option to save his winery—a crime for the ages to save a floundering business that no one would ever care or read about.

This would cost him more than money.

Jack opened the encryption app and dialed.

"Well," the old thief said when he answered, "the prodigal son returns a phone call."

"I'm sorry I've been out of touch, Reg. I've been dealing with some things, and," he paused, "it's been a little complicated on my end."

"I can imagine," Reginald said in an odd way that had Jack cock his head and raise an eyebrow.

"I wasn't trying to keep you at arm's length or anything, and I don't want you to think it was about that job. It's just that..." Jack paused. He felt like he was reading from a script and the speechwriter had simply stopped writing in the middle of a sentence.

"Jack, it's fine," Reginald told him in a flat, dry voice. "You don't need to apologize for anything. You have a separate life outside our work." And then Reginald punctuated it with a quick, forced laugh, as equally dry as his voice and totally out of place in the conversation. It was like an exclamation point in the middle of a word. "Look, bygones, right?"

"Thanks, Reg," Jack said hesitantly. "I appreciate that."

"So, what's on your mind?"

Jack walked to the edge of the deck, resting his free hand on the sun-hot wood. "Well, I wanted to talk about that job."

"The Carlton? Forget about it. Slate's clean. I appreciate your reasons for turning it down, and maybe I was a little pushy. Jesus, we sound like a therapy session," he said and chortled again. It was the throaty sound of a big-block engine at idle.

"That's not what I mean. I'm not calling to apologize. Well, I am, but that's not all. I want to do the job."

Long moments of dead silence followed. Jack heard nothing, literally nothing on the other end of the line, like he'd dialed outer space.

After about a hundred years, Reginald spoke. When he did, his voice was different and carried a strange resonance. "That job's not available anymore, Jack."

"What do you mean, it's not available? They cancel the exhibition?"

"No, they didn't cancel it. I just gave it to someone else."

"You did *what*?" Jack tried to force as much indignation into his voice as he could.

"You heard me, Jack," Reginald said with the hard edge of finality. "You told me in no uncertain terms, and quite emphatically, I might add, that you wanted nothing to do with that job. So I gave it to someone who did. I'm sorry."

"You can't be serious. Who else do you know who could possibly pull this off?"

Reginald let out a heavy, wet "heh" that could've just as easily been a sarcastic laugh as emphysema. "You think you're the only person with light fingers in this business? You're not the only thief I know, Jack. Look, maybe there's a life lesson in there somewhere. I don't know what it is, but you weren't willing to take the risk for this one, so it's probably for the best that you didn't. This isn't the sort of thing you want to try if you're not a hundred percent committed. And you weren't, so let's just leave it at that."

"Things have changed."

"Yes, they have." His words hung in the air.

"Whoever you've got running this isn't as good as me, and we both know it," Jack said in a unique and wholly uncharacteristic spoken arrogance. "Tell them something came up and give me the job."

"It doesn't work that way, and we both know that too. You want me to pull a crew I've lined up at the last minute now that they've got all the details? Or add you and tell them that now, all of a sudden, they've got to split the take? You know what an eighty-five-million-dollar grudge looks like?" Reginald blasted. "Well, fucking neither do I." Before Jack could drop a word of reply, he continued, "And I don't aim to find out today." Jack heard Reginald exhale hard on the other end, an exorcism. "Look, Jack, this one isn't going to work out. I'm sorry for whatever trouble you're in, but aren't you the one always telling me 'never steal out of necessity'? Makes you reckless? Ring any bells? You're always preaching me the Gospel of Saint Jack, so maybe this time you should say one of your own prayers instead of telling them all to me. Go relax, have a glass of that Cabernet you like so much, and when I've got work for you, I'll give you a call. I gotta go."

"Reg—" Jack started, but Reginald had already hung up.

Jack knew that they were long odds for Reginald to let him in on the crew at this stage. Either he'd have to fire the leader and create an enemy (who also knew about the job) or force everyone to take less of a cut. Neither of those were good business decisions. Like Reginald said, Jack didn't really want to find out what an eighty-five-million-dollar grudge was like. Of course, it was possible that Reginald hadn't found someone to run the crew, or he was going to give it to Jack's crew, in which case they'd probably take a smaller percentage to have him on the job. But the other reason he called LeGrande was to find out if he was still doing the job at all. Jack didn't really believe Reginald would pass on it, but it was always possible. Knowing he was still going after it was important because that told Jack two things.

One—time was a factor.

Two—he had to cover his tracks perfectly. There was absolutely no room for error.

Reginald would never believe that Jack would do this alone. The job violated all of the rules Jack lived by, the ones that ensured he was never caught. As cautious as Jack was about planning scores, Reginald would never think of him trying something like this without months of preparation.

He thumbed through his contact list until he came up with the fake name he used for Enzo. Jack stared at the number for a long time before he closed the phone. Enzo was his good friend and an old one, and while Jack didn't think that Reginald would try to tap that crew without Jack leading it, he didn't *know*. He couldn't go into a job like this where there was even the potential for divided loyalty. There was also the very real chance that they'd fail or have to walk away from it for any number of reasons. Jack had done that plenty of times. A score could look great when you plan it, but when you go to pull the job, something might just be *off*. If that happened and Jack had coerced Enzo away from Reginald, he was now putting Enzo in a position where he might feel like he needed to choose between his friend and his livelihood. As much as Jack wanted him in on this, he just couldn't take the risk that Enzo might not want to cross Reginald.

Eighty-five million reasons, Reginald had said.

Something else was gnawing at him. The fixer's comment: *Go relax, have a glass of that Cabernet you like so much, and when I've got work for you, I'll call.* What he said was odd enough, but the strange and sarcastic emphasis Reginald placed on having a glass of wine struck Jack with an unsettling resonance that was punctuated by the abrupt sign-off.

Jack ran a hand over the smooth wood of his deck railing, stained a deep brown and already just south of hot in the summer sun. He loved it here. Truly loved it. Jack could see most of Sonoma Valley from his deck. He spent countless cool evenings drinking a glass of wine on this deck, most often his own, with Miles Davis or Coltrane playing in the background. It was strange how much being a winemaker gave him purpose. At least being a proprietor, but he was learning. Megan told him in her own overly frank way that while he didn't know anything about the business, he had an innate sense of whether something was good or not, and those instincts couldn't be taught. Given time, she and Hugh told him, he could be one of the greats, and Kingfisher could be great too.

People depended on him, and Jack found meaning in that also.

He'd be goddamned if someone was going to take this away from him.

Jack opened a secure browser on his phone, one that wouldn't leave any search history in case the phone was ever confiscated. He looked up Ari Hassar. The top hits were all a variation on the first: "Israeli Diamond Mogul Promises Spectacular Show."

Buddy, you have no idea.

Jack set his phone down and thought for a few moments, rolling the words *spectacular show* around in his mind.

Reginald's team would likely target the opening. After that, there would be too much traffic at the InterContinental Hotel.

Jack dialed one of the few contacts in his directory that wasn't a dummy. The other line answered on the second ring.

"Jack," the voice said, sounding sly and on the edge of a smile.

"Rusty, I'm going to need a few things. And I'm going to need a car."

8

According to his watch, Jack spent the better part of two days getting to Cannes.

He caught a red-eye to London. Jack cooled down somewhat as he crossed the Atlantic. Reginald was right. Jack had passed on the job, and Reginald wasn't going to just give that opportunity up. His friend would be furious when he learned that Jack stole the jewels first, but Jack figured that cutting Reg in for his usual five percent would put a lot of salve on those wounds.

He landed in London in the early afternoon and then hopped to Marseilles, deciding it was best if he avoided flying into Cannes directly.

Jack met Rusty in Marseilles to collect his car, passport, and credit cards.

Rusty was an American expat living in Europe and was the sort of character you only expected to find in movies. Jack used him to clear local hurdles and to quietly procure the hard-to-find things that thieves tended to need on short notice. But Rusty was equally effective as an information broker.

The details were never made clear, and Jack never pressed, but he knew Rusty had once been with the FBI. Rusty joked once that he was the guy who enforced the "FBI Warning" you saw when you first watched a DVD. Based on how quickly and thoroughly Rusty navigated the obstacles, Jack had no doubt there was law enforcement in his background and that it likely wasn't always above reproach.

Rusty met Jack at Marseille Provence Airport. The ex-fed dressed like how most Americans envisioned Italian gigolos— gray sharkskin pants just south of shiny, short-sleeved navy shirt, pointed-tip tan Italian loafers, and large sunglasses with a blue tint. Rusty had a suit coat slung over his shoulder like he'd never intended to wear it. His hair was probably brown, but it was kept to a length that was just above military-grade stubble. He was fit and carried himself in a way that suggested he wasn't often challenged. They shook hands, vamped big smiles, and Rusty put a hand on Jack's shoulder—like old friends meeting.

They turned and walked for the door.

"I got you a Maserati GranTurismo Sport." Rusty turned to Jack, his face serious. "Yes, it's *Rosso Mondiale*, before you ask." He knew his customers. "Passport and credit card are in the glove compartment. The name is Peter Edward Ramsey, and you're from Los Angeles. The card is a ghosted Visa Black Card, so it should be good everywhere. There's no limit, but just be careful about patterns. I know you know all that, but I have to say it. If you're only using it for a few days, we should be cool. I've also put two thousand euro for walking-around money in there as well as a Beretta 92FS."

Jack nodded. Rusty always amazed him with how fast he could turn around an order—getting a high-end Italian sports car, pistol, and a passport (he kept stock headshots of Jack) on two days' notice was a near legendary skill in the fixer community.

Jack didn't want the gun, but it was a reasonable precaution when working by himself.

They left the main terminal and stepped into the dry, mid-seventies air. It felt good after spending so much time on a plane. Rusty turned his head, clearing left and holding up a polite hand to the oncoming car. "I found out who LeGrande is using in Cannes like you asked, and I don't think you're going to like it. He's got your current roster of regulars: Enzo Bachetti, Gaston Broussard, and Gabrielle Eberspach." Rusty waited a beat. "He's also using Ozren Stolar."

That complicated things more than a little.

Jack shook his head as they stepped into the parking lot. It was disturbing that Reginald would use Jack's own crew but not all that surprising. Every thief Jack knew that had served time was either born-again risk averse or a pathological daredevil. Definitely the former, Reginald would not leave this to chance. He'd use the people that Jack trusted, that Jack had brought along in the hopes that they still had some trace amounts of Gentleman Jack's magic in their systems.

An ugly, heavy, sour feeling formed in Jack's stomach. He'd always known it was a possibility that he'd be going up against his former team. Though, he'd honestly believed Reginald wouldn't do that. Jack thought it more likely Reginald would use a fresh crew with no ties to Jack because it would be too easy for Jack to guess the team's moves.

Jack and Rusty left the terminal and walked across to the parking lot, enveloped by the hot sun and thick, salty air.

They reached the car. A GranTurismo, with its limited-edition factory-special paint, was a hard thing to miss. The car was objectified elegance and speed. The GranTurismo had the famous Maserati long, shark-nose front end and wavelike lines over the front rim, dipping ever so slightly before rising again to encompass the passenger cabin. The rear window sloped more steeply to meld with the trunk. Rosso Mondiale was the shade of red you would expect on the lipstick of a high-end escort, so ostentatious it was inherently masculine. It was a color that only an Italian could dream up.

Rusty flipped Jack the keys, smirking.

"Gentleman Jack, it is always a pleasure. Most of the people I work for ask for Fiats, VWs, and BMWs with fake plates and clean histories. I have to say, I appreciate your taste as much as I do the challenge of satisfying it."

Jack smiled back. "Thugs steal purses. Gentlemen steal jewels." Jack briefly ran his hand along the door before settling on the handle and opening it with a gentle tug. "You need a ride somewhere?"

"No, I'm good."

"Thanks for everything. What's your schedule the next couple of days?"

A grin broke on Rusty's face. "I've got some work around here. My Spidey sense told me you'd be asking, so I decided to stick around."

"You're a good man, Friday."

"Get out of here, you criminal." His face cracked into a wry smile. "I can't afford to be seen associating with people like you."

Jack climbed into the GranTurismo, set his leather bag on the seat next to him, and popped the glove box to verify the contents. He placed the money in his wallet and the pistol in the bag, burying it beneath his clothes. He also placed the passport he'd used to get here in the bag.

Jack guided the car out of the parking lot, relishing the

engine's growl in the low gears. The seats and dash were cappuccino colored, though the seat backs and cushions were black, as was the roof and fiberglass accents. She had just over four thousand miles.

Jack made his way to the A8, glad to be putting Marseilles behind him. The city was dirty in a way not easily remedied. Her streets were covered in a veneer of grime that couldn't seem to be washed clean. Even when it rained, it just spread the dirt around. Those same streets were also choked with urchins and petty criminals—pickpockets, frauds, purse-snatchers, and muggers, refugees of France's imperialist forays into Morocco and Algeria. Rather than assimilate into their new society, they chose simply to steal from it. Stealing, like any trade, Jack believed, should be left to the professionals. If one couldn't do it with skill and, to be fair, a certain degree of panache, it shouldn't be done at all.

The trip to Cannes would be just under two hours, which would put him there in the early evening. That was a perfect time to begin scouting the hotel, as it would be buzzing with dinner traffic. Jack put the pedal down and stepped through the gears, accelerating onto the highway and feeling the Maserati's engine begin to stretch its legs and pull away.

He merged at just under a hundred.

As the car accelerated and Jack felt the familiar push back into the seat, the scenes outside the car began to blur, the distractions faded into the background. As a thief, he knew there were "today problems" and "tomorrow problems." A thief who couldn't parse those things, worried about the things they couldn't control or affect today, was someone who was not focused on the job. Finding Paul Sharpe and the money he stole, saving the winery, even the fallout of Reginald using Jack's own crew against him...those were "tomorrow problems." Jack had his immediate work cut out for him.

But right now, his job was to drive, and he felt free.

Rusty set up Jack with a villa rented under the Peter Ramsey alias that was a five-minute drive to the InterContinental. Jack changed into a cream-colored summer-weight suit with a blue gingham shirt and a rust-colored cotton pocket square that had been firmly pressed into exacting creases. He walked back down to the carport to the Maserati. The car was an extravagance, true, but it was also part of his cover. One didn't drive up to one of the world's exclusive hotels in a Peugeot and expect to blend into the scenery. This was Cannes, and if Jack was going to fade into the background, he had to look like he belonged in it.

To say that the Carlton Intercontinental was merely one of the most famous hotels in the world was to fundamentally misrepresent the grandeur of the place almost at the molecular level. So too was that an understatement of its importance to French culture. The Carlton was the epicenter for the Cannes Film Festival, and for a few weeks in May, it was the axis upon which the film industry spun. The InterContinental had more in common with the Palace of Versailles than it did the run-of-the-mill luxury hotels that it shared geography with on the Boulevard de la Croisette.

Jack approached the hotel on the two-lane, palm-lined boulevard that ran along the beachfront. As he neared the Carlton, he spotted the gaudy pink-and-white signs advertising the Hassar diamond exhibition beginning its run on the twenty-eighth of July. Jack pulled off the boulevard into the U-shaped carport, dotted with palms. A maroon-jacketed valet was at his door instantly as the car stopped, asking if Jack was a guest of the hotel. Jack knew just enough French to say that no, he was simply here to dine, and handed the valet his keys. The valet accepted the keys with a disinterested air and welcomed Jack with the arrogant hospitality that was so singularly French. As Jack walked toward the entryway, he spied a nuclear-orange Lamborghini Aventador angle-parked in the upper left corner of the carport. The exhibition space was directly behind it. He took a moment, apparently to admire the car, as he slowly slid his valet ticket into his trouser pocket.

The single showroom extended out from the hotel's northwest corner. The salon had floor-to-ceiling windows, though gaudy pink fabric awnings overshadowed them. Each awning had a message announcing Hassar's pending exhibition. The awning extended to entirely cover the short patio, letting only a slit of light through. He could just make out the outline of a door. Jack made note of this too. A waist-high concrete wall separated the patio from the street and the awning. The patio was elevated above the sidewalk by several feet and connected to it by a long ramp.

Jack made a final pass over this with his eyes and committed it to memory. Thirty seconds total. The valet pulled his car away, and Jack stepped across the asphalt patch and into the hotel, guided by a doorman with an extended arm.

Walking into the hotel, Jack ran down the checklist in his mind. The show opened in six days.

Task one: case the hotel. He had to learn the layout, the security, and the staff patterns intimately.

Task two: find the competition. He needed to figure out what their approach would be so that he could try to guess when they were going to make their attempt. At this stage, only Gabrielle would be inside the hotel. If he could make her, he could start figuring out their plan and reverse engineer it. This would be where the danger was, as he could only accomplish this by shadowing them and that meant he risked being spotted himself.

Task three: plan his own approach and escape. Reginald was probably right. Operating alone, this would have to be smash and grab, or as close to that as Gentleman Jack Burdette got. Jack would probably be fleeing to a chorus of alarms followed by a command performance of police sirens, and he would be captured by the many exterior cameras. He'd have to keep his face covered until he was about a block away, and that would be conspicuous. Additionally, his take would be limited to what he could fit in a briefcase or backpack.

Jack stepped into InterContinental's foyer and took in the lobby.

The lobby was both exquisite and, oddly, less grand than he expected. Built in 1911, the interior style and furnishings were styled after France's Belle Époque period—what everyone who wasn't French would call Victorian. The walls and floor-to-ceiling columns that lined the walkways were a regal white, now pinkish-orange in the setting sun. The floors were a diamond pattern of creamy marble with a wide, tan marble outline. Walkways of tan marble, flanked by columns, connected the various sections of diamond-patterned floor. The concierge and reception desks occupied opposite corners of the entryway and were greatly understated in the typical fashion of European hotels.

Signs of a similar bright pink-and-white styling stood upon easels on the left side of the lobby, directing casual passers-by to the exhibition hall. There were four such signs precisely spaced in between the columns on the chance that someone would fail to see the first three and thus miss out on the exhibition of Ari Hassar's finest. Jack paused a beat in the center of the foyer, pivoted, and walked toward to the concierge desk on his right.

The concierge greeted him in French, and Jack replied "good evening" in English, knowing that most cultures appreciated it if you made the attempt to speak their native tongue, but the French took such pride in their mother tongue that it was an insult to their ears, if not their entire cultural heritage, to misspeak the language. If you were not fluent, it was best not to attempt it. The concierge responded in a beautifully accented English.

"I couldn't help but notice," Jack said with the attendant irony, "the Hassar Exhibition." Jack reached into his pocket for a card wallet, drawing out an embossed business card on heavy blue bond. Gold filigree identified him as international wholesaler with offices in San Francisco, New York, London, and Milan. By the time Jack said, "Exhibition," the card was in his hand, hovering just below eye level. He watched her eyes read the card, then he withdrew it with a magician's flourish that made the concierge smile.

"Do you have a ticket?"

"Unfortunately, I do not. I was here on business...in as much business as one conducts in Cannes," he said with a knowing smile that she returned. "I'm here to meet a colleague and noticed the signs and wanted to inquire about getting a ticket."

The concierge clasped her hands together. "I am sorry, sir, but it is a private event. It is invitation only."

He leaned in, placing a single hand on the counter, and stage-whispered conspiratorially, "How does one go about getting an invitation?"

The concierge smiled softly, apologized, and said it was not possible. "I'm afraid these were all coordinated well in advance."

"So there's nothing we can do?"

"Well," she said with a sly smile, "Mr. Hassar is going to do a walk-through on Sunday afternoon before the show opens on Monday. I suppose you could ask him yourself." She smiled again politely, but in a way that said the conversation was over and that she had actual work to do.

Jack had no expectation that it would work, but it was worth a shot.

Jack thanked her for her time, placing a twenty-euro note in her hand with his right and placing his left atop hers, appearing to give an affectionate handshake. He winked and turned on his heel. Jack strode across the lobby to the opposite corner where there was a small bar. That was the best place to post. Jack ordered a Campari and soda and rotated in his chair so that he could face the entire lobby.

To maximize his time, Jack figured to work the first two of his three objectives in parallel. As he was figuring out how he was going to pull the job, Jack needed to also think how his team—ex-team, he corrected himself—would approach it.

He didn't begrudge them the chance at an eighty-five-million-dollar take. Jack would've done the same in their position. But he couldn't deny the surreal feeling of playing against a group of people he'd worked closely with for many years.

Enzo would be the leader.

That pained Jack the most. The others were all good at what they did, and Jack enjoyed working with them, but their relationships were simply transactions. Enzo Bachetti, however, was one of the only true friends in Jack's life, aside from Reginald. They first met in the Italian city of Turin. While the city was infamous for its organized crime, it was positively famous for its tradition of thievery. Jack and Enzo met in the mid-nineties, both on the run from pasts they'd just as soon forget. They found a kinship in stealing jewels, racing cars, and drinking grappa.

Jack arrived in Turin alone and on the run in 1995. Reginald sent him there after an armored car job went sideways and he needed to get out of the country for a while. Jack was sent to study under an old colleague of Reginald's, a thief named Vito Verrazano. Vito was a thief in the old tradition and Jack took his apprenticeship seriously. Eventually, that brought him into the orbit of Niccoló Bartolo and his infamous "School of Turin." That was how Bartolo referred to his organization, a network of some of the most skilled thieves, con artists, and electronics experts in northern Italy. This was where he met Enzo.

Il Orologiaio. That's what they called Enzo in Turin. The Watchmaker.

When Enzo turned to crime and reapplied his exacting precision, patient hands, and considerable skill to safecracking, his occupation stuck with him, as did the name. Criminals loved nicknames.

Jack shook his head as though that would dismiss the memory and forced himself to focus.

How would Enzo approach this?

Enzo and Gaston would be the inside team. They would most likely move in at night and hide until the exhibition staff brought the jewels in. The hotel security systems were professional grade but not bank quality, and Gaston could easily disarm them. They would have to come in from the street. The lobby was too well lit, and they'd be under constant observation by the staff—unless they were trying a Trojan Horse play in hotel staff uniforms. Jack reconsidered his assessment of their play. Gaston was a native speaker and thought fast on his feet. A Trojan Horse removed the complexity of the alarm system, which would give them more time on the inside. He made a mental note to think through this more thoroughly when he returned to the villa.

He'd never had to plan a job where he was racing against another team before, and he found himself second-guessing his assessment of their plans. You could generally guess what the police would do and how, as the patterns of law enforcement were nearly universal.

He needed to focus on Gabrielle.

Gabrielle's job was recon and intelligence. She would map the interior of the hotel, describing the positioning of staff and noting their shift changes and would make every effort to get into the exhibition itself. Enzo and Gaston would need her to describe the interior layout of the hall and the guards' positioning.

Gabrielle Eberspach was the daughter of a Bavarian father and a northern Italian mother, both descendant from nobility and readily made that known, not so much in word as in deed. Gabrielle grew up straddling the Alps—her parents separated when she was young—and spent much of her teenage years at a Swiss boarding school where she majored in skiing and modeling. Gabrielle's father, an industrialist, eventually grew tired of her jet-setting at the expense of his pocketbook—despite having plenty to spare, but he was German, so he abhorred flash and waste—and made her choose which parent she would live with. Offended at the prospect of having to choose between either of them, Gabrielle chose her mother to spite Heinrich Eberspach, who then severed all ties—filial and fiduciary—with German efficiency.

Jack didn't know exactly how she came into the criminal life, but he knew that her mother didn't have the ability to afford her own lifestyle, let alone Gabrielle's, and that well very quickly ran dry when her father cut her off. Gabrielle was beautiful but was a little too voluptuous to make it as a model in the "heroin-chic" late nineties. Likely, she got involved with the wrong kind of man, and he showed her how she could maintain the lifestyle she wanted by being a little less than honest about how.

Jack spotted a leggy brunette in a green dress. She was walking with a man who Jack guessed was at least fifteen years her senior, but he carried it well, and the disparity wasn't such that it was obvious she was playing to his vanity. Gabrielle was a blonde, but she often wore wigs or dyed her hair, and she used colored contacts. The woman steered the man toward the bar, and Jack's pulse quickened. Jack grabbed his drink and made to leave.

They had crossed the lobby and were approximately halfway to him. The bar was becoming crowded, and there were several collections of mostly full tables between Jack and the rest of the lobby, but they hadn't made him yet. He paid for his drink and kept his profile to the lobby so he could keep an eye on them without being totally exposed.

Jack looked around for the exits. The bar was in the back corner of the lobby with a few clusters of Belle Époque–style tables and chairs set on a farther orbit out from the bar. He thanked the bartender in French and stood, looking down at his phone to hide his full face. Jack maneuvered through the bar area, weaving around chairs, still with his face stuck in the iPhone. His pulse raced.

Jack chanced a look. He had to know whether he'd been made or not.

His eyes tracked up from the phone still held not far from his face.

The woman in the green dress and her older escort were right in front of him.

It wasn't her.

Jack stared at the woman dumbly for a second, as if he was unsure of what to do next. He recovered his composure a moment later and stepped out of their way, apologizing in

French. Jack exhaled. Bullet dodged, but he let the feeling sink in. He had to be mindful of the fact that his team would be alerted to his presence. Gabrielle would be looking for him inside, Enzo and Gaston watching for him outside. The only thing Jack *could* count on was the fact that the element of surprise was gone.

9

Jack returned to the Carlton the next morning.

He wore the same suit as he had the night before, only now sporting a lavender shirt and a striped purple tie. Jack also wore a pair of Persol Steve McQueens that he kept on indoors as he scanned the lobby. Satisfied, he removed the glasses, folded them, and slid them into the suit's breast pocket. Jack ordered a coffee from the bar and found a seat in the lobby that gave him a comprehensive view of the place. Over the next two hours, he pretended to read a copy of yesterday's *Le Monde* while he observed the lobby and committed it to memory. There was no sign of Gabrielle yet. Jack broke at eleven for an early lunch, which he took at the Carlton's restaurant. Jack opened his leather-bound folio and made notes, transcribing everything he'd discerned regarding security, the staff, their shifts, and the flow of the place. He also sketched the lobby, noting the exits and the hallway leading to the exhibition salon.

After lunch, Jack decided to take some chances.

He followed the equally ubiquitous and ostentatious pink-and-white placards right into the exhibition salon. The doors were closed but unlocked, and Jack could hear work on the other side of them. He opened the double doors and stepped through. The salon was well lit, even with the white curtains drawn, as three sides of it consisted of large French windows. The column motif of the lobby repeated here, though the floors were different. These were parquet as opposed to marble, which Jack suspected was for dancing. Jack counted six workmen assembling secure display cases. A number of the cases had already been completed and were positioned around the columns and along the walls. Jack was intimately familiar with this model—the glass was shatterproof and hardened against blunt force, like a hammer strike, as well as resistant to piercing from, say, a pick or even a small-caliber bullet. Emptying the cases would take entirely too long, unless he made his move at night *and* they left them unguarded *and* they left the stones in the cases overnight. Both scenarios Jack discounted out of hand.

Burdette took in the entire room, committing it all to memory.

"*Qu'est-ce que vous voulez?*" one of the workmen asked, lazily, more annoyed at having to ask what the interruption was about than at the interruption itself. He was a round-faced man with wiry brown hair, cut close, and a very deep tan. The room smelled of mineral oil. The workman held his mouth open in a half-exasperated expression, as if expecting Jack's answer to come from his own lips as much as Jack's. When Jack didn't immediately respond, the Frenchman jerked his head and popped his lower jaw, adding astonishment to his irritation.

Jack held up his hands and said, "*Mon erreur.*" Then he took a tentative step backward, showing the angry Frenchman that he'd just realized his mistake.

The workman muttered, "*Connard*," and went back to his work.

Jack closed the door behind him, smiling. The minute he'd spent looking around that room was more valuable than nearly any other intelligence he could've gathered today. He now knew the layout of the exhibition and the type of cases they'd be using. He would never have planned on smashing the cases to retrieve their contents, but knowing that wasn't an option was helpful not only in forming his own plan but in trying to guess what the team would try. Gabrielle's focus over the next few days would be to get inside that room and get as much detailed information about it as possible, if she hadn't already, because that would formulate the foundation of their approach. Unless they had inside information as to where the jewels would be stored when they weren't in the display cases, or if they planned to hit them in transit. The latter was certainly higher risk, and the former played to the team's strengths. They had one of the trade's foremost safe crackers, after all.

Jack returned to the lobby, found an unobtrusive chair, and quickly sketched the layout of the salon, noting the columns and the number of cases that were already constructed. From there, rough math would tell him about how many cases he could expect, and that would give Jack a sense of the overall volume he'd need to plan for.

After completing his sketch, Jack returned to surveillance.

He spotted Gabrielle shortly after two, and this time there was no mistaking it. She wore a white dress with large black dots that jealously hugged her curves, large sunglasses, and a wide-brimmed sun hat. Her hair was red, most likely a high-quality wig. Jack wouldn't have made her but for Gabrielle removing her sunglasses when she stepped inside. She took a seat in the center of the lobby, which gave her a relatively unobstructed view of the entire place. She was there for maybe five minutes before a man—Jack placed him in his mid-forties, wearing a summer-weight navy suit—approached her, offering his hand. Gabrielle accepted it, standing as she did. They exchanged short words, the corners of Gabrielle's mouth turning up slightly at a timed and practiced smile. Then the man waved an arm at the exhibition hall and guided her toward it.

The lobby swelled with midday elegance. Women who were all leg strutted about in thousand-dollar swimsuits that would never see a drop of water. As often as not, professional gentlemen of leisure, whose attire was not that dissimilar from Jack's own, escorted the women through the lobby. He only saw one sheikh, which disappointed him, because the internal odds had been at three. He did spot an actor, the British guy with the raspy voice and granite stare who had a habit of making the same movie over and over and just swapped out the titles.

Jack didn't begrudge him, though. He could appreciate steady work.

Gabrielle and her guide reappeared approximately twenty minutes later, conversing casually as they walked. Jack could tell from the body language and the interaction that Gabrielle was affecting a businesslike air. She asked short, pointed questions and nodded at the answers, as if making mental notes. The man escorted her down the columned walkway to the center of the lobby, where they exchanged pleasantries for a moment. Jack lip-read a "thank you." Interesting that the conversation was in English rather than French. There was a final handshake, and Gabrielle made for the street. Jack studied Gabrielle's companion for a moment and memorized his face. Jack might need to make a play on this guy himself. He suspected the man might be Ehud Arshavin, one of

Hassar's most trusted number twos and the director of the exhibition. Jack filled the hours between San Francisco and London by researching Hassar's inner circle. The man's appearance fit the profile. Eastern European, middle-aged but took care of himself, jet-black hair close cut and parted the same way every day. His suit was Savile Row, gray, with a white shirt and a light blue tie that had a very slight pattern. Jack would recognize that tailoring anywhere.

Jack paused a moment and followed, timing his pursuit so that they wouldn't be in the carport at the same time. He paused inside the door, pretending to respond to an all-important message on his phone while the doorman held the door for him. Jack looked up and saw Gabrielle get into a cab. He apologized to the doorman in the perfunctory way an asshole would, saying the words because that's what was expected in this situation, and stepped into the summer heat. He asked for a cab, and one appeared immediately from that alternate universe accessible only by the luxury hotels of the world, designed specifically so that their guests did not have to wait for a ride. Jack palmed the doorman a ten-euro note and stepped into the cab. He directed the driver to follow the cab in front of them, offering the unnecessary explanation that straight-world people always did to justify doing something a little out of the ordinary. In this instance, his friend was in that other cab, and that Jack had *just* missed her. They were going to the same place, blah blah blah. The driver shrugged and did as his fare asked. It was all money to him.

The trip was about a mile.

Jack noted that she didn't just have Ozren drive her, but they were probably trying to minimize exposure and not have multiple crewmembers spotted together on hotel surveillance cameras. He took a certain pride in seeing them avoid the avoidable mistakes that were so often the downfall of people in their profession. Reginald always said that there were only two things that you could control that would land you in jail—rookie mistakes and girlfriends.

Gabrielle's cab exited a traffic circle onto Avenue Isola Bella and stopped. Jack's driver's eyes flicked to the rearview mirror, awaiting instructions. Jack nodded and said, "Here's good."

The driver pulled over just outside the traffic circle saying only, "Twelve euro." Jack handed him two notes, a ten and five, not wanting to take the time to dig for correct change. Creating a coin to represent the two most common denominations given as change instead of a note was emblematic of the foolish decision-making, bureaucratic inefficiency, and national groupthink that plagued the European Union. However, that same mindset was also one of the things that made crime in this part of the world so easy. They fought crime the same way they governed—by committee.

Jack nodded and got out.

Jack stood on the corner of Avenue Isola Bella at the top of a small hill where the avenue dropped slightly with the traffic circle on one side and Rue du Lys on the other heading back toward the Mediterranean. This was a quiet, residential neighborhood composed of villas and low apartment buildings, both sequestered behind fences and walls of varying styles. It was nearly impossible to see many of the buildings from the street because of the dense coverage of cypress and palm trees with thick green bushes and smaller trees occupying seemingly every possible space.

Gabrielle moved gracefully through a waist-high metal gate and into a four-story apartment building. Jack crossed the street and watched her enter the building. Now he just had to figure out which one they were in.

Jack lost Gabrielle as she entered the apartment building.

Because of the walls separating the properties from the street
on either side, there was no good place to stake out and watch
the building. The rolling shutters on most of the windows
were down anyway. Jack quickly crossed the street to the
apartment side and walked around to the back, finding a large
patio and garden area. He decided that it was too risky to poke
around there in broad daylight, figuring they would probably
have the shutters up. A man creeping about in the afternoon
wearing a suit and carrying a leather folio might look just a
touch out of place. Not to mention, Gabrielle may have seen
him from afar and not made the connection, but even trig-
gering the recognition would place him at both locations, and
that would certainly clue them in that someone was following.
Jack turned around and walked back to the traffic circle to pick
up a cab. Still, he knew approximately where their safe house
was, and that alone was something useful.

The cab that took him back to the Carlton reeked of stale
cigarette smoke and staler sweat. Jack paid the driver when
they pulled through the hotel's circular carport and stepped
out into the warm, Mediterranean air. Jack barely had time to
consider the cab's putrid diesel cough as it accelerated out of
the Carlton's roundabout. A soft breeze coming off the sea
lapped at the palm trees, rustling their fronds and whisking
away the scent of the cab. With Gabrielle back at the team's
safe house, Jack knew he had a few precious hours to himself
in the hotel and needed to make the most of them. He turned
about and quickly walked inside. The doorman welcomed
him back.

Jack stood in the lobby for a moment, planning his next
move, when he spotted the man Gabrielle met with earlier
walking toward the bar. He allowed Hassar's man a few of the
hurried, purposeful steps that were the sole provenance of the
functionaries of the world and followed. Arshavin sat and

regarded the woman already at the small round table. A waitress appeared immediately, and Arshavin pointed two fingers at his companion's champagne flute. The waitress smiled, spun on her heel, and flitted back to the bar. Arshavin—he was sure of it now—accepted a black leather folio from the woman, opened it, and began reviewing the contents. Arshavin's left hand balanced on the side of his face with his index finger extended and the others gently cupping his chin.

Jack reached the bar, deftly weaving in between the chairs, occupied and not, now swelling with the afternoon crowd. Women who could be models, if it didn't require so much bloody effort, relaxed uncomfortably in the Belle Époque chairs. Jack slowed his pace and drifted past Arshavin's table, casting a downward eye at the pages in the folio. Jack's Italian was good. He could hold an interesting conversation with most adults who weren't physicists, and he could read at an eighth-grade level. He could function in Germany, though they rarely worked there because German police didn't recognize civil-rights violations in the course of law enforcement. But for some reason, the French language eluded him, and despite two passes with Rosetta Stone, Jack still spoke like a tourist, and an ignorant one at that.

But at least he knew this much: the word at the top of that page, *Programme*, meant "schedule."

Jack walked up to the bar, ordered a Campari and soda, then found a table next to them. He opened his own folio and appeared to busy himself with the papers inside while he eavesdropped on Arshavin's conversation. Naturally, this was in French. Either they were talking about the set-up activities or what to put on a baguette, Jack couldn't be certain. The waitress arrived with his drink. He paid her, stirred the drink exactly three times before discarding the black swizzle stick, and drank.

Arshavin went through each page in the folio once—there appeared to Jack to be about twenty—and drained his champagne cocktail. The conversation had moved on from the exhibition and was now clearly in social territory. Jack didn't need a third pass through Rosetta Stone to know Arshavin was clearly hitting on her. Bad flirting was the universal language of men worldwide. He was anxiously trying to get the waitress's attention, but she was both a Frenchwoman and notionally preoccupied with other customers, which meant she'd get to it on her own time. After two minutes of this, Arshavin began to get exasperated. Jack knew the type instantly. Arshavin's boss was notoriously impatient, seemingly at the molecular level, and that translated to Hassar's cronies because the transitive properties of slack were an immutable law of organizational physics. If they weren't getting any, they sure as hell weren't giving it.

Jack leaned over in his chair, saying conspiratorially in English, "My friend, I had the same problem yesterday afternoon. It took so long to get a cocktail, my companion even left me for another man." He emphasized "left" with mock indignation. "Best that you order at the bar and not keep your lady waiting." He winked at Arshavin's companion, who smiled back coyly.

"Yes," Arshavin replied sourly, annoyed that someone had solved the problem for him and further irritated that there was still a problem to be solved. He excused himself and walked up to the bar. Jack killed his drink, stood, and turned to face the woman.

"I'm sorry to hear your companion left you for another man," she said. She smiled at their shared, private joke.

"Well, he had a bigger yacht."

She raised an eyebrow. "Perhaps you should try more discerning women."

"Do you know any?"

"I might."

"I wouldn't want to appear rude to your friend, because I think he fancies you, but perhaps I could call you."

The woman waved a dismissive hand. "He's from the Middle East. He'd sleep with anyone. They're not particular. Do you have a pen?"

Jack set his folio down on top Arshavin's still open one, flipped to an open page, and handed the lady a pen. She elegantly drew out the nuclear-launch-code-length European mobile number and playfully pushed the folio an inch toward Jack, signaling that she was done with it. He reached under his and scooped as many of Arshavin's papers as he could. It felt like better than half and pressed them against the bottom of his own folio to keep them concealed.

"*Bon après-midi, mademoiselle,*" Jack said with a wink and a smile, and he left as Arshavin was returning to the table with a pair of champagne cocktails.

Jack made the front door fast.

10

Enzo twisted his thick, hairy fingers around the bottle opener and popped the cap off a Peroni as Gabrielle entered the apartment. He gave her an offhand greeting and walked back around the counter to the small dining room table. The apartment had two bedrooms and an otherwise open floorplan with the living room, dining room, and kitchen all sharing the same space. It was cramped as hell with the four of them, but after this Enzo would be living on a yacht permanently anchored off Monaco, so he could suck this up for a day or two. The table was a haphazard collection of laptops and notebooks, all of which would be acid-bathed at the end of the job. Gaston was lounging on the couch, switching between a preview of this weekend's Formula One race and an Arsenal match.

They'd practiced enough for the day. One of the lessons Jack taught him was on the dangers of overtraining. People needed downtime to keep their minds fresh. Being overworked, on top of being nervous, on a job was a perfect formula for making a mistake and getting caught.

Ozren, however, paced.

Gabrielle set her things down on the table and pulled a chair out. The meeting with Ehud Arshavin, one of Hassar's innumerable lieutenants, had gone exceedingly well. She had gotten an intimate look at the exhibition space and, more importantly learned that in order to be ready for Hassar's pre-show walk-through Sunday afternoon, they would be moving the jewels from the hotel vault to the showroom floor Saturday night. Arshavin didn't admit this directly, of course; he merely made an offhand comment about needing to orga-nize a dress rehearsal for his boss before the show opened, and Gabrielle was able to fit the details together from that. Arshavin spoke with the surety that came with being a key functionary of a person with real power, and while it was just south of bragging—gentlemen, after all, do not brag; they merely tell things as they are—Arshavin made it clear to the beautiful woman he was escorting around the salon that he was indeed an important man because he was entrusted with the exacting execution Hassar expected. From what they'd gathered on him, Hassar possessed a level of patience so minute that it couldn't be measured and a wrathful temper that seemed to be created exclusively for billionaires by the universe with the sole aim at making them insufferable. Taken together, his people would move heaven and earth to have the exhibition ready for his appointed viewing, even if it meant cutting some corners with security to do so. For the drones setting this up, it was a binary choice—skirt some "rules" in order to meet the boss's timeline or follow them and risk getting fired if everything wasn't in order by the time he wanted to go.

Enzo and Gabrielle discussed the logistics involved and deduced that Hassar's people would be working through the night to have the jewels positioned just so before transferring ownership to the security detail for a few hours until Hassar arrived. Enzo and Gaston would access the hotel through one of the service entrances. The hotel staff had a habit of leaving those open at night. They already had a pair of hotel uniforms, having found out where a lot of the staff takes its dry cleaning. They'd be in and out in ten minutes.

"I can't believe they're actually leaving them in the cases like that," Enzo said, shaking his head at the sheer stupidity of it. Security on Hassar's part, so far, was terrible. French law prohibited private security from being armed, but he assumed that a man of Hassar's considerable resources would be able to...convince...the *Commissariat de Police* to have an armed presence. Also, Enzo found it particularly peculiar that Hassar would hold his exhibition in a salon that was accessible by the street—one of the busiest streets in Cannes—and on the ground floor.

Gabrielle shrugged, her mouth twisting in the corner: *What do you want me to say?* She couldn't believe security was as lax as it apparently was, but that's what she'd learned. Gabrielle took off her wig and began pulling out the pins that held her golden Alpine hair in place. "I'm going to take a shower."

Enzo nodded and sipped his beer. He was pleased. It was a good plan. Hassar had made some major mistakes, or his people had. Enzo suspected it was the way it always seemed to be with powerful men. None of their cronies were willing to call them on their stupidity for fear of retribution. Business, governments, or the mafia in his own country, it was all the same. Well, this time it would cost Ari Hassar. Not to mention the army of yes-men circling him like so many remoras, it would cost them as well. Enzo smiled, imagining them being summoned to some executive conference room within Hassar's Tel Aviv headquarters, blond wood and cream-colored carpeting, looking out over the city—Hassar leaning over the table, all five feet seven inches of him, bullet head and hairy knuckles, screaming at them behind his giant sunglasses, frothing at the mouth for the incompetence that couldn't even be calculated, it was so stupid and so extreme. All of them fired. Eighty-five million dollars he'd get back from the insurance company almost immediately. Enzo envisioned that check would actually be in Hassar's pocket by the time he was executing his staff. God, to think an insurance company would go along with an exhibition with such porous security was truly amazing to Enzo.

Enzo tried not to second-guess himself, but it was difficult not to. He wondered if Jack did this. In the days and hours before a job, if he poked holes in his own plan, if he worried over the things that he hadn't thought of or hadn't thought through fully. Or was the cool that Jack showed on the job just because he'd done this so many times, he had a sixth sense where the holes were and knew how to fill them? Enzo still couldn't believe Jack turned this one down. Like, he got it, on a certain level. Of course, Hassar didn't just *sound* dangerous, he *was* dangerous, but the reward had to outweigh this. It was a million-to-one job. He wished he could call his friend now, ask his opinion, but Reginald said Jack was strictly off-limits.

Enzo drank his beer slowly and focused on his notes. These would all be burned when they were done. He reviewed the timeline and reviewed the two alternate escape routes they had. He might take a stroll in a minute, clear his head, and then get back to it. He still needed to think through what would happen if he and Gaston walked into a different situation when they got inside. What if there was more security?

What if it was Hassar's personal security and not the rent-a-cops? What if the crew was ahead of schedule and the jewels were already in their display cases? You had to think through these possibilities, however outlandish or remote they might seem.

It was the things you didn't see that got you.

11

Jack reached for the bottle of white Burgundy in the carafe sitting on the table next to his patio chair and refilled his glass. Beads of condensation threaded their way down the terra-cotta cylinder in tiny rivulets. Half-melted ice chunks softly crashed together when he lifted the bottle out and again when he replaced it. He tasted the wine, savoring first the light citrus and grass flavors and then, amazingly, strong honey as he swallowed. It was getting a little dark to read, but then, he'd already memorized the fifteen pages he'd lifted from Arshavin this afternoon.

The patio was designed in the fashion of a Roman garden. Tall cypress and palm trees dominated the background, surrounded by nearly impenetrable thickets of smaller trees, bushes, and ferns. The back wall was hidden by a reasonably manicured hedge about fifteen feet tall. Hanging plants with yellow-green leaves draped over the side of the stone wall that surrounded the pool, expertly placed to appear slightly overgrown. The pool itself was green, though that was more a reflection of the plant life surrounding it rather than an indication of the owner's attitude toward upkeep.

A gentle burst of wind pushed through the patio and rustled the small sheaf of papers on the table. The stolen documents were a veritable gold mine. From these, Jack had learned that the cases would be loaded in the low hours on Sunday morning, presumably because they believed that to be the least risky time. The cases had to be ready by eight. This was circled twice and underlined twice in pen, because Ari Hassar would be doing his own walk-through around lunchtime. There would be two guards watching the entire thing between the end of loading and Hassar's walk-through.

Jack marveled at how poor the security was. An actual fortune sitting behind casual centimeters of impact-resistant glass and two unarmed security guards who could, at best, yell for help and make ungentlemanly suggestions about Jack's parentage. It could be that Hassar had planned this himself, and telling him it was a bad idea went against the hardwiring of the yes-men he surrounded himself with. Or Hassar knew that his reputation preceded him and knew no one would be dumb enough to steal from him.

Jack took another sip of wine. The plan was beginning to come together now.

Jack would go Sunday morning, just after eight. The streets of Cannes would be relatively clear—probably the quietest they'd be all week. He'd use a motorcycle, which Rusty could arrange quickly enough. That could be parked out of sight in a nearby alley, and given the time of day, Jack would be able to get out of town very quickly. It would also help him elude the police, should it come to that.

Now, he just needed to figure out how Enzo and Gaston were going to play this.

He thought again of his friend. Nothing was so dangerous as a troubled man with just the company of his thoughts. And wine, Jack mused.

What agonized Jack was not so much that he was working against the Watchmaker. He'd rationalized that already as a survival mechanism. Instead, it was that his friend of nearly twenty years took the job. Yes, it was an absolute fortune, but he'd wished Enzo said no for all the reasons that Jack did. If he had, they would be available *now*. Not only would Jack not be working against them, but he'd possibly be working with them against whatever B-team crew Reginald could assemble at the last minute.

Would they? Would the team he trained, had led on dozens of successful heists and, through his meticulous planning, kept out of jail—would they do this without him?

Of course they would.

This was a sum of money that brooked no loyalty.

Jack sipped the wine and forced his thoughts back to California and his own winery. The dark paths of revenge would do nothing good for him tonight. The job, the crew, and reverse engineering their plans would keep until tomorrow. He'd looked over the purloined documents, his notes, the layout, everything he had to work with until his eyes threatened to roll back in his skull. Preparation was important, but so was a rested mind.

Jack closed his eyes and focused on nothing but the wine and the wind.

Jack enjoyed the complexity and the sophistication of French wine. It was truly a craft. The climate and terroir of France was so unlike that of California wine country that even the same varietal, in this case chardonnay, would have a radically different taste on the palate. Well, that and for the last decade or so the trend among California chardonnay producers was to infuse as much oak as was chemically possible outside of floating wood chips in the glass so that drinking it tasted like sucking on a stick of butter. Though

Megan came from the Italian school, she still maintained a very old-world approach to winemaking, and the oak craze infuriated her to no end. Kingfisher made the obligatory white, a chard they called "Goshawk," but it was done very much in the French style with minimal oak.

Jack absorbed her passions by osmosis. Megan's personality was so strong she practically radiated this kind of psychic energy that gradually eroded your own opinions about things until eventually you agreed with her. Also, she had an Irish temper and had been known to throw things on occasion to make a point, up to and including shovels.

Jack smiled, remembering the moment. It was funny...now.

They were building something special. That's what Megan told him about Kingfisher before he left, and she was right. Jack bought the winery because he was looking for a way to establish a legitimate identity that he could settle into after his career was finished. He didn't want to be like Reginald, running jobs until he got caught and then fixing jobs until he died to make up the difference. Jack's original plan was to be an almost silent partner in his own winery, pump his money into it and turn it over to smarter people, but he found that he truly loved it. Making wine spoke to him in a way that nothing else had. It gave him purpose and something to strive for.

The idea first came to him about ten years ago. He was reading the in-flight magazine during one of his transcontinental hops and came across an article about how all these Silicon Valley millionaires were buying wineries, looking for something to do with their newfound fortunes.

The idea was so perfect, he practically shouted on the plane. Jack discovered a love of wine when he and Enzo were running and gunning in Torino. Later, when he returned to the States, Jack found himself vacationing in wine country more and more when he was in the low months between jobs. He found peace among the solitude and serenity of the vineyards and mottled green and tan mountains. It also had a frontier feel to it. No one cared where you were from or what you did so long as you were passionate about the wine. What better way?

The next morning, Jack woke early and moved through a yoga routine by the pool while the coffee brewed. It was Thursday, which meant he had three full days to keep tabs on Enzo, Gaston, Gabrielle, and Ozren.

He knew the earliest that Enzo and team could go would be in the overnight hours between Saturday and Sunday because the jewels wouldn't be delivered until then. Unless, of course, Gabrielle had charmed the location of the vault the jewels were being stored in out of Arshavin, but most likely those weren't even in country yet. There were simply too many minuscule, oddball permutations to think about, and Jack just wasn't going to waste the time running all those scenarios down. Instead, he'd just watch them.

Jack alternated between watching the safe house and tailing Ozren as the driver practiced various escape avenues from the hotel. The Serb was also checking the roads, making sure that there were no major obstructions, like last-minute roadwork, on their getaway route. Ozren tried several paths but ended up at the D4085 heading north toward the French Alps and, ultimately, to the Swiss border. That would buy them crucial hours as the French authorities coordinated with their Swiss counterparts to pick up the chase. They could well be in Austria by the time the border closed.

On Friday morning, Jack posted in front of the safe house, parking the Maserati on an adjacent block out of sight but near enough that he could get to it quickly if he needed to. Before coming over, Jack drove to the Carrefour on Rue Meynadier. Carrefour was a kind of French Wal-Mart, though God help the American who drew that particular parallel in mixed company. There, he purchased gardening equipment, a pair of coveralls, a wide-brimmed hat, and sunglasses. Jack changed in the bathroom and, now garbed like a gardener, drove his hundred-thousand-euro Italian sports car to the safe house. Once there, Jack walked the perimeter once to make sure there weren't any legitimate gardeners on the premises and then located the column of apartments he'd seen Gabrielle enter two days prior.

The complex housed what looked to be about twenty units. The apartments were grouped in stacks of four, with each stack having its own dedicated doorway and stairwell. Jack slowly walked past each unit, inspecting the plant life, checking to see what needed to be pruned or trimmed. This also gave him a chance to look in each of the windows in a group of units and see which ones had the shutters open. Jack knew now that he did not need to figure out Enzo's plan so much as he simply needed to know when the group intended to execute it. He drew up several scenarios, using his knowledge of his old friend to red-team Enzo's operation, but there were still so many variables and so few clues. Jack could not settle on one he was willing to commit to. His best bet was to wait until they were out of the apartment so he could break in —the locks would be laughably easy to pick—and try to learn when they'd go.

Jack was pretending to look at the foliage in an adjacent unit when he spotted Ozren, wearing black jeans and thin gray polo shirt, walking out of the doorway and up the short concrete path to the waist-high metal gate, which he promptly opened and stepped through, barely breaking his stride. The Serb opened his flip phone—he'd never trusted smart phones —and made a call. He checked the street once, again without breaking his stride, stepped off the sidewalk, and made his way quickly to a gray Mercedes Sprinter parked across the street. Stolar got into the van and sped off, never paying the gardener a second glance.

Jack had a decision to make. Follow the Serb again and risk him spotting Jack's car and making the connection of a red GranTurismo two days in a row, or stay here, hoping that the crew had their windows open and Jack could eavesdrop, reasoning that they likely had one car and would stay put with Ozren gone.

He chose Ozren.

Jack left the bucket of gardening tools on the low concrete wall that ringed the front of the building, pushed up against a bush that looked like it needed attention, knowing that anyone walking by would just assume a lazy gardener had abandoned it until he felt like cleaning it up. Judging by the state of the shrubs and hedges out front, this wasn't a hard sell.

Jack quickly made his way across the street, rounded the corner, and broke into a full run for his car. He spotted the Serb's van about a half mile west of the safe house. Ozren was sticking to the main roads and obviously wasn't thinking about a tail. Ozren turned right onto the Boulevard Sadi Carnot, one of the city's major north-south arteries, and followed that until it merged with D6285, becoming a four-lane divided road heading northwest until it crossed the A8, at which point it became the D6185. Navigating in France had always confounded the hell out of Jack, though he had to admit it was better than Ireland, where road names and designations and even the widths would be dictated entirely by the county they were in with no real semblance of central organization or management.

Ozren stayed on 6285 as it became 6185 and was clearly intent on leaving Cannes.

Whatever the reason, unless he followed Stolar to his destination, Jack could only speculate at the motive, and he was in far too conspicuous of a car to pull that off safely. There were enough high-end sports cars on the streets of Cannes that a Maserati just blended in with the background noise. But once they left town, Ozren would pick him up in a flat second. Jack watched the gray Sprinter grow smaller through his passenger window as he turned onto the A8, accelerating to merge speed, then up to a hundred and twenty for a few miles until the D6007 exit on the western edge of town.

Jack met Rusty at his villa shortly after two to take possession of the motorcycle, a gray-and-red BMW R 1200 GS. The R 1200 was a sport bike that doubled as a touring cycle. As one of the top-selling bikes in its class and immensely popular throughout Europe, it would not stand out at all. Though the bike was quick and handled well, the real reason they'd chosen it was the detachable briefcase-style side case that would easily hold the take. Rusty told him that the plates were clean, but the registration was forged. Whatever Jack was planning with the bike, it'd probably be best to strip the plates and acid-bath them when he was done.

The meeting was brief. Rusty wished him luck and said he was heading back to Marseille for another job, reassuring him with a laugh and a smirk that Reginald LeGrande had nothing to do with that one. Jack smiled back. Rusty was the very definition of a rogue—rakish and sly in both style and speech, his work and his appearance an immaculate simulacrum of the other.

Jack didn't tell Rusty what he was doing here, but he'd

know immediately as soon as the story broke. Jack planned to give the fixer more money as a bonus, and if it were anyone else, he'd be afraid of them thinking that they could come back to the well. Of course, if it had been anyone else, Jack would never have called.

He drove back to the apartment complex on Avenue Isola Bella. He slowed as he rolled up on the building but decided not to stop. The Sprinter was not parked out front, so he drove around the adjoining blocks to make sure it wasn't anywhere nearby. Without the van there, he didn't know if Ozren had come back and gotten the others or if he was still out. So, Jack couldn't break into the apartment because he had no way of knowing if someone was in there or not.

Deciding there was nothing else he could do, Jack returned to the villa, where he spent about thirty minutes swimming laps in the pool and then another thirty doing a yoga routine to burn off some nervous energy. Still in his swim trunks, Jack opened a Sancerre—this would be his last, as there was no alcohol consumption the day before a job. As Jack sat in the Mediterranean sun, drinking the '07 Domaine François Cotat in a villa on the French Riviera, even he had to laugh at the outward hilarity. This was the pregame routine for one of the world's most notorious thieves.

He called Megan to check in, but it went straight to voice-mail. So, he simply reclined and enjoyed his wine, trying to calm the turbulence in his mind.

He really just wanted to hear her voice.

Jack wasn't exactly sure what their relationship was anymore, or more importantly, what it should be. But he certainly missed her when he was gone. They'd been attracted to each other immediately, and shortly after she'd started working at the winery, they'd gotten drunk and had some inadvisable sex. In the cold light of morning and aided by sobriety, they'd agreed not to do that again for the good of their working relationship. They'd slipped up a few times since, and Jack heard from Corky that most of the full-time staff assumed they were together anyway. Recently, they'd admitted to each other that the feelings were still there and that neither of them were sure how to approach it. For his part, Jack said he was happy that she was in his life, personal and professional, and whatever they decided to call it didn't matter as long as the substance didn't change. Megan said that was fine with her too.

Jack hesitated, not only for the obvious reason that it put a very tangible stamp on the lie that was Frank Fischer, but also because he had almost pathological difficulty forming personal attachments. When Jack was young, he made a very, very bad mistake, and the only way he saw to answer for it was to disappear. If he stayed, the people he loved would be punished. So, the lesson that Jack learned was to never attach himself to something he couldn't walk away from. Even Kingfisher, he knew, he could drop and run if he had to. But letting himself fall in love with Megan was an entirely different matter. That was not something he could just run away from.

An hour later, Jack walked back into the villa from the patio for a bottle of water. The television droned in the background in the other room, and something caught his attention. He kept it turned to CNN International because that was the only station he could understand. Piqued, Jack walked quickly into the living room, dialing up the volume. Frozen in place, Jack watched the silver-haired American broadcaster repeat his breaking news statement with the practiced cadence designed to sound urgent but measured and extemporaneous.

Two inmates had escaped Prison de la Croisée in Orbe, Switzerland, in a brazen, audacious, and well-planned breakout the night before. According to the reporter, a car charged the outer gate and then sped up to an inner fence surrounding the prison's exercise yard. The driver exchanged gunfire with the guards while an accomplice pushed a ladder up and over the fence before opening cover fire himself. The two inmates then used the ladder to scale the fence and jump into the car. The car raced back through the gate and disappeared before the guards or the local police could launch an effective pursuit. Swiss authorities found the car's charred remains in a town not far from the prison. The reporter said that the French, German, and Italian border crossings were being monitored as well as the airports. There was an inset map at the lower right corner of the TV screen showing Orbe's location in southwest Switzerland, not far from the French border.

"Shit," Jack said aloud, softly first, drawing the syllable out. His second "Shit" was much louder and harder. His own escape plan called for him to leave France overland to Italy. If the borders were already being monitored, what did that mean for his plan, especially considering that by the time he arrived at the checkpoint, the news of the Carlton heist would be all over the radio.

Then the reporter said something that made a cold pit form at the bottom of Jack's stomach. The two escapees were known Serbian criminals and suspected members of the Pink Panthers, a notorious syndicate of international jewel thieves, most of whom came from the miasma of anarchic Balkanized chaos that was the former Republic of Yugoslavia. Most of them were suspected to be former soldiers in the Yugoslav Army, particularly their special forces, who turned to crime when Yugoslavia broke apart in the 1990s and descended into lawlessness.

The Pink Panthers, in that vein of spite and sarcasm

unique to the English, were so named by Scotland Yard in a sardonic homage to the Peter Sellers film after gang members stole a single diamond from a London jeweler valued at half a million pounds. The Metropolitan Police intended the moniker to infuriate and embarrass the thieves, but instead, the gang embraced it, particularly after their successful high-profile jobs made the police look as incompetent as Sellers's Inspector Clouseau. Soon, they became known for daring jobs reminiscent of Hollywood heist films by employing elaborate costumes, flashy executions, and daring escapes. In a 2009 job on London's New Bond Street, the thieves made no attempt to hide their identities, which led authorities to speculate they'd used makeup and prosthetic features, speaking of a cold, premeditated calculation and thoughtful planning, whereas before the police ascribed them only thuggish luck.

Ozren volunteered little of substance about his past, and if Reginald had any indication, he certainly never shared it with Jack. But he had long suspected that even if Ozren wasn't actively affiliated with the Panthers, he had most likely gotten his start in that group. As Jack understood their cellular organizational structure, it was more of a criminal franchise than a syndicate. The group would train prospective members and turn them loose on the world, with cells occasionally providing logistical support or intelligence on juicy scores. There was no notion of a centralized command or hierarchical structures of Western organized crime enterprises. This confounded European law enforcement for the better part of a decade. They simply couldn't reason over a criminal network that looked more like metastasized cancer and less like the mafia. Last fall, Jack and Rusty met up in Sorrento to talk about work, and the ex-G-man gave Jack a master course on the Panthers over a couple buckets of beer.

The pieces began to fit together in Jack's mind, and he considered the broader implications.

When Jack followed Ozren earlier, on what he assumed was the group's escape route, Ozren was really heading north on a road that eventually led to the Swiss border.

Jack grabbed his keys and ran outside to the car, not bothering to turn off the television or even lock the villa behind him. Jack made fast time to the apartment complex on Avenue Isola Bella, keeping his eyes peeled only for the gray Mercedes Sprinter. Jack drove around the block and then each of the surrounding blocks for a quarter mile in any direction.

The van was nowhere to be found.

Ozren must have thought that with Jack out of the picture, this score would be ripe for the taking. He probably made plans with his former colleagues to go for it themselves. Most likely, they were going to wait until Enzo and Gaston made their move with the hope they could steal the take from them after rather than make a play themselves.

Jack had to warn them. If that crazy Serb was coming for them, Enzo had to know. He paused. If he told them, Reginald would find out that Jack was making a play for that score. Jack would certainly have to cut Enzo, Gaston, and Gabrielle in on the score. Reginald would be angry, but the cut would ultimately be the same. They would just be trading Ozren's cut for Jack's. Better to have a cut of something than all of nothing. But Ozren and his fellow Panthers would need to be dealt with, and if the stories were true, they were most likely trained soldiers in addition to being exceptional thieves.

A darker thought entered Jack's mind as he played through the permutations.

There was a nagging question of exactly where Reginald's loyalties lay and how many angles he was playing. Pangs of guilt stabbed at Jack as quickly as he thought of it. He wasn't surprised that Reginald would cut him out of the job considering how Jack spurned him initially and then tried to come in at the last minute. Jack might well have reacted the same way if the situation were reversed. But he couldn't banish the knowledge that LeGrande found and recruited Ozren. The Serb was cunning in the way animal predators were, but he was no mastermind. As hard as it was to contemplate, Jack knew he had to allow for the possibility that maybe his old friend was playing both sides.

Reginald had no specific loyalty to Enzo, Gaston, and Gabrielle, and he didn't know that Jack was here.

Still, Enzo was his friend, and Ozren was almost certainly going to double-cross them.

And where are your *loyalties, Jack?* he asked himself. *Is it to a bunch of criminals, or is to Megan, Lincoln, and the rest of your employees who are on the street if you fail?*

Jack's eyes tracked up to the car's roof as his mind searched its hallways for answers.

He coolly reached for his phone. It was time to make a call.

12

Enzo opened the sliding glass door and stepped out onto their second-floor balcony, pulling it closed behind him. His impulse was to check his watch, but he knew it couldn't have been more than fifteen minutes past the last time he'd done that, so at most, it was seven o'clock. Where the fuck was Ozren? He was supposed to be back four hours ago. Enzo himself was so tense he thought he was going to crawl out of his skin. He was doing his best to keep a lid on it, to put a good face on for Gaston and Gabrielle, but he didn't know how much longer he could keep this up. Finally, he stepped outside on the balcony for some fresh air, knowing that if he didn't, he would probably scream.

The Serb never would've pulled something like this with Jack. It's not that Ozren was afraid of Burdette, but the boundaries that Ozren would try to push with Jack had limits. Apparently, that same recognition didn't seem to translate to Enzo. It was simply one more thing to deal with, and Enzo wondered how Jack ever kept it straight in his own head while managing to look so cool.

Enzo never wanted to run a crew of his own. He had his

specialty and was very, very good at it. Enzo enjoyed the exacting precision of safecracking. He enjoyed the puzzle of it. But as Enzo tried to think through every possible angle on this job, he realized that he liked only being responsible for his own function and not having to also know everyone else's job well enough to plan it. Again, he wished Jack were here now. Reginald LeGrande told him that Burdette was out of this one, said it was against his "rules," and Reginald scoffed when he said it. Enzo had called Jack to confirm it. "It's too risky," Jack told him at the time. "I'm walking away, and you should too." Enzo said he understood.

"Never steal from someone with the resources and the will to come get it back," Burdette told him once. Reginald was clear on one thing—Jack could not know they were the ones behind this. Reginald said it's best that you not ever reveal that you pulled a job to a colleague or a friend. Jealousy is a breeding ground for bad decision and worse actions, he said. Enzo protested, and Reginald said in a cold, low voice, "You don't know him like I do." He sounded scared.

Enzo begged to differ on that score but left it alone.

Maybe Reginald was right.

So Enzo went along with it, because eighty-five million dollars.

But that was in the rosy planning stages when one simply waltzed into the Carlton InterContinental and walked out a multimillionaire.

Hell of a job to cut your teeth on as a crew runner.

Now, a day out from the job, Enzo wasn't sure they'd actually be able to carry it out, and Gaston and Gabrielle would be looking to him to make a decision—do they go, or don't they? Enzo honestly could not answer that question.

Enzo heard the glass door open behind him, and Gaston said, "Hey, man."

Enzo turned. Gaston had two beers, both opened. He held one out to Enzo, who accepted it gratefully, wishing it were something stronger.

"Figured you could use one."

"Thanks," Enzo said. He moved to the side, avoiding that stupid hanging plant someone was always seeming to bump into.

Gaston smiled in the half-light but said nothing. He didn't have to, and Enzo was grateful that he didn't offer the hollow platitudes people so often did in moments like these. The two men stood in silence and drank their beers. They were friends as well as colleagues and knew each other well. They'd been to each other's homes. Normally, a cardinal sin in the trade. Gaston knew what was on Enzo's mind and respected him enough not to pry.

For Enzo, it wasn't just a matter of Ozren being available to drive the van after the job; Gabrielle could do that. Of course, the plan called for her to be out of the country by the time the job went down—you never had the face involved in the execution phase. But Ozren's other job was surveillance. He was supposed to be watching the building and the surroundings while Enzo and Gaston were inside. Ozren knew how to spot police, knew how to tell plainclothes security from a tourist in baggy clothes. He knew where to park the van so that it hit the fewest number of security cameras—or better, was in the seam between them. Or, the biggest risk of all: they do the job, succeed without him, and that crazy Serb comes to collect.

Yes, they *could* do the job without a driver or by having Gabrielle do it. They practiced each of these scenarios. They had to, because on any job someone could get cold feet and bail, they could get made, they could get hung up in a traffic accident or some other freak thing the universe threw at them. Everyone had their specialties, but they were all cross-function. What was making them nervous was why Ozren wasn't there. Knowing why someone wasn't there and planning around it was one thing. Having someone missing and *not* knowing was trouble.

"Do we go without him?" Gaston asked.

Enzo looked at his friend. "I don't know. If he was arrested, we're walking into a trap. If he decided to sell us out to some associates, we're walking into a trap."

"Do you think he would? Either of them?"

Enzo smirked, shrugged, but said nothing further. He didn't want to respond out loud because they both knew the answers to those questions and neither of them wanted Enzo to vocalize it, make it real.

"Well, we don't know if he's wanted here for something else. Or," he reasoned, "it could've been Europol. Who knows? Ozren has a pretty long history in Yugoslavia, and God only knows what he did there and who he pissed off."

"That I can believe," Gaston said and pointed with the tip of his beer bottle, as though Enzo had just shown him an exhibit.

"I'll tell you one thing's for sure," Enzo said, looking out into the semi-dark of the lawn and bright sliver of skyline. "If he shows up back here, I'll shoot him myself."

"So, back to the original question. Do we risk it? We'll have to change the plan, we'll need to get a new car, and Gabrielle will have to drive," Gaston said.

Enzo nodded but said nothing. They were breaking a lot of their rules on this one, but they'd also be making enough that none of them would ever have to work again.

"But where do we get a car on such short notice?"

"I'll be honest," Gaston said into the mouth of his beer bottle, "that's about the only thing I've never stolen."

"Me either," Enzo said. "We could rent one, but that's going to leave a trail."

Jack had a guy that did this sort of thing for him. Guy was a magician. Found cars, passports, airplane tickets. Shit, he'd even managed to get them a boat once for that thing in Nice.

Enzo didn't have a guy.

"Could we do this without a car?" Gaston asked.

"Just walk out of town?"

"I don't see that we have a lot of other options."

"This is what we'll do. We've got the credit card Reginald gave us. I can hire another car on that. I'll call LeGrande and tell him Ozren skipped out on us—he'll need to know that anyway so he can figure out what to do with the son of a bitch. I just want to make sure that the credit card is still good. This thing doesn't need to be a Porsche, it just has to drive. What is it Jack always says?"

"I don't know. He says a lot."

Enzo half laughed. "That's true. No, he says that if you're in a position to be in a car chase with the police, you're caught already. The only one who doesn't know it is you." Enzo killed his beer. "I'll call Reginald right now. It's late morning where he is."

Gaston nodded in agreement. "So we go?"

"We can't pass this up. Not even for Ozren and whatever the fuck he's doing right now. If you're willing to take the risk, then so am I."

"No bullshit, my friend. French prison isn't anything to scoff at."

Enzo flashed a sour look. "You're served wine with dinner."

"I said we were bad jailers, I didn't say we're barbarians." After a moment: "Enzo, I mean it, if we get caught, we'll never see daylight again."

"That was true when we started this thing. Gaston, we have their schedule. We know every move they're going to make. We know exactly when the collection is going to arrive, and we have a good idea of the corners they're cutting so that it's done on time. Having Gabrielle as the driver is a risk. I mean, let's face it, she sticks out in a crowd. Even in this town. But I think the odds of her getting made are slim. It was always you and me on the inside. It's not like we're losing anything there by not having Ozren with us."

"I agree with all of your points. I just owe it to you, to all of us, to make sure you're thinking about all the angles. But there's one thing you haven't mentioned yet."

"What's that?"

"You haven't asked Gabrielle if *she's* okay with it."

Enzo was reaching into his pocket for his phone to call the American and thinking through how he'd broach the subject with her when Gabrielle called out from the living room. Enzo opened the sliding glass door and saw she'd turned the television on; he'd left it off all day so he could think.

"You two need to get in here!"

13

Sunday morning found Cannes gray, cold, and damp. Rain had come in off the Mediterranean in the early hours, and though it hadn't been drenching, all of the surfaces and the streets were wet and would be until the sun burned it off. By the look of things, that wouldn't be for several more hours. Jack didn't know exactly what Enzo's timetable would be but surmised it would be later that night to execute the heist in the final few hours before the show opened.

The real variable was the prison break.

Jack would normally have done a final dress rehearsal the day before, but instead stayed hidden at his safe house. He had to assume Ozren was making his own play. If that was true, they'd be casing the hotel, and Jack needed to stay away.

It was too great a coincidence to think that the information about this job was on the street, Ozren Stolar knew about it, and then some of the Pink Panthers broke out of a prison in Switzerland yesterday. While he could ghost Enzo's moves and be fairly confident about it, the Panthers were incredibly unpredictable. He wondered whether he should warn Enzo about the Pink Panthers but ultimately decided against it, as that would confirm that Jack was here and going after the same score. They'd figure out soon enough that Jack beat them to it, and by then, the Panthers would be sidelined as a threat.

Jack left his villa at eight thirty. He took a long, circuitous route to the hotel. It was a Sunday morning and the streets were clear. The air was cool and heavy. Jack approached the hotel from the west, having gone the long way around and looped back. He pulled onto Boulevard de la Croisette, the long and elegant road that ran along the beach, the street that Cannes wanted to present to the world. The boulevard had two lanes in both directions, separated by a median that was beautifully landscaped with palm trees and smaller plants. The seaward side of the street had palms and broad coniferous trees that reminded Jack of a kind of cypress he saw in California. Jack rode the motorcycle. He chose it because it gave him more options on the escape, should he need it. When pulling a job with a crew you could, if needed, have someone create traffic problems for the pursuers, such as causing a minor accident along the escape route after the driver and the take had passed. Those times were rare, but Jack had needed to use it on occasion. Going alone, however, the bike gave him the ability to ditch a route if he needed, or even to weave through traffic on the existing one.

Jack passed through the wet shadows of wide cypress trees. Taking a moment to glance out to sea, Jack saw more wealth floating just offshore than he would ever steal in a lifetime of thieving. There was little foot traffic on the sidewalks and fewer cars, except for delivery vehicles. Hotel workers were preparing their private beaches, opening cabanas and setting beach chairs in long rows. Umbrellas were stuck in the ground, though left unopened, in the event of either rain or bright sun. Jack saw more than one attendant looking up at the sky and wondering if the gods of tourism held them in their favor today.

Jack spotted his target.

The Carlton loomed like a monolith, a relic from a previous age that still held power over the modern world. The Carlton was a huge hotel and occupied nearly an entire city block. Jack turned left just before the hotel to the next block. Midway up that street, a road split the block on his left, dividing it into two different hotel properties. Jack parked the motorcycle on that street, in between those two hotels but still somehow in the shadow of the Carlton InterContinental.

He removed the motorcycle helmet and secured it to the bike, then opened the side case and replaced the helmet with a black ball cap and aviators, keeping his head low and aimed at the street. He was dressed in a long-sleeve white T-shirt and jeans and had a large, loose scarf around his neck, styled to look like a regular bandanna that motocross and mountain bike riders wore. Finally, he removed the Beretta from the side case and tucked it against the small of his back. He got a sick feeling as he did it. Jack hated guns and despised violence, but without a crew to back him up, control the crowd, and add mass to the equation, Jack knew he needed the weapon to put the odds in his favor.

The bike was equipped with a silver side case that looked like a small suit- or briefcase, intended to give the driver the ability to bring clothes and personal effects with them on long trips. Jack detached the case from the bike and crossed Rue François Einesy to the sidewalk next to the Carlton. Jack briskly walked the two hundred feet or so up to Boulevard de la Croisette, Cannes's seafront and palm-lined Miracle Mile. Hassar's propaganda machine was in full effect. Gaudy pink-and-white banners hung at both corners of the salon's raised exterior patio and from the concrete wall topped by a balustrade that separated it from the street. Further, to fill up the visual space between the street and the salon, they had extended the gold-and-white striped awning to cover the entire patio. Three additional bright pink banners advertising the show hung in the space between the awning's edge and the top of the balustrade. The patio floor was eye level for the average person standing on the street, so someone would have to be standing right there and looking at him to see him enter or exit from the street-side door.

Jack scanned the street once more. It was sleepy. A jogger in hot pink moved along the seaside sidewalk and there were a handful of walkers on either side of the street, but little traffic otherwise. Jack counted two cars moving. There was no law enforcement present; he didn't even see any hotel security. The other thing he looked for was a van.

If his crew followed their typical plan, Gabrielle's phase of this would be done. Enzo might pull her in to make up for the reduced manpower (assuming Reginald didn't add to the crew with some of his others), but Jack didn't think Gabrielle would go for that. She only did this because of the solid deniability she had when the jobs went down.

No, he was looking for Ozren. Jack didn't *know* that Ozren was behind the prison break, but he didn't see how else the Pink Panthers would have known about this job, and again, the coincidence was just too much to ignore. The news report said that it'd been a van matching the description of the one he'd seen Ozren driving. Still, without intel on this, he had to assume that they would hit it in the early hours before the show opened—tomorrow.

Jack took one last look up either street and saw that it was clear. It was now or never.

Jack walked the length of the long patio, conscious to keep his head low but not obviously so, then turned in and quickly ascended the short steps that connected the patio with the street. Jack stepped under the awning and into the shade. He counted off two sets of French doors and placed his gloved hand on the carefully polished brass handle of the third. He pulled. As promised, the door opened with a soft, barely audible click.

Jack pulled the scarf up over his nose and mouth and stepped inside the salon.

As soon as he cleared the door, Jack's right hand went from the handle to the small of his back and the Beretta 92FS pressed inside the waistband.

There were five men in the salon under the bright lights. If the room could be described as organized chaos, it was just barely so. The jewelry cases had been assembled and positioned around the room, and there were now display stands near some of them providing a detailed description of the contents. Each of the cases had a piece of printer paper on it with a large letter and number combination. Jack assumed that corresponded to a similar code matching the contents of the various hardshell transit cases that were set about the room. The papers had writing in French and Hebrew, neither of which Jack could read.

Jack looked to the occupants—Ehud Arshavin, two other men in suits—one Middle Eastern and one European—and a pair of uniformed security guards. Jack checked their hips and ears. They didn't even have radios, let alone sidearms. Arshavin noticed him first, followed by the guards. By the look of it, they were running way behind schedule. Only half of the jewelry cases had been filled, and the rest of the exhibition was still in its transit cases.

Four steps and Jack was in the center of the room, pistol out in front of him.

"You two," directed at the guards, "on the ground facing away. Hands above your heads. Now."

The guards dropped to the floor. They clearly weren't being paid enough to pretend they didn't understand English, though a pistol was a universal language. Jack's head remained fixed forward, but behind the glasses, his eyes flicked from the guards to the other three, making sure they weren't about to try something stupid. Jack waited a few solid breaths until he was sure there weren't any heroes in the room. Then he addressed the others. "Empty out the display cases. Put the jewels in the sacks and put the sacks in this case." Jack dropped the side case and pushed it farther into the room. Arshavin and his companions stood frozen. "Now!" Jack said sternly, implying the threat instead of overtly stating it.

Arshavin cleared the fog first. Tentatively, he reached over to one of the black velvet-lined sacks that sat folded on top of a display case, which he unlocked, an anxious hand unsteadily guiding the keys, and began loading its contents into the sack. Hands shaking, Hassar's lieutenant scooped up diamonds and other loose jewels by the handful and dumped them into the sack. Then he moved on to the next case. The other two followed Arshavin's lead, emptying the display cases and the transit boxes, per Jack's instructions. Jack supervised with his Beretta, keeping an eye on the salon's interior doors.

For scared men, they worked quickly.

The whole thing took a little over a minute.

"Th-that's everything," Arshavin said.

"Close it," Jack told him.

Arshavin bent back down and closed the case, securing the latches. When that was done, he looked back up for instructions.

Jack tapped the air twice with his pistol, indicating to

Arshavin to back up. When he did, Jack stepped forward and bent down, not taking his eyes off the men in the room, picked up the case, and started backing toward the door. Jack stuffed the pistol into his front pocket, opened the door, stepped out, and closed the door behind him. Under the cover of the awning, Jack pulled the T-shirt up over the pistol and pulled the scarf down off his nose and mouth. He made fast steps for the balustrade, planted his free hand on the white cement, and leaped over it.

But Jack dragged his foot just slightly and caught it on the edge of the balustrade as he vaulted over. The impact threw the timing of the jump off just enough that Jack rolled slightly off-balance in midair. Reflexively, Jack let go of the case to brace for impact. The anodized steel box crashed onto the sidewalk next to him. He landed with a hard smack and bounced his knee off the pavement. A shock of pain shot through Jack's leg. The force of the impact caused the case to open like a shiny, drunken clam, vomiting its contents all over the sidewalk.

Jack pulled himself into a crouch and looked around to survey the damage. He quickly scooped up as many of the loose jewels as he could into his hands, dumping them back into the case. He might have missed a few, he wasn't sure, but he didn't have time to search. Hotel security would be alerted and they would be calling the police right now

Jack was on the corner of the Boulevard de la Croisette and Henri Ruhl. Still in a crouch, he looked up from his diamond grab long enough to see he'd earned the attention of at least a few pedestrians. Fortunately for him, most were on the far side of the boulevard, which was a four-lane road divided by a palm-lined median. No one was close enough for a credible eyewitness account. They probably thought he was just some drunkard or clumsy oaf who tripped and fell. Still, Jack swore under his breath, turned his back to them, and pulled the Beretta out from his pants, which he thrust into the case. He'd never liked the idea of a handgun in his crotch and always thought the people he saw do that in movies were idiots begging for disaster. Jack grabbed the case, stood, and dashed across to the opposite corner where he'd stashed the motorcycle.

Jack checked his surroundings once more to be clear of onlookers. There was no one in the alley. He traded the ball cap for the helmet, depositing the cap into the case before locking it and starting the motorcycle. Before securing the case to the bike, Jack quickly inspected case to make sure that it wasn't damaged from the fall and would close securely. It appeared that it was just the shock of impact that forced the latches open, which seemed like poor design for something to go on a motorcycle. Jack tried the latches a few times, opening and closing them, and they seemed fine. He attached the case to its connector on the bike, locking it into place. The bike had a case on the other side, which was where Jack stored a tightly packed, ballistic nylon motorcycle jacket. He put this on and closed that case as well. He thought about transferring the contents of the damaged case to this one but decided against it. It would take too much time, and he was now putting himself at risk.

Jack got on the motorcycle and started it up. His plan was to take a similarly circuitous route back to the safe house, but in any case, getting away from here as quickly as possible while avoiding the main streets. The police would establish a perimeter quickly, and he needed to be out of here before that happened. Police sirens began to dot the background noise, lancing the lazy serenity of the Mediterranean morning with a chorus of alternating wails that grew in number like a haphazard orchestra.

14
_____

Enzo paced and drank water like a man in the desert. His nervous habit was not to chain-smoke, drink, or talk to himself, like he'd seen so many of his counterparts do over the years. Instead, when his nerves were up, Enzo's language grew fouler and fouler until it was just a stream of expletives. This was different. Enzo's mouth went dry, and he spent nearly every free moment pouring water down it to quench his seemingly insatiable thirst. He wasn't sure how many bottles of water he'd gone through that morning, but there was a stack of the plastic carcasses scattered about the counters and table in their apartment.

Someone beat them to it. *Someone*, he thought sourly. *Ozren*.

They each handled the news differently.

Enzo's plan was for he and Gaston to enter the exhibition through the outer doors late Sunday night. According to the reconnaissance that Gabrielle had done, that would be an easy enough lock to pick, and even if they tripped an alarm, he figured they could be out of there in less than three minutes.

Enzo and Gaston hadn't wanted to wait until Sunday night,

but Gabrielle learned through Arshavin that the jewels wouldn't be in place until daylight hours Sunday morning because their flight from Dubai had been delayed. Enzo didn't want to risk a daylight attempt. Apparently, he was the only one with that concern.

As soon as they learned about the Swiss jailbreak and, more importantly, the identities of the escapees, they knew that Ozren's disappearance Friday was neither coincidence nor an ill-fated run-in with the police. Perhaps Ozren had planned it all along—intending to use their plan instead of doing his own legwork and then busting his crew out to do the deed. That seemed a little complicated for the Serb, but then Enzo knew the Panthers were a cunning lot. At this point, Enzo didn't know or care—the simple fact was that Ozren betrayed them and took the score right out from under their noses.

The story broke onto local news during lunchtime. A single thief entered the salon from an outer door facing the street, subdued the two security guards with a pistol, and then forced the men setting up for the exhibition's Monday opening to fill up a briefcase with the jewels. Reports varied, but some eyewitnesses said that the thief fell leaping down onto the street and spilled the contents onto the sidewalk, which he promptly scooped up before hurrying across the street and disappearing around a corner.

His current whereabouts and identity were unknown.

"So, do we go after Ozren?" Gaston finally asked.

"Gaston, we don't know where they are," he said, trying to force some reason and calm into his voice. "We don't have any guns, and even if we did..." Enzo's voice trailed off. Enzo knew his way around a pistol and had a pistol with him, stashed in his things—he almost always carried, a simple precaution necessitated by his way of life, but he'd still never used it in anger. Enzo kept the piece as a hold-out, something to show. He'd never used one outside of a practice range. Gaston had military training and could hold his own, but Gabrielle had never touched a weapon in her life. The news report said two Pink Panthers had broken out of that prison. Enzo knew their background because Ozren had bragged about it enough on jobs. These weren't the kind of people he was going to just hold up.

"I just don't see how we can sit here and—"

"Enzo is right," Gabrielle said sternly, cutting into the debate. "What are we going to do to them, Gaston? They are trained killers."

"We could leak his name to the police," Gaston offered.

"Then the police get the jewels. That doesn't get us any closer."

"No, but it puts him farther away," Gaston bit back. "Fucking bastard."

Enzo walked up and put a hand on his friend's shoulder. "I hate this, but I don't see how we can get the jewels from them unless it's by force. And even if we had the means, we don't know where they are. If we tipped the police, as much as I'd love to see his face plastered all over the fucking television, he'll just say that we were accomplices." Enzo let out a long, sad breath. So, he thought to himself. This is the taste of failure. Up until the moment when Gabrielle called them into the living room Friday night, Enzo was decorating his yacht in his mind and puzzling where he'd put his Ferrari collection. Eventually, he said, "I'm going to call the American and tell him what's happened. Maybe he can at least make it harder for Ozren to sell them off." Enzo knew it was hollow consolation to his friends and knew as well that there was nothing to be done. But it was his responsibility and that ultimately, the fault was his. If he'd acted fast enough, acted boldly, been *deci-*

sive, they'd be racing for the border right now. He silently cursed Jack and LeGrande both. Whatever the hell had passed between them, whatever tarnished that relationship that they hadn't been able to put aside—even if just for this job—cost them all.

The depression was all-consuming.

Enzo had lost a wife once. She was beautiful and young and vibrant, fiery the way only his people can be. But she also had a taste for fine things—the best clothes, the best jewelry, elegant cars which she herself never wanted to drive but simply wanted to be seen in, the best cocaine, all things that Italy had in abundance for the privileged few. His wife's tastes came from hunger and shame; she was born poor and believed that she was above it. Enzo first became a thief, taking jobs on the side, to supplement his legitimate trade as a watchmaker. His wife, once she whetted her appetite on luxury, could not be satisfied with the occasional gift of jewelry or weekend on the Riviera. Soon, Enzo was away all hours of the night, taking jobs to chase the lifestyle that his wife demanded and doing so because he believed that's what love was. What was important was that he loved *her* and believed she loved him for the sacrifices he was making. When he lost his job as a watchmaker because it was simply one too many times that he didn't show up for work, Enzo told his beautiful wife that they would not suffer. She believed him.

It was not until he was caught that she left him.

Now he was a *penale*, a criminal. A woman of his wife's stature (or rather, what she perceived it to be) couldn't possibly be married to a criminal. Enzo turned twenty-five in prison. It would be another five agonizing years before his divorce was final, thanks to Italian marital law. In that time, he only spoke to her attorney.

Enzo felt the remembered pain and sadly saw how agonizingly parallel it was. In the span of a few hours, they went from being on the cusp of retiring at leisure to having that snatched away from them, betrayed by one of their own. No, Enzo corrected. Ozren was never one of their own, and perhaps that was the problem. Jack was right not to trust him. Enzo now wished that he'd had the same foresight.

Gaston had been fuming for the past few minutes, Enzo now noticed, with Gabrielle trying fruitlessly to calm him. The debate stopped when they each heard the sound of the apartment's lock turning over and watched the deadbolt rotate to the unlocked position. Seeing a door unexpectedly unlock from the inside was unnerving to say the least. It was enough to make someone believe in ghosts. Enzo, Gaston, and Gabrielle each shared the same look of openmouthed confusion watching the door open, seemingly of its own accord.

When Ozren Stolar appeared in the doorway with the shadowed forms of two men behind him, Enzo found himself completely unable to process the scene. He stood transfixed for a span of moments that could well have been hours and watched as though he were watching an image of himself staring at the door, dumbfounded. This made no sense, there was no reason for Ozren to be in the doorway. This was too surreal to comprehend. Enzo stood dumbly staring as his life turned into a Dalí painting.

Nothing made any sense.

Gaston was closest and he simply reacted, the current of loss and betrayal too strong to override better judgment. Gaston lunged. This, too, Enzo watched in slow motion. Gaston didn't see the pistol in Ozren's hand, but Enzo did. Ozren raised it coldly, emotionlessly, and fired three times. His face bore no hint of expression. It was simply an action. Gaston's body jerked backward, a marionette thoughtlessly commanded by a petulant child. The Frenchman sailed through the air, upending one of the dining room chairs on his way to the floor. Gaston was dead before he hit the carpet.

Ozren pushed into the room. The two men behind him, still formless masses of shadows. Their only corporeal features were the pistols in their hands.

Enzo's ears continued to ring and his nose was filled with the smell of expended gunpowder. His own handgun was in his bag, hidden under tightly folded clothes. It might as well have been in the Pope's sock drawer.

Ozren held the gun up to Enzo.

Not now, the Italian thought sourly. *Not like this and not by him.* His life could not have led to this moment.

"Where is it?"

Enzo said nothing. He just looked to his friend's dead body.

He was dimly aware that Gabrielle was screaming, but it was a far-off sound and he was having a difficult time processing her terror.

"Where is it," Ozren shouted at him again. When Enzo didn't immediately answer, Ozren looked to one of his companions, who effortlessly shot Gabrielle twice in the chest. She collapsed with a childlike cry.

"I'm not going to ask you again."

"Where is what, you dirty Yugo fuck," and the reality of the moment collapsed in on Enzo Bachetti, immediately hyper-aware of everything. He went from formless, disembodied fog to an almost supernatural awareness with a rocket-launch velocity.

Ozren swung his pistol in a wide arc aimed at Enzo's head, but the Watchmaker, with his momentary omniscience, saw this and brought a hand up to block the strike. Ozren's face twisted into ugly fury. He punched Enzo in the face with his free hand, and as the Watchmaker staggered, Ozren brought the gun up a second time and smashed the flat side of the pistol into the side of Enzo's head.

Enzo crumbled with the impact, falling to the carpet. He caught himself as he fell, landing on his hands and knees, head hanging between his shoulders. Blood poured freely from the site where Ozren's pistol hit him.

"One last time, Enzo. Where are the jewels? I know Jack had help. Was this the plan all along?"

A shock went through Enzo's body. What did Ozren say? He knew Jack had help doing what? Why was Ozren asking for the jewels if he was the one who...

The one who...

Enzo took a deep breath and launched off with his legs, propelling himself toward the bedroom door that was both ten feet and a million miles away.

Ozren fired. A shot exploded into Enzo's left shoulder, and the force of impact drove him back to the floor. He bounced once, crashed on his opposite shoulder, and rolled, finally sliding into the bedroom door. He'd almost made it.

Enzo heard one of Ozren's companions barking at him in their native language. Unsurprisingly, he sounded angry. Enzo's last thought before blackness took him was *Jesus, Ozren can piss off anyone...*

15

The story broke overnight and had been picked up by most of the US news outlets by now, but they had already begun to repeat their information, which Reginald knew meant that they hadn't learned anything new. Still, he sat in the small parking lot for a short while flipping between BBC World Service and the cable news stations that simulcast over satellite radio, just in case they had a breaking detail.

He'd been awake. Waiting.

When he didn't get the expected call from Enzo, Reginald grew concerned. He knew the Italian wouldn't walk out on him. Reginald knew too many people who could get to him, and Enzo was well aware of that. Reginald began to suspect Jack's involvement when the realization of what happened sank in. The timing of his call the other day was too coincidental, the indignation a bit too fiery for Jack's usual response. In hindsight, the usually measured man was trying to appear furious, and Reginald had to admit that he'd bought it at the time.

Then Enzo failed to contact him.

Then Reginald saw the news.

There were things he didn't want to believe Jack was capable of, and certainly would never have given him credit for, but now seeing for the first time that Jack was obviously leading a parallel existence, LeGrande didn't know how far Jack would go.

Reginald sighed.

There was no use delaying the inevitable, he reasoned. Reginald was truly sorry it had come to this, but he didn't see that he had any newer, better options. And Jack had placed himself in this position. All Reginald was doing was protecting his interests. Well, perhaps there was a little more to it than just that.

He shut off the rented Impala and got out, gravel crunching under his feet. He'd never spent any time in wine country, but Reginald could understand its appeal. He set the tall Peet's cup on top of the Impala and stared across the half-full parking lot to the long hacienda-style building. Reginald retrieved his coffee and walked inside.

The Kingfisher tasting room was cool despite the warm July day. He counted six people standing at the bar attended to by a pair of young, smiling staff members. An older man with steely hair stood back a bit, occasionally checking in on his people but otherwise busying himself with a clipboard and lists of paper. The man Reginald assumed was the manager didn't acknowledge Reginald until he approached the bar and became a customer.

"What can I get you?" the man asked him affably.

Reginald removed a pair of reading glasses from his sport coat's breast pocket and examined the menu standing on the bar inside a clear plastic stand. He scanned it for a moment and selected the merlot. While the manager was pouring his wine, Reginald looked around the bar, finally settling on a photo of a group of seven or eight people standing outside this very building, a twenty-dollar bill taped to the picture frame. Sure enough, Gentleman Jack Burdette was right there in the center with one arm around a woman's shoulder and the other around the tasting room manager. The photo was captioned, but Reginald couldn't read it from as far away as he was.

So this is what you do, Reginald thought. He'd tracked Jack's phone—the one Reginald gave his erstwhile protégé—using the device's GPS and knew from the number of hits that this was where Jack spent most of his time, but Reginald didn't know in what capacity at the time.

Patterns began to form, and empty puzzle pieces came together.

Jack was building a business to move his money through. Interesting.

The manager turned back around, set the merlot on a round paper napkin that bore the winery's name, and asked Reginald if there was anything else he'd like.

"Actually, I'd like to speak with the owner, if that's possible." Reginald paused for a moment. "I'm a distributor."

Part of Reginald honestly wished the man's response would be, *He's right out back, let me get him for you*, and then have Jack appear. There would be an awkward conversation followed by a heated exchange and certainly burned trust for a time, but that all could be repaired. What it would mean was that Jack was here and Reginald had been *wrong*. Jack hadn't gone to Cannes and stolen those goddamned jewels.

"Well," the man behind the counter said in a long way. "He's away on business, but our head winemaker is here, and she runs things when he's gone." The man laughed. "She kinda runs things anyway."

Reginald sighed, and the corners of his mouth dipped in a half frown that could just as easily be interpreted as annoyance. He genuinely was sad. He breathed in the cool yeast-and-grape smell of the tasting room and considered his thoughts for the briefest of moments. Finally, he simply said, "Even better."

The manager dug an iPhone out of his pocket and thumbed out a text. His phone chirped a response a few seconds after, and the man told Reginald that she'd be in to see him shortly.

"That's a nice photo," Reginald said, looking at the picture with the twenty taped to it and chinning once in a kind of reverse nod.

"Oh, yeah," the manager said. Reginald finally picked up on the accent—Southern, deep, but gradually fading into a California patois. "Took that when we opened the tasting room. That was a great day."

"I bet." Reginald smiled and leaned in, squinting. "Who's that standing next to you? Is that the owner?"

"Frank? Yeah. Frank Fischer."

"Ah, Kingfisher Wines," he said, rolling it around his tongue. "I get it."

"Frank's a clever one."

"I bet," Reginald said again, but this time his voice flattened. The manager didn't pick up on it.

A woman in dusty, faded blue jeans and a UC Davis Aggies T-shirt entered the tasting room. She spotted Reginald immediately, but then he was the only one in the room pushing sixty and wearing a sport coat, so he probably fit whatever the manager had typed.

Reginald placed her in her mid-thirties. She was attractive but had that worn look of people who had lived a life and were undecided which way the scales were going to tip in the end. There were trace freckles across her cheeks, and her nose tipped up slightly, which gave her a girlish look. Reginald liked her immediately, or would've, he corrected himself.

"Megan McKinney," she said, extending a hand.

"Reginald LeGrande," he told her. Reginald thought about an alias, but he didn't have anything to back it up. Everything in his wallet said Reginald LeGrande, but more importantly, the point of this was for Jack to know that he'd been here, so the ruse would only be for the lady. The only way this was a problem was if Jack had told her who he really was, and if he did, that story would no doubt include Reginald.

Judging by her reaction, Jack had not.

Interesting, Reginald thought. Here Jack was, living and working as this Frank Fischer. He'd concocted an entire life and had been living this for at least the last four years, but probably longer.

"So, Steve tells me you're a distributor. Who are you with?"

"Yes, ma'am." Reginald took another sip of his merlot and set the glass on the counter. He knew from the article that there were only a small number of national distributors anymore, three or four, he couldn't remember, but there were still plenty of state and regional ones. Anticipating the question, he said, "D and L Wines." It sounded innocuous enough and had a ring to it. "I'm based out of Long Beach myself, but most of my trade is in Orange County. My clients are boutique wine shops and mid-scale to upscale restaurants with curated wine lists." Reginald repeated that almost verbatim from a blog he'd read on his flight up here from Long Beach. "We've had our eye on you since your '09 Osprey but wanted to give it a few years for the brand to develop."

More bullshit he'd read, swapping whatever wine was in the blog post with one of theirs he found scanning the menu.

"Anyway, despite what Jay Lewiston says in *WineScout*, we like your label and think you'd be a good fit for a lot of our clients."

Megan was smiling, but Reginald could tell that she was being guarded. He didn't know if name-dropping the wine blogger was a good idea or not, but he wanted to show her that he'd done his research. One of the blogs he'd read on the way up here was a series written by a wine buyer who said that his strategy was always to select a wine that had a poor rating in a series of good ones and to try to buy it at a discount.

Megan asked him some questions about what price point he'd sell the wines at and how much he wanted. Reginald rattled off some figures that he was mostly making up on the spot, trying to recall what he'd read. He needed to be convincing enough for her to get Jack on the phone. Jack needed to know without a shadow of a doubt where Reginald was calling from, and there was only one way to guarantee that.

The banter went on for a few minutes, and Reginald found he was running out of things to say, reaching the limit of what he'd learned about wine distribution on the flight here. "So, what do you think?"

Megan's poker face cracked. "Well, I think it all sounds very good. I'd like to run the numbers by Frank to make sure everything makes sense. Can I call you in a couple days?"

"I can certainly understand that, but I came all this way and I'd hate to leave without a yes." Reginald flashed her a bright, soft smile. "Could we call him? I'd love to close this deal in person."

Megan looked down at her watch, and Reginald could see her doing the time zone math in her head. Then she reached for her phone. "Frank is in Switzerland this week on business. It'll be a little after nine." She dialed.

"Frank? Hi...How's it going?...Good. Good. Listen, I'm sorry to bother you so late, but I've got a distributor here...yeah. Sounds like it, yeah. No...I know...but he'd like to talk to you about it too. Okay."

She handed Reginald the phone.

16

Jack made the calculated risk to stay in his Cannes safe house
the night of the robbery. France and Italy had an open border
because they were each members of the Schengen Area,
which meant that travelers could pass between them freely.
However, that border could still be closed down by either side
for security purposes. Jack reasoned that between the Swiss
prison break, which was not far from there, and the Carlton
heist, there was a strong probability that the border would be
checked. Law enforcement would also quickly make the leap
that the Pink Panthers who escaped from Orbe were the
leading suspects for the Carlton. However, these would be
temporary measures, and neither government would stand up
to the pressures of keeping the borders restricted for long.

Jack didn't want to chance that he make it to the border,
only to have his car stopped and inspected. The forged passport he was fairly confident in, the case full of jewels would be
a little harder to explain. He believed that the risk of staying in
Cannes an extra night was lower than trying to make the
border, which had been the original plan. Certainly, he could
find a hotel within driving distance, but the police would be

looking for exactly that. It was too risky to try and have Rusty get him another safe house.

This place was clear and he'd ditched the motorcycle in a crowded public parking garage on the other side of town from the Carlton. Jack took the plates with him, draped his jacket over the carrying case so it looked a little less obtrusive, and hailed a cab. By the time Jack made it back to his villa, he was certain that he hadn't been tailed and that any connection between him and the hotel was erased. Jack's phone rang not long after he arrived. If it were anyone else, he wouldn't have taken the phone call. He was exhausted and edgy, and sitting around in Cannes frayed his nerves, even if he believed it was the safest choice. He saw Megan's picture pop up on his phone and immediately wondered what it was on a Sunday afternoon that would make her want to call. Maybe she just wanted to talk, but probably it was business. Whatever the reason, he just wanted to hear her voice. Normally, he didn't take his Frank Fischer phone with him on jobs as a security practice, but with everything happening at the winery right now, Jack felt he couldn't leave them like that.

Megan said there was a distributor there to talk to them about Kingfisher. Jack smiled. It was good to hear her, and it was good to hear her sound happy. This wasn't the time, and he would have to get rid of this person as quickly as he could, but doing something for Megan gave him something else to think about and it made him happy. He could have a short conversation with this distributor, inform them he was on a business trip and would look forward to catching up in person when Jack returned to the States the following week.

"Frank Fischer, it's good to finally meet you." There was a pause. "I've heard *so* much about you."

That excitement evaporated the instant Jack heard that

voice, like words dragged over wet gravel rather than being spoken.

The elation Jack felt at just pulling off one of the largest jewelry heists in history dried up.

Think fast, Jack. "Don't say another word, Reginald." He waited a beat, giving Reginald a chance to hang himself or utterly fuck this up. Reginald said nothing. "Now, say your number like you were giving it to me to copy down." He did, and Jack could practically see the sanctimonious "gotcha" look on the bastard's face. "Say you'll talk to me soon and hang up. Leave my tasting room. I will call you back in exactly three minutes."

Jack disconnected the call. He went to his bag, dug out the iPhone that Reginald set up for him, then shouted, "Goddamn it!" He shook his head. "That's how the son of a bitch did it."

Reginald, whom he trusted, who'd set him up on jobs for years, arranged forged passports, ghosted credit cards and false identities, who gave him a "clean" phone so that they could communicate. iPhones had GPS receivers and a program that allowed the owner to track them in case they were stolen. Jack had disabled all of these things, but Reginald could easily have installed an app that allowed him to do this without Jack's knowledge. He'd been tracking Jack's location, probably for years, all the while Jack believing he was living in anonymity.

Jack set the Frank Fischer phone to airplane mode so that it would stop transmitting. Once the phone was safe, Jack went through and disabled the location services: Wi-Fi, Bluetooth, anything he could think of that would broadcast his location. Reginald hadn't known about that one until just now; Jack had purchased that himself. He then went through the same process on his Jack Burdette phone. He also called up the phone's settings to see what was running in the background that he might not be aware of.

Jack was furious at the invasion of privacy, but he still couldn't guess at what Reginald's game was. They'd settle that issue and a few others when he returned to California.

Jack opened the encryption program and dialed Reginald's phone.

"What are you doing there, Reginald?" he said as soon as LeGrande answered.

"Well, imagine my embarrassment when I heard this morning that someone ripped off a jewelry exhibition in Cannes and then I find out that you're in Europe on business."

"What can I say?" Jack said, his voice flat. "You told me the situation changed. So I changed it back."

"You changed it back?" Reginald said. "Do you have any idea what you've done?"

"I asked you to let me back in, and you wouldn't do it. You didn't leave me much of a choice."

"Wow," he said, "you are one cold-blooded son of a bitch, Jack, but I guess you do what you have to do. Those lives are on you, though, and that wasn't my fault."

What the hell is he talking about?

Reginald continued: "You should've taken the fucking job when I offered it to you, and this never would've happened."

"You can obviously see that I'm trying to ease myself into another life. When you first offered me the job, I wasn't in a position to take it."

"So, you're telling me there's a *right* time and *wrong* time to try and steal eighty-five million dollars?" He let out a short, terse laugh. "Jesus Christ, I want your problems."

"Why am I talking to you right now, Reginald?"

His old mentor sighed audibly. "I want the eighty-five, Jack, every shiny goddamned penny of it. Or, rather, the thirty-five you're going to take home from your fence."

"This is your idea of a joke? I've seen your wardrobe, Reginald. I know you have terrible taste, but even you can't think this is funny. Look, I was planning on giving you your cut anyway to smooth things over, so there's no need to get touchy."

"I'm not joking, *Jack*." Reginald put a hard emphasis on his name. "You're going to give me the entire take."

"You wanted the money, you should've let me do the job or hired a better crew."

"You're right there," Reginald said softly. There was a tone in Reginald's voice that he couldn't quite place. "I honestly didn't think you had it in you, Jack. But it is a lot of money, and I've never known you to let anything stand in your way. Not even friends." LeGrande breathed a heavy breath into the phone, and it created a burst of static on the line. "In a way, I guess it makes this easier for me, knowing what you did. I don't have to feel guilty about what I'm going to do next."

There was something off in the way Reginald delivered that line, but Jack couldn't puzzle it out. Instead, he closed his eyes and breathed, forced himself to calm down. "Why are you doing this, Reginald? I took care of you. You'd have been on the street if it wasn't for me." There was a bitterness in his own voice that he didn't intend.

When Reginald spoke again, his cadence was slow and his voice almost sad. "What can I say, Jack? Things change. The world was a different place when I got out." There was a gravity to those words rather than a simple statement, and something about it pulled Jack toward them, telling him there was so much more than what Reginald actually said. They were both quiet for a few awkward moments, neither of them knowing quite what to say or what to make of the conversation they'd just had. "I didn't want things to end this way, Jack. I really didn't. But you forced my hand. There was just too much money to pass up, and I don't have enough years to nickel and dime it like you do." Then he said simply, "I'm sorry."

Reginald breathed, and it was a soulless push of air against the phone's speaker, a ghost. "I'm giving you forty-eight hours before I call the FBI. I'll make it so you can't stay in Europe and you can't come back here. I'll tell them everything. It's not a big enough world for you to hide in forever."

"You can't turn me in without implicating yourself, or did you forget the fact that you've set up almost every job I've ever done?"

"But not this one," he said flatly. "And after this, after what you did, they won't care about the rest. If I don't hear from you by this time Tuesday, the feds are going to know everything about you. I'm not sure how much longer you're going to keep that little operation of yours afloat if that happens. Thieves are one thing, killers are another."

Jack bit back the words he wanted to spit out, the ones that explained how many people were counting on him, how Reginald had no right to threaten their livelihoods, but Jack knew those were hollow words that would bounce off unhearing ears. What the hell was Reginald talking about *killers*?

"I wonder," Reginald said, "what you're more afraid of? The police finding out who you really are or that lady friend of yours."

"She's not my lady friend."

"Yes, she is. Everyone knows it but the two of you."

"You touch her, and I'm coming for you," Jack said in a cold and emotionless tone that left nothing to question.

"Oh, I don't doubt it," Reginald responded. "That's why I'm not giving you the chance. You're not doing me like you did

Enzo, Gaston, and Gabrielle." Reginald let that hang in the air between continents for a minute. Then he said, "You have two days, Jack."

Reginald hung up just as Jack was asking what in the hell he was talking about.

17

Outside the house, Ozren fidgeted. They'd been sitting in this van for hours just watching for any sign of Burdette. Ozren wasn't sure this was the house; they'd followed Burdette from the hotel, but he'd lost them on the road. Ozren thought this was the place but couldn't be totally sure. Not that he was going to admit that to Milan Radić. Ozren desperately wanted a smoke, as did his companions, but he'd said that would give them away too quickly. At least once an hour, Milan demanded they just go in and take the jewels, and at least once an hour Ozren told him that was stupid.

Carefully.

Ozren didn't need the reminder that Milan Radić was a dangerous man. Ozren's and Milan's paths first crossed in 1989 in the Serbian Special Forces. Ozren had just been selected for the elite 63rd Parachute Regiment, and Milan was the training sergeant. The 63rd was a Serbian Army unit that traced its lineage back to the Second World War, after which it had been dissolved and then reactivated several times, and in 1967 it was incorporated into the Yugoslav People's Army and headquartered in Niš. Ozren loved the army—rather, he loved jumping out of airplanes, loved running through the forest and over mountains. He loved the challenge of an operation. It was like solving a complex problem. The army gave him purpose, gave him meaning.

Then the Republic of Yugoslavia crumbled as though it were built out of sand.

Slovenia and Croatia, bristling under the perceived Serbian hegemony forced on them by Slobodan Milošević, took up arms in protest. Ozren never possessed an interest in politics, and he didn't really know or care how the Yugoslav Wars started. His sergeant told him to fight, so he fought. First the Croats, then Slovenians, then the Bosnians, and then the Macedonians all decided they didn't like the way things worked, the way things had always worked in that country, and revolted. June of 1991, Ozren's unit deployed to a peace-keeping operation inside Slovenia. They were riding in heli-copters and escorting the First Armored Brigade where they seized the airport at Brnik. It was the most exciting thing Private Stolar had done in his life to that point.

Sergeant Milan Radić approached him the afternoon of June twenty-seventh. He was collecting the best troops for a special mission and wanted to know if Stolar was interested. Of course he was. Radić gave him a time and place to meet, an out-of-the-way corner of the Brnik Airport well after dark, and he was to tell no one, not even—especially not even—his command chain. It was *that* secret.

When Ozren arrived, there were three others. Radić and two more showed up shortly thereafter. They climbed into a civilian delivery truck and drove into the Slovenian capital, Ljubljana, where Radić informed them they were hitting a strategic target. It turned out to be a Slovenian national bank. Getting into the bank was little trouble for six Serbian Special Forces soldiers, and they weren't especially concerned about raising attention. Radić actually said they *wanted* to be conspicuous. They wanted to remind the Slovenians that Serbia called the shots. What belonged to Slovenia belonged to Serbia by extension. Within fifteen minutes, they had a truck full of dinars and were speeding back toward the airport. Radić gave them a couple thousand each as payment and told them to keep their fucking mouths shut. When one of their secret cabal was "killed by the enemy during maneuvers" two days later, the others guessed what had happened. He ran his mouth. No one else spoke of it, not even to each other.

The situation in Yugoslavia continued to deteriorate throughout the early nineties, and Ozren had little desire to spend the rest of his life fighting what looked to be a war against seemingly everyone, so he processed out in 1993 before he was going to have to make another half-assed attempted at peacekeeping, this time in Bosnia. So, he got out of the army and immediately wished he hadn't. There were no jobs, and there was barely any food. There was nothing.

The United Nations, led by the Americans, were sanctioning the hell out of Yugoslavia because of the "war crimes" perpetrated by Milošević and his cronies. Of course, the president didn't feel the bite of the sanctions, only the Yugoslav people did, and the country was already disrupted by the chaos of three years of instability and two of outright warfare. Stolar had no idea this was happening. He'd never cared about politics and had never read a newspaper. He didn't keep in touch with his family, didn't really care what was happening to them, so when Ozren left the bubble of isolation that the army formed around him, he found a very different world than the one he'd left.

In this new world, it was very hard to put food on the table. At least if you were trying to do that with honest work, but there was none of that to go around. Ozren had skills, sure. He was an expert marksman, physically fit, a problem solver, all these things the special forces taught him in order to outsmart his opponents. So he put them to work. Ozren became a thief.

At first it was petty crimes, stealing to eat, but once he had his basic survival needs met, Ozren wanted to expand, to improve his life. The first time he'd ever had money, real money, was when Milan Radić recruited him to rip off that bank in Ljubljana. Belgrade was largely untouched by the unrest that was shredding the Yugoslavian State around him, so Ozren relocated there to ply his new trade.

It was there, in 1996, that he once again came into Milan Radić's orbit.

Radić offered him a job. Said he was recruiting men from the 63rd, men he could trust, men who knew how to use the skills the army taught them. As before, of course, Ozren was in. Radić, in time, went on to explain that he was part of a loose affiliation of professional thieves, most of them Serbs, and many of those ex–Serbian Army with a high concentration of special forces.

The Pink Panthers were more of a series of franchises with no central organization or leadership. Instead, a Panther cell would provide training and resources to someone who showed potential. Then they would turn them loose on the world. Radić trained Ozren, and the two worked together frequently throughout the rest of the nineties and early 2000s, until the two of them had a falling-out over a beautiful Hungarian woman they often used to scout their jobs. Milan Radić was not a man to cross, and Ozren learned that was a mistake he could only make once.

Ozren found himself on the outside of the Panthers. Radić circulated word that he was not to be trusted. Stealing another man's woman was as unpardonable a sin as it was an ancient one. Eventually Ozren found his way to an American fixer by the name of Reginald LeGrande, who put him on crews with his golden boy, Gentleman Jack. Ozren hated the pretentious ass but had to admit he was a good thief, as good as any of the Panthers and certainly with his own flair for the dramatic. Most importantly, they never got caught.

But it was cold on the outside, and working with the Americans was dangerous. They had a different kind of code, and they were only as loyal as the moment.

It wasn't until Radić got popped in Geneva that Ozren had an opportunity to get back into the fold. He learned through his network that a breakout was being planned. A mutual acquaintance and fellow veteran of the Ljubljana bank job was organizing the effort. Ozren approached him and asked if he could help. The man laughed in his face, so Ozren said, "What if I knew about an eighty-five-million-dollar job? The exact details." Ozren offered to help spring Radić and then, as a grand act of contrition, would tip him to a major score that would be ripe for the picking. The contact passed it to Radić, who agreed.

The moment that idiot LeGrande recruited him for the Carlton, Ozren began formulating his plan. Once LeGrande told him that it would be Enzo Bachetti and not Jack Burdette leading the crew, he practically came in his pants with excitement. Bachetti and Broussard were both soft. He'd get a better fight out of the woman.

"I'm sick of this shit. Let's go, Ozren." Radić put a hand on the door.

Careful, Ozren told himself. "We have to be patient, Milan. Cannes is a city practically without crime and certainly without murder. If we kill Burdette now, and he won't go quietly, the police will be on top of this place before we're even out the door."

"I know how to kill a man with more than just a gun."

"He doesn't," was all Ozren said in return. "The world, literally the entire world, already thinks it was you who pulled the Carlton job. You broke out of prison two days before the theft." Ozren held a breath, exhaled, and let his words sink in. This was his moment. Radić would either kill him out of blind fury, or the words would drain into that impossibly arrogant, stubborn head of his. Softly, steadily, Ozren continued.

"Jack has to leave the country. None of the fences he works with are in France. He won't fly. There's no way he's going to take those jewels on a plane and risk them getting discovered by security. His only option is to drive, probably through Italy, east. He normally deals with a Turkish syndicate that he meets with in our backyard." Ozren held up a steadying hand. "If we can, we'll take him on the road. If not, we'll get him—quietly—when he stops. Okay?"

"You'd better fucking be right, Ozren." Then Radić added unnecessarily, "Your second chance was getting me in the car."

18

Danzig learned about the Carlton heist from Giovanni Castro, but by then it was already all over the news. She turned CNN on while she was talking to him. The theft occurred at approximately eight thirty on Sunday morning, Central European Time. Danzig found out by early afternoon. It took about seven or eight hours for word to get to the transnational trafficking task force, which, by European standards, was like moving at the speed of light. Castro told her what they knew, which at that point had been very little—a lone thief had entered a street-facing salon, which surprisingly had an unlocked exterior door. He was described as wearing a hat, bandanna, and sunglasses over his face. Castro remarked, dryly, that he sounded like one of the bandits in a Sergio Leone film. He had a handgun. It was over in about ninety seconds. They had security guards in the room, but they weren't armed. The collection belonged to an Israeli jewelry magnate named Ari Hassar. The French authorities were reporting the collection as valued at eighty-five million.

Castro also told her that the day prior, there had been a prison break in Orbe, Switzerland. Two members of the Pink

Panthers had escaped. The Panthers were Europe's criminal boogeymen, and Danzig believed that her European counterparts, but particularly the French and the Swiss, tended to blame those guys for everything. If there was a jewelry store robbery, it was the Panthers. If there was a bank job, it was the Panthers. If a football team lost a match, it was the Panthers. Castro told her, not surprisingly, that INTERPOL was already saying they were behind the Carlton heist.

"It doesn't fit their profile, though. Surely you guys have to see that," she told him. The Pink Panthers were not subtle, or subdued, or secretive. When they pulled a job, they wanted people to *know* it was them. Law enforcement now knew the origins of that group, former soldiers from the fragments of Yugoslavia and most of them ex–special forces. They were brazen and audacious, as if flaunting their abilities in front of Western law enforcement. Their first credited job was a jewelry store in London, where they'd broken in wearing elaborate disguises and dressed as women. The Pink Panthers crashed Audis into storefront windows and used MP-5s for crowd control. This thing in Cannes felt...different to her. It was brazen and audacious in its own way, but not *their* way.

"*I* see that," Castro said. "But everyone here is scrambling for leads. It's still very early."

Danzig knew that Castro was just informing her as a professional courtesy. There wasn't much that she could do in terms of help at this point. But as a task force member, the US government would lend assistance if asked. This was exactly the reason that the task force had been created. Danzig knew that there were two likely destinations for those jewels. First, they'd be broken down and taken out of their settings. Then they would either be sold on the gray market in Europe to unscrupulous wholesalers who weren't concerned with the provenance of their product. Danzig had interviewed a few of them during her time in Europe following a sting they'd run. One guy actually had the audacity to liken the practice to recycling.

But the greater danger was that these were going to end up in the hands of al-Qaeda, Hizballah, or some other collection of scumbags. Because jewels were untraceable, they were a favored form of currency for the world's terror organizations. Al-Qaeda in particular had been moving in on the world's emerald trade because of the vast mineral wealth in the parts of Afghanistan they still controlled. Eighty-five million in dark money could fund a lot of bad things around the world.

Castro finished his update and was quiet, waiting for her to speak. Danzig thanked him for the call and told him to let her know if there was anything she could do to help. The Bureau's resources were at his disposal and all that. Castro told her that an INTERPOL Red Notice, their version of an APB, would be going up tomorrow for the two escapees from Orbe Prison. He was sure that they'd want to tap the FBI for intelligence support once they got organized. He remarked how a Sunday was about the worst time for something important to be stolen in Europe because it was hard to make anyone care until Monday morning.

Once she'd finished with Castro, Danzig called the FBI's LEGAT in Paris. The LEGAT was an FBI agent stationed at the US Embassy and was America's chief law enforcement representative in that country. Their primary job was to facilitate cooperation between the US and the law enforcement activities of the host country, but they were also responsible for counterespionage and counterterrorism. Particularly over the last decade. Danzig identified herself as the FBI's representative on a transnational gem and jewelry trafficking task force and said that she frequently liaised with Europol and INTERPOL. The Bureau hadn't officially been asked to lend support yet but, if he needed anything, to just ask. She gave him her cell phone and office numbers, email. He took it down and thanked her, said he'd be in touch. The agent did say that the French government hadn't asked for any cooperation yet. He'd learned about the theft by watching the news.

Danzig hung up and set her phone down on the counter. She walked across the hardwood to the kitchen island where the thermal carafe was and poured another cup of coffee. Danzig lived in the Brooklyn Heights neighborhood, not far from the bridge and very close—as one measured time and distance in New York City—to the FBI building in lower Manhattan.

Danzig reached over, picked her phone back up, and called Darren Givens, who was her boss and the agent in charge of the Gem and Jewelry Program. The Bureau wasn't involved in this yet, but this was the biggest jewelry heist in ten years and Katrina Danzig wasn't sitting on the sidelines for it.

"Hey, Darren, sorry to bug you on a Sunday...but are you watching the news?"

19

Jack left shortly after eight in the morning so that he would hit the border around lunch, in the thick of the noontime traffic. Once Jack got onto the A8, he opened the GranTurismo and was all but gone. Not that anyone was looking for a legitimate American businessman driving an Italian sports car. He couldn't put distance between himself and Cannes fast enough. Jack kept his speed around a hundred and ten, a respectable amount for this kind of car. Once he crossed into Italy, Jack knew he'd probably draw more attention if he kept the Maserati below the speed limit, so he pushed it up just enough that he wouldn't piss off any police and force them to pull him over. Speed was a way of life in Italy. Only assholes and foreigners drove slowly on the interstate.

He had wiped the villa down as best he could before he left. Jack also took the BMW's plates and forged registration with him so that he could dispose of them when he had time. Rusty would have a cleaning crew in there to make the place hospital-worthy later that day, but Jack was nothing if not cautious.

The trip was roughly eight hours, and Jack spent much of

that listening to BBC Radio to get updates on the Carlton heist. Few, if any, new details emerged during his drive to Rome, but the reporters were already speculating the theft was an inside job. It was just too easy.

The other story they reported was far more troubling.

There was a triple homicide at an apartment on the Avenue Isola Bella in Cannes. The identities had not been released, but they were reported as two men and a woman. Jack already knew their names.

Enzo.

Gaston.

Gabrielle.

They'd been found, murdered by gunshot, Sunday afternoon by another tenant who'd found the apartment door ajar, looked inside, and saw the bodies. Police were saying nothing, but the reporters were already speculating that three murders the same day as a historic jewelry heist could not be a coincidence.

During his drive, Jack also replayed his conversation with Reginald, and now everything made sense.

I've never known you to let anything stand in your way. Not even friends.

I don't have to feel guilty about what I'm going to do next.

You're not doing me like you did Enzo, Gaston, and Gabrielle.

You are one cold-blooded son of a bitch, Jack.

Reginald actually thought *Jack* killed his old crew because they got in his way. Thinking that Jack would stop at nothing, Reginald tried his scorched-earth play, threatening to dime Jack to the FBI.

Fucking Ozren. It only could've been him.

Jack had warned Reginald that the Serb was dangerous.

He'd pieced together Ozren's plan Friday when he learned of the prison break and spent most of that night wrestling with the decision to call Enzo or not, to tell his friend that the Serb was coming for them. He didn't call. Jack decided that he couldn't trust Enzo, despite their friendship, because Enzo had cast his lot with Reginald when he'd signed on for the Carlton job. Because of that, Jack didn't believe he could count on those three beyond any doubt, didn't believe that he could trust them in the way he used to with the depth required for a job like this. You had to be able to anticipate the actions of your crew, and with the uncertainty his reappearance would cause, Jack knew he couldn't, so he chose to go it alone.

Jack had actually believed that when Ozren found the crew empty-handed, the Serb would just let them go. Maybe that's just what Jack told himself so he could live with it.

People often waxed about the worth of a life.

Jack knew the answer to that question now. Right down to the penny.

Compounding his feelings about his crew and adding to that mountain was the depth of Reginald's betrayal. It sunk in as he drove and had the time to truly consider it. Reginald had brought him up in the trade, discovered Jack when he was boosting cars and selling them. He'd taught Jack, made him a *thief*. In their heydays during the mid-nineties, man, they pulled some crazy, reckless, and dangerous jobs. They lived fast lives. Then Reginald sent him to live in Europe for a while, let things cool down after an armored truck heist went bad.

Jack lived a couple years in Turin during the middle part of the decade, and it was something of a renaissance. In parallel, law enforcement, particularly the feds, were getting pretty good in the nineties. Jack suspected that since the FBI wasn't chasing Soviet spies anymore and had basically broken the mob, they could focus their attention back on criminals. Their technology was starting to catch up with the criminals as well. But Europe was another story. Jack spent two years working back in the States before he decided it was too risky. But Reginald wouldn't listen. He wouldn't accept that Jack refused to pull a job at home anymore. He tried to get Jack to go in on it with him. It was supposed to be a quick million, an exclusive boutique in Beverly Hills. Jack passed—too risky—and tried to talk Reginald out of it. The stubborn bastard did it anyway.

And he got caught.

And he'd gotten ten years in San Quentin.

While Reginald was in the system, Jack provided, because he knew that when Reginald got out, he was done. If Reginald got popped again, he'd go up forever. So every job Jack took, he put some aside. By the time Reginald got out four years into his term, he had a kitty of just over a million dollars to start his life with. Jack also talked his mentor into semi-retirement. Stop taking jobs, stop taking risks. Jack convinced Reginald to use his connections both in the US and the ones they'd made working in Europe and become a fixer. Reginald would set up jobs for several crews of thieves that he knew and trusted. Jack pointedly advised Reginald to spread the wealth around. While he did his best to keep crews isolated, crooks talked, and it was still known in certain circles that Reginald and Jack were working together. By not reserving the high-profile jobs just for him, Jack reasoned, Reginald was less likely to incur the wrath of the thief who thought he should be getting bigger scores. Jack wanted nothing to do with those kinds of jobs.

Because of Jack, Reginald had a steady, reliable, and relatively safe source of income. Without that, the old thief would have gone and done something hasty, trying a large score to make up what he'd lost to the government, and he would have gotten nailed. He'd have gotten twenty-five years, which, at LeGrande's age, would've been a death sentence.

Reginald's betrayal was as inexplicable as it was unfathomable.

Jack hit the outskirts of Rome around four in the afternoon with no more answers than when he started. From there, it took him another hour fighting Roman traffic to get to the house that Rusty set up for him. The place in Cannes was nice, a perfect Mediterranean retreat from which a gentleman could plan and execute a job in both comfort and style—as a gentleman should. But this one, this was a place where Jack could *live*. The home was a long, single story of yellow stone with large square windows, totally hidden from the street by a twenty-foot-tall hedge that encircled the entire property and cypress trees that were three times that. The grounds, the only fitting description, were a sprawling expanse of cypress and palm in which sat a secluded ramada, its latticework covered by grapevines.

He took a lot of grief for his expensive, seemingly pretentious lifestyle and his penchant toward the finer things, even when on a job. Sure, Jack enjoyed those things, but that wasn't why he did it. That was something people like Reginald would never understand and people like Rusty always would.

The police never looked for jewel thieves in Roman villas.

Jack parked the GranTurismo, grabbed his bag and the motorcycle case, and walked to the front door. The key was in a lockbox attached to the handle. He input the code Rusty had given him and unlocked the door. The interior was white walls with light walnut shelves and accents, recessed lighting, and marble floors. The home was classically decorated with Italian artwork and sculptures, some of which he suspected were originals. He found the master bedroom and set his things down. Then he made a quick tour around the place. There was a window on nearly every exterior wall, which made for some spectacular natural light, but Jack was also a little paranoid. Otherwise, the home had everything—five bedrooms, a sauna, and an exercise room, even air conditioning, a rarity for most European homes. Rusty had even left him some gifts. There was a bottle of twenty-five-year-old Talisker, a 2001 Villa Cafaggio Chianti on the kitchen counter, and a takeout container of penne arrabbiata from one of Jack's favorite Roman cafes. There was also a note, not in Rusty's handwriting but a flowing feminine Italian script, reading, "Enjoy your stay, Mr. Hendricks."

As an added layer of protection, the Peter Ramsey alias was left behind in France, and this house was paid for with a new account and new name.

Jack leafed through the drawers until he found a foil cutter and split the protective covering around the scotch and the wine. Then he hunted for a bottle opener so he could let the Chianti breathe for a few hours before dinner. Jack poured a scotch and walked into the study. He liked this room immediately. You entered it through the antique walnut bookcase that formed the entire inner wall. There was a low, square table in the center and a plush, cream-colored couch on the far wall beneath a wide window that ran the length of the room. Jack sat, put his feet on the coffee table, and clicked on the flatscreen television set into the bookcase. He clicked through the local stations. He was unable to find CNN International on this cable system, but his Italian was a lot better than his French, and Jack could follow the local news well enough.

Deciding instead on accuracy, Jack scrolled through various news sites, mostly British, on his phone, his Frank Fischer phone—though GPS location was disabled on that as well—and learned that if there were any substantial leads in the Carlton job, the Cannes police weren't sharing. In fact, other than a basic recounting of the events, there wasn't much reporting that offered insight beyond the initial stories from the day before, and there was no mention whatsoever of a motorcycle.

The reports did, however, state that the thief had apparently "jumped out of a hotel window" and that when he landed on the street, he spilled the contents of his briefcase, which he hastily scooped up. Jack sipped his scotch. The only thing to pull him out of his black mood was the knowledge that he'd executed a nearly perfect job. The only mistake he'd made was mistiming his jump from the patio—the media even got *that* wrong—and lost a few jewels. He could see why eyewitnesses would think he'd jumped out of a window. No one had seen him clearly, and it was probably the motion of his jumping from the balustrade to the street that drew attention.

The declared value of the jewelry collection was much higher than the eighty-five million initially reported. It appeared now that Hassar insured the collection for nearly double its originally reported value, declaring the loss at one hundred forty-five million dollars.

But then, Jack already knew that.

Here's to being a step ahead of the competition. Solemnly, sadly, he raised his glass. Thinking of Enzo, he said, "Sorry, old friend."

Tears welled in Jack's eyes, and he did his best to force them back. The waves of loss and grief and guilt came at him like high tide. Enzo was his friend and he was dead because Jack didn't warn him, because Jack chose a score over him. Jack couldn't help but picture the look of shock, confusion, and surprise that must have been on all of their faces when Ozren turned on them. They probably weren't even armed and had no chance to defend themselves.

He didn't even have time to grieve. Enzo got to occupy Jack's thoughts for the exact time it took for him to finish the drink, and then he had to bring his focus back to the trouble he was in.

Jack would meet his buyer in the morning. He'd get paid, though it would be nothing close to what Reginald demanded.

He had between now and then to think of a plan to resolve the Reginald question.

Jack ate dinner around seven, reheating his dinner on the stove with olive oil rather than the microwave. It was something to do. He took his meal at the antique-looking table underneath the ramada and a perfect Roman summer sky. He tasted nothing. After dinner, Jack had another glass of wine, looking to numb himself, and watched the sun set. As the evening sky faded into night, Jack grabbed his glass and the wine bottle and walked back inside. He needed to think, and to do that he'd need a clear head.

Jack stepped into the house, accessing it from the patio door off the kitchen, and set his wineglass and bottle on the counter to the immediate right of the door before turning around to slide the door shut behind him.

As soon as he put a hand on the door handle, Jack heard a hammer click.

He turned to the sound.

Ozren Stolar stood in the center of the kitchen with a glass of Talisker in one hand and a pistol in the other.

It would've been hard to see Ozren when he first entered the kitchen. The counter next to the door extended out about eight feet where it housed the stove, above which was a large hood that extended down from the ceiling. Ozren was in the center of the kitchen, standing at a diagonal from Jack. The Serb held up his glass of scotch but never took his eyes off Jack. "I helped myself. Hope you don't mind."

Jack's pistol was in the bedroom on the other side of the house. To get it, he'd need to execute a serpentine dash, weaving through the house designed like a child's pencil maze. It could be done, Jack thought quickly. The dining room was to his left. From there, he could dash across the main living room, cutting behind Stolar. If he got to the hallway before Ozren could shoot him, Jack could duck into the study and from there to the hallway. Then finally Jack would have to weave around to the master bedroom. The odds were better than even that Ozren had tossed the house while Jack was outside drinking and stewing in his guilt, which meant that he'd already have both Jack's gun and the jewels.

Ozren picked up on Jack's thoughts immediately.

"Don't," he said, setting the glass of scotch on the counter while keeping his stare fixed on Jack. It'd served its purpose. "I've got two men outside covering the exits. You step one foot out that door..." The Serb let his voice trail off. There wasn't the superior ring of satisfaction that Jack would've expected to hear.

Jack considered his options, and they were none of them good. Jack was not a violent person and had never resorted to it throughout his long years in the trade. He carried a gun like most people carried life insurance. It was a bet against the world that he never expected to call in. Jack had only ever fired at a target range, and that was worlds different from trading shots with an ex-commando who had done it for real. Jack's close-quarter possibilities weren't any better. The best Jack could hope for was to rush Ozren, try to knock him off-balance, and wrestle the gun away.

And hope he didn't get shot in the process.

"Let's not waste a lot of time, Jack," Ozren said quickly. "Place your hands behind your head."

Jack complied.

"Now, slowly, kneel down."

"Fuck you, Ozren. You killed Enzo."

The Serb only shrugged in response. He wore a nonchalant look on his face. Jack lowered his arms in a show of defiance. He didn't care. The Serbian fuck could shoot him.

"And Gaston and Gabrielle," Jack continued.

"On the floor, Jack. Now."

"How'd you find me?" Jack said instead of moving to the floor.

"It wasn't easy," the Serb said, indulging him momentarily. "But I'd gotten a tip that you might be here. I knew you needed to go to a major city and you probably would avoid Paris for obvious reasons."

I'd gotten a tip. Jack rolled the words around in his mind. Even *thinking* them felt like bile in his mouth. *Reginald fucking LeGrande.* That's the only person that could have tipped Ozren to Jack being involved, though based on their conversation the other day, Jack guessed that Reginald didn't think Ozren was going to murder Enzo, Gaston, and Gabrielle in cold blood.

"The problem for you is that your pal Rusty and I know a lot of the same people in Rome. I was able to call in some favors and buy a few more. I'm more than happy to spend the money I'm about to make."

"No," Jack said. "I mean in Cannes. How did you find me in Cannes?"

"We were watching the hotel. Enzo's plan was to go on Sunday, and I assumed he'd move up the timetable after I left, so we staked it out for two days, waiting for them. Then I saw you. Of course, I didn't know it at the time. You and Gaston are built about the same. I lost you coming out of the hotel, so I just went back to the crew's safe house to collect. Unfortunately, they didn't have the take." Ozren shook his head slowly, in mock sadness.

"And then you killed them. Even though they had nothing to do with it. You knew they were innocent and you murdered them anyway." Jack stared cold hate into the Serb's eyes, but Ozren only shrugged.

"They knew I was here. What else could I do?"

"You're a fucking coward, Ozren. And you're scum."

"The words of a dead man echo in no one's ears, Jack."

"What is that, some bullshit Serbian proverb?"

"No," he said, sounding perplexed. "Sounds like it, though, doesn't it?" Then Stolar cracked a frozen smile. "I've had enough of this," he said in a clipped tone as he raised the pistol into a modified Weaver stance. "Now, on your goddamned knees."

Silently, Jack lowered himself onto the floor.

Jack knelt with one knee on the hard tile. His left leg was still up so that he could propel himself forward if he saw the chance. There was about five feet between the two of them, so it would have to be a fast and powerful lunge if he was going to hit. Jack needed to push Ozren back before he could get a shot off.

But again, Ozren seemed to sense Jack's intentions and shook his head, just slightly, side to side.

"Don't," a voice said from the shadows of the living room. "Lower the weapon." The speaker was firm but calm, clearly trying to avoid provoking or startling Stolar. When the Serb didn't immediately comply, the speaker informed him, "I've got a forty-caliber Glock aimed right between your eyes. Bad luck for you, it'll need to go through your brain to get there. So, why don't you use that brain and do exactly as I tell you."

Rusty stepped into the kitchen from the living room. He was wearing a tan linen suit, an open-collared lime-green shirt, alligator shoes, and a .40-caliber Glock. There were a handful of people in the world who could pull that look off, pistol or no.

"Who the fuck are you?" Ozren spat.

"You were right about one thing, Ozren. You and I do know a lot of the same people in this town. Problem for you is they all think you're an asshole. Oh, they'll take your money and answer all your questions...but the next phone call goes to me," Rusty said.

"What does that say about your friends?"

"I never said they were my friends, just people I pay."

"You must be Rusty," Ozren said.

"That's right. Now, I know for a fact you've been arrested before, so you should be pretty familiar with this next part. I want you to get down on your knees, slowly, with your hands out to your sides." Ozren did. "I want you to very carefully lower the weapon and then set that weapon on the ground. Easy now," he said like he was a firing range instructor. Ozren lowered the pistol and brought it to his side.

Jack saw something flash in Rusty's eyes.

"Jack, down!" Rusty shouted, pivoting his stance about five degrees and firing three shots just as Jack cleared the space the bullets traveled through. All three rounds went through the sliding glass door behind him in a tight group. Jack heard nothing but the sharp crack as they passed through the glass and then a hard thud of something falling behind him. Jack hit the floor, going as prone as he possibly could. Kissing tile, the stove and its ensconced peninsula of cabinetry blocked most of his view of the kitchen, but he could still see Ozren grabbing his pistol off the floor and then raising it as he turned around to face Rusty. Rusty, having pivoted toward the unknown assailant behind Jack, was at a terrible angle in relation to Ozren, and the Serb was already inside his reach. Ozren would have his pistol into Rusty's gut before the other man had a chance to react.

Jack watched Ozren move into position, as if from a stop-motion camera, and Rusty countered much too slowly. Just as the Serb was about to fire, another form appeared out of an open doorway next to Jack.

Enzo Bachetti emerged from the shadows with a pistol in his hand and coldly shot Ozren twice in the side of his face.

The other side of Ozren's head exploded with the exit wounds, spraying blood, bone, and brain matter in a wide arc. The body dropped to the tile, a limp mass of dead meat.

Enzo Bachetti walked over to Ozren's body and stood over the lifeless form. Then he spat on the Serb's body.

"That was for Gaston, you fuck. He was my friend."

Jack picked himself up and stood.

Enzo dropped his pistol onto Ozren's corpse, as if suddenly detesting the very existence of the thing, like it was poison in his hand.

Behind him, Jack heard the sliding glass door push violently open, landing at the end of its track with a hard bang. A hunched-over figure emerged from the darkness, one hand holding a large pistol and bracing against the open door-way. The other hand clutched at his midsection. He was a large man and well-muscled. He looked familiar to Jack but wasn't someone he could immediately place, like a half-remembered detail from a dream. The man stumbled into the kitchen, growling curses in a guttural language. He brought his pistol over from the doorway.

Jack was the closest and the only one in a position to act. In one sweeping pivot he reached for the scotch bottle on the counter, and, turning the motion into a lunge, he stepped toward the man with the gun. Jack connected, braining his attacker with the Talisker bottle, sending a dull wet crack through the otherwise silent kitchen.

His attacker staggered back, dazed. Then the pistol came up again.

"Goddamn it, Jack, *get down*," Rusty shouted.

Jack dropped to the floor still white-knuckling the bottle, now stained with an ugly smear of blood.

Rusty walk-fired twice. Both shots connected, but the large man stayed on his feet. The man spoke, but it was nothing more than a spiteful growl. He knew where he was going but was intent on taking someone with him. He raised his pistol a few inches so that it was level with Jack, now on the floor.

Then Jack placed the man. Milan Radić, one of the escaped prisoners. The man's balance became unsure. He staggered backward and stumbled, losing ground on the shards of broken glass on the tile. Radić fell into the darkness outside.

"I know that guy by reputation," Rusty said after a few seconds. "I'm surprised that's all it took. Jack, go check for a pulse. I want to make sure he's dead."

Jack stood and brushed off the bits of broken glass from the patio door, shot through several times, and walked over to Radić's body now just outside. He knelt and felt the Serbian's neck. Finding nothing, Jack shook his head.

"Okay," Rusty began. "Plus the one I took out guarding the front door, that makes three." Satisfied, Rusty removed his silencer and put the pistol into his shoulder holster. He retrieved his phone and placed a phone call before any of them spoke another word. Rusty issued short instructions in Italian, provided their address, and then he hung up the phone. That would be the cleanup crew. All the shots fired had been from silenced pistols, so they didn't have an immediate fear of the police, but they still couldn't stay here long. This had to disappear—fast.

Rusty went to cupboards and opened several of them until he found the glasses. He gripped three tumblers with his thumb, index, and middle finger, pressing them together for stability, then slid his left hand underneath, where he guided the glasses to the counter. "I suppose you've got some questions," he said, looking over at Jack.

"You might say."

"Let's go outside until my crew gets here. Bring the bottle." He tossed Jack a dishrag for the blood on it.

Jack bent over and grabbed the motorcycle case and followed him. Enzo came last. Once the initial shock of seeing him faded, Jack realized Enzo had his left arm in a sling and could see the mass of bandages beneath his collar. Rusty padded across the grass to the ramada and sat. Jack joined him, choosing a seat to Rusty's right at the end of the table, followed by Enzo, who sat across from Rusty at Jack's right. Rusty poured a healthy amount of scotch into each of the glasses.

"I think this is the part where you say, 'I thought you were dead,'" Enzo said without mirth and drained the glass. Then he grabbed the bottle and poured another.

Jack looked over to Rusty for some kind of explanation. Rusty immediately picked up the cue.

"I heard about the shooting from my police contacts in Cannes as soon as it was reported. A couple hundred euro in the right palms, and I learned that Enzo here wasn't actually dead, just really, really close. The police were keeping the knowledge of his survival a secret because they were thinking that might lure the killers out into the open, and they, rightly, assumed it was connected with the Carlton theft."

Jack looked over at his friend. Enzo drained the second and poured a third. He was drinking like a man who'd just killed someone. "I was running for my gun when Ozren shot me—upper shoulder blade. Since it was close range, the bullet went right through. Another couple inches and it would've been my heart." Enzo shook his head. "He never even said anything. He asked us for the take, I said we didn't have it, and he shot Gabrielle. Then me and Gaston."

Rusty picked the story back up. "So, I was able to buy my way into the hospital and got to talk to Enzo as soon as he came to. This was this morning. I asked him who shot him, and he told me it was Ozren and two others."

Jack shook his head slowly, sadly. If Reginald had just fucking listened to him.

"I can help out here," Jack said. "I don't know how long you were listening, but Ozren told me that he picked me up at the Carlton, thinking I was Gaston. They were watching the hotel, planning to ambush you after you'd pulled the job. I caught them off guard going so early and they lost me. So they went back to the safe house looking to pick up the take there. When they didn't find it on you, Ozren realized that I must have done it and he came here to Rome."

"How'd he know to look here?"

"He had help," Jack said flatly.

"Reginald?"

Jack only nodded.

Rusty said, "I came in right when Ozren was telling you to get on the ground, so I must have missed all of that. Anyway, I figured it was a good bet that Ozren was coming after you, so I snuck Enzo out of the hospital, and we hauled ass here. While we were on the road, I got a phone call from one of my associates that Stolar was looking for you. I tried calling you, but I couldn't get much of a signal when we were on the road, and when I could, there was no answer." Jack's phone was in the bedroom with the gun and the jewels. "We got here just after they did."

Jack exhaled hard and leaned back in his chair. Finally, after taking a long, slow sip of scotch, he said, "Thank you," first to the table. Then Jack looked up. "Both of you. Enzo, I'm sorry about Gaston and Gabrielle."

"Where the fuck were you, Jack?" Enzo challenged. Scotch and Oxycodone were not the ideal cocktail for diplomacy. "Why didn't you take the job when Reginald offered it? Ozren never would've pulled this shit if you were there."

"Oh, I doubt that very much," Jack said with the knowing gravity of a rabbi. "The way it looks now, Ozren Stolar planned to cross you the minute Reginald told him about the job." Reading the anguish that was all over Enzo's face, Jack calmly told him, "You're not responsible for their deaths, and don't fault yourself for not seeing it. I didn't. I never trusted the son of a bitch, and I told Reginald he was too dangerous to work with, but I never figured he'd try to double-cross us. Not like this." Jack's mind immediately went to Paul Sharpe.

Now it was his turn to drink.

"We talked about it," he said after a healthy pull. "My reasons are complicated, and I'm not sure this is the place."

Enzo poured another rail and knocked back half of it. The Oxy in his system was probably handling the physical pain. Enzo was trying to drown his guilt. This was something Jack knew well.

For Rusty's benefit, Jack said, "Initially, I didn't think it was a good idea. There was too much money out in the open for it to be that easy to get to, and I didn't like the setup. Plus," he added dryly, "I make it a point not to cross Israeli billionaires known to employ ex-Mossad hit men as their security guards."

Rusty nodded his head softly, acknowledging the logic. But Enzo bit on the line. "You seemed to have an easy enough time with that money in the open."

Jack let it pass.

He continued, ignoring the interruption. "I also had some things in my personal life, my private life, that demanded my full attention. I decided it wasn't worth the risk, so I passed. I assumed Reginald wasn't going to do it without me. I had no idea he was going to try and talk you three...four...into it." Indeed, sourly recognizing Ozren as part of the team.

Enzo, riding a wave of scotch and opiates, tore into Jack about the two lives they'd left behind. Jack just let him go because he knew that Enzo needed the exorcism...and because he was right. When Enzo finished, both the tirade and his third drink, he poured a fourth with a shaky hand and descended into a dark bog of loathing for Jack, the world in general and seemingly everything to have come out of the shattered remains of Yugoslavia and himself.

"So," Jack said finally, behind the burn of his scotch. "Where do we go from here?"

"Wherever that is," Rusty said evenly and looking at his watch, "we need to be there in less than twenty-five minutes. I don't want you two within five miles of this place when my cleaning crew gets here. Both of you are a little too well known in these parts to risk it."

"What about the money?" Enzo asked, his speech starting to resemble a poorly made cocktail.

"That's an interesting question, isn't it," Rusty asked.

Jack said nothing, did nothing as he carefully considered what to say next.

"I'm prepared to pay you both seven million dollars. You saved my life and—" He looked at Enzo, but words failed him.

"Why can't we just take our cut out of the stones? Cut out the middle-man?"

Jack looked to Rusty for help, but he only shrugged.

"Enzo has a point," was all he said.

"You won't be able to move them. I can all but guarantee that no one is dumb enough to take them off your hands, not once they realize what they are. In fact, I think the diamond market is going to dry up for a while until people are sure this lot is off the streets."

"What are you talking about? Why wouldn't they?"

"Because they will know who the stones belong to and don't want to fuck with them. Anyone you talk to is going to tell you they don't know you and then, as quickly as they can, call the rightful owner, who will hunt you down and get his property back. And then he will kill you for putting him through the trouble."

"That didn't seem to stop you from stealing them."

Enzo knocked back the remnants of his glass and reached for the bottle, but Jack beat him to it and pulled it out of reach. Charity and understanding only went so far, and Enzo needed a clear enough head if he was going to be able to make a decision.

"But we're not going to get to that point because I'm not giving you any of the stones. I made a deal to bring back all of them, and that's what I'm going to do."

It was the scotch and the drugs as much as his pain, physical and psychological, talking, but when Enzo popped off, he was clearly angry. "So, I suppose the great Gentleman Jack Burdette can move them when no one else can?"

"Who do you think my buyer is?"

"Wait," Rusty said, his speech catching up with this thoughts.

"What are you talking about?" Enzo asked in a foggy voice.

This was it. There was no going back now.

"Ari Hassar," Jack answered. "He paid me to do it. Hassar is broke. Not flat, but the kind of broke that only people like him and small nations can get. He hired me to rip off the exhibition so he can collect the insurance money plus whatever he realizes on the gray market for the stones."

Rusty shook his head and smiled. "He's doubling his money."

"Bingo." Jack shrugged. "It's small change compared to what he lost."

"Enough to retire on," Rusty said, but Jack shook his head.

"Not guys like him. He's going to gamble every cent from this scheme to get back to where he was. The ethics of this doesn't even enter his mind. It's simply a game of numbers and how quickly he can make his money back. From his perspective, he's just making a shrewd play that his competition wouldn't have expected." There was more, but he was cautious about how much he should tell Enzo with his friend in the state he was. Hassar knew someone was organizing a run at his exhibition, so part of Jack's involvement, perhaps the largest part, was for him to steal the jewels before anyone else had the chance. Enzo could probably take knowing that Jack had simply beat him to the score. Knowing that he never had a chance and that Gaston and Gabrielle died anyway would be too much for him to bear.

"Wait," Rusty said. "This is a little too clean for me. How is it that Hassar knew to call you to set this little scam up?"

"He didn't," Jack said nonchalantly. "I called him." Jack paused and let that sink in. "Reginald originally pitched me on the job, and I turned him down. I thought stealing from Hassar was risky and stupid in a life-altering kind of way." Jack leveled a hard gaze at Enzo. "For the record, I still do. So I called him. Told him who I was, that I knew a crew was going to come after him at the exhibition. I was actually hoping he was just going to beef up his security and pay me a tip-off fee. The theft was actually his idea. I'm starting to think he may have had something like this in mind."

"So why are you telling us this?" Enzo asked, suddenly and amazingly lucid.

Rusty shot him a glance but said nothing. He'd obviously figured this out already.

"It's an insurance policy. The three of us go pretty far back, but if you wanted, you could double-team me and take the stones. I can't stop you. But like I said before, you can't move them on your own, so I'm telling you this to buy a little trust."

Jack put just a touch more scotch in his glass and took a quick sip.

"You can't sell them, and I'm the only one who knows how to get to Hassar. If anyone but me shows up, Hassar's men will just kill them and take the diamonds. By telling you about my arrangement, I'm counting on you to let me walk out of here with this," he patted the case, "so that I can make the exchange with the understanding that I will pay you what I promised as soon as I have my cut." He leaned back in his chair and took a drink.

Hassar was paying him thirty million, roughly a fifth of the full value of the collection. The Israeli initially offered a much lower sum, but Jack countered by saying this was still an actual theft with an actual risk of jail time if he got caught. If he was going to do this, he wanted to make it worth his while. The subtext was Jack wanted enough money to convince him not to steal the collection for real like Reginald asked him to do. He'd never actually do that, but it was an incredibly effective bargaining chip. Hassar appreciated chutzpah.

The fourteen million was a hit, a big one, but not an insurmountable one. It would still leave Jack with sixteen, and that was more than enough to cover what Sharpe had stolen and to make back a bit of his savings.

Rusty's words had to find their way past a gut-born chuckle. "Jesus Christ, you've got a pair on you, Jack. I'm in. Hell, before you offered, I'd have done my part for free just to see if you could pull it off."

A smirk crawled up the side of Jack's face for the first time in what felt like a lifetime.

"No take-backs, asshole."

They both looked to Enzo, who just shrugged sullenly.

"Seven million dollars," he said softly, and the others could guess that he was weighing the value.

Enzo held his sour face for a perfect second before he broke into a laugh as well. A full-hearted belly laugh, one that brought tears to his eyes. Jack held his smile for a time after he regained composure. He knew there would be many dark nights ahead, but it was good to see his friend happy, even if it was fleeting for all the hell he'd just seen.

"So," Jack finally said, "we do have one problem."

"What's that?" Rusty said.

"Reginald LeGrande." Jack said the name like it was an old-world curse, something you possibly didn't believe in but were still wary to vocalize. "He knows I did the job, he knows I succeeded, and now he's trying to blackmail me for the full amount." Jack paused so they could grasp the gravity of it. They all knew how far back his and Reginald's professional association went, so there wasn't a need to tell it again. "But he's also figured out that I live under an assumed name and that I have an exit plan set up with that life."

Rusty nodded knowingly. "How'd he puzzle that out?"

Jack shook his head. "He sets me up with a clean phone every few months. I never thought to turn off the GPS tracking. I mean, I knew the phone had a GPS but I didn't realize someone else could track me with it. I also never considered the fact that Reginald was spying on me." Jack looked off to the eggplant-colored sky with the bubble of light from Rome coming up from below. "If I don't confirm that I'm going to pay him by tomorrow, he said he's going to dime me out to the FBI, give them every job I've ever pulled plus this one, and he'll give up my other identity. That doesn't just have consequences for me."

"You can't pay him, Jack." Rusty's eyes flicked to Enzo as he said this. "I don't say this out of a sense of self-preservation for Enzo and me. Well, not entirely," he allowed with a slight smile, though there was no humor behind it. "But I can tell you from experience that blackmailers don't stop when they get their payout, even if it is every red cent they asked for. It might last for a while, sure, but they almost always come back to the well. Could be a favor, could be another job. Hell, I had a case once where a guy was blackmailing people into being the business end of a murder-for-hire ring. The point is, it's not just the money, it's the power he has over you based on the strength of the information. He's banking on the fact that whatever he's got on you is worth more than the price of what he's asking in exchange," Rusty extended his index and middle fingers, tapping the table to punctuate each of the next two words, "in perpetuity."

Jack drained his scotch. "Even if I were inclined to pay off the double-dealing fuck, and let's be clear that I am not, I'd never go back on Ari Hassar. That guy's enough to scare me into going straight."

"Let's not be too hasty, there," Rusty said.

Jack and Enzo both smiled again. "Don't worry," Jack said. "I have no intention of giving Reginald our money. What I don't know is how can I prevent him from going to the FBI."

"So what if he does? You'll have more than enough money to disappear," Enzo said.

"It's not that, my friend. It's what I'd be giving up."

"Do you have anything that you can use to leverage Reginald?"

Jack shook a negative. "Not without implicating myself. He's run other crews, some of whom I know," he gave a half-hearted wave in Enzo's direction, "but I couldn't dime Reginald on that without implicating a lot of people who have nothing to do with this."

"You could scare him off," Enzo said. His lucidity was cresting as the scotch caught up to the pain meds. "Especially if Hassar is as dangerous a character as you say he is."

"I thought of that. Problem is, one of the conditions of my deal with Hassar was my silence. Now, I broke that with the two of you on a calculated risk that I can trust you, but I can't use that as a lever with Reginald. Besides, he would be just as likely to use that knowledge to get money out of one of Hassar's competitors. That comes back on me in a big and very bad way."

"Is Hassar an option?" Rusty asked.

"What do you mean?"

"Tell him about LeGrande. Likely, he'll just take out the bastard as a precaution."

Jack had considered that as well, but he had always stopped short of having Reginald killed. Jack abhorred violence of any kind. He had never practiced it and wouldn't work with people who plied it in their trade. There was a cold, easy logic to what Rusty was suggesting. It seemed the only logical response to a betrayal at such a fundamental level, and yet Jack couldn't bring himself to do it. This was still taking a human life. For as much as crime and violence were romanticized, even glamorized, in popular culture, it was a line that Jack knew he would not, could not ever cross. Someone threatened him once, threatened his family. It was a lesson he never forgot. There would always be a solid line between him and people like that.

He chose a different rationale in his response to Rusty, though he suspected the ex-cop knew the truth. "Hassar came to me because he wanted this done quietly. I can't go to him and say that someone else knows about the job. If I tell him about Reginald, his people will figure out who Reginald contracted. Eventually, that would lead them to Enzo." Jack looked at his intoxicated, pained friend. "I wouldn't put you at risk to save myself. Ever."

The two held each other's gaze for a time. Then Enzo nodded.

Rusty's phone buzzed. He checked it and then set it back on the table, facedown. "Okay, my crew is about five minutes away. You two need to get out of here now. Enzo, you're in no condition to drive. I'll take you somewhere to lay low for a bit until you're well enough to drive on your own. Just stay out of sight until I'm ready to leave. It won't be long. Jack, I'll put some feelers out, and if Reginald does give you up to the FBI, I should be able to find out about it. Meantime, try to think of anything else you've got on him." They stood and began walking back inside. Rusty put a hand on Jack's shoulder. "Maybe I can run some interference once he contacts the Bureau, try to preemptively discredit him."

"Jack," Enzo said suddenly. "What happens if you don't come back?"

"I don't follow."

"You said Hassar is broke and was doing this to make his money back."

"What's your point?"

"What if he decides, once he's got the diamonds, that he'd like to have that thirty million too?"

"Well," Jack said and drew in a long breath of warm, fragrant summer air, "if that happens, you'll be in the same place as you are now, broke and with a bullet wound. But you'll be alive."

Jack entered the house and avoided the kitchen, instead moving through the dining room and around through the living room to the den, hallway, and finally the master bedroom, where he collected his bag. Rusty caught up with him when he was climbing into the GranTurismo.

Rusty handed him a flip phone inside a Ziploc bag.

"This is a totally clean phone with no GPS. There's one number in it, which is mine. Use this only to call me. Break it apart and toss it in the trash when you leave Rome."

"How do we get Enzo out of here?" Jack asked. "I shouldn't be seen with anyone, just in case Hassar has people watching for me. They're all ex-Israeli intelligence, wouldn't put it past them."

"I've got him. My crew knows what to do. I don't need to be here. It's probably better that I'm not."

Jack nodded and tossed the Ziploc bag on the front seat next to his bag and the motorcycle case.

Jack drove.

For once, he wanted to stay in a place that someone didn't set up for him—one that couldn't be compromised.

He traveled across town to the St. Regis, valeted the Maserati, took his two pieces of luggage to the hotel desk, and asked for whatever they had available. There was a suite for fifteen hundred a night.

Perfect.

Jack handed the woman behind the counter Frank Fischer's credit card and passport. He also told her that he was here on a sensitive negotiation for his business and would appreciate discretion if anyone called asking about him. She understood. It was a common request given the number of celebrities that often stayed there. Before he left, he asked for an eight a.m. wake-up call.

Jack went to his room and fell into one of the deepest, blackest sleeps of his life.

21

Jack woke on the hotel staff's fourth wake-up call.

He asked room service to send up breakfast and a pot of coffee. While he waited for breakfast, Jack stretched out on the floor and went through a yoga routine to loosen up. After breakfast, Jack took a shower, bringing the case of Carlton jewels with him into the bathroom. After the events of the past two days, he was not letting them out of his sight.

At ten a.m., he finally powered on his phone and called Hassar, or rather, Hassar's lieutenant. His actual number two, not the army of executive functionaries, like Arshavin. This was an undisclosed number, likely on a cell phone that would be smashed and discarded after this call. Hassar's assistant, if that really was the right way to think of him, told Jack to meet them at the Rome Cavalieri Hotel. The assistant would meet Jack in the lobby himself and escort Jack to the penthouse suite.

Jack wore his cream-colored suit with a robin's egg Oxford, a blue-and-gold striped tie, and his McQueens. The Beretta was tucked inside the glove box. Jack knew he'd be searched as soon as he got into Hassar's hotel room—that was to be expected—but if the events of the past twenty-four hours had taught him anything, he wasn't making the trip across town empty-handed. Jack allowed himself to be caught off guard last night. That wouldn't happen again.

Jack took a circuitous route across town, doubling back several times and making turns that would have confounded the GPS in his phone if he'd had that on. Luckily for him, Rome was a city he knew well.

He arrived at the Rome Cavalieri at 10:40. Jack guided the GranTurismo counterclockwise through the wide roundabout that circled a perfectly manicured garden with trees and a small pavilion designed to look like an ancient Roman structure with a triangular roof supported by columns. The hotel itself was a massive, sprawling structure set in the center of a fifteen-acre park overlooking central Rome. Lush, leafy plants hung from each of the hotel's three hundred seventy private balconies to appear like an ancient hanging garden. Prior to the hotel's acquisition by the Hilton chain and subsequent inclusion in their Waldorf Astoria collection, the Cavalieri sported one of the finest art collections in Italy.

Jack stepped out of the car with the case in hand, accepted the valet ticket, and told the valet that he was not a guest, would not be staying long, and would prefer his car to be kept out front. He handed the man a twenty-euro note to make sure that happened and then walked around the front of the vehicle as he fastened his jacket. He entered the lobby. It was ostentatious, even for his taste.

The central lobby sat beneath a ring of large, globe-shaped lamps, though the ring itself was also lit. Four huge white marble columns just inside the ring linked the floor with the slightly vaulted wood ceiling. The bank of reception and concierge desks sat along the far walls beneath long rows of recessed lighting, over which hung Renaissance paintings. Jack allowed himself a smirk when he noted that the floors were a similar style to the Carlton InterContinental in Cannes, golden marble with ivory accents. Burdette walked quickly to the center of the lobby beneath that giant ring of lights. He was absolutely on edge but considerably less so than if they were meeting in a truly private location. A double cross was certainly possible, but his initial, albeit natural, fear of it being a lethal encounter abated somewhat knowing that they were in one of the most exclusive hotels in Rome, if not the world. One could likely pay to keep a high-profile tryst secret in a place like this, a murder not so much.

Still, betrayals didn't always end in body counts.

It was a risk, Jack knew, but one he would have to live with.

"Mr. Burdette?"

Jack turned to the heavily accented voice. He wore a gray suit, open collared with no ornamentation, no cufflinks or pocket square. It was well made, as were his black oxfords, but simple. He was naturally tanned, with close-cropped blond hair and eyes whose color were hard for Jack to place in the lobby, which was still somehow dimly lit despite the constellations of lights overhead. The man said, "Follow me, please."

Jack noted that he did not introduce himself.

Jack followed the man in the gray suit to a bank of elevators where he produced a key card and pressed the button for the penthouse suite. They rode up in silence, but Jack's mind was far from quiet. He was nervous for all the expected reasons and a few that were not. This wasn't a business built on trust; it was built on the tolerance of risk. Jack knew he couldn't *trust* Hassar not to kill him and save the payout. He'd simply calculated that the mogul would not. If Hassar was going to do it, it wasn't going to be here at the rooftop of Rome.

The elevator stopped on the top floor. Hassar's man

stepped into the hallway and began walking, saying only, "This way, please."

Jack followed.

The man stopped at a door after several steps and again produced the key card, this time holding the door open for Jack. When Burdette looked to him, the man simply nodded, and Jack stepped into the suite. The doorway opened to the corner of a short hallway so that anyone entering the room couldn't immediately see into it. Hassar's assistant stepped around Jack and walked into the living room. There was a wet bar to his right set inside a beautifully designed wood cabinet that occupied most of that side of the room. Two men, similarly dressed as his nameless guide, sat on a plush couch watching the television that Jack saw was to his immediate right. The men on the couch looked up at him as he entered to register, but not acknowledge, his presence.

Hassar's assistant stepped into the living room and motioned with his hand for Jack to follow, indicating to a carpeted stairway set into the wall. The landing was a wide, rounded step, and each subsequent step was slightly smaller until they twisted around the corner and disappeared. Jack caught a glimpse of the bedroom as he stepped into the staircase. There was a Warhol on the wall. It was a *Dollar Sign* painting—four dollar signs, each one a different color and style, all looking like they came out of a comic book.

But it was worth a small fortune because of the name attached.

The attendant irony was not lost on him.

Jack was not searched.

A practiced eye could discover whether someone was hiding a gun.

Or they simply knew he'd never be that stupid.

Jack walked up the narrow stairs and found himself on a

private terrace casually peering over the Eternal City like he was a Caesar. Even now, it was hot. There was a small Jacuzzi to the left, its surface placid, beneath a large cloth pavilion. Under the pavilion there was a rattan-and-canvas outdoor sofa and two chairs arranged around a glass table. Beyond that there was an open-air patio with a line of deck chairs that ringed the hotel pool and the sprawling undulating Roman landscape.

Ari Hassar, diamond mogul, billionaire-ish, sat basking in the heat looking out over the city. He wore a loose-fitting white linen shirt, turquoise linen pants, and sandals. There was an empty deck chair next to Hassar, and between them was an ice bucket with a bottle carefully wrapped in a white cloth towel that Jack could easily guess was champagne. All of this was for show—the penthouse suite with the goddamned Warhol in one of Rome's most exclusive hotels, the entourage, the name-less functionary who provided only cursory instructions, even Hassar's positioning when Jack arrived on the terrace, with his back to Burdette's arrival and the chilled champagne at eleven in the morning. All of this was to build the pretense that Hassar didn't desperately need the money that Jack held in his hand.

Jack waited for a second, guessing that this was all for face. He decided to let the mogul enjoy his moment and then said, "Good morning, Mr. Hassar."

Ari Hassar stood. He was deeply tanned and while he still possessed a squat, powerful frame, his prime was clearly behind him. He had a wide face and struck Jack as looking more than a little like a Middle Eastern version of Albert Finney. He couldn't make out much more of Hassar's face, as it was largely hidden behind his enormous sunglasses. He was mostly bald with a low halo of stubble around the back. Jack found it curious that a man of such crippling vanity wouldn't shave, not even for control. The other striking thing about the man was how short he actually was. Five five, five six, tops.

Hassar smiled broadly and extended a big hand.

They were the paws of a man who built his empire by hand, stone by stone.

Jack stepped tentatively out from under the pavilion and into the sunlight. He shook Hassar's hand and then drew the McQueens out of his jacket, flipping them open with his right hand and put them on. He couldn't see Hassar's eyes for the dark lenses, but he knew they were on the case in Jack's left hand.

"It's a pleasure to finally meet you," Hassar said.

"You as well, Mr. Hassar."

Hassar smiled. "You live up to your name, I'll give you that." Then, "I like that in a man." He gestured toward the other deck chair. "Please."

"Mr. Hassar, perhaps it's best that we not do this out in the open. I don't think it's a good idea that we're seen together."

Hassar only laughed to spite the heat. "An overabundance of caution, my boy. You and I are the only two here who weren't Mossad. I can assure you that we're quite safe."

Jack knew that insurance investigators at this level were dogged pursuers, sometimes on par or better than the police themselves and often better resourced. But, in seeing that they were on a hill above central Rome and at least a few miles from a suitable vantage point to take photographs, which could be done, but the equipment required was the kind that the US intelligence agencies possessed, not Lloyd's of London, Jack relaxed, but only a touch.

As Jack moved to take the seat, Hassar motioned to his man—still no one had addressed this guy by name and the suspense was starting to eat at Jack—who walked up and made to take the case, saying only, "Sir." Jack hesitated for a moment—he hadn't been paid yet—but at this point there was little he could do. He handed the man the take from the Carlton and took a seat next to the collection's rightful owner. The aide withdrew to beneath the pavilion, likely to inspect the contents without the glare.

He sat, and as he did, he saw Hassar accept a nod from his man.

The mogul, still standing on ceremony, reached into the bucket and drew out the wine to the sound of cascading ice. He poured two flutes and handed one to Jack. Another man in Hassar's position would have had an assistant do this very simple thing, but again, this was part of the show and the message. Hassar was a man who did things himself. Jack raised the glass and said, "Success, to crime."

Hassar laughed and said, "Indeed." The reference was apparently lost on him. It was Sam Spade's toast with the two detectives and his recognition of the dangerous game he was about to play.

"I must say, Jack, I admire your style. The one thing we lack in my country is panache. We don't have the luxury, I'm afraid."

"Mr. Hassar," Jack said with a slight smile, "I don't think anyone would try to make the point that you don't have style."

That earned a belly laugh.

"But not like you, my friend. I'll admit, I was expecting some elaborate scheme, perhaps. Instead, you simply walk into the exhibition like one of your famous Wild West bandits and," Hassar's free hand jumped out in a finger-gun, "stick 'em up," followed by another heavy belly laugh. Hassar held up his flute, the delicate crystal incongruous in the man's hairy-fingered paws. "To Gentleman Jack Burdette."

"Well, I didn't have the men for something a little flashier, but then, flash is not exactly my style. Tipping me to Arshavin was a big help," Jack said, sipping the champagne. Jack assumed that was Reginald's inside man. Then, with a smile, "And the door," he added, just in case there was a sub-rosa motive at play here, making it clear that Hassar was as much a part of this as Jack was.

If Jack's statement bothered him, Hassar said nothing.

Jack breathed deep and allowed himself to relax.

Jack had met with Hassar in Miami, not long after he'd passed on the job. He kept Reginald's name out of it initially because he didn't want him to get hurt. Jack was cagey about where he got the information from, and Hassar seemed to respect that. Hassar said he had some holes in his organization to fill and that he was more than capable of doing so. Jack reasoned that if something happened to Reginald after that, well, it likely would have happened anyway. On Hassar's yacht, the mogul pitched Jack on the idea of stealing the jewels in advance of the theft that was expected to happen. Hassar told him "the word was on the street" about the diamonds. This was a man who'd probably done shadier things in business than Jack would ever do in actual crime and was talking like a movie character because he thought that's how criminals actually talked. He gave Jack the intel on Arshavin and made sure the salon door would be open.

The news outlets were already reporting that a furious Hassar was threatening a lawsuit against the hotel for such a "monumental oversight."

Jack had pushed his luck on the boat.

He'd told Hassar he'd do it, but he wanted to know why. If Hassar was worried about thieves, why not just step up security. Jack needed to know why so he knew that he wasn't walking into a trap.

"I will tell you why," Hassar had said. "We will have this secret between us, and then we will have trust."

Ari Hassar was broke, or as close to it as measured by men like him. One of the first casualties of the Great Recession was luxury goods, and Americans were the world's leading consumers of diamonds. Hassar was losing millions a year in excess inventory, and the growing instability in Africa following the Arab Spring only compounded his troubles. Though the countries that his diamond mining operations were in were largely spared, Hassar lost access to valuable ports and eventually major segments of his construction empire because the newly installed religious governments wouldn't do business with an Israeli.

This was an emergency fund, a kind of golden parachute that could only exist in the kinds of orbits that men like Hassar occupied. Though he was rebuilding his businesses and the diamond market was gradually coming back around, there was the legitimate possibility that Hassar would never fully recover, and so this three-hundred-million-dollar scheme, minus expenses, of course, was to be a fail-safe, just in case he wasn't able to bring his empire back into the black. He would be able to sell off the businesses he had and live out his days as his contemporaries would expect of him, sparing himself the considerable embarrassment of having to admit he'd gone broke. Instead, he'd appear a shrewd investor with strong hedges against failing business and global instability. He'd win where his peers had lost everything.

As with LeGrande, Jack had initially rebuffed Hassar's offer. He had a winery to run. Jack was given a number to call if he changed his mind.

Then, Paul Sharpe.

Jack waited until he was down to his last option. When he knew that he had no better choice, and when his faith in the criminal justice system was proven hollow, Jack called that number and told them he was in.

Jack accepted the deal. He negotiated them up to thirty million from the laughable starting price of fifteen. Hassar believed that Jack's initial refusal and later acceptance was all an elaborate negotiating tactic and that it was a shrewd, audacious play.

Hassar's man appeared at the once and future mogul's side, bent low, and exchanged some words in Hebrew. Then he disappeared. Hassar turned to Jack in his chair. "I am informed that we have transferred the agreed-upon funds into your bank in Vanuatu, less a bit for some stones that I understand ended up on the streets of Cannes."

"How much less are we talking?" Jack asked cautiously.

"One dollar." And then he practically bellowed, enjoying the expression on Jack's face.

Twenty-nine million, nine hundred ninety-nine thousand dollars. Actually, as Jack thought on it, it was pretty fucking funny.

"I must say that I have enjoyed being a 'victim' of the great Gentleman Jack Burdette."

Jack didn't like where this was going. Of course, Hassar would only want to be stolen from by the best and might enjoy the cache that brought him in certain circles. Jack was reminded of the Warhol hanging downstairs.

"Well," Jack said with a disarming smile, "I hope you didn't enjoy it too much. I'm afraid this one won't be making my résumé."

"A pity," Hassar guffawed. "You're now the most successful jewelry thief in history, and you cannot even talk about it. It's a shame, in a way, that no one knows but the two of us."

Partially true, Jack corrected silently.

"It would've made a great movie," Jack allowed. There was no stopping Hassar from talking about this, he knew. If he was going to brag to his billionaire friends that he'd been robbed by the notorious thief Gentleman Jack Burdette, it would be worse if he had to explain to his billionaire friends who Jack actually was. The questions would come, certainly, long after the international law enforcement community resigned this to be a cold case, after the story faded from the headlines, and after Hassar's promises to "find those responsible" became little more than echoes. There would still be questions from Hassar's peers who would ask, rightly, how it could be that his personal security staff, some of the most highly trained intelligence operatives in the world with access to Hassar's seemingly limitless resources, could not discover the perpetrator's identity? He could only hope that Hassar's discretion would outweigh his vanity, his bluster, and his compulsion to brag about the operation.

There would also be questions from the press, typically triggered by the anniversaries of such events. Would someone get the itch to investigate the theft, already being described as the "Crime of the Century"? *At least it's a new century*, Jack thought ruefully.

He stood, straightened, and then buttoned his jacket. "Mr. Hassar, it's been a distinct pleasure doing business with you." Jack extended a hand. "I think, in other circumstances, you and I would've been great friends...but I'll be damned if I ever play poker with you."

Hassar laughed heartily, stood, and accepted his handshake. The mogul wished him good fortune and hoped their paths crossed again in the future.

Hassar's man saw Jack out to the elevator, again saying nothing until he pressed the elevator's lobby button. Jack fought the urge to ask him what his name was. "Good luck, Mr. Burdette, or whomever you may be," he said softly. "Walk with God."

Jack got the GranTurismo from the valet and drove back to

the Rome Cavalieri by a circuitous route that added about another fifteen minutes onto the trip. His eyes scanned the rearview mirror for possible tails, but he knew it would be next to impossible to spot one car during the chaotic crush of noontime Roman traffic. He'd be lucky to get the Maserati back without a ding in it, let alone spot a tail. Still, he drove in the most nonsensical, haphazard way back to the hotel. If anyone was following him, they'd think he was blind or the most inefficient tourist in history, or both.

Jack spent the rest of the day inside at the Rome Cavalieri, mostly in his room watching the news and contemplating what to do about Reginald. The theft remained the leading story, even though none of the news outlets had anything new to report. The investigation was now turning inward to the hotel staff, with speculation mounting that it was an inside job. How else could security have been that incompetent to leave the salon's street-side door unlocked? Hassar did not appear on camera, but a spokesman released a statement that said he was cooperating fully with the authorities—Jack actually laughed out loud at that—and that they too had questions about the hotel's handling of the matter, even though the exhibition's security was ultimately their responsibility. Jack knew that the finger-pointing was part of Hassar's strategy to make this as murky as possible. It was also exactly the move a man in his position would make.

Part of the arrangement was that Hassar would assume responsibility for covering tracks at the hotel.

That solved, or at least mitigated, Jack focused on how to deal with Reginald. Having roughly fifteen million to work with, he could attempt to pay off LeGrande. The challenge there was that Reginald would be expecting a significantly larger sum. Fencing jewels, both finished pieces and loose stones, typically netted between thirty and forty percent of their market value. If Jack were selling these himself, there's no way that he'd be able to move the entire take at once. Rather, it would've been cautiously done over the course of several years and with a variety of different fences mostly, if not exclusively, in Eastern Europe or Asia, where such transactions could be conducted with greater ease and far less scrutiny. Were he to sell these on his own, Jack would've been looking at something between fifty and sixty million dollars total profit, only spread out over five years. That's what Reginald would be expecting.

LeGrande put him in an impossible position, by design.

Reginald would know Jack couldn't sell the jewels and jewelry in one go and realize anything but a fraction—probably a third of the total value. It had to be done over time in order to spread the risk around as well as to increase the profit. Not to mention there were very few people in the world who could pull off that kind of transaction. Jack began to wonder how deeply and thoughtfully LeGrande weighed this before launching his blackmail. Impossible choices were fine if the game was to make one side lose, but Reginald wanted money. If he wasn't giving Jack any flexibility, how was he supposed to get it? What wasn't he seeing?

Jack thought of options and just as quickly crossed them off his list, for none of them ended in Reginald either walking away or lining his pockets with the expected amount. "What if I just pay the fucker off?" Jack finally asked himself. Hand Reginald the money Hassar had paid him and walk away. Was fifteen million dollars worth it to have a chance at a legitimate life, a public life, and a life that included Megan, in whatever way that meant?

Yes. Unequivocally.

But if he paid Reginald off, how did he save Kingfisher? They were still ten million in the hole, and even if they got the full amount back from Sharpe, which was unlikely, the winery would be bankrupt by the time the check cleared. Perhaps they could find a bank that would stake them. Certainly, Hugh could put him in a room with someone who would at least hear them out, though what they were asking for was still an incredible sum.

The question was if Jack had the ability to lead them out of their situation even if he did get the money. He was finally able to admit to himself that the winery's problems were largely his own making. Instead of trusting people who knew better than him, Jack assumed that running a winery was a complex operation and therefore equivalent to running other complex operations. He, to his fault, didn't draw a distinction between the kinds. Jack micromanaged nearly every detail in an effort to appear that he was an expert businessman. He also put his trust in people who didn't deserve it, and they all had paid the price.

Jack dismissed the idea of a loan and, by extension, the possibility of paying Reginald off. LeGrande would know that Jack couldn't have moved the stones this quickly unless he had a single buyer lined up in advance, and that would immediately draw suspicion and speculation. Reginald would press for the details because he would rightly deduce that Jack had something up his sleeve. Worse, Reginald would think there was another well to tap.

Jack was almost willing to let him try.

He dialed guest services and had them send up a Nero d'Avola.

He was suddenly very tired. Tired of running, tired of the balancing act, and tired of the questions for which there were no good answers.

22

Jack nursed the bottle over a period of several hours, taking care that he kept his wits, if not about him, in sight. He remembered a quote from Hemingway that he pulled out of an in-flight magazine once in an article about Key West. "Write drunk, edit sober." The author's point was that Hemingway's creative juices flowed better when the actual juice was in his veins. Maybe that worked for Pappy, but this wine wasn't unlocking any brilliant ideas. Jack could barely calm his mind enough to think through the problems at hand, plan his next move.

He'd leave for California in the morning. That was at least a step in the right direction. Jack had an eight a.m. flight the next morning out of Fiumicino with a connection in Frankfurt and then direct to SFO, landing around four in the afternoon, Pacific time. Jack wanted nothing more than to put all this behind him, and there were a hundred problems he needed to sort out with the winery. He also knew it would be a long time before that happened. He wouldn't be safe until Reginald was dealt with. His original plan was to swat Reginald with a few million dollars and hope that was enough to salve whatever perceived bullshit wounds Reginald invented. But now, after he'd shown up at Kingfisher and implied a threat against Megan. Well, there was no turning back from that.

Jack stared at the glass of Nero d'Avola for a long, long time.

He couldn't imagine what had made Reginald turn on him like that. Even Jack passing on the job initially shouldn't spur this kind of...vengeance? Is that what this was? But there was no reason for it that Jack could see. Reginald was not only his friend and his mentor, but Jack had made him a lot of money over the years. Reginald made a comment that he didn't have as long to wait as Jack, didn't have time for this, what did he call it..."nickel and dime shit." Jack could understand that. He could get that Reginald wanted out of the game and that explained why he pressured Jack into the job in the first place. But that didn't explain why Reginald would threaten to expose Jack, destroy everything he'd built. Those were acts of vengeance...but vengeance for what?

It was approaching midnight and Jack had finished the wine. He'd since moved on to a glass of scotch that he'd gotten from the minibar in his room. He was no closer to answers. There didn't seem to be any way to neutralize Reginald short of paying him the money he demanded, which of course Jack could not do. Well, there was one option, but Jack would never do it. Whatever Reginald had done or was doing, Jack wasn't going to kill him.

Jack was halfway into the second scotch and just a shade south of drunk when Megan called. She was frantic and confused.

"What's wrong?" he said slowly, concentrating on each word.

"Frank, two people from the FBI are here. They demanded

to see you and wanted to know if I knew anything about a guy named Jack Burdette. Do you know what this is about?"

Jack's blood turned to ice, and he felt a queer, queasy sensation in the pit of his stomach. His heart rate immediately redlined. He'd heard people describe accounts where they were drunk or high, recounting that they had some kind of sobering event where they somehow had total control of their mental faculties. This was bullshit. Jack was still half-cocked, and he knew he was still half-cocked, but the fuzzy-robe feeling you got after drinking a bottle of red wine was quickly replaced by a sensation that felt a lot like being on the deck of a ship skippered by a particularly incompetent captain navigating a hurricane. Still, it seemed like someone dunked his head in ice water, and things were all the clearer for it.

Think fast, Jack.

"No. No idea. Jack Burdette?" He said the name, rolling it around on his tongue. His words sounded thick and heavy to his own ears. "Did they say what they wanted him for or why they wanted to talk to me?"

"They seem to think you know him or know how to find him. They didn't say what it was for, only that it's in our best interest if we tell them immediately. They wanted to know when you were coming back and were really pushy about it. I didn't know what to say. I told them you were in Switzerland on business but would be back in a few days."

"Okay, Megan, I want you to call Hugh Coughlin. Call him right now. Tell him everything that happened. Are the FBI people still there?"

"Yeah, they're out in the parking lot on their cell phones."

"We've got nothing to hide and we've done nothing wrong, but you already know how I feel about the government. If they don't have a warrant, they can fuck themselves."

"Frank."

"Sorry. I just don't like the thought of them bullying you." Then he quickly added, "If they talk to you again, tell them that we're happy to cooperate with them, but it will be in the presence of our attorney. Don't take no for an answer. If they give you any shit, you tell them that we have every right not to trust them and that they can talk to our lawyer."

"Frank," she said at length, "I don't know if we want to play hardball with these guys. They're the FBI, and this is kind of scary."

"I know, Meg, but we're also not going to let them push us around." Jack pressed his eyelids together and scrunched his face. Maybe he could force the tension out by sheer force of will. He prayed he sounded sober. "Look, we don't have anything to be afraid of. We haven't done anything wrong. I don't know who this guy is or why they think I'd know, but I promise you we'll get this sorted out as soon as I get home."

"When will that be?"

"I land at four in the afternoon, your time." He paused a moment. Even through the fog of intoxication, Jack saw this for what it was. Reginald. He'd telegraphed his moves when they'd spoken on the phone. If Jack didn't come through, Reginald was going to dime him to the FBI. This was just his first shot at that, get Jack to think that he'd done it. So that meant Reginald wasn't acting alone. The son of a bitch had a crew.

"Frank? Are you still there?"

"I'm still here, Megs. I'm sorry. I think I know what's going on."

"Well, I'm glad someone does."

"I had an old business partner once, and he's unfortunately shady. A con man. I just found out too late. You met him the other day. He was the guy who showed up at the winery and pretended to be a distributor. He's saying that I owe him money from the sale of this business that I'm arranging now. I don't, but he's trying to strong-arm me. I think those 'FBI agents' are people he's using to scare me into paying him off."

"But why would he do that?"

"We cut him out when we thought he was dealing under the table. I think this is some get-back. He knows what the business is worth. Please call Hugh. That should at least scare these guys off."

"Do you want me to call the sheriff's department?"

That was the actual last thing he wanted.

"They didn't do shit when Sharpe stole our money. I'm not sure what good they are going to be now." Megan protested, but Jack didn't relent. They said their goodbyes, and Megan promised her next call was going to be to Hugh Coughlin.

Jack paced the length of his hotel room, furious. He gripped his hands so tightly his fingernails dug into the heels of his palms. It was all he could do to keep from screaming at the top of his lungs. Reginald gave him forty-eight hours, so where in the hell was that? Why didn't he honor it?

After a fast eight minutes, fury, alcohol, and anger beat out discretion.

He grabbed his Burdette iPhone, powered it on, and dialed Reginald from the encryption program. LeGrande picked up on the third ring, and when he answered, his voice was smug, haughty, like a teacher delivering an answer from the instructor's edition.

"Hi, Jack. I wondered when I'd hear from you."

"Cut the shit, you lying fuck. You said I had forty-eight hours."

At first, all Jack heard on the other side was soft chuckling. It sounded like an old engine that was barely turning over.

"What's so fucking funny, Reginald? I don't remember making a joke."

The chuckling continued for a few beats, then Reginald deadpanned, "I'm blackmailing you for eighty-five million dollars, and you're quoting Robert's Rules. That's very funny to me."

"You said I had forty-eight hours," Jack repeated through his teeth.

"You *do* have forty-eight hours. This was just a little reminder to let you know that I'm serious."

"You sent the FBI to my place of business," Jack said in a low voice.

His voice even, Reginald said, "I told you I was going to do that. When I didn't hear from you, as I knew I probably wouldn't, I set certain things in motion just to make sure you knew it wasn't an idle threat." Reginald paused. "This can all be turned around, Jack. Nothing is irreversible, not yet."

Jack decided to play along with it for now. He didn't want Reginald to know that he'd figured out those guys were in on it.

"What, and live with the FBI hanging over my shoulder for the rest of my life? What am I going to tell my employees? They're going to need to know why the feds were there asking questions and looking for me."

"Tell them whatever you want. I think you've got this double-life thing down pat by now."

"I've got a way into a normal life, and you're taking it personally. Are you angry that I have a parachute and you don't, is that what this is about?"

"Don't get sanctimonious with me, Jack. Yeah, you kicked me a couple nickels when I got out of prison, but you forget that they took everything I'd ever made. Think you could keep *your* lifestyle up on that?"

"A couple nickels, huh? I made sure you had something to count besides ten years of probation," Jack shouted back.

"And I made you a lot of money in the years since. I was even going to cut you in on some of this score until you pulled this shit."

"Cut me in? I tipped you off to it. You wouldn't have even known about this if it wasn't for me."

"Once you told me another crew was on it, I became a free agent."

Why not just tell him you're working for Hassar, Jack scolded himself. What did one-upping Reginald get him other than tipping his hand?

Finally, Jack said, "It wasn't my fault you went up, Reg, and you sure as hell aren't making me suffer for it now. You don't like how your life turned out. I'm sorry, but I'm not paying for your mistakes. Maybe you shouldn't have taken that job." Jack had to clamp his mouth shut before the words "like I told you not to" practically bounced off his teeth. This had escalated enough already.

"Maybe you can give me another lecture on your rules."

"I've never been caught, have I?" Rusty doesn't count, Jack told himself. He was already bent by then.

That laugh again, though this time Jack knew it was forced. "Not yet."

Jack's head swam against the current of betrayal, rage, alcohol, and incomprehension. All he wanted to do was put his hands around LeGrande's neck and squeeze. If this conversation had happened face-to-face, Jack wasn't sure he'd have been able to stop himself.

Blackmail was a sin of an entirely different order.

It was calculated, it was designed, and it was a bespoke crime.

Questioning it, reasoning it, Jack finally realized through the fog of alcohol and fury, was pointless. Reginald knew exactly the outcome he was trying to get and had weighed the risks and concluded that the tradeoff, Jack, was worth every penny. Appealing to him would be wasted air.

"I'm waiting, Jack. I want my money, and I want it now. Pay up before this gets a lot worse."

"See, that's the thing, Reg. You know that, at best, the take is forty-five or fifty once you fence them, and that's spread out over several years. No one is going to buy these in bulk for anything close to that. There's no way I'm selling these anytime soon."

"That, Jack, sounds like a problem. I'm not interested in problems. I'm only interested in the money. I'll tell you what. My original projection from the sale was thirty-eight million. I'll cut you some slack because we go back so far. I don't care how you raise it or even if it comes from the sale of those particular stones, so long as the next time we speak, you are able to hand me thirty-eight million dollars."

"You know I can't do that. If I had that kind of money, I wouldn't have done this job to begin with." When Reginald didn't immediately respond, Jack said, "You never intended for me to be able to pay you that money, did you? You just offered me an impossible choice."

"Maybe I wanted you to understand what that felt like." Then Reginald said, "No, I fully intended for you to fucking pay me. And you're going to, or I'll take everything you have."

Whatever Reginald's game was, and Jack was admittedly having a difficult time seeing it for the fog in his head, he now knew that part of that strategy was to make Jack twist on the line for a time. Reginald wasn't done yet, and the money wasn't his goal, not in total. He just wanted Jack to know a level of panic first before he revealed it.

So what, then?

Jack had to buy time. He needed to put Reginald on his heels, at least long enough for Jack to figure a way out of this.

He'd always hoped he'd never have to play this particular card.

"All of this assumes one thing, Reginald."

"Oh," he offered with a tone that was both banal and smug. "And what's that?"

"You offered to hand the FBI Gentleman Jack Burdette. You're assuming that's who I actually am." Jack let that float in the static between Rome and Long Beach for a time. "Your plan only works if you can corroborate your accusations about Burdette, which you can't actually do."

"What are you talking about? Of course I can. We've worked together for twenty years."

"So you say, and I'm sure that's something you'd tell the authorities. Once they bust you, of course. More on that later. Maybe it never occurred to you that perhaps Jack Burdette isn't a real person. Perhaps when the FBI shows up at Frank Fischer's door, Frank Fischer doesn't know anything about you or Jack Burdette. See, Frank Fischer is a real person with a very long, very verifiable history. You've got a name someone gave you, and you always assumed he was telling you the truth." Jack's annunciation was succinct and matter of fact and more than a little condescending. "I think the way the FBI is going to interpret this, and the way Frank Fischer's very good attorney is going to interpret this, is that Reginald LeGrande is an opportunist looking to blackmail money from a prominent businessman. But for you to come forward to the FBI, you're going to have to prove that you know the hows and whys of Jack Burdette's career. That'll take a lot more knowledge than 'some guy you met in prison.' You can't out me without outing yourself, and you don't have shit to trade." Jack paused again. "You're about to make some people very angry, Reg, unless you come to your senses very, very quickly. I'd better not hear of you or anyone connected with you going to Kingfisher again."

Jack hung up the call and shut the phone. He wished he hadn't had to say the last part, but he needed something to put Reginald back on his heels a little, buy some space. Yes, Jack flagged that he was working with someone. But Jack believed that would worm its way into Reginald's psyche, maybe get him to think again about his next moves. It was just intended to buy Jack some time and hopefully get Reginald to trip up a little.

After all, a little paranoia could go a long way.

23

Katrina Danzig stood at the front of a long conference table, and there was a long, thin smile on her face. This had come together quickly, building like a wave, and she had been in exactly the right position to ride it. Turned out, this was her set. It started with an informant, though not the one she'd been expecting. She'd gotten a call late in the evening two days prior from Kurt Sinclair, the Assistant Special Agent in Charge of the San Francisco Division. Kurt had been her boss during her tour in Europe—her mentor and friend. Kurt's agents were working a joint operation with the California Highway Patrol and had a confidential informant that fingered Gentleman Jack Burdette as the perpetrator behind the Carlton InterContinental heist. Knowing that she'd been the Bureau's lead on the investigation into Burdette, Sinclair called her to see if she could corroborate. Danzig told him that the Gem and Jewelry Program was supporting the investigation, or would, if the Europeans asked for help. Which they hadn't. In fact, apart from her one phone call from Giovanni Castro, there had been dead silence on either side of the pond. She'd mentioned about how she'd tried to get the gem program into the game, but without an American involved, her boss didn't see the need. Sinclair opened some doors, as the number two agent in charge of a major division could do, and two days later, Danzig was on a plane.

The operation was coming together quickly, though she suspected that some parts of this had already been in motion before she had gotten involved. Danzig wouldn't be the operational lead on the case, that would be the San Francisco agents, but she was here as a representative of the trafficking task force and subject matter expert on their target. That alone made it worth strong-arming her boss to get here. There was still a prosecutorial question of who would try the case, the US Attorney in San Francisco or the Southern District of New York, the issue being the crime was committed in France but the suspect would be arrested in California. That wasn't Danzig's problem. This was the first credible lead they had on Jack Burdette's identity and his whereabouts in the United States. Further, it was from an American. Castro hadn't seen Jack since 1997, and she doubted that his identification would hold up in court. She had called Giovanni to let him know and also to check with *his* informant, who had allegedly been on Burdette's crew in Valencia earlier that year. If they could get two informants to testify to his identity and his involvement in that crime, they would have him.

Danzig had flown into San Francisco the evening before. She and Kurt met for drinks to catch up. Sinclair's wife, Rebecca, had also joined. They were a Bureau family, Rebecca Sinclair was an agent too and something of a minor legend in the FBI for having done a lot of undercover work during the early parts of her career. She was also a trailblazer, and Danzig looked up to her. The Sinclairs had kind of adopted Danzig during their European assignment, personally and professionally. It was good to see them. More than that, they were both very proud of her, and that meant the world.

Danzig orbited at the front of the long conference table where she would be delivering her presentation. She hated small talk and hated mingling. Yes, she could do it and knew how and when to turn that on, particularly if she was working a source or the times she herself had been undercover, but right now she wanted her head clear. Kurt walked her through who would be in the room the night before, the representatives from CHP, the Assistant US Attorney as well as his people, and tried to give her a little insight into how each of them might react to her presentation. Even though Danzig had been after Burdette the longest, that was a new facet of a broader investigation and she was an outsider here. He encouraged her to proceed with a measure of caution. The one person she knew already was CHP's Lieutenant Brian Valero. Valero had been running an informant for several years and provided a wealth of information over the previous forty-eight hours to help her construct her presentation.

Danzig focused on the room, on her talking points.

She was dressed in a black skirt and jacket, light blue blouse. She kept her hair short anyway, but it was pulled back in a tight, efficient tail that looped her dark hair to the back of her head. She was ready. This was her moment.

Kurt was near the door, glad handing and welcoming guests as they filed in. His brown hair had a gray flash at the temple. He was in Brooks Brothers pinstripes over navy blue, purple-and-blue striped tie, and an American flag lapel pin. Sinclair had been an athlete in college and told her that he'd taken up cycling during his time here in San Francisco. Better on the joints, he'd said.

Sinclair walked over and joined her at the head of the long table with his coat unbuttoned and hands on his hips so the jacket spread like lazy wings. There was a coffee mug on the table in front of him with the FBI shield on it, though it was faded from a lot of washing. Next to him, there was a large screen displaying the title slide of Danzig's presentation with her name next to the words "Gem and Jewelry Program." Beneath that read, "Transnational Trafficking Task Force." Danzig's eyes briefly went to the window and the impressive view of the San Francisco Civic Center and its famous mayor's office. She suspected this room was for the benefit of their California Highway Patrol liaisons. In addition to protecting California's highways, since the nineties, CHP has acted as California's state police.

"Ready?" Sinclair asked.

Danzig smiled. "This is going to be fun," she said.

Sinclair returned the smile and gave her a quick fist bump.

Sinclair waited for the last of the guests to file in. He had a couple more fast words with Valero. They spoke with an ease and familiarity that suggested they'd met before. Sinclair shoulder-clapped him, and they agreed to a lunch. While she wasn't trying to eavesdrop on her ex-boss's conversation, listening without looking like you were listening was a valuable skill, and she was as much of an outsider here as Valero.

"All right, let's get started, shall we?" Sinclair waited the obligatory three seconds and then continued. "There's water and coffee over there on the table." He motioned to the two pitchers and glasses. "I apologize in advance. The coffee isn't Philz, but what do you want? We're the government." Polite, perfunctory laughter and knowing nods punctuated his punch line. "Before I turn this over to Katrina, let's do a quick round of introductions so we know who's who in the zoo. I'm Kurt Sinclair, I'm the ASAC here and will try my best to stay out of your way." Sinclair favored the room with a rakish smile. "I say that, but I've got a pretty deep background in the subject matter. Before coming here, I was the legal attaché at the Hague and ostensibly attached to Europol to help coordinate transnational gem trafficking. Prior to that, I'd done a tour in Kabul, which is where I was first introduced to the problem that gem trafficking presents in supporting terror networks. I can tell you firsthand what we're going to start here today has some very real national security implications for our country. Special Agent Danzig," he extended a hand in her direction, "was my number two at the Hague and was and still is the Bureau's chief representative to the transnational task force. All this is to say, I'll help in any way I can, and my Rolodex is totally open to you." He nodded. Sinclair motioned with a hand to the CHP officer to his left. "Lieutenant Brian Valero is here representing California Highway Patrol. It's the strength of one of Valero's informants that really kicked this off."

Valero brought a handful of CHP officers with him, whom he then introduced. Sinclair continued when he was finished. "Special Agent Matt Riordan is one of mine. Matt is currently making waves on our white-collar squad. I knew him by reputation before I got here as one of the most dogged fraud cops in the Bureau."

Danzig had heard of Riordan too—a good cop, but "one of the best in the Bureau" was overselling it a bit, she thought. Sinclair introduced three other special agents in the room and Preston Turner, the Assistant US Attorney who would be prosecuting the case.

"Finally, again, the star of the show today, Katrina Danzig. Katrina's with the Gem and Jewelry Program's Transnational Task Force out of the New York division. She's on loan to us for as long as we need, right?"

"That's correct," she said.

"Katrina is one of the toughest investigators I know, and

we'll all probably be working for her someday. SAC Lattimore and I both agree that she's the right person to take point on this, so she'll have operational control of the investigation." Sinclair favored her with another rakish smile and returned to his seat at the opposite head of the table.

That was new news. But Sinclair always liked to spring surprises that way; he thought it was funny as hell.

"Okay, Katrina, why don't you tell us why we're all here," Sinclair said.

Danzig stood, straightened her jacket, and grabbed the small remote on the table. "Thanks for that, Kurt. Matt, Brian, gentlemen, it's good to meet you all in person, and thank you for your time this morning. Thank you, as well, for all the background info you provided. I've incorporated the most relevant pieces into my presentation today. This is a pretty complicated affair, and I think it makes the most sense for us to review these events chronologically so we all have the same sight picture." She advanced the slide, and it showed a photo of the Carlton InterContinental Hotel in Cannes.

"Three days ago, a single thief robbed a jewelry exhibition at this hotel in Cannes. It was originally reported to be eighty-five million dollars, however, a statement released by the collection's insurer has placed that closer to one hundred and forty-five million." One of the CHP officers whistled. "We have a CI who believes that he can identify the thief as one Gentleman Jack Burdette." Danzig advanced the slides. Reginald LeGrande's mugshot appeared, along with his incarceration dates, significant crimes, and the conviction that sent him to prison.

Danzig gave a nod to Lieutenant Valero. "This first bit is courtesy of CHP. Brian, I think I've got everything captured here correctly, but please jump in if there's anything I've missed. Reginald LeGrande is a career jewel thief, mostly active in the greater Los Angeles area with occasional activity in Reno, Las Vegas, Phoenix, and here in San Francisco. LeGrande was arrested and later convicted for robbing a Beverly Hills diamond wholesaler in February 2001. He was sentenced to ten years at CSP San Quentin. Almost immediately, LeGrande tried whatever he could through his lawyer to get out. He was over fifty and didn't think he'd last long inside. Eventually, he got onto CHP's radar and struck a deal. This was to inform on current criminal activities and known associates." Danzig acknowledged Valero with a nod.

Valero said, "That's exactly right, Katrina." He then turned to face the table. "It's worth noting that LeGrande's lawyer is also crooked. LAPD nailed him for money laundering in '06. He was disbarred and served a five-year stint in Lompoc."

"Now, in exchange for his release," Danzig said, picking up her thread, "LeGrande agreed to become a CHP asset. Under the conditions of his agreement, LeGrande would provide material knowledge of open, unsolved cases and would offer to set up active suspects in sting operations." Danzig advanced the presentation a slide, and it displayed a list of open jewelry thefts with their dates and locations going back to the early nineties. "Based on LeGrande's information, CHP was able to close eleven unsolved thefts since 1996."

"That's right. Not all of these happened in our jurisdiction, but we were able to do some good cooperation with sister agencies. Bought us a lot of goodwill," Valero said, nodding. "CHP considers this a good trade."

"While they were running LeGrande, CHP discovered another skill he'd picked up: forgery. This is how he got onto the FBI's radar. LeGrande had become a fairly competent passport and identity maker." She motioned to Riordan. "Matt's team believes that given the tradecraft and skill they've seen him apply, LeGrande has likely been doing this since before his incarceration."

"How did we find out?" Sinclair asked.

Riordan leaned forward. "His name first came up in that sting we did last year when we did that passport-for-hire scam. One of our suspects rolled on him pretty fast. I ran the name and came up with the hit that he was a CHP asset. So, I called Lieutenant Valero and filled him in on what I knew. We didn't have anything we could charge him on, but I shared that he was linked to a passport forgery scheme."

Sinclair nodded, satisfied. Danzig continued. "Knowing that he was still dirty, CHP began putting the screws to LeGrande, telling him that he needed to give them a bigger fish. So, LeGrande gave them Gentleman Jack Burdette."

Danzig paused a second for effect and flashed her eyes between Riordan and Valero.

"Burdette is suspected in at least fifty jewelry heists and several banks in Europe going back to the late nineties. To the best of our and Europol's knowledge, Burdette has never been questioned, arrested, or fingerprinted by any law enforcement agency. He is believed to travel under a variety of aliases, rarely using the same ones twice and never sequentially. He's also an expert in disguise. This is according to LeGrande, who claims to be Burdette's mentor, fixer, and logistician."

"Never been arrested? That seems unlikely," Riordan said.

"Not really. LeGrande tells us that Burdette worked almost exclusively in Europe since the mid-nineties, and he's believed to take only midsized scores. Small, mostly independent jewelry stores and usually not in major cities. There's specula-tion that he was involved in a bank job in Turkey in 2005, but I find that unlikely."

Riordan acquiesced a nod but didn't appear convinced.

"Burdette is incredibly well trained and a meticulous planner. He usually works with the same crew and only with people that he vets in advance. Burdette is believed to have been in the School of Turin." Danzig broke eye contact with Riordan, looked up, and addressed the entire room, as though she were giving a lecture. "For those unfamiliar, the School of Turin was an organization of thieves who operated in Turin, Italy, in the nineties. They were led by Niccoló Bartolo. If that name is familiar to you, it's because he was the one behind the 2003 Antwerp Diamond Centre job. Bartolo's group operated throughout northern Italy, western France, and Switzerland. Bartolo handpicked each one, and most of them had a particular skill set—safes, alarms, computers, electronics. They are known for several daring, high-profile jobs, but Burdette is believed to have been on the 1997 Fiat payroll heist. The original School of Turin was broken up in 1997 as the result of a six-month undercover operation run by the Italian state police. One of their officers, Giovanni Castro, was the undercover and knew Burdette personally. Burdette escaped. Almost everything official that we have now comes from Inspector Castro. As far as we know, Burdette is the only foreigner known to have operated in that group."

"How did you come by all of this?" Riordan asked, now genuinely curious.

"Good question. During my European assignment, I met Inspector Castro, who was on an exchange tour with INTERPOL and a task force member. Castro was based in Turin and was a special investigator targeting, among other things, the School. A Turin mafia captain had placed a hit on Castro, but he was warned off by an informant and fled before they got him. A sympathetic judge had Castro transferred from the state police to the Guardia di Finanza, which is the Italian economic police. He's still with them today."

"Thanks."

"We've since corroborated this with other sources as well," Sinclair offered.

"So, as I said, LeGrande was getting nervous that he hadn't provided a substantial lead in some time, so he named Burdette, who he trained, mentored, and was close friends with. By the way, LeGrande lives in a two-million-dollar oceanfront home in Long Beach."

"He also maintains a one-bedroom shit box apartment, mostly for his parole officer's benefit," Valero said. "He's got a bogus job punching a clock at a local construction company. We're working with Long Beach PD to roll that operation up when we bust LeGrande."

"How long did CHP suspect that LeGrande was still dirty?" Sinclair asked.

"Oh, we never thought he was clean, Kurt," Valero said with a wry smile. "But between the cases he allowed us to close and the other people he's set up for us over the years, it's been an acceptable trade. Now, I think the passport fraud is a different level. That's got broader implications than knocking over jewelry stores."

"Now, on to the reason we're all here." Danzig paused for a side conversation to settle and advanced her slide. The title was "Jack Burdette." There was a small box for known aliases, and beneath that the heists he was implicated or suspected in. On the left side of the slide was a picture of the ubiquitous cartoon bandit from the neighborhood watch signs, beneath it the caption "artist's rendering," which drew a short laugh. "It's funny, but that is about as good as we have to go on. Burdette works mostly in Europe and typically with the same group of people, which is organized by LeGrande. He earned his nickname 'Gentleman Jack' because he treats his people very well. Everyone gets an equal share, and they tend to be fairly loyal to him. We—and I'm including INTERPOL and

Europol in this—have never been able to get anyone to flip on him. That's one of the reasons we've had so little to go on regarding physical appearance. That is, until recently. Castro had actually been running a CI that made his way into Burdette's organization. His name is Ozren Stolar. He's Serbian, former special forces, and believed to be a member of the Pink Panthers. Stolar is currently missing and is believed to have fled. Interestingly, Stolar was also in the employ of Reginald LeGrande and is one of the thieves LeGrande ran."

Riordan looked across the table at Valero, pen dangling between his thumb and forefinger like a broken pointer. "Didn't LeGrande give you guys any physical evidence to prove that he knew Burdette?"

Valero broke in, "When he first told us about Burdette, we said that it sounded like something he'd made up to keep us interested. That's when he spilled about the passports and organizing the crews. We told him that we wouldn't prosecute him for the forgery if this Burdette lead turned out to be legit. That's when we contacted the Bureau. This was in March. He said that he'll turn everything over to us as long as he gets a written guarantee of immunity."

Riordan started, "So how—"

"Anything we provide will only be for the State of California. He won't be protected from federal prosecution. We didn't tell him that, of course."

"No, but a lawyer will know that," the AUSA added. "Does he have counsel?"

"Not that we're aware of," Valero said, "but we should assume he does. We'll vet his lawyer a little more closely this time." Valero smirked.

Turner looked over to Sinclair, clearly concerned. "Kurt, I do need to advise you that this part sounds shaky to me."

Sinclair said he understood and agreed, but then asked Danzig to please continue.

"So where does that leave us?" She vocalized the thought in everyone's mind. "Monday, LeGrande contacted Lieutenant Valero and said he had reason to believe that Jack Burdette was behind the theft at the Carlton InterContinental Hotel in Cannes over the weekend. French police also reported a triple homicide the day of the robbery about two miles from the Carlton. The victims were known accomplices of Burdette, but we aren't sure what that connection is yet, if any, and neither do the French. It's a strange coincidence, to be sure, but Burdette is explicitly nonviolent."

"Hundred million dollars makes it pretty easy to forget that rule," Valero said.

"How certain are we that Burdette pulled this?" Sinclair asked. Danzig knew she was teeing him up, using an old lawyer's tactic to establish doubt and then blow it away with fact.

"On the surface, the job doesn't fit his MO. One of the reasons Burdette has kept such a low profile for so long is that he only takes medium-sized scores."

Valero said, "LeGrande says Burdette has these rules he operates by and that he never breaks them. The first and most important one is that Burdette doesn't do big jobs. He takes three or four moderate scores a year, exclusively in Europe. LeGrande figures Burdette nets between two fifty to three hundred a year. He launders that offshore in a tax shelter and then invests it domestically. He makes a good bit off the stock market."

Danzig stepped backward toward the screen and pointed at the cartoon. "This is what we had to go on until Monday." She tapped a button on the remote, and the neighborhood watch cartoon dissolved and revealed a picture of a handsome, middle-aged man with brown hair, brown eyes, and a youngish face. The picture was professionally taken and appeared to be some kind of corporate headshot. "LeGrande said that Burdette has been living under the alias Frank Fischer, a winemaker in Sonoma County, for the last several years. This picture was taken from promotional material available in the winery's press packet." She paused a moment to let everyone in the room fix the image in their minds. "Frank Fischer allegedly made a killing in the tech boom in the late nineties and early 2000s. When he retired around '06, he bought a winery. Fischer was in Europe on business when the Carlton was robbed. Riordan and his partner, Special Agent Chapman," Danzig nodded to the agent, "went to Fischer's winery on Monday to question him, but he wasn't there. They told us he was in Switzerland."

"Wasn't there a prison break in Switzerland over the weekend?" Sinclair asked.

"That's right. Two men known to be Pink Panthers escaped from a Swiss prison on Friday. I should mention that the leading theory at Europol is that the Pink Panthers are behind the Carlton job. However, the Panthers source their membership almost exclusively from former Yugoslavian and Soviet Bloc countries, most of them have military training. Again, Ozren Stolar is believed to have been a member of that group and has been on Burdette's crew once or twice, but that is believed to be Burdette's only connection to them."

"Still, this is a little too coincidental for my tastes," Sinclair said. Others around the table nodded. "Katrina," he said, scribbling something down on the notepad in front of him. "I'll take action to call my folks in Europe and see what the talk is. I'm wondering if maybe Burdette helped get these guys out of prison."

She nodded in reply. That was a red herring, but she

wasn't going to tell him that in public. "So," Danzig said. "We have the statements from an informant known to be a reliable source who allegedly has photographs of the suspect in his possession. The suspect was in Europe at the time of the theft. We have another informant who can corroborate another of Burdette's thefts and provide visual ID, but he's currently in the wind, and we'll need to locate him. I think we have enough for a warrant." Danzig waited for a few moments to let the room absorb it. In particular, she was focused on Turner. The attorney's expression was unreadable, probably something he picked up for court.

Sinclair leaned back in his chair at the far end of the table. "Brian, does CHP think LeGrande is a flight risk?"

The tall patrolman turned in his chair to face the Assistant Special Agent in Charge. "Without a doubt. He definitely has the means. We assume that he's got a bug-out bag ready to go with a clean passport and money. But will he? I've always believed that'd be a last resort. LeGrande likes being the Duke of Long Beach. He's got this little game he's running down there, and I think he means to keep it up. LeGrande doesn't think we know about this side hustle. He'll feed us people every so often. They're good enough to keep us interested and to satisfy his obligations to the State of California, but we know they're basically minnows to middle fish. He's been using us to take down his competition and, we believe, save choice scores for his crews. We haven't been able to prove the latter part yet, which is one of the reasons that he's still on the loose. But, as I said before, we're cleaning up a lot of crews and closing old cases, so again, we think this was a good trade." Valero paused and took a drink from the bottle of water in front of him. "The forgery racket is a new wrinkle, and I think this is really where LeGrande has been making his money over the last several years. He doesn't think we have intel on it."

"And you're running him from headquarters?" Sinclair asked. Valero was based out of CHP's headquarters in Sacramento.

"I am, but I'm keeping Southern Division looped in as well as Long Beach PD. We've got a good relationship with them."

"Okay, " Sinclair said. "What does winning look like for him? What's LeGrande's end game?"

"He wants his slate cleaned to end his obligation with us."

"And you expect his intention is to keep his operations up once he does that?"

"Without question." Valero smiled, but it was more a humorless crack in his face. "We have no reason to believe that he'll stop if he gets a deal from the state. We'd need to launch a new investigation to break open whatever racket he's got, and that will take time. Plus, whatever Burdette has done is outside of our jurisdiction. You're in a better position to nail LeGrande for forgery, and that could have broader implications, depending on who he's making passports for. That lets us all take him off the streets now, and it's a cleaner prosecution since he's been a CI of ours for so long."

"Bet the CT guys would love to take a crack at him too," Riordan said. "See who he's making passports for."

Sinclair turned back to the front of the room. "It's your call, Katrina."

But Turner interjected before she could speak. "I'm not entirely convinced yet that Fischer and Burdette are the same person. LeGrande has concocted a pretty elaborate story, and this Fischer seems like an odd fit for it. I think it's very possible that LeGrande has the relationship that he claims with Burdette, but I also think there's a strong possibility that this could be a false flag. This feels like he could be protecting his friend."

"Why would he frame an innocent man," Sinclair asked, "let alone go through the trouble of finding someone to be a patsy?"

"We don't know that Frank Fischer is innocent. If LeGrande knows him enough to set him up, he's probably an enemy of his." Turner's face was twisted in a concerned frown. "Now, I will allow that LeGrande fingering an innocent person —innocent of jewelry theft, at any rate—won't hold up in court. And it seems like an odd move, so I'd want to understand from CHP a little more why we think he's doing this."

"Well, we investigate this Fischer and figure out he's dirty, arrest him on whatever that is," Riordan said. "Takes him off the board. That seems to be a lot of LeGrande's pattern."

Danzig was losing control of the briefing. A bunch of alpha personalities were diving in and directing it toward their own agendas, rather than focusing on the task at hand. She'd experienced this before, particularly when briefing very senior agents in the Bureau. The story here was not LeGrande. They had an opportunity to bust one of the most prolific and elusive jewelry thieves in the last twenty years. And if Burdette really was behind the Carlton heist, he had just taken down the biggest score in history.

"I'm sorry, Agent Danzig," Turner said, "but I can't authorize an arrest warrant on what you've presented here today. If you had this other CI, this," he looked down to his notes, "Ozren Stolar? I might be able to move forward. At least then we could have him back up what LeGrande was saying. But since LeGrande has a well-established track record of using law enforcement to set up rivals, I just don't believe we can arrest this Frank Fischer."

"Let me interview him," Danzig said hurriedly, before

anyone else could jump in. "I agree it appears thin, but this is how cases start. We have a CI who is offering up information on a major crime. We have an obligation to run that to ground." Danzig stopped herself when she saw a dark flash go across Turner's face. *Careful*, she told herself. *Pissing off the AUSA is not going to get you a warrant.*

Sinclair turned in his chair to face the attorney. "I'm comfortable with this approach, Preston. I agree with all of your concerns, but if this Burdette really is as slippery as they say, we've got no reason to believe he'll stick around now that he's got a hundred and forty million on his hands. I trust Katrina's judgment on this, but I'll have some of my people go with as well. They'll interview Fischer, probe his alibi, and then we'll make a call."

"But on what grounds?" Turner said. "We can't just go bothering citizens because a known criminal gave us a name."

How does this guy think cases are made? Katrina asked herself, trying to maintain composure.

"Kid gloves, Agent Danzig," Turner admonished. "If it turns out that this Frank Fischer is dirty, we will prosecute him to the fullest extent of the law." Danzig had to restrain herself from rolling her eyes. She wondered if federal prosecutors were taught in law school that they always had to use that line in these situations. "But," Turner said, "I do not want the FBI harassing a legitimate businessman. Are we clear." Turner's tone clearly conveyed it wasn't a question.

"Yes, sir, we are clear."

Sinclair stood. "Everyone, I want to thank you for your time here today. Brian, especially yours. We wouldn't be here today without your assistance and your cooperation."

"We appreciate that," the lieutenant said. "What about LeGrande?"

"Let's run this to ground. If LeGrande's information proves

to be true and Frank Fischer *is* Jack Burdette, we'll need to weigh his value as an informant with the value of the collar. I suspect there will be some kind of a plea deal to be made, but we take passport forgery and identity theft very seriously. He won't walk on those things."

"Good. I'm glad we agree."

"Of course, you'll be free to get him on whatever the State of California wants to throw his way. If LeGrande's information on Fischer is not correct, then we should reconvene and see how we want to proceed." Sinclair turned back to Danzig. "Katrina, is there anything else?"

Danzig scanned the room for a moment, watching the eyes track back to her. Her presentation didn't go exactly the way she wanted, and these guys were being way too cautious. But she had a chance to look this Frank Fischer in the eyes and start poking holes in his story. If he was the guy, she knew she could unravel that. Federal investigations usually took months to get started, and they had an opportunity to possibly make an arrest within a few days. Danzig would take what she could get.

"I think we're good here," she said.

24

Burdette landed at SFO in the early afternoon, but his body had little clue of where on Earth it was. He'd cleared immigration and customs using a passport Reginald knew nothing about, so whomever he was working with wouldn't know what identity Jack used reentering the country. Rusty maintained several for him to use in emergencies, like if one of his identities was burned. This was entirely a precaution, because Jack spent the entire flight working through what he believed Reginald's game to be, and he was more convinced than ever that his initial intuition was correct.

There was no FBI.

Reginald was running a rather elaborate con.

Forging the credentials would be no problem for him, and Jack knew that badges from every conceivable law enforcement agency could be had if you knew where to look. It was a smart play on Reginald's part, Jack had to give him credit for that. When most people were confronted with seemingly legitimate authority figures, they tended to fall in line. Reginald had already given Jack the threat. Now he was simply showing part of his hand to establish that he was for real. This was Reginald's way of scaring Jack into compliance.

Jack's first call leaving the airport was to Megan. Hers was the only voice he'd wanted to hear that entire interminable flight, and he felt like he was actually going to crawl out of his skin at times because he couldn't talk to her and knew it would be hours before he could.

"Yeah, I just landed," he said after her greeting. She sounded worn, worried.

"Is everything going to be all right, Frank? I'm...I'm scared."

Jack's first reaction was, *There's nothing to be scared about. It's being handled.* On the continuum of things Jack could be threatened with, blackmail was the least of the sins. But he forced himself to remember that this was the first time Megan was faced with a criminal act. Well, Paul Sharpe embezzling from them, but he didn't exactly cut a threatening figure. He was just an asshole in Tommy Bahama who took money out of the collection plate when no one was looking.

"Well..." His eyes flicked to the rearview to clear left before changing lanes and accelerating, the throaty supercharged V8 opening up in a familiar growl. Not the same as the Maserati, though. "I think it will be."

"Why would he do something like this?" After a moment, Megan added, "Your business partner."

"Well, he's an ex-partner, for one thing." Jack paused. He didn't want to get too deep into a lie about Reginald; that kind of thing might be hard to walk back later. "It's no secret that I made a lot of money in the stock market, and God knows they made such a big deal out of that when we started releasing wines. Remember the piece that *Spectator* did when we released the '09 Peregrine last year?" That had been the first hit of big publicity Kingfisher got, and at the time it had scared

Jack more than nearly anything in his life. He hadn't wanted to do the piece at all, but Megan unknowingly forced his hand. She knew a reporter with the magazine and called him to let him know they were releasing their first high-end Cabernet. The reporter immediately picked up on Frank Fischer's back-story of another wealthy tech guy buying a winery and what made *Frank Fischer* any different. Obviously, Jack hadn't wanted that kind of scrutiny but was forced into it. His para-noia, however well justified, wasn't necessary. The piece was favorable, and it was as much about Kingfisher's debut as a winery as it was another rich guy dabbling in winemaking. During the interview, he'd deflected questions about the companies Frank Fischer was supposed to have worked for. Jack portrayed Fischer as a recluse who was singularly focused on winemaking and redirected any discussion about his business. He wondered if that's how Reginald figured out where he was.

"He figured me for an easy mark," Jack continued. "I've got a lot to lose. He could have hacked my email to see when I was going to be out of town to pull that FBI routine. Or someone was just following me. If you think about the money involved, it's not that farfetched."

Megan was silent for a few moments. Jack could see her brow creasing the way it did when she was thinking through something. Despite his exhaustion and foul mood, he smiled.

"So you don't think that was really the FBI?"

"No, I think it was someone posing as the FBI to get me to do what they want." Jack paused. He knew he needed to tread carefully here. The logic of the con was that unless Jack complied, LeGrande would tell law enforcement about Jack's alter ego. There was no logical reason the FBI would be inves-tigating Frank Fischer, so all this hinged on Megan believing

Reginald was attempting a scare tactic. But it was thin and he knew it.

"The guy you spoke to at the winery, the one who said he was a distributor."

"Yeah, what about him? He gave me a kind of a creepy vibe."

"Well, when I spoke to him, he said that I had two days to pay him a couple million dollars or he was going to send the FBI after me."

"What!" The words erupted from Megan's mouth before she probably even knew what she was saying. "But what interest would the FBI have in you, or in us? Did you...is there something you're not telling me?"

Now there's a question without an easy answer. Only literally everything about me except that I like wine, Jack thought sourly.

"It's because I keep so much money offshore. Everything is perfectly legal," Jack said. *Not really.* "I have to bring my money into a US-registered bank in order to use it, so I pay taxes on that like anyone else. I've been trying to piece together what I think the scheme is. I think he figures that if he told the IRS that I was keeping a bunch of money offshore, they'd start an investigation and it'd cost me millions and years in court to resolve it. So, cheaper to pay him now to keep him quiet."

As he thought through it, Jack actually thought that might be part of Reginald's scheme, actually.

"Why didn't you tell me? We have to call the police. Right now. Frank, this is extortion."

"Meg, I didn't tell you because I didn't want you to worry while I was gone. I also didn't want you contacting the police without me. I just wanted to be here when we did it, is all."

"Well, I'm pretty fucking worried now, and this isn't the time for a bunch of libertarian bullshit."

"It's not..." Jack stopped himself, redirected. "I know, and I'm sorry."

This was all happening so fast, and what Jack really needed was time and space to think. The decisions he made in the next few hours would impact not only him but also his employees, potentially for the rest of their lives. They were all good people who didn't deserve getting pulled into his conflict with Reginald. Two people were already dead because of that. Well, technically five, but three of them Jack had a hard time feeling sorry for.

Jack would not allow anyone else he cared about to be injured because of Reginald LeGrande.

Jack justified keeping his money in offshore tax shelters because Frank Fischer was a kind of hyper-libertarian Robin Hood. Fischer didn't agree with how the government spent his money, so he was going to try and limit how much of it they could get. Megan thought this was batshit crazy but most of the time wrote him off as an eccentric millionaire.

"Everything I do with my money is perfectly legal. Hugh wouldn't do business with me if it wasn't. Besides, the government is taxing the hell out of the winery, and every time I put my money into that, they're getting their cut." Jack was silent for a short while as he considered his next move. "The next time they show up, I'll have Hugh and maybe a sheriff's deputy waiting."

Megan was quiet again for a while as well. Then, "Does that mean we can finally call the police?"

"I promise I will talk to them."

Jack began to calm somewhat, and though he was still on edge, he was not as precariously balanced as he was when he and Megan started their conversation. Maybe he bought himself some crucial time, even if it was just an hour or two, to think through a plan. Then Megan said, "But the FBI guys...

they were asking about someone named Jack Burdette. They said you know him. Who is he, and what does he have to do with all this?"

Goddamn it, Jack mouthed, wishing he could shout it. In his haste to wrap this up quickly, he'd completely forgotten that Reginald's fake feds had mentioned him by name. That was Reginald's bowshot, that he knew about Jack's double life. Shit. Whatever he'd just built up with Megan was now unraveling. "I'm not sure what any of that is about," he said at length. "I think it's part of whatever con they're setting up. Look, I'm piecing this together with the information I have." That much was true, at least. "I should be up there in about ninety minutes. Why don't you let Corky handle the closing and meet me at my house. We'll talk this through once I get cleaned up, okay?"

"Okay, Frank," she said tentatively.

They said their goodbyes and disconnected. Jack called Hugh Coughlin.

"I was wondering when I was going to hear from you," his attorney said in a loaded voice when he picked up the phone. Hugh had a law degree from UC Berkley and an MBA specializing in the wine industry from UC Davis. He was one of the foremost experts on the mechanics and the laws of the business and hadn't spent one brain cell on criminal defense since law school. Which was in the seventies. Coughlin stood on the shorter side and was edging in on the pudgier end of the spectrum, which wasn't surprising since his clients were all winemakers and restaurateurs. However, people who discounted him because of his stature did so at their own risk. Coughlin paid for his undergraduate degree with the GI Bill after serving in the Marines in Vietnam. Jack had seen people underestimate him on occasion, and Coughlin had subsequently taken their heads off and hadn't stopped there. Hugh was a dogged and relentless negotiator. Reginald's fake FBI agents were in for a fight. Even though Hugh had never practiced criminal law, he at least *knew* the law, which was more than could be said about the opposition. Jack was confident that Hugh would make short work of them.

"Busy couple of days," Jack said honestly.

"I'll bet," he said. When Jack didn't say anything else, Hugh opened up. "Now you want to tell me what the holy fuck is going on here, Frank? Why in the hell am I getting panicked phone calls from Megan that the FBI is at your winery? And who is this Jack Burdette?"

"Hugh, someone is trying to blackmail me. They dressed up a couple thugs to look like the gestapo and sent them into the tasting room to scare me into paying."

"Well, how the hell do you know all that?" Hugh snapped, not necessarily at Jack—Frank, rather—but more at the logic of his response.

"Because the blackmailer told me, Hugh," Jack deadpanned. "Guy shows up on Sunday pretending to be a distributor and gets Megan to call me. Once he gets me on the phone, he says that I need to pay him ten million dollars or he's going to tell the FBI that I launder money overseas."

"Goddamn it, I knew that tax haven shit was going to get you in trouble, Frank. But you never goddamn listen."

Jack smiled in spite of himself and the situation. Hugh Coughlin, who looked every inch a wine industry lawyer, was still a true vulgarian down to his bones. He could paint a tapestry of profanity like an old-world master and turn a soccer hooligan blue. "The blackmailer," Jack said, "to prove he's legit, sends a couple guys pretending to be FBI the next day. I don't think it'd be all that hard to get a fake badge and credentials. Christ, you could probably get an actual badge on eBay, for that matter. Even if it was fake, our guys wouldn't know the difference."

"We need to get the police involved, Frank. And we probably need to talk to a criminal attorney. We should've done it already."

Jack had already thought of this. Call Reginald on his bluff and double down on the Frank Fischer legend. Of course, Reginald would just hand them the passport photos he had, recount their years of debriefings, which for all Jack knew had been recorded. It was an option, but not a good one.

"Hugh, I held off on calling the police until I got home. I couldn't manage this from Europe. Don't lecture me about letting people do the work for me again." The words came out with a raw, unvarnished anger that Jack had not only not seen coming but also had not intended in any way. "I'm sorry to snap at you. I'm just worn pretty thin. We've got this thing with Paul that's already out in the open. If people find out that I'm being blackmailed too, they're going to think that something real is going on."

"Something real *is* going on," the old attorney said in a soft but stern tone. "Frank, are you being totally up front with me? Why have you been so reluctant to call the police?"

"Yes, I am being up front with you." But when he said the words, it brought him a heartsick pain. Hugh had been good to him, had mentored him in the wine business the way a father would. How many nights had they spent in Hugh's backyard or walking the grounds at Kingfisher? Over countless bottles of wine, the cagey old lawyer schooled Jack in the mysteries of this business, lessons that would've taken Jack a lifetime to learn on his own. The two formed a deep and lasting bond over the last ten years, and it was Coughlin, again not unlike a father, who tried to point out to Jack what should be so obvious—that Megan McKinney was far and beyond the best thing in his life. Lying to him in this way was as tangible and visceral a betrayal as it was consummate.

"I promise I will call the police," Jack said, echoing what he'd said to Megan just a few minutes before. "Look, I've just flown across half the world. I need to get some sleep. I will talk to you first thing in the morning, and we'll figure out what to do next, okay?"

"Okay, Frank."

Jack drove on in silence through the rolling, golden hills bathed in the orange light of evening. His windows were down, and the rush of crisp, fresh air felt good on his face. He'd made stupid, uncharacteristic mistakes over the past two days, and he could not think of a way to undo that damage or even minimize it. Nor was the right next step clear to him. He'd backed himself into a corner with Hugh and Megan because any normal person in this situation would contact the police and report being blackmailed. Jack could have used that but would have needed to make up a thing to be blackmailed about, because he certainly couldn't tell them the truth. Then he'd be living under the specter of a false secret that would be worth several million dollars to a made-up blackmailer. That was a long lie to keep up.

Now the two closest people in his life were expecting him to contact the police because it's what *Frank Fischer* would do. There was no logical, rational reason for him not to do that.

Jack cried out a deep, bellowing roar of frustration, fear, and confusion. He screamed because he didn't know what else to do. It was a raw and anguished sound, like that of an animal. Not one that had been tortured or cornered, but rather one that had been separated from its pack and did not know the way home.

Jack continued for a time trying to calm down. He was failing.

His phone buzzed, and the number that flashed across the car's infotainment screen was not one he recognized. Jack rolled up the windows and closed the sunroof. "Hello, this is Frank Fischer," he said.

"Good evening, Mr. Fischer. My name is Special Agent Katrina Danzig with the Federal Bureau of Investigation, and I'd like to ask you a few questions. What is a convenient time for me to meet you?"

25

Jack Burdette needed a drink.

And so did Frank Fischer.

Burdette rolled slowly to his home on the ridge over-looking Sonoma because every inexorable foot brought him closer to realities that he did not want to face and questions for which he had no answers.

Jack could no longer see the game Reginald was playing, because it appeared as though the woman he just spoke to on the phone was very much a federal agent. It was hard to envision Reginald LeGrande informing to the FBI, but Jack just couldn't see that it could be anything else. If Reginald was indeed running a game, Jack was wholly unable to see it for what it was.

Jack sat in the Audi's dark cockpit for a long time, pressed back into the seat because of the angle of his driveway. It made him feel like he was strapped to a rocket on a launch pad he couldn't control, headed for a destination that he didn't know.

The air was cool and light when he exited the car, but it brought him no comfort and did nothing to calm his racing blood. Jack slowly trudged into his house, lifelessly showered, and then changed into a pair of loose-fitting jeans and a light blue Kingfisher T-shirt.

He walked into the kitchen and pulled a Robert Biale Pagani Ranch Zinfandel from his in-counter storage unit, grabbed two glasses, and walked barefoot out to his deck. Jack poured himself a glass and leaned against the railing, watching the sunset over the Sonoma Valley. The sky was a darkening orange, and already the valley below the mountains was fading to a dusky blue. Evening light bathed the mountains on the far side of the valley in a crown of fire. Below him, the trees and the vines on the slope that his wooden deck lorded over stood silent in the cool, burgeoning night. How many more times would he get to enjoy this view?

If this was a con, Danzig gave a command performance. Jack pushed back where he could test her, and she parried well each time. She even told him that she wanted him to come down to the Federal Building in San Francisco tomorrow to answer some questions, strictly voluntary, of course. That was an incredible gamble for a con artist, because the entire thing folded if Jack called them on the bluff. He thought through the scenarios and realized there were any number of ways they could play it to avoid going into the Federal Building that also got him out of Sonoma for the entire day, thereby separating Jack from anyone who might help. *Still*, he thought.

Jack told her calmly that he wasn't going to the Federal Building. If she wanted to talk to him, then Danzig would have to come to his house, where Jack would have his attorney present, as well a Sonoma County Sheriff's deputy to prove that Danzig actually was a federal agent. Danzig gave him a variation on that universal cop line about how only guilty people asked for lawyers and that she could assure him she was, in fact, a federal agent. Danzig also said that if he liked, she would call the Sonoma County Sheriff's Office herself and save him the trouble. Or the state police, if that was his preference. Jack responded with Frank Fischer's long-held distrust of the government to counter the former and something about the correlation between the quantities of nickels in relation to the number of times someone posed as a government agent to scam him out of money. They finally agreed that the meeting would take place at Hugh Coughlin's office the next morning.

Jack did a reverse number lookup on her number, but it came up blank. Then he called up the website for the FBI's San Francisco field office and dialed the number. He went through a series of prompts asking him if he had a tip or was asking for general information before finally getting to an operator. He asked for Katrina Danzig. The voice on the phone said it was after duty hours but would relay a message if it was urgent. Jack said it wasn't and would call back in the morning.

Jack realized they probably wouldn't confirm or deny the identity of an agent over the phone for security reasons, but this didn't leave him any more settled. The odds were starting to stack up in Danzig's favor that she was who she said she was.

Reginald was really pushing this thing all the way.

Jack began to puzzle out the cold, Machiavellian logic behind Reginald's giving Jack to the feds. If they arrested him for tax evasion or money laundering, in Reginald's mind that probably meant that the Carlton score would be hidden somewhere. He was counting on Jack to hide the stones somewhere, probably in his house. God knows, Jack preached to Reginald numerous times over the years that one of the reasons you never took big scores was that you couldn't move all those jewels at once. You had to sell them slowly over a span of years both to avoid arousing suspicion and because few people had the resources for making big buys. Knowing how strongly Jack felt about this, he'd assume that Jack either had the jewels on him now, having smuggled them into the US somehow, or that he'd stashed them in Europe somewhere. Either of these would be solvable problems from Reginald's perspective, if Jack was behind bars.

Jack told his attorney of his phone call with the alleged Special Agent Danzig. Jack said he didn't know why the FBI had contacted him and said they hadn't even told *him* what it was about. They agreed to meet an hour before the agents arrived.

He took a drink and tried to forget it for now, knowing full well that he couldn't. Jack hoped that he could at least push it below the surface of his mind.

With his free hand, Jack texted Megan, and she said she'd be over in a few minutes.

Jack drank slowly. Equal parts of him longed to see her and dreaded her arrival. He thought of hard truths.

Megan arrived in her beat-up Wrangler, wearing dusty jeans and a shirt that was faded from the sun. She wore her hair up in an absent-minded ponytail, and there were traces of pink on her cheeks from being outside all day. Jack met her on his front step. "I left as soon as we closed up shop," she said.

"I told you Corky could handle it."

"We're running a business, Frank," she said in a scolding tone.

This was already not going the way he'd hoped. Jack said, "Come on in," and waved her toward the door. Megan looked down at the Kingfisher logo on his shirt and smiled. "I love that shirt," she said as she passed, patting the winery's emblem on his chest. Her mood seeming to lighten, and Jack felt an electric surge when she touched him. "That was such a fun day."

The shirt was from the release party for their 2010 vintage.

Jack led her into the kitchen. The orange-red Spanish tile was cool beneath his feet. Jack's kitchen was a huge open space in the center of a long room that was mostly windows. There was a dining area with a long table in an open space to the left of the kitchen. To the right was a space just large enough for two Manhattan chairs to look out of the windows that gave a two-sided view of the Sonoma Valley.

They stepped out onto the back deck.

"Will you please tell me what in the hell is going on? First the FBI shows up and wants to talk to you, and then you tell me that it's some kind of scam. Frank, I don't even know what to think anymore."

"Well," he said slowly. "It's complicated, but I think I can explain it."

"I don't see what's complicated. Either the FBI is looking for you or they aren't."

Jack poured two glasses, and Megan immediately put up two hands.

"I don't want a drink, Frank. I want you to tell me why the FBI was at our winery. Did you do something? Is this about that stupid offshore stuff?"

Jack drank deeply and then exhaled, thinking of not only what to tell Megan but how. He thought he'd settled on a path, but the call from Danzig changed things. Jack was convinced that she was what she said she was, which could only mean that Reginald was working with them in some way. That changed the game significantly.

The Frank Fischer identity was the best that money could buy, but with their resources, the FBI would eventually unravel it, and Reginald would be able to give them a hell of a head start. When that happened, all Jack could do was disappear, leaving everyone he loved behind.

Jack had done that once before, and those were scars that had yet to heal.

It was not something he was eager to try again.

But in this moment, Jack didn't see how he could survive with the Fischer identity intact, let alone the life that was built around it.

There were no good options here, just a handful of dirty bad options and the choices between them.

And even if Jack found a way past the feds, he knew Reginald would keep coming at him because the amount of money at stake was just too much for him to ever let go. Reginald wouldn't stop unless he was dead, and Jack knew that was a line he would never cross. Reginald knew that too.

So what was the other option?

Reginald was going to expose Jack unless he paid up, and Jack wasn't about to do that. He couldn't. He didn't have the money to give. He couldn't tell Reginald that, however. Hassar warned Jack what would happen if he ever disclosed the nature of their deal. But even if Jack did, Reginald would just use that as a way to keep him working for him for years, but not the kinds of relatively safe jobs Jack had become famous for. Reginald would force him into high-risk, high-dollar scores because Reginald knew it wouldn't be his ass on the line if Jack were caught.

I can't see him stopping unless I pay him off or kill him. So, we're back to that, he thought darkly.

Jack thought about offering a payoff of a much lower sum than what Reginald was demanding. There was a chance that Reginald would be willing to accept the fifteen million Jack had left. But that, too, had risk. Reginald would expect to know why he wasn't getting the full amount, which Jack couldn't disclose. Plus, he would assume that Jack was deceiving him and that there was more money to be had. Even if Reginald went along with that plan, it brought Jack full circle to the original risk that Reginald would just push him into a series of risky jobs until he burned Jack out or got him caught.

But maybe that was the game all along.

Reginald admitted on the phone that he'd left Jack with an impossible choice because he wanted Jack to "know what that felt like." Once he knew he'd gotten Jack to his breaking point, he'd force Jack into paying him whatever money he had, maybe even selling off the winery to cover the debt. Then a cold stone formed in the pit of his stomach. It was what Reginald had said when Jack confronted him on the phone, but Jack was too drunk or too angry to pick up on it. *I just wanted you to stay hungry enough that you'd keep working for me.*

Paul Sharpe.

How couldn't Jack see this until now? He'd been so used to living behind that veil he'd constructed that he'd gotten complacent. He didn't see this for what it was.

Sharpe was a plant.

The timing was too much to be a coincidence. Reginald pitches Jack about the Carlton job, Jack passes on it. Two, three months later and *just days* before the Carlton job was supposed to have gone down, Sharpe disappears with ten million from the winery's accounts. That put Jack in a position where he'd have to do the job just to stay afloat. And, since Reginald now had something over him *and* he knew how desperate Jack would be, Reginald wouldn't settle for the five percent finder's fee he normally got for setting gigs up. He'd want the whole take.

All that time leading up to this, the years that Sharpe was managing Kingfisher's books, he was probably skimming the entire time. Bleeding the profits just enough that Jack had to keep working for Reginald in order to remain solvent. A winery was like a ship with a thousand holes. They leaked money everywhere, especially in the early years, and most sank. It took at least three before you even had a product that you could release, and it could be ten before you saw a profit. Sharpe could quietly siphon money and they wouldn't even notice. Didn't notice.

Jack realized something else, and that knowledge was visceral, painful, and embarrassing all at once.

Reginald had used Jack's own rules against him. It was what he'd based this entire con upon, one last fuck you to let Jack know that he'd one.

Never take a score large enough for someone to notice. Never steal from someone with the will or the means to get it back.

Sharpe had taken care of that first part for years, and Reginald would assume that Jack would do anything to protect his new identity, satisfying the second.

"Son of a bitch," he said.

"Frank?"

"Sorry," he said, just then realizing that he'd been silently swimming against a rip current of thought for a while. Jack looked across the short space between him and Megan. She wore a pensive, nervous, and confused expression. It was the look of someone who knew they were about to walk into a bad situation but had no idea of the depth of it.

"This is complicated and a little hard for me to explain."

Jack's head was swimming. This was a hell of a time for an epiphany.

"You can tell me, Frank." She leaned in and touched his knee. "Whatever it is."

Jack breathed deeply and wondered if that was true. The night air was quickly turning crisp. He closed his eyes for a few moments, and when he opened them, he saw Megan's stare in the soft, lingering light of dusk. "I am being black-mailed. The gentleman you met the other day, the one pretending to be a distributor, is a former...business associate of mine. His name is Reginald LeGrande."

"Why is he doing this?" she asked. If she thought of Jack being deceptive in his previous explanation, she said nothing about it.

"Well," Jack said slowly, "my name isn't really Frank Fischer. I've been living under an assumed name, and Reginald knows that I'll go to some pretty great lengths to keep that a secret. He's demanding that I pay him an insane amount of money or he'll tell people I care about, tell the police." Jack indicated to her with an open palm.

"Well, if he's blackmailing you, why not just tell the FBI? I don't understand."

"That's where it gets complicated."

"Are you in witness protection or something?"

A flash of inspiration hit him, and Jack thought she'd just teed up a perfect exit ramp for him, but he decided against it just as quickly.

"No," he said, shaking his head. "It's nothing like that."

"Why would he care if you're living under an assumed name? Changing your name isn't illegal."

"Not when you do it through the courts, it isn't."

Megan's face went ashen, and she whispered, "Oh."

Jack clenched his teeth and tried to think if there was another way around this. There wasn't. When he spoke, hot tears welled in his eyes, and he hoped Megan couldn't see it. "I did some things when I was younger that I'm not very proud of. I made some mistakes, stupid, dangerous ones. I had to run away, and when I did, I created a new identity to protect my family. If I'd have done it the legal way, some very bad people might have found out, and my family could've been hurt. So, I moved out here and paid someone to give me a new name. Then I just lived my life."

"Your money," she said flatly. "Is that why you keep it offshore?"

"Originally, yeah. I didn't want the IRS digging too deep into my past."

Megan stared down at the table, but there was a faraway look in her eyes. Long moments passed in silence. Jack studied Megan's face. Other than an occasional tic around her eye that she sometimes got when she was straining, Jack couldn't deduce what she was thinking. She picked up her wineglass but just held it in both hands, cupping the bulb the way you did a coffee mug on a cold day as she stared out at the darkening valley. He could see the line on her jaw tighten and then relax as she clenched and unclenched her teeth.

Maybe minutes had passed in the stiff silence, or maybe it was just seconds. Jack knew how nerves could play on your sense of time. He'd experienced it on the job often enough, waiting, waiting, waiting for some trigger, some action for what felt like hours, stiffly crouching only to look down at your watch and see just minutes had passed. The blank stare, the utter lack of reaction...Jack couldn't stand it anymore. He had to know.

"Meg," he prompted. "I know this is a lot to take in." Jack spoke softly and cautiously.

Megan didn't respond. She just nodded, but when she did so, she started rocking back and forth in her seat slowly, as if the action required every muscle in her body. She just said, "Yep," and kept rocking.

"If you didn't do anything wrong, I don't understand why you can't just go to the FBI and tell them that this LeGrande guy is trying to blackmail you. Surely that's worse than whatever it was that forced you to change your name."

"Well, that's hard for me to explain."

Then Megan exploded. "You keep saying that." Her voice was just shy of a shout. "Why is it hard to explain?" Finally, she turned in her chair to look at him, twisting her body so that she could lean across the arm of the chair. It was an aggressive, challenging position. "Explaining cancer to a child —*that's* hard to explain. Telling your parents that a marriage is falling apart and that it's both your fault and his, *that's* hard to explain. Losing something you've worked your adult life to build because it was *your* mistake, that's hard to explain. I know because I've done all three of those, so I understand 'hard to explain.' So tell me, Frank, what's so hard about it?"

"Megan," Jack said softly but firmly. "No one knows my real name, and that's to protect my family. I made a mistake a long time ago, and in order to keep them safe—particularly my little sisters—I disappeared. I wouldn't risk their safety, not for anything. What I'm about to say, I've never shared with anyone. Literally, no one, and if I tell you, I need your word that it's not going to get out. You can't tell Hugh, you can't tell the FBI, no one. I will leave out certain facts, but I'll be as honest as I can. Hopefully, you can at least understand some of the decisions I made, even if you don't agree with them. Do I have your word?"

"I can't promise that," she said softly. "I'm not going to lie for you, Frank," she said. "If the FBI asks me, I'm going to have to tell them."

Jack closed his eyes for a moment, knowing she was right.

Then she put her hand on his knee and said, "But I won't tell anyone else. You have my word."

He inhaled a breath of cold and took a drink to steel himself. "I grew up in a Chicago suburb, and when I was a kid, my family was pretty well off. My dad was an investment banker. I'd always been into cars. My dad got me into them, and I started racing karts at an early age. I was pretty good. When I was fourteen, and doing really well on the amateur racing circuit, my dad's business partner swindled him. I don't know if what my dad was doing was totally aboveboard or not, he never talked about it, but when his partner ran out with the money, a bunch of people came to collect.

"We lost the house, their retirement, college savings, everything. Lawsuits took whatever was left. We were on food stamps by the time I got my driver's license. My racing career was over. I started working at this garage in Cicero to help make ends meet. I knew cars pretty well and was helping out as a mechanic, changing oil and whatever they needed. Turned out some mob guys owned the place. By then they knew who I was, knew the shape my family was in, so they asked me if I wanted to make some extra bucks driving cars for them. Errands, driving guys to meetings, stuff like that. I didn't know exactly what they were into, but then I didn't much care either. Money was money, and we needed all we could get. So, this goes on for a couple of months, and the money was pretty good, you know, so I didn't ask questions. They started to trust me more. Sometimes I'd go out with them, and other times I'd just drop a car someplace. Like, delivering it to someone."

Jack saw the anticipated next question forming on her lips and preempted it. "I didn't ask. All I knew was that my dad, who was spending all of his time with lawyers either trying to get back what his partner took from him or trying to stay out of jail or both, didn't have to worry about putting a little bit of food on the table."

Jack paused the story and walked back into his kitchen. He retrieved a bottle of '09 Peregrine and returned to the deck with the opened bottle. He filled both glasses, knowing he'd need some insulation against what was to come. Jack took a deep drink, savoring both it and the warmth of the wine as it hit his stomach. He continued. "So, one day the guys at the garage gave me an assignment. Gave me the keys to a car, some old beater Lincoln, and told me to drop it at some address." He moved the hand holding his wineglass in a circle in the "as-you-do" gesture. "But this time, they tell me, 'Don't look in the trunk.' And they were serious about that. But I was a seventeen-year-old kid. You tell me not to look, of course that's the first thing I'm going to do." Megan smiled, not understanding that it wasn't a joke. "I drove a couple miles, and it was killing me, so I stopped and popped the trunk. By now, I knew these guys were gangsters, but I figured it was like crap games and unions and shit. What I found in the trunk was a couple pounds of heroin."

Jack stopped, his own eyes going to the horizon. Then he took a drink and continued. "An idea hit me. I didn't know how much any of this was worth, but I knew it was a lot, maybe enough to solve our financial problems." Jack pinched his eyes shut and rubbed them with his free hand.

"Please tell me that you didn't do what I think you did."

Jack nodded slowly, heavily, sadly. When he opened his eyes again, they were moist. "I did. All I could think about was being a hero. A seventeen-year-old boy doesn't think about consequences, he doesn't even think about the inevitable and logical question his parents would ask—like, 'Where did you get this money?' He only thinks about being their hero. I drove the car into Cabrini-Green, quite possibly the worst place on Earth for a teenage white boy with a trunk full of heroin to be. I can't even describe in words how stupid that was. I roll up to some guy selling shit on a corner and ask him if he wants to make a deal. He looks at me like, 'Are you for real?' Then he asks me if I know where I am. He tries to sell me something, so I tell him I'm not buying. *I'm* selling. I get out, walk over to the trunk, and pop it, like some big shot. I don't know what I expected, that he's going to introduce me to someone. I don't know. Like some fucking corner thug is going to give me a half a million dollars for what's in the trunk of my car instead of what he would do...what he *did* do, which was to pull a pistol on me. I moved to close the lid of the trunk, and he knocked me upside the head. I went down, and he kicked me a few times before getting into the car and taking off. So, now I'm in the middle of hell, and I have to walk out. Got jumped a couple blocks later, beat to hell, and had everything I had stolen. They even took my shoes so I would *have* to walk out of there."

Megan's hand went to her mouth, stifling a gasp.

Jack exhaled, steeling himself.

"I couldn't go home. It's not that I didn't think I could explain the beating...or the shoes." He paused long seconds to compose himself. "I just couldn't face them after I failed. So, I wandered around most of the night barefoot. And now, the realization of what I'd done started to hit. Anyway, it didn't take the mob guys long to figure out what happened, or at least that I didn't do what I was told to do, so they came looking for me. By the time I made it back to my part of town, it was just after dawn. They found me. They grabbed me and threw me in the trunk. I was pretty sure that was it. Took me to the garage and asked me where the car was, so I told them. I told them everything I did and why. They said that I'd just cost them about half a million dollars—this is the eighties, mind you. We're talking about a lot of money."

Jack leaned against the railing and looked at the dark shapes beneath him that he knew to be vines. "To this day, I don't really know why they spared me, and there were days I wished they hadn't. At the time, they said that the lesson was worth more than killing me. Whatever that meant. After keeping me in the garage for most of that next day, they piled me into the car, and we drove to my neighborhood. They said they were going to let me live because they understood why I did what I did, but that if I was in trouble, I should've come to them instead of stealing from them. So, I had to leave.

"They said if they ever saw me again, they wouldn't do anything to me, but they would hurt one of my little sisters as an opener. To prove their point, they drove me by my youngest sister's school as it was letting out. They slowed the car to a crawl, and one of them pointed her out to me." Jack hung his head in shame and in grief. "Jennie was walking down the street, pigtails and a lunch box. She looked over at the car and saw me, and it took her a second, but then she recognized me. I remember her looking confused, like why was her big brother in this car and not stopping. They held us there for a few long seconds and let that sink in. The last image I have of any of my family is my six-year-old sister with this confused look on her face, starting to wave to me and then stopping as the car drove away. That was the last I ever saw of them, of any of them." Jack's voice warbled, and then it broke. His shoulders racked with sobs.

Jack waited until he could compose himself, and then he continued. "They drove me a couple miles from town and dropped me in a parking lot. The one guy got out of the passenger seat and dropped a pair of white-and-red Nikes next to me. Said I needed shoes for all the walking I was going to do. Then they left me. I waited until they were gone, and I stole a car to spite them. I'd walked enough."

"Didn't you ever try to go back?"

"I couldn't."

"You don't think they'd want to know you were alive? After all this time? Those mob guys can't possibly still be in business, and even if they are, do you really think they care about something that happened, what, thirty years ago?"

"When I disappeared, my family thought I was dead. My father killed himself later that year. It was just too much for him. He'd guessed that I was probably doing something illegal that got me killed. They knew about the garage, about the people who owned it, but they looked the other way because they needed the money. My mom raised my sisters on her own. I learned all this about ten years ago after I had the same thought you did, that I could just go back, that the people I was mixed up with wouldn't possibly remember me. Once I realized what I'd done to my family, I knew that there was no way I could go back to them. It would just open those old wounds, not to mention how much hurt was compounded over the years."

Worse, he knew, was that they would rightly blame him for the ruin of their family, and that was something Jack could neither face himself or put his mother and sisters through.

"I couldn't legally change my name because that would reveal that I was still alive, which then sets in motion all of the horrible things I just described to you. At this point, I could probably do it, but again, there's always the possibility that my mom and my sisters will somehow find out."

"You don't think that if you explained that to them, to the FBI I mean, that they'd understand?"

Jack scoffed, actually scoffed, aloud at the thought. "They're cops, Meg. They only see things one way."

"Ugh," Megan practically shouted. "Blackmail is a hundred times worse than anything you did when you were a seventeen-year-old. Surely, Frank, they won't fault you for what you did. Particularly in light of what's happening now. But even if they did, I have to believe the statute of limitations on being an idiot has run out. Now you're putting everything you've worked for—*we've* worked for—at risk, and for what?"

"Because they'll shut the winery down if they find out that I'm not really Frank Fischer, and they'll expose me for who I am. Then my name gets out and my family finds out that I'm still alive, and they get twenty fresh years of pain. You told me you understand about hard choices. I kept my identity a secret for twenty years because I was afraid that my family would get hurt. Then, once I knew the mob guys were probably too old to give a shit, it was too late. I could never explain to them, in words they'd understand, why I'd stayed hidden for so long. They thought I was dead, and they made peace with that." Jack's voice was elevating now, and he stopped trying to fight it. "How self-centered would it be for me to just show up and tell them, surprise, I'm alive. Your grief was all a sham."

"No. It's goddamn self-centered *not* to." Megan stood so abruptly that it pushed the thick patio chair back a foot. He simply deferred to the harsh scrape of the chair legs on the deck. "You don't want to tell them because *you* don't want to face it, not because you're keeping them from it."

Jack knew Megan McKinney well enough to know that she would have one of two reactions to what he just told her. She would either explode with the full force-of-nature fury that only an angry Irish woman possessed, or she would run. Jack had hoped for the former. An argument implicitly meant there was a position that could be countered, even reconsidered.

Flight meant resolution.

Jack stood, but she pushed past him and maneuvered around the chairs to the door leading into the house, pausing only to look back at him. "If you don't tell the FBI the truth, they're going to believe whatever LeGrande tells them about why you're hiding, and you'll have to take your chances with

that. If you do that, you're going to lose everything, Frank."
She stopped a few steps away. "Everything *else*."

And she was gone.

Jack wanted to call after her, but he knew it wouldn't do
him any good, so he resisted the urge. If she was anything,
Megan was both willful and defiant. Her mind was set that she
needed time, and if Jack pushed her now, he knew it would
only end one way, and that was badly. She fast-walked
through his house, now out of sight, marked by the sound of
echoing footfalls to the front door. Then a car door, ignition,
and the sad sound of car tires on pavement carried her away.

Jack heard that final sound of her Wrangler backing out
onto the road and quickly fading into the night, and he fought
off every urge, every base instinct to go after her. All he wanted
was to scoop her up in his arms and tell her all the ways this
was going to be fine. Even if he knew they were lies. But Jack
wanted to say them anyway, because he wanted Megan to stay
at whatever price that came at.

When the sounds of the Jeep driving away faded into
silence, Jack said, "It would've been easier if I'd have just told
her I was a thief."

26

Jack barely slept, and when he did, it was fitful.

He finally gave up at four, ground beans, and put on pot of coffee. Jack occasionally sat but mostly paced until the sun rose over the Sonoma Valley. Jack had largely pushed thoughts of his family back into his subconscious. The human mind was a miraculous thing, but it could be tricked into believing something was true when it was not, given sufficient passion and repetition. Police and attorneys on both sides of the courtroom used that to their advantage, coaching witnesses to the desired conclusion by assisting recollection. If you said something enough times, the mind started to believe it was true. Jack repeated the mantra of avoidance for years until his mind accepted cowardice as simple truth. There were a hundred ways Jack could have contacted them before or after his father's suicide that would not have put his sisters in any danger. He could have at least given them some semblance of closure, if not an explanation. At the absolute worst, he could have given them a locus for their anger.

Instead, Jack ran as though every mile was one farther

from his guilt, and he convinced himself that it was the only choice he could have made.

Gentleman Jack Burdette was a construct born of necessity. It was a cutout persona designed to fit a narrative, to make living this kind of life a little easier, a little safer, and to give him some much-needed security. And it was a far cry from the boy he was when he ran. Jack didn't know who *that* person was anymore.

Frank Fischer was who he truly wanted to *be*. Fischer was a successful businessman and entrepreneur. Someone who'd gambled on himself, won, and was now in a position to carve out a comfortable, fulfilling life as a reward. Fischer earned the right to honestly reinvent himself. Frank Fischer was a man who'd left his other life behind. He maintained no ties with his former business associates, with ex-bosses or old rivals. Now, he lived his life according to the rules that he made for himself, because he'd earned that right. Frank Fischer spent his days doing something that gave him purpose.

Fischer had a past, an expertly crafted one and further refined over the years as situations required. He was also a man who didn't believe much in talking about where he was from and believed very much in where he was. More than once when, in a quiet moment, an employee asked him about his life, the way one did in trying to figure out a boss, Fischer would simply motion to the mottled tan-and-green hills of Sonoma underneath a perfect lapis sky and say, "Who cares what no-name town you came from when this is where you ended up?" Part of the persona was that he wanted to come across as the rakish, enigmatic businessman, the slightly eccentric guy who kept most of his money offshore because he didn't trust the government to hold it. Frank Fischer wanted to keep people guessing because that made him interesting, but not interesting enough to dig any deeper.

As Jack, he was simply a master thief, and questions about his past were easily dodged. People tended to talk on jobs, it was a natural tendency to want to fill the nervous hours, but Jack was always cagey about this. He worked under aliases when he was with people he didn't know, and even as Jack Burdette he simply refused to talk about himself. Enzo and Rusty now knew that he was a winemaker in California, but he trusted them. Inasmuch as you could trust anyone in this business.

Trust was a matter of economics, nothing more.

When distilled down to its essential components, the fabric of trust was held up by the value of the knowledge possessed. Did the person with information have more or less to gain by maintaining that trust or by betraying it? Enzo wanted a quiet villa on the Riviera or Lake Como or both. Jack knew that the Watchmaker wanted to travel on a long dime and eventually settle down again, try life with a higher-caliber woman than he had the first time. His cut, which Jack was happy to pay, would help Enzo get the second chance at the life he'd originally wanted. Jack wasn't worried about him.

Rusty was an enigma and had his own secrets to bury, but as sure as he was of anything, Jack believed Rusty wanted to keep playing the game as he had been. He'd probably be disappointed to know that Jack planned to retire and focus on the winery, not because of the money Jack would pay him, but because Rusty lived for the kinds of challenges Jack threw his way. Still, Jack had a feeling that this wouldn't be the end of his relationship with the fixer. If anything was clear over the last few hours, it was the knowledge that Jack would need a full-time damage controller for some time to come.

Jack believed Enzo and Rusty knowing about his alter ego

was an acceptable risk. Their knowledge of his identity would not jeopardize him. Nor was Jack concerned about the identity itself. The Frank Fischer driver's license, social security card, and passport were real—it was the documents to get those things that were fake. The SSN he'd been using belonged to a dead person, and he'd gone through a fairly elaborate con to convince a mid-level drone at the Social Security Administration that it was his death that was falsely reported, as part of a larger identity theft scheme. They'd issued him a new card (keeping the existing number) but removed his records from the so-called "death database" they maintained. As far as the US government was concerned, Frank Fischer was a real person.

But even that tightly constructed lie would only hold up under so much scrutiny. The Frank Fischer legend would pass a civilian background check or any credit inquiry or serve as proof for ID, and it had for some time. Jack never intended for this to hold up against a serious and persistent criminal investigation. It might take them a few weeks, but eventually the FBI would be able to prove that Frank Fischer was a cutout. At that point, they would dive into Jack Burdette and find that name was also fake. That would eventually lead them back to Jack's birth identity and his family and renew a lifetime of buried pain. At a minimum, they'd have him on felony counts of fraud, tax evasion, and falsifying documents, to say nothing of the charges that he'd face if they were able to connect him with Jack Burdette's résumé.

Jack reasoned that Reginald had been working with the FBI for more than a decade. They'd probably gotten to him when he was in prison. The early-release story now made much more sense. Looking back on it, when the second- and third-tier guys Reginald crewed over the years periodically got pinched, Jack simply assumed that was the cost of doing business, the risk you ran in being a thief. Now it was clear that Reginald was just handing them over to the police. Likely, it was part of the deal. But what really troubled Jack was when he thought of the post-mission debriefs he and Reginald conducted. It had become a ritual to him, both a shared experience and a chance to learn from a master thief. Now it was plain that his mentor was simply gathering facts all along so that one day he could hand Jack over, too.

How could he have been so blind to a decade-long con?

Fury boiled up inside him.

He could picture his hands closing around Reginald's neck, or the look on that weathered and liver-spotted face when he saw Jack at the other end of a pistol, that silver-blond mullet billowing out with the force of impact before he fell to the ground. The thought was satisfying for a moment, but Jack knew it was fantasy and nothing more. Killing Reginald would kill the investigation of Jack Burdette, professional thief, but that would just birth the investigation of Jack Burdette, first-degree murderer. He also knew that no matter what Reginald had done, Jack was no killer. He just wasn't. Jack was a career criminal, fine, but the gulf between thievery and murder was so wide it was impassable in his mind.

So, how to stop the investigation?

How to convince the FBI that Reginald was just some kook scam artist coming after a legitimate businessman?

Another, darker question swirled in his mind. Reginald had said that if Jack didn't pay him, he would turn Jack over to the authorities. Jack hadn't, and Reginald seemed to have made good on this threat, and yet, he was still asking for the money. How would he plan to walk that back?

Jack watched the sunrise, or rather, watched the western sky brighten as the sun rose behind him, knowing that he had no answers to the questions that plagued him throughout the night. Then he showered, changed into a navy Zegna suit and pink micro-stripe shirt that he left open-collar, and drove into town. Jack had breakfast at Grace's Table in downtown Napa, which made the best cornbread he'd ever tasted. From there, he walked two blocks to Coughlin's office, which was on the second floor of a peach stucco shop complex that shared a block with the Andaz Hotel. Jack walked up the exterior flight of stairs and into Hugh's office. Coughlin preferred to do most of his business from his home, which was a modest house in the foothills with a much nicer view than the parking garage he was looking at right now. He was pissed off that he had to come into the actual office, pissed off that he had to wear a suit, and pissed off that he had to meet with federal agents.

They arrived a few ticks before noon.

Danzig was taller than he expected, for some reason. Jack figured she was about five foot eight, five nine, and looked to be very athletic. He could tell by the angles in her face. She kept her brown hair short, and it curled around her ears, doubtless to conform to some bureaucratic notion of style. Danzig dressed in a dark gray pantsuit and white open-collared shirt. She didn't wear any jewelry that Jack could see. Smart. It left less for a potential combatant to grab onto. She had a handbag, but Jack suspected that was more to carry the interview tools, so she could lose that in a scuffle. He could see from the slight bulge on Danzig's hip that she carried her service pistol on her person rather than in the bag.

The other agent was taller, and Jack judged him to be in his mid-thirties. He was decidedly less athletic than his partner. The man had the look of someone whose physical glory days were about fifteen years ago but who worked out, as though he were still clinging to that particular ghost. He wore Brooks Brothers, though not particularly well. The suit had high armholes designed to give a slimmer look, but the agent got his height from his legs rather than his torso. He appeared to be carrying about ten pounds too many, so the suit gave him more of a bell-shaped look. The salesman should've known better. Then again, if this guy could afford a five-thousand-dollar suit, he wouldn't be in the FBI.

Danzig looked both Jack and Hugh up and down, clearly sizing them up, and then introduced herself. When she spoke, her voice was deeper than he would've expected. Not quite raspy but it clearly had some miles to it—Kathleen Turner as a private eye. "Good morning, I'm Special Agent Danzig." She held out her badge and credentials for them to see. Jack always wondered why they did that. The average person wouldn't be able to tell if they were real or not. "This is Special Agent Riordan." She leveled her dark-eyed gaze at Jack. "Mister," she began, then laid in an intentional pause as if she were searching her memory for the right name. "Fischer, I presume?"

"That's correct," Jack said, nodding. "Frank Fischer," he said for her benefit. "This is my attorney, Hugh Coughlin."

There was a brief and curt exchange of greetings, at the end of which Coughlin led them over to a conference table in the back of his office that sat beneath a window looking out on the second floor of a parking garage. On one wall, there was a series of portraits taken of the same perspective at the same vineyard in each season, meant to show the progression of time. On another wall, a framed copy of *Wine Spectator* where Coughlin made the cover, standing next to two now-legendary winemakers. The lead story was about how he'd brokered the deal to merge two highly successful operations into what was now a multimillion-dollar viticulture empire. Other artifacts of Coughlin's career hung about the office, all of which identified him as a businessman and wine expert.

Jack was already second-guessing the logic of having the meeting here.

"Shall we get started?" Coughlin asked when they were seated.

Danzig reached into her bag and removed a black leather folio containing a legal pad and several documents.

Danzig spoke, her voice slightly elevated and authoritative. "Today is Thursday, August first, 2013. My name is Special Agent Katrina Danzig, and I am conducting this interview with Special Agent Richard Riordan" She looked at Jack. "Please state your full legal name, date of birth, and occupation."

Jack paused a moment, noting that she clearly stipulated his "legal" name but didn't prompt him with one. Obviously a bowshot.

"My name is Francis Thomas Fischer. My date of birth is February second, 1968. I am the owner and proprietor of Kingfisher Wines."

"This interview is taking place at the law office of Mr. Hugh Coughlin, Mr. Fischer's attorney. Thank you," Danzig said. She asked Jack to provide his current address and cell phone number and then turned to Coughlin to do the same. "You stated, for the record," she placed heavier than normal emphasis on the latter, "that your legal name is Francis Fischer."

"I prefer to go by Frank," he said convivially.

"I'd like to get a little bit of background on you, if we could, Mr. Fischer. We performed a cursory search, but there was very little public information available on you. You don't maintain any social media accounts and have been relatively hidden from public life."

"Maybe I'm just not that interesting," he said. When the joke didn't land, Jack said, "Technology and music are kind of like a train, Agent Danzig. At some point, everyone chooses their stop, and they get off. Mine was a while ago. As for being 'hidden,' that implies I have something to hide. I think it's more accurate to say that I'm just a private person."

"Indeed," she said. "Let's go back to something you just said about technology. Were you or were you not a 'technology consultant' for a number of years? How is it that you could effectively perform that service if you, as you say, got off the train?"

"Using something doesn't make you an expert in it. The key to understanding social media is understanding how people think and act, not wasting your time with your face in your phone. Besides, my consultancy was more with advising others on how to run a technology business. I leave the engineering to them. The winery has a Twitter feed and a Facebook page. You're welcome to 'like' us," Jack said, his voice smug.

"That'll do," she said. "What we're trying to establish is the type of relationships you maintain. In this day and age, it stands out when someone doesn't communicate with people from various stages in their life, given how easy it is."

"Maybe I'm just old-fashioned." Jack's response was intended to sound like a dodge, and it was.

"Where are you from, originally?" she asked.

Jack noted that Danzig didn't pursue her previous line of questioning any further, despite his laying the trap of his evasive answer. This was useful information for him. A less-experienced interviewer would have bitten or even openly challenged him.

"Chicago suburb," he said.

"What high school did you attend?"

"Morton East, class of 1986. John Denver went to my school, though it was a few years before me, obviously."

"Are your parents still in Chicago?"

"My parents are dead." Jack's tone was cold, flat, and emotionless in a way that conveyed a very deep pain, something that was so profoundly painful to him it made it sound as though he were totally empty.

Danzig set down her pen and looked up at him. "How did they die?" Danzig asked, just as emotionless, though hers was clinical.

Jack took a moment to answer, though the look of abject horror and offense on Coughlin's face spoke as loudly as Jack's silence.

"I fail to see how this is relevant," Coughlin broke in.

"No," Jack said in a tone that was purposefully devoid of emotion. "It's fine. My mother died of cancer when I was fourteen. My dad took to the bottle. He was a full-on drunk by the time I could drive."

"Alcoholism run in your family?" Danzig asked.

Jack recognized the tactic. She was trying to set him off, raise the temperature of his blood to force a hasty answer, to get him off guard.

"I said he was a drunk, not an alcoholic. Do you know the difference? Alcoholism is a disease, like cancer. You can't decide if you get it; you just decide if you'll make it worse. Being a drunk," Jack stabbed the air between them with two of his fingers, "that's a choice. When I graduated high school, I ran as far and as fast as I could. I came out here and I never went back. Told him I'd talk to him again when he dried out. I was angry with my father for spending more time with Jack Daniel's than with me after Mom died. He lasted about two years. One night he drank a fifth of whiskey and shot himself in the head. I think people blamed that on my leaving, so no, I don't keep up much with my family." Jack leveled a flat gaze at the agent across the table from him to let her know that she'd gone too far.

"I'm sorry to bring that up, Mr. Fischer. Please understand that we need to be thorough. You said you came out here and attended college?"

"San Jose State, though I didn't finish. I got an internship with a software company and they hired me full-time in my junior year."

"What company was that?" Danzig asked, not looking up from her notation.

"Pinnacle Software, though they aren't around anymore." The cheerful, carefree, almost wistful lilt returned to his voice. "Netscape bought us in the mid-nineties. I stayed on through ninety-five or so before I quit. I had a ton of Netscape stock, which I cashed out shortly after the IPO. I took a sabbatical for a few years."

"Seems like an odd move for a mid-level software engineer in his late twenties."

"I had about a million dollars in the bank by the time I was twenty-seven. Most of us lived like hermits because all we did was code, never had time to spend any money or enjoy being in our twenties. At that point, I'd seen two places in the United States—Chicago and Silicon Valley. I wanted to travel, and like most twenty-seven-year-olds, I thought a million dollars was a legitimate fortune."

"Spend any time in Europe?" she asked, now looking up.

"Little bit. France, Italy, Spain. Kind of funny, really. I spent a couple years traveling Europe and ended up staying in places that looked a lot like California."

"How about Turin?"

Jack noted that she referred to the city by its proper Italian name rather than the Americanized "Torino." That wasn't a mistake.

The charming, chatty expression Jack wore drained away. "I don't think so. Why do you ask?"

"Oh, no reason. Like I said, we're just trying to establish who you are." Danzig held her gaze, locking eyes with Jack for a long breath.

Jesus, LeGrande had been thorough. While Reginald hadn't been present for any of those years, he certainly knew about Jack's exploits in the notorious School of Turin and seemed to have handed over those details to the FBI, key details from which they could begin deconstructing the Frank Fischer legend and establishing him as Gentleman Jack Burdette. Danzig was intentionally telegraphing her strategy here—essentially saying, *We know who you are.*

They said nothing further about Turin.

Riordan took the lead and launched into questions about Frank Fischer's background that plodded on for another hour as they dutifully and painfully reconstructed Fischer's life in the nineties and aughts. They repeated questions or asked them in a different way, often circling back to things he'd said before in other lines of the conversation, looking for holes, holes that lined up with whatever information Reginald fed them. Jack told them about how he'd made a lot of money in Netscape's IPO, which was true, and then lost nearly all of it when the tech bubble burst a few short, heady years later— which was also true. He told them how he was running a technology consulting practice by '01 and bet big on Google, which obviously paid off.

By '05 he was mostly playing the stock market and had largely moved his consulting practice to Europe because they were about a decade behind the US in software development. The Europeans were hungry for his knowledge and the lessons the Americans learned in the nineties. He founded

Kingfisher in '06 and formally retired from the tech scene to make wine.

Danzig asked how often he traveled overseas, and Jack's answer was several times a year while he was consulting, not quite once a month but close. She countered with specific dates and locations over the last decade, all of which Jack knew to be times where there were specific thefts committed that Reginald would have knowledge of. Each time, Jack rebuffed, saying he didn't remember the specific dates or places he traveled to, but most often it was the UK, Germany, Switzerland, and later, some Eastern European countries that were starting to build a technology base.

Riordan, voice impartial, added, "So, you'll have these specific dates in your corporate files, I assume? You'd be billing these trips to your clients, no?"

"I think you're giving my 'files' a little too much credit. If I'm traveling for Kingfisher, like, say when I was in Italy a few months back to meet with some Sangiovese growers, I'll have records for that. The consulting stuff I don't keep too close a tab on."

"But there are records. Invoices, ledger entries, that sort of thing?"

"I don't maintain that business anymore, so I'm not really keeping up with the books, you know?"

So this is how they were going to come at him, Jack mused. Start by breaking apart his decade-long alibi by trying to prove Frank Fischer was never in a consulting business. Once they did that, he wouldn't be able to disprove he wasn't doing jobs with Reginald. In fact, their strategy might even be to just get Jack on the fact that he was living illegally under an assumed name with fraudulently acquired documents. Or at least have that as a backup in case they couldn't prove he was a thief.

"But you do have these records? You can prove that you were in Europe on those dates, meeting with clients?"

"Where are you going with this?" Coughlin demanded. "Are you investigating whether or not my client was a good accountant?"

"Mr. Coughlin, we don't think Mr. Fischer was ever meeting with clients. The dates on this list indicate when jewelry thefts occurred at various locations throughout Western Europe. We believe these thefts were planned and executed by a man named Jack Burdette. A credible source has provided convincing evidence that your client's real name is Jack Burdette. Further, we have reason to believe that your client is implicated in dozens of jewelry thefts conducted in Europe dating back to the early nineties."

"This is outrageous!" Coughlin thundered. "He was a programmer in the nineties."

"Did you know him when he was working as a programmer?"

Coughlin said nothing, recognizing the old courtroom trick for what it was.

"What do you have to say to this, Mr. Fischer?"

"That I think you have me confused with someone else."

"I wonder if I'm actually the one who has you confused with someone else." Then she added, "As I said, I have an informant who says he's known you as Jack Burdette since 1991. His description matches you exactly, and he even provided these photographs of you." Danzig drew a small envelope from her folio, opened it, and removed several head-shots of Jack that Reginald had taken to forge his travel documents.

"Do you recall these photographs being taken?"

Coughlin, now red-faced, held a hand up. "Frank, don't say anything else. This interview is over."

"Mr. Coughlin, we can have the interview here, or we can arrest your client and continue this in an interrogation room at the Federal Building. Which will it be?"

"There's no proof that those were given to you by this supposed source," Coughlin broke in angrily. "For all we know, those are old DMV photos or corporate headshots from the winery."

"We've already established that your client intentionally maintains a very low profile and does not engage in social media. Therefore, by his own admission, there are going to be very few places where his photograph will appear online and could be co-opted, as you suggest."

"I just gave you two."

"I can assure you that's not where they came from."

"Actually," Jack broke in, tapping his finger on the table near the photos but careful not to touch them. "These look like pictures we took for the winery." Jack kept his tone and cadence slow and somewhat hesitant in the beginning, as though he were recalling some filed-away facts. He added confidence to his answer as he continued. Turning to Hugh, he said, "We did a bunch of promotional shots early on, remember? We had a lot of press events, and we always sent photos out with them to include in the articles. It wouldn't be hard for someone to get ahold of those. And there are plenty of pictures of me in various trade publications. Anyone with a reasonable skill in Photoshop could doctor those to make it look like that." Jack pointed at the photos on the table.

"Why would someone want to do that?" Riordan asked.

"Why else? To blackmail me." Before either Riordan or Danzig could pick that up and run with it, Jack continued. "A few days ago, I got an anonymous phone call from someone saying that he was going to tell the police I was a career criminal, just like you say, unless I paid him several million dollars.

He said that by the time anyone figured out the truth, the damage to my winery would've been done. Said that I should, and I'm quoting here, 'invest in silence.'" That was one of Reginald's favorite phrases, and he used it often, particularly when Jack was referencing one of his rules. If these feds had spent any time with LeGrande, it was a good bet they'd heard him say it.

"So you're saying that someone contacted you and attempted to blackmail you. What day was this?"

"Monday."

"Did you report this to the police?"

"No."

"Why not?"

"Because if you've actually done your homework, you'll know how I feel about the government and its law enforcement. I don't have a lot of faith in the system, and I'm right not to. I came forward when my CFO embezzled close to ten million dollars from us. All I got from the State was a bunch of bullshit about how these things take time but that I should be prepared for the fact that I probably wouldn't get my money back. You know how much it takes to run a winery? Ten million will fucking bankrupt us, and where is your *system*? Where are the *authorities*? Instead of finding—"

"Frank," Hugh said in a calming voice, patting his hand on the table.

Jack dialed it down. He took a breath.

"But I guess the word got out, and that obviously signaled to someone that I had deep enough pockets for a blackmail run. You can appreciate why I didn't want to come forward. Now, just after you accuse me of being a thief," Jack air-quoted the word derisively, "then you have the gall to question why I didn't come forward after the blackmailer called. Jesus Christ."

"What did this blackmailer say your next step was?" Danzig asked, ignoring Jack's invective. "How are you supposed to contact him?"

"He said he'd be in touch. I assumed that's what you're intended to be. When you and your partner first rolled up to my winery, I thought you were part of the scam. You show up asking about jewels, and then I expect that I'm going to get a phone call in the next day or two with payoff instructions. The implication is that if I do, you guys go away."

Smelling blood in the water, Coughlin jumped in. "You've got unsubstantiated allegations from someone claiming to be an informant and a very real threat of blackmail perpetrated against my client. What is the FBI going to do for us, Ms. Danzig?"

The two agents shared a look, but Jack couldn't read it.

"One last question, Mr. Fischer. Where were you on March fifteenth of this year?"

"I'd have to check my calendar. I have no idea. The days tend to run together in this business."

"Ever been to Spain?"

"Yes."

"Familiar with the Falles Fiesta?"

"No."

Jack did his best to maintain his composure, keep his face a mask, but she was asking about the festival that they'd used as cover for the Valencia job. She'd *only* know that if she had someone on the inside. The only people who'd known about that were him, his crew, and Reginald. Of that list, only Jack, Enzo, and LeGrande were still alive.

"I think we have what we need for now, Mr. Fischer. We'll be in touch with the next steps."

"What about the blackmailer?" Coughlin demanded to know.

Jack grimaced inwardly but said nothing. He didn't want Hugh to push this too far.

"Well, that depends entirely on your client's willingness to participate in the investigation." Danzig closed her leather folio.

Coughlin handed Danzig his card as he stood up from the table. "If you'd like to speak to Mr. Fischer, you can go through me."

Danzig and Riordan stood and collected their things. They did not shake hands. When Danzig had placed everything back in her bag, she looked at Jack. "Mr. Fischer, blackmail is a very serious crime. I can assure you that the FBI will give this allegation the attention it deserves, and if it is indeed true, we will bring that person to justice. But if I find out this is a dodge on your part, I will bring the full measure of the US government down on your head. Are we clear on that, Mr. Fischer?"

"I'm glad we understand each other," Jack said.

The agents left.

Jack bought himself a few days at most. He could tell from the shift in body language and tone that the FBI had not considered the fact that Reginald was playing both sides of this game. Their next action would be to pull him in and ask what in the hell he thought he was doing. That would give Jack just enough time, he hoped, to make that answer indelibly clear.

Danzig and Riordan walked out to their car. Riordan was driving, so Danzig walked around to the passenger side. She placed her things on the roof and stared across the gap at the other agent. She thought he was a good investigator, but he seemed a little wooden to her. Riordan was clearly a white collar crime guy and was the kind of agent that could happily go an entire career without getting his hands dirty.

"He's lying," Danzig said and looked past Riordan back in the direction they'd come.

"Hundred percent," the other agent said.

"I'm going to call the US Attorney. We've got more than enough for a warrant now."

27

Jack landed at LAX, picked up a cab that offended his finer sensibilities and that took him north to the Hollywood Hills. The private investigator Jack hired to locate Paul Sharpe came through just before Jack had left for Cannes. Apparently, he wasn't that hard to find. When the investigator told him where he'd found Sharpe, Jack called the state's investigator. The drone read off a pro forma response of how these things took time and that it was best that Jack didn't interfere with the investigation. Jack snapped at him, saying he'd just done the hard work himself. All they had to do was arrest him. The investigator actually said he could appreciate Jack's frustration but that he would need to be patient while the system worked. He also said they weren't allowed to take a private investigator's word and that was an unlawful invasion of a citizen's privacy.

Meanwhile, Paul Sharpe was hiding out in a multimillion-dollar home in Laurel fucking Canyon. Didn't even have the good sense to leave the country.

Sharpe was counting on how slowly the justice system worked.

Or he just didn't know how to disappear. Jack took for granted that he knew how to make himself invisible, how to hide out. Just because he could make money disappear didn't mean Sharpe could pull the same trick with himself. He didn't speak any other languages that Jack knew of. Sharpe couldn't manufacture a false identity and didn't know where to get one. Put simply, absconding abroad was something that was going to take him some time to figure out how to do.

Jack crawled from Inglewood to Hollywood over the course of the two hours, finally arriving at the address his private eye had given him, just as the sun was nose-diving into the Pacific. He'd also had the detective check out the property value of the place. It was a four-and-a-half-million-dollar home, but Sharpe was only renting it. Apparently, you could do that in LA. The Ferrari he was driving, however, Paul had bought. The house, a stunning and unique architectural style of exact angles and aqua windows sat on the outer elbow of a snakelike road called Miller Place. From his backyard, Sharpe had a perfect view of the Los Angeles skyline, which was currently backlit by a burning streak of orange, upon which floated a layer of blue that was quickly deepening to indigo. It looked like a Cubist architect designed it as a set piece for *Miami Vice.*

Jack paid the cab driver in cash at the bottom of the hill about a quarter of a mile from the home, according to Google Maps. When the cab was gone, Jack quickly walked the distance. Jack pulled on a pair of tan leather driving gloves. It was dark, and this was one of the richer sections of goddamned Hollywood, anyway. A lone guy walking and wearing driving gloves wouldn't even break the scenery.

All the lights were on, and Sharpe didn't have any curtains drawn to obstruct his amazing view of Los Angeles, though the house sat atop a nine-foot-tall concrete rise. From the house, there were no good angles to get a detailed view of the street unless something was on the far side of it. Jack kept his head down, power-walking as a man deep in thought, and continued along the road, walking the length of the home. Once, he did look up, catching a glance of Sharpe standing in the window, drink in hand, admiring the view. Jack already knew he was home, though, because he'd called the house pretending to be soliciting a charity for crippled Yorkies. Sharpe declined interest in giving.

The garage was detached and offset from the house, seemingly in a separate wing. The garage door was the same aqua tone as the house's windows but opaque. There was no door handle or keypad, meaning it could only be operated by a remote control, which was likely in the car, or from the inside. Jack walked around the far side and stepped into the garage's shadow, obscuring himself from the street view. There was a dark-brown teakwood fence spanning the ten-foot distance between the garage and the concrete pillar that formed the outer edge of the gray stucco wall that surrounded the neighbor's yard. There was a door, or at least the outline of one, in the fence, but like the garage door, it didn't appear to be accessible from the outside.

No matter. Though the lack of exterior handle or lock was a slight setback, the fence was clearly designed for aesthetic as opposed to security. The top of it was perfectly flat, keeping with the architectural theme of the rest of the house, and Jack was able to pull himself up over it easily. He dropped to the other side as quietly as he could, avoiding the giant green trash bin as he started searching for a side door into the garage. He found it on the side facing the house, next to a bamboo garden that stood behind a wall of that same opaque aqua glass used on the garage door.

Jack removed a thin black leather case from his jacket

pocket, opened it, and drew out his lock picks. He set to work on the lock. Even in the dark, he was in the garage in less than a minute. There it was—a powder-blue metallic Ferrari California.

"He should be arrested for spending my money on this color alone," Jack muttered. He walked along the car, running his gloved hand along the curves all the way to the door handle. Jack opened the door and sat down, sliding behind the controls. A sly smile cracked on his lips. He popped the armrest and found both the key fob and the control for the garage door. Jack opened the garage and then, gleefully, pressed the bright red "Start Engine" button on the steering wheel. He waited for the initial growl to drop to a throaty purr, then tapped the accelerator once to rev the engine, then twice more, each time spiking the tachometer higher.

Paul Sharpe was an accountant, and he committed the kind of crime accountants knew how to do. He left the keys in the car because he assumed they were in the garage and the garage was locked, so therefore they were safe. He was too lazy to bring them back into the house, a bad habit he'd carried a long time. Jack used to give him shit about that, and now it felt somewhat prophetic. "Someone is going to steal your car, Paul," Jack repeated softly and without humor.

Jack backed out onto Miller Place and hammered the throttle, hitting forty-five before he reached the end of the house and then quickly braked so he could make the turn. He didn't know if Sharpe had seen him or not. No matter, he'd know soon enough. Jack wound his way out of the hills and headed south, enjoying the drive out of Hollywood infinitely more than he had the drive up.

Jack cleared the hills and headed south.

His phone sat next to him in the passenger seat, opened to a police scanner app that he hoped would give him a warning if Sharpe reported the Ferrari stolen. The app was poorly designed and crashed at random every few minutes, but Jack was hopeful it would work long enough for him to make the hour-long drive to Long Beach. Jack guided the Ferrari down the 110 and then opened her up...for about three hundred feet until he hit Los Angeles freeway traffic and dropped it back into third for the long crawl south.

The app died thirty-five minutes into the trip, and nothing had come across the scanner before it did, but by then, Jack figured he had enough of a head start on the police that it wouldn't matter.

He rolled into Long Beach underneath a dark sky that held traces of horizon fire, as if from a canvas painted by a disoriented god.

Jack had been to Reginald's home many times over the years since the fixer left prison. Jack fronted LeGrande the money for the place and had obviously made enough for him over the years to keep the bastard in style. The house was a three-story Mediterranean style on the exclusive Naples Island that overlooked a marina. About five years ago, LeGrande's rackets made him enough to add a boat to it. He actually christened it *Second Chances*, which Jack promptly told him was just as likely a middle-tier Panama City strip club. The townhouse was bobbing just under two million when Reginald bought it the decade before, and it had certainly doubled in value by now.

It never ceased to amaze Jack how little effort an over-worked parole officer put in. Jack doubted they'd ever even peeked in the windows at the cutout apartment Reginald maintained across town or spoke to Reginald's landlord, his neighbors, anything to prove that Reginald actually lived there. Maybe the feds just told them not to worry about it. The thought made him bitter.

Luckily for him, unlike much of Long Beach, this was the kind of neighborhood where a Ferrari California would look right at home. Jack parked it farther down Reginald's street, Lido Lane, and reached for his phone, the one Reginald had set up for him. Reginald picked up in three rings.

"The prodigal son," he said in his gravelly voice, infused with smoke and bourbon.

Jack sighed loudly for effect before speaking, as though he'd been agonizing over the call, fingers hanging over the screen, too afraid to dial. "You win, Reginald." Then he paused, to give the impression that he was still wrestling with his next words. "I'll pay you the money. Just call off your fucking dogs, okay?"

Reginald chuckled softly on the other end, and it sounded like an old engine choking. "Feds put a scare into you, eh?"

Listening to this fucker gloat was worse than the perception that Jack was paying him off. "Yeah, well, they make a convincing argument."

"I can imagine," Reginald said flatly. All the levity from just a second before drained out of his voice.

I'll bet you can.

"So, look. I stashed the stones in a box belonging to a numbered account in Switzerland. I'll give the account information, but it's going to be in person."

"I'd rather you just wired me the money."

"I'm sure you would, but we're not negotiating terms here. You know goddamned well that I couldn't have moved that many stones this fast and that I also wouldn't have risked bringing them stateside. You should also know that if I had fifty million on hand to give you, I wouldn't have taken the job in the first place. So, if you want the stones, you can have them, but on my terms."

"What if that doesn't work for me? How do I know I'm not getting set up?"

"Too risky. First of all, if I'm trying to double-cross you, there's always the possibility that it doesn't work. If it doesn't and it gets out, it's a good bet that the knowledge I pulled the job comes with it. There won't be a rock big enough for me to hide under if that's the case. Second, part of my price is that you're going to tell the FBI that you had the wrong guy."

"Your price, huh?"

"Yeah, and we're not negotiating it. I want this over, Reginald, and over now. I've got enough money that I can probably make it well enough on my own, so you get the jewels, and you already have the connections to move them. Even if you're stupid with it, you should be looking at fifty million dollars clean."

Jack was about to launch another string of invective when Reginald cut him off.

"Fine, goddamn it. I'll do it. If you just shut up about it. When do you want to make the exchange?"

"I'm in town now."

"Okay," Reginald said, drawing the syllables out. "Well, you remember how to get to my place. Come over and we'll do it here. I've got steaks. No reason we can't be civil about this."

"Fuck you, Reginald, and fuck civil," Jack said in a flat, even tone. "I don't trust you—at all—and I'm not doing this on your turf." It wasn't hard for Jack to summon the fury for his voice, even if it was for show. "I'm going to be at a restaurant in Beverly Hills. Call me when you get to Rodeo, and I'll tell you where to meet. If I sense anything is out of order, like I see someone with a government-issued haircut and a Brooks Brothers suit, I'm fucking gone. You understand me? And so is the money."

"Jesus, I get it," Reginald snapped. "But it's going to take me an hour and a half to get there at this time of night."

"Then I guess you better get moving." Jack hung up.

Jack had chosen his line of attack precisely, if not his exact words. He knew Reginald wouldn't go for it if Jack didn't appear to put up some kind of a fight or try to twist the situation into an advantage for him.

He watched Reginald's house for a few minutes. The street-facing side showed a slanted roof over a balcony that overlooked the front door and short lawn. Stubby palm trees covered most of the front of the home and reached up to the balcony with two larger palms extending up to tickle the roof tiles. From his vantage point three houses down the street, Jack could see Reginald exit the house but then lost him as he disappeared around the corner to the carport. Reginald didn't go for modern cars. Instead, he bought and restored classics. He'd bought the '69 GTO Judge convertible not long after he'd gotten the house and spent a few years resurrecting it. Even if Jack couldn't see the nuclear-orange paint job, there was certainly no mistaking the GTO's engine as it pulled out onto Lido Lane. From there, it was a short jog to Second Street, which would take him off the island and into Long Beach proper.

A pang of regret flashed in Jack's chest as the car throttled away. He was genuinely disappointed that he wouldn't have a chance to steal that car out from under Reginald.

Jack waited a long ten minutes before exiting the Ferrari. He wanted to give Reginald time to forget something and come back or to think better of accepting the terms of the arrangement. When the ten minutes passed, it was clear that Reginald was going through with it and wouldn't be coming back. Jack stepped out of the Ferrari and into the warm California night. Depending on traffic and Reginald's patience,

Jack figured he'd have between ninety minutes and two hours with the house. Well, less than that, depending on what Sharpe did about his car. He smirked.

Jack walked up to front door and removed his lock picks. Reginald didn't have an alarm system. The last thing in the world he wanted was for the police to respond to a break-in. Instead, he'd simply have very good locks on all the doors. In fact, Jack recalled a conversation on Reginald's deck shortly after he'd bought the place where the old thief said exactly that. Jack was inside in less than two minutes.

It was a little more difficult working the lock while wearing the driving gloves because it messed with his "feel," but that was one of the scenarios that Jack practiced for. He still worked locks in his spare time to maintain his proficiency and ran himself through drills like working with gloves on, in the dark, or against a stopwatch. The lock clicked, and Jack slid inside the dark house. He tapped the flashlight app on his phone. Jack padded across the foyer to the cream-colored carpeted staircase that snaked up to the second floor.

LeGrande's house was impressive, even in the dark. There was a guest suite and living room on the first floor, family room, gourmet kitchen, and bedroom on the second. Jack would be spending most of his time in there. But first, he walked up to the third floor, which held the master suite. There was a second wet bar in there, because apparently the original owner couldn't be bothered to walk downstairs to the main bar most nights. Jack knew from experience that this was where Reginald kept his good liquor. Reginald drank cheap when they were together, Jack Daniel's and rocks usually, because he was thumbing his nose at Gentleman Jack and his proclivities toward expensive libations. Jack knew, though, that LeGrande had developed an affinity for high-end scotches. Reginald even had a bottle of Macallan twenty-five, which went for just under a grand, and had bragged that he was saving it for his "retirement."

Jack found the wet bar and the scotch, still in its wooden container at the back of the bar. There were a lot of rare whiskies in there...it was almost a shame that no one was going to be able to enjoy them. Jack removed the Macallan, slid it out of the box, and split the foil, pouring a healthy dram into one of the tumblers on the bar. If his plan worked, he wasn't going to have to worry about Reginald finding the evidence. Glass in one hand, bottle in the other, and a smirk cracking the left side of his face, Jack returned to the second floor and stepped into the kitchen. He took a sip of scotch, savoring the vanilla and cherry burn and the *long* finish. It was incredible, exquisite.

This was a lady you spent the night with.

Jack grabbed the landline phone in Reginald's kitchen. Jack didn't keep one himself, but he knew Reginald's paranoia about communications. Jack dialed Paul Sharpe. Sharpe had gotten a new cell phone, but the private eye had figured that out and gotten Jack the number. Jack had a white noise app that he used when he was sleeping on planes. In addition to white noise, it had a variety of different ambient sound samples, including one called "Crowded Room." He selected this and set the phone on the counter. The background noise would help disguise Jack's voice and make it sound less like he was calling from someone's silent kitchen.

"Hello?"

"Is this Mr. Walter Willis?" Jack asked, using the name on the car's registration.

"Who's calling, please?"

"This is Triple A Towing in Long Beach."

"Did you say Long Beach? I'm sorry, I'm having a hard time hearing you."

"Sorry, it's a busy night here. Mr. Willis, do you own a 2013 Ferrari California?"

There was a long pause before Sharpe said, "I do."

He had to have bought that off the showroom floor. There's no other way Sharpe could've gotten that car that fast.

"Look, I got a call to pick up your car about fifteen minutes ago," Jack said, making it clear he was annoyed. "You left the car in a handicapped spot on Ocean. Normally, I'd just tow the thing, but it's a really nice car and I don't want to ding it, you know. Last time I did that, I had a guy try to sue me. Besides, dealing with the insurance companies is a pain in the ass for cars like that."

"I'm sorry, but you've got the wrong guy. My car is in the garage, and I've been here all night."

"You sure? I gotta run the plates on every car we get, make sure they weren't reported stolen. Well, I did, and your name came up. This is your car." Jack had no idea if this was true or not, but it sounded good. He knew Sharpe wouldn't know the difference either.

"That's impossible."

"So, look, you want to park in handicapped spots, that's your business, but unless you got a tag, I gotta tow ya. I'm trying to do you a solid here and let you come get the car—you're, what, at dinner or something?"

"I'm at home in fucking Hollywood," Sharpe snapped. "Hold on." Jack could hear him walking, huffing as he moved, occasionally muttering to himself. Jack took another sip of the scotch as he listened to Sharpe exit the house, walk down the pathway to the garage, and then explode into a fugue state of profanity that probably registered on the Richter scale when he saw that his car was gone.

Unable to resist turning the screws, Jack said, "Maybe it was your wife?"

"I'm not married! My fucking car was stolen."

"Well, look, it's at the corner of Ocean and South Termino, parked in the handicapped spot at the Jack in the Box. If you can get down here in the next thirty minutes, I won't tow it."

"Thirty minutes! I'm in fucking Hollywood. How am I going to get down to Long Beach in thirty minutes?"

"I'll hold off as long as I can, but you better hurry." Sharpe was about to try and bargain for more time when Jack interrupted him. "I got another call. You got a half hour, or it's a tow and two hundred and fifty bucks. And I'm not liable for anything that happens to your car." Jack hung up and put the phone down, smiling. He took another long, satisfying drink. Sharpe was most definitely on his way.

He refilled the glass another two fingers' worth and walked into the third bedroom that Reginald had converted into an office. The back wall was essentially a large window. To the left was a bookcase that occupied that entire side, to the right a desk with an iMac and a photo-grade printer. Jack started with the bookcase. Using his phone flashlight, he found the books on the third shelf that covered the wall safe. Jack pulled those off the shelf and let them drop, revealing the small safe set into the wall. Were it anyone else's safe, he'd wish Enzo Bachetti and his watchmaker's hands were here, but Jack knew Reginald. He knew where the old thief's tradecraft was excellent and where it lacked. Jack tried six numbers on the keypad —04-14-03—followed by a resolute *click*.

The numbers were the day Reginald got out of prison.

Jack opened the safe and aimed his phone's light into the space. The safe was filled with documents of all sizes, most of which were organized in manila folders or Moleskine notebooks. Jack put the phone in his teeth and flipped through them one by one until he found what he was looking for— his. Reginald kept a meticulous accounting of all the different identities he'd created, the types of documents he'd used, be it passport, social security card, driver's license, whatever. The books were organized by the person's name, with their associated aliases and forged docs listed below, ledger-style. Curiously, Jack's was in one by itself. He quickly thumbed through each one to make sure that he was only mentioned in the one book. That red Moleskine listed every identity that Reginald had ever created for him and had a variety of different headshots, all passport-photo sized. This was what he'd come for.

Jack returned the rest of the documents to Reginald's safe but didn't close it. Next, he went over to the desk and tapped on the keyboard of LeGrande's iMac to wake it. The machine popped to life, showing the home screen, which was a picture of a sunset over the Pacific, presumably taken from Reginald's boat. "You're getting soft," Jack muttered. It wasn't password locked, because no one who lived alone did that, regardless of what they had on their machine. Jack removed the memory stick he carried with him and plugged it in and selected the one file on it—a headshot of Paul Sharpe that he'd once used for staff bios. Reginald's default photo app launched when Jack clicked the thumbnail. He printed a sheet of the photos, photo-booth style.

Given his experience with the efficiency of the State of California thus far, Jack couldn't rely on their ability to put all of this together and connect Reginald with Sharpe, so Jack decided he was going to give them a little help.

Jack picked up the glass of scotch and walked over to the printer and sipped while it pushed out a single sheet of sixteen headshots against a generic blue field that could be the background on any driver's license or passport. Smiling, Jack removed the printed sheet, careful to touch only the edges with the tips of his gloves, and walked back over to the open safe. He pushed the photo sheet into the space, closed the safe, and replaced the books in front of it.

Jack finished his Macallan and set the glass on the table, toasting the empty air with his final sip.

Jack returned to the kitchen holding the notebook. Reginald had three candles in pewter stands all in a row in the center of his dining room table. Clearly someone had decorated for him. Jack grabbed one and lit it with a cigarette lighter he found in a junk drawer. He set that on the breakfast bar at the far end of the kitchen. Jack then walked over to the professional grade, six-burner gas stove and quickly turned each knob to high, turning on the gas flow and bypassing the pilot. He took the notebook and the bottle of scotch and bolted down the stairs. He made fast steps to the front door, slamming it closed as he passed.

Jack tore across the street to the Ferrari, making no effort to be inconspicuous. There was no time, and being seen was also something of the point. He dropped into the car, started the ignition, and pressed the accelerator down. The Ferrari jumped to life and sprinted to the end of Lido Lane, engine roaring. The kitchen exploded as the car took off. Jack saw a flash of orange light and black smoke pouring out of the second floor windows, smearing the light of the streetlamps. He whipped around a traffic circle that spat him onto Appian Way and a winding route around the outer edge of the island to Second Street.

Jack took the Second Street bridge and continued for several blocks, hanging an impossible right on Pomona, barely slowing down to forty miles an hour and earning a long horn from some poor asshole he cut way off. Jack screeched into the parking lot behind a taco shack and hard braked as soon as he hit the asphalt. He dropped the Ferrari into a dull, throaty idle and eased his way through the parking lot, exiting the other side. He parked the car along the curb, next to a dumpster. It was illegally parked but not overtly obvious. Jack shut off the Ferrari and gingerly exited, taking the notebook and the scotch. He locked the car with an over-the-shoulder shot from the fob and briskly walked to the street.

A siren wail broke the air, and another joined it almost immediately. Soon, there was a distant, terrible chorus.

Jack's heart rate shot up, and he could feel panic forming at the edges of his psyche. This was the first violent act he'd ever committed and his first crime on American soil in almost twenty years.

Jack dropped the Ferrari's keys in a blue postal service mailbox on Second. If the car was still sitting there when the mail carrier emptied the box the next day, he was in for a surprise. Jack handed what was left of the Macallan, a good three-quarters of the thousand-dollar bottle, to a homeless man sitting cross-legged in a doorway asking for change. Jack told him, "Cheers" when he gave over the bottle. A dirty face looked back, seemingly incapable of speech. The vagrant looked at the bottle, confused, trying to puzzle out the meaning of the gesture before abandoning the train of thought, opting instead for a healthy swig.

Jack hailed a cab and told the driver to take him to LAX and not to worry about the red lights. He had a flight to catch.

The cab picked up the 710, and Jack watched with vacant eyes as Long Beach blurred into the seemingly endless line of identical neighborhoods hanging off the freeway. The cabbie tried to make conversation, but Jack ignored him, if he even heard him at all. Jack was fighting the urge to tell the cabbie to drive instead to Beverly Hills and the restaurant that Jack told Reginald he would be at. Jack wanted to look Reginald in the face, to tell his mentor that he had figured out LeGrande's game, had outplayed him. Jack burned to see the look of haughty, self-assured arrogance drain away as he took the call from the Long Beach Fire Department telling him that his house, his life, was in ashes. Then to see Reginald begin to connect the pieces before Jack's eyes, to see him realize that he had been beat.

He chastised himself for the lack of discipline. That kind of thinking was what got him in trouble in Rome.

But Jack had learned his lesson from that event. Learned that sometimes the act of revenge itself was enough, had to be. His drunken, enraged call to LeGrande a few days before revealed that Jack was on to the fixer, and it had cost him not only time but also the element of surprise. Jack would not allow himself to make that mistake again. Reginald would tell his FBI handlers that Jack lured him out of his house and then set fire to it. He would do this anyway, but if Jack met him in person, there would be people who could place him in Los Angeles, and that would make his denial of involvement so much harder to believe. As it was, he'd need to be seen out and about in Sonoma tonight to establish an alibi. Jack would simply have to trust that Reginald would piece together Jack's hand in his undoing from a prison cell.

He just wished he'd had time to steal Reginald's goddamned boat too.

28

Katrina Danzig walked up Frank Fischer's driveway in her dark blue FBI raid jacket flanked by Riordan and their CHP liaison, Lieutenant Valero. They had four other CHPs with them, all wearing tactical vests, two several steps ahead, walking toward the front door and two moving around back to cover the rear exit. They disappeared into the predawn darkness. Two more CHPs were at the end of the driveway watching the road. Danzig followed the lead CHPs to the door and waited until the radio crackled, signifying they were in position. She nodded. One of the CHPs, a no-necked former Marine named Tomlinson, hammer-fisted the door. "Police officer," he barked. "Search warrant."

Danzig's heart rate picked up, anticipating the confused look on Fischer's face when he opened the door to find five cops on his doorstep with an arrest warrant. Danzig dropped the smile before anyone saw her. This was a major victory for Danzig—wrapping up an international jewelry trafficking ring that she had literally happened upon. Unless something broke their way with the French, they would not get Burdette for the Carlton InterContinental job unless he actually had some stones on him, and everyone believed Burdette was too smart for that. LeGrande couldn't actually testify that Burdette was in France at that time, just that he'd set up the job for him. But they could get him on several open and unsolved jewelry heists going back nearly a decade, based on LeGrande's information and his testimony.

Then they'd nail LeGrande for forgery, and if they couldn't get anything solid on him, she was sure that the counterterrorism guys in DC would want to speak to him about who he was making passports for. Danzig had seen his house in Long Beach—his actual house, not that bullshit flophouse apartment he rented and was conning his PO with. LeGrande was doing well for an ex-con working as a "construction foreman." She seriously doubted that jewel thieves were his only passport customers.

This was shaping up to be a hell of a week.

A few moments passed, and Danzig realized everyone was looking at her. There was no answer at the door, and they waited for instructions on whether to break down the door.

The trend in law enforcement over the past twenty years was to use SWAT to serve high-risk warrants. Increasingly, that meant a squad of police officers wearing body armor and carrying long guns. But there had also been a trend in police departments getting warrants wrong—serving at the wrong address or even getting into shootouts with gun-owning homeowners who believed (rightly or wrongly) that their homes were being invaded. The SAC was specific on this point —there was nothing in Fischer's profile that said he was violent or that this would be a high-risk service. In fact, their interviews with LeGrande suggested the opposite, a man who abhorred violence and didn't own any personal weapons. Layered on top of this was a recent surge in police violence against civilians and the attendant public backlash. Approval to seek an arrest warrant for Jack Burdette/Frank Fischer came only after Danzig, with support from ASAC Sinclair, convinced Mark Lattimore, the Special Agent in Charge of the San Francisco division, that Burdette was a significant flight risk. Danzig argued that if they didn't take him down now, he'd escape overseas, where he likely had the resources to stay hidden.

Lattimore was a careful, meticulous investigator and had a reputation for both playing the game well and the upper echelons of the Bureau. The word was he had his sights set on a position at one of the DC-based national intelligence fusion centers that would be a major stepping stone in his already immaculate career. He wasn't about to risk that by blowing a major investigation because his people went for the grab too soon and let their target escape.

Lattimore argued that the evidence was insufficient, but Danzig knew he was just burdened by an abundance of caution. She was new to him, and he hadn't yet evaluated whether to trust her judgment or not. The SAC knew her reputation, both good and bad, and Danzig was plainly aware that she carried those bags with her. But Sinclair was in her corner, and she knew that he'd pressed the SAC not to block her on this. Sinclair was of the older tradition of agents with law degrees, and he was able to explain how a judge would evaluate the warrant. Sinclair was convinced that the evidence Danzig presented would indeed satisfy a judge, and after a short but heated closed-door debate, SAC Lattimore agreed to let them put the warrant in front of a magistrate.

Lattimore and the US Attorney acquiesced to the warrant, but there were conditions. First, they would have to involve California Highway Patrol in the warrant service. Danzig suspected that stipulation was SAC's way of spreading the risk around. If someone got jumpy and used force, it would be easier for Lattimore to distance himself if it was from another law enforcement agency. Next, they absolutely could not use SWAT or CHP's Warrant Service Team, a decision that nearly caused Valero to pull out of the operation entirely. Lattimore was clear that this had to go forward cautiously, and the stated objective was to take the subject quietly or they wouldn't go at all. They were not going to have a shootout in the middle of wine country.

Danzig didn't care about who served the warrant. One local cop was as good as another in her opinion.

Thinking on that, she felt Tomlinson's eyes on her, staring back from Burdette's door, waiting for further instruction. She caught him flicking his eyes over to his lieutenant, but she couldn't tell if it was to see if guidance was coming from Valero instead or if it was something more malignant. "Hit the door again," she said.

Tomlinson hammer-fisted the door with three hard hits and bellowed, "Police officer. Search warrant."

Valero radioed his team in back to see if they observed any activity inside the house. They responded instantly with a negative—no lights, no motion.

"Do I go in?" Tomlinson asked, irritation heavy in his voice. Danzig could almost hear the "or what?" at the end of his question.

The SAC had filled her with enough doubt about the repercussions of being wrong that she was starting to second-guess herself. If Frank Fischer wasn't actually Burdette's alias, they'd blow their opportunity to nab the real Burdette, for one. Secondly, and more importantly, they'd have a public relations scandal for forcing entry into the home of a wealthy and well-liked Sonoma businessman, who would undoubtedly sue the bureau and CHP. Danzig looked to her partner, hoping to read a vote of support or urge of caution in his face.

Riordan wanted to nail Burdette on general principle, because he'd been so thoroughly outmaneuvered during their interview two days before. He wasn't a guy who enjoyed losing, and that could sometimes cloud his judgment.

"I say we go in," Tomlinson announced, as though there had been a debate about it and it was his turn to offer an opinion.

With some trepidation, Danzig nodded her head in the affirmative.

"Go," was all she said.

The highway patrolman that accompanied Tomlinson to the door—Danzig hadn't bothered to learn his name—brought the battering ram up and smashed in Frank Fischer's front door. The wood exploded around the deadbolt with a sharp crack that split the dry morning air and seemed to echo down the quiet street. Six highway patrolmen boiled into the house, shouting their presence and hearing nothing in return. Danzig and Riordan ran in immediately on their heels, cognizant that they needed to grab the suspect first.

The shouts from the police were met only with silence.

Danzig moved through the quiet, dark home, the morning light now beginning to stream into the windows. She visually verified in every room that the suspect was nowhere to be found. From the master bedroom on the second floor, she distantly heard the voice of a patrolman saying there were no cars in the garage.

They rallied in the kitchen where she issued instructions —sweep the home. Someone asked her what they were looking for. Danzig doubled down. She ordered them to upend every drawer, every cabinet, and every box in every closet. They were looking for jewels, finished stones, and jewelry, and they were looking for passports not named "Frank Fischer." They were looking for cell phones and computers. She admonished them to be cognizant of false bottoms and panels. Whatever they were looking for would be well hidden.

Danzig started in the bedroom, knowing that psychology often led people to keep their secrets in the place they felt the safest, the most secure, which was the place they slept. She started with his drawers, dumping the contents on the floor and tapping every part of the bureau and the drawers for false bottoms or hidden compartments. She asked Riordan to help her move it away from the wall to make sure it wasn't hiding anything either on the wall or in the floor.

Riordan's phone buzzed, and he stepped over the window for better reception. Danzig moved to the closet.

She heard Riordan end the call. When he didn't immediately say anything, Danzig turned around and looked at him.

Riordan wore a flat expression. "That was the overnight watch in LA. Somebody set fire to Reginald LeGrande's home in Long Beach last night and burned it damn near to the ground."

"What the fuck is going on?"

"Oh," Riordan said, "it gets better."

The next few days evaporated into the ether for Danzig as they spent nearly every waking hour trying to piece together what in the hell happened to their case. What had been a straightforward investigation had, overnight, become a municipal, state, and federal clusterfuck. The Long Beach Fire Marshal determined, almost immediately, that the fire was arson, and that it had been set by turning the gas range on and then having an open flame in the room, likely from a candle. Neighbors also reported seeing a man run out of the house, get into a vehicle—a rather unsubtle Ferrari California—and speed off. Long Beach PD recovered the Ferrari a few miles from the house, ditched on a side street.

The car's owner was none other than one Paul Sharpe who, until June, had been the CFO of Kingfisher Wines and was the subject of an embezzlement investigation. Sharpe had been "hiding out" in the Hollywood Hills under an assumed name, rather luxuriously and essentially in plain sight, as he figured out his next move. When pressed jointly by Long Beach PD and the Highway Patrol, Sharpe couldn't produce a convincing argument as to how he'd come to relocate to Hollywood in such style. CHP arrested him on the embezzlement charge and suspicion of arson.

Sharpe did try to argue that his car had been stolen, though there was no corroborating report with LAPD, Long Beach PD, CHP, or the LA County Sheriff. Sharpe also claimed to have gotten a mysterious phone call from a towing company in Long Beach alleging that his Ferrari was illegally parked and that he'd have to come get it. The responding officers assured him that no tow truck operator on Earth was that magnanimous and told Sharpe directly they thought he was lying. Sharpe offered no other explanation for having been in Long Beach that night.

Things didn't get weird until the police opened up the fire safe that LeGrande had in his office. It was one of the few things in his house to survive the blaze. Inside were the notebooks that LeGrande kept on the various identities he'd created for people over the years, something of an accounting ledger for a master forger. It initially struck Danzig and Riordan as odd, given that it amounted to an admission that Reginald LeGrande had, in fact, been creating fake identities for over a decade. But it was Riordan who figured out why. LeGrande had been trading people to various authorities for

years, and he needed a way to keep track not only of the ones
he was selling out but also the identities that they'd be living
under. It was probably the only way that he could keep things
straight in his own head. The notebooks weren't all they found
in that safe, however. There was also a sheet of passport-sized
photos of none other than Paul Sharpe.

Once they'd made that discovery, theories began to
coalesce.

Sharpe had embezzled tens of thousands of dollars from
the winery over a five-year period and one final amount of ten
million before he disappeared. Burdette/Fischer—Danzig
refused to think of him any other way—reported the crime to
CHP when it happened. Burdette's attorney, Coughlin, had
actually filed charges with the Sonoma County DA's Office in
June, who had, in turn, kicked it up to a state investigator,
where it was in a queue.

Sharpe's connection with LeGrande was still unclear to
Danzig and Riordan. Was it Sharpe who initiated the contact,
approaching LeGrande to create the travel documents necessary to get out of the country on an assumed identity? Or was
it LeGrande who enticed Sharpe with the promise of an easy
score for a cut of the profits? That was the likely theory in
Danzig's mind, given that Sharpe had no prior criminal background and didn't seem like the person to have access to a
passport forger. What was clear was that LeGrande had the
materials necessary to make a passport for Sharpe. But why
would he need to? No law enforcement agency was looking for
Sharpe yet, otherwise he wouldn't have been living in a rented
four-million-dollar home in the Hollywood Hills and driving a
Ferrari.

Unfortunately for Danzig, it appeared they'd stopped
listening to her.

Riordan's working theory, which was the one the brass had

latched onto, was that Sharpe initiated the contact and was likely bragging to LeGrande about how much he was taking in from the winery. Riordan challenged the assumption that because Sharpe had no record, this was his first criminal act. Riordan knew that embezzlement was rampant in the wine industry and used that to bolster his argument. He suggested that Sharpe had likely been running this scam for years with various unknowing clients. To be a successful winemaker, one had to be part artist, part chemist, part marketer, part salesman, and part businessman. It stood to reason that very few people could do most of those things well, so they hired out the things they couldn't do to the Paul Sharpes of the world. Riordan argued that it was an embezzler's paradise.

LeGrande then, according to Riordan's hypothesis, decided to see if there was anything left in the well and tried his own blackmail game. Fischer corroborated this in their interview. Sharpe panicked once he learned that the FBI was involved. He wouldn't know that LeGrande had been an informant for the better part of a decade. He traveled to LeGrande's house and set fire to the place, hoping to destroy any evidence of his and LeGrande's relationship, not knowing that LeGrande had the fire safe.

Times like this, Riordan said, it was a wonder that society still needed cops.

In a last effort to save her investigation, Danzig pointed out that there was still no conclusive link between Sharpe and LeGrande, but Lattimore shut her down quickly. He said that would come out in the interrogation and that it didn't appear the Gem and Jewelry Program had any remaining interest in this investigation.

She'd asked about Burdette.

Lattimore's response had been final. "What do you have other than the word of a con man?"

Danzig had gotten into trouble for ordering the entry to Fischer's home, even though the warrant authorized it. The justification of probable cause was now being questioned, and Fischer's lawyer was raising hell over it. Danzig tried explaining to Lattimore that Fischer was Burdette, that he'd been named as the chief perpetrator in a jewelry store heist in Valencia, Spain, by someone on the crew, and that same person said Burdette was behind the Carlton InterContinental heist. Lattimore said, "Fine, you produce an informant and I'll give you another chance."

But that wasn't going to happen either.

Castro's informant was dead.

Stolar's body turned up a few days ago in Rome. There were no leads, and the Italians had already closed the case. They weren't burning a lot of effort solving the murder of a foreign criminal in their country on a forged passport.

So that left Danzig with very few options.

Danzig still believed, still *knew* that Burdette was behind all of this. Though she kept those suspicions to herself now. SAC Lattimore believed "Jack Burdette" was a fabrication LeGrande created to sell his blackmail. Danzig argued that was a convenient story to fit the facts, but the SAC wasn't hearing it. She wasn't one of his agents, and he wasn't about to go out on the ledge for a jewelry cop from New York. Sharpe had motive and intent and was seen in Long Beach not two miles from LeGrande's house. When they interviewed him, Sharpe repeated the same bullshit story about a towing company that he'd initially given to the Long Beach Police. Even Danzig had to admit that sounded like something a bad liar would make up on the fly. Long Beach asked the court to include LeGrande's phone records in their search warrant and discovered a phone call made from LeGrande's home to

Sharpe's cell about the time he said that he'd received the call from the mysterious, benevolent tower.

Lattimore cancelled the warrant on Frank Fischer.

They arrested LeGrande on the forgery charges and conspiracy to commit blackmail. In parallel, the State of California was pursuing a decade of parole violations.

Lattimore wanted them to arrest Sharpe as well, but Long Beach PD and CHP were flexing to see which agency's charges had primacy. It looked like Long Beach was going to win that particular pissing contest, since CHP couldn't prove they were actively investigating Sharpe for the embezzlement charges first. Sharpe was looking at twenty-five years in state prison for arson and another ten years of federal time for the embezzlement.

It appeared that all the FBI was going to come away with was a forgery and a conspiracy to commit fraud conviction on an informant CHP had run for ten years. The State would get him on the conspiracy to commit blackmail.

They were already expecting LeGrande's attorney to call attention to how CHP ran him as an informant and then simply handed him over to another agency for prosecution, a strategy that would make it look like the one government agency had used him and then handed him over to yet another government agency to arrest him on something else. It would look to a jury like dirty politics.

And no one was talking about jewels.

Danzig couldn't understand it. LeGrande was the one who gave CHP Burdette's name in the first place—he could identify Frank Fischer as Jack Burdette. But again, Lattimore wasn't having it. Any evidence that there might have been burned up in the fire, and Lattimore wasn't letting go of the story that LeGrande made up the Jack Burdette/Frank Fischer connection as a way of selling the blackmail. She offered to show him her files, years of investigation into Jack Burdette, but again, Lattimore wasn't hearing it. He said that without someone else to confirm Burdette's identity, it was over. With Ozren Stolar dead, she didn't have anyone else that could do that.

She just couldn't understand it.

Then, as she thought of it, she could.

Lattimore was a climber, a careerist. More than that, he was a company man. He was going to protect the Bureau, and by extension himself, from any harm that might come from going too far out on a limb for a case he thought was built on a dodgy premise. The worst thing for her, though, worse even than the dressing-down SAC Lattimore gave her in front of her mentor and friend, was the Assistant US Attorney, Preston Turner, having the gall to say, "Agent Danzig, do you know why the Department of Justice has a ninety-nine percent conviction rate?" Of course she fucking *knew*. That's the first stat they give you in the academy. It's in the fucking pamphlets. Turner then said in the most condescending, bullshit, government weasel lawyer voice he could possibly conjure, "Because we only take up the cases we know that we can win."

Danzig was done in San Francisco.

Lattimore directed her to turn over any information that was pertinent to the LeGrande/Sharpe investigation and return to her duty station.

Which she did. Mostly.

Frank Fischer didn't add up.

Whatever these clowns were doing out here was fine, but Fischer would remain a person of interest to the Gem and Jewelry Program, and she would use that to dig into his background. Danzig had an informant identify Frank Fischer as being Jack Burdette. That was enough for her. She was certain that, given time, they'd discover he was a fabrication. But was he one of the world's most notorious jewel thieves? Danzig believed he was, but she also doubted that a single person could possibly have pulled off the Carlton job. That also gave her hope because they and their allies at Europol would eventually start to piece together how that job was pulled, and from there, who was involved. In fact, she'd already gotten approval to go to Cannes. She'd be meeting Castro there in a few days.

Danzig knew that when she stripped the layers off Frank Fischer's story, she'd find a jewel thief named Jack Burdette. That identity would line up with several unsolved jewelry heists alleged by LeGrande. Once his trial was over and LeGrande was back in prison, he'd be ripe for the picking. Danzig would dangle a deal in front of him for him to roll on Burdette, and she'd get everything she needed. It was just a matter of time. Time, she had.

After all, we only take the cases we know that we can win.

29

The tasting room was cool and quiet beneath the soft overhead lights. The last guests were finishing their glasses, and Jack was in no hurry to kick them out. They were a nice local couple who he'd seen there more than once. The husband was a chef, and the wife was in commercial real estate. They were finishing their second comped glass of Osprey and chatting it up with his tasting room manager. Jack hung back and busied himself with inventory. Real work was a welcome distraction from the last few weeks, and Jack was happy for it.

Because he'd spent every waking minute on edge.

The couple finished their glasses in time, bought a few bottles to take home, and thanked Steve for his time. They promised to be back soon, and the chef said he'd like to have their wines on his menu to see how they did. Steve beamed and took the man's card. Jack walked over, introduced himself, shook hands, and said they were honored and would send a case over for them to try out.

Then he sent Steve home, saying he'd finish closing up the tasting room.

Jack poured himself a glass of Osprey that Steve had left

and enjoyed the silence. It took him the better part of a day to clean up the mess the FBI made in his house, and Coughlin was practically frothing at the mouth with righteous indignation to sue them for falsely accusing his client. Of course, Jack wanted nothing to do with that and was laboring to come up with a justification for pulling Coughlin back. It was the sort of thing that an outraged private citizen would do in this day and age. The idea that was gaining traction in his mind was not suing because they would not want to further cloud their case against Paul Sharpe.

Jack's phone rang. It was Meg. He stared at the screen, at her face, for a long second before answering.

"Hey," he said tentatively.

"Hi, Frank, or..." Her voice trailed off. "I don't even know what to call you."

"Just call me Frank," he said, but the name sounded strange to his own ears.

"Where are you?"

"Tasting room. I'm just closing up." Then he said, "You could come by? Have a drink?"

Meg was quiet for a time. "I don't know."

"Look, I know this is...strange...but I think we can figure it out."

"Can we?" she said, and Jack detected a hint of anger in her voice. "I care about you, Frank, and I often thought that we'd have some kind of a future together. Running the winery...and us. But now, I'm just not sure of that. Of anything."

"Meg," he started.

"Let me finish," she said. It was clear to Jack that she'd been working on this for some time. "I thought I was in love with you, but now I don't know what that was based on, now that I know that man doesn't exist. Not really."

"Of course I do," Jack protested.

"No, you don't! You made up Frank Fischer like he was in a story or something. None of the things that make Frank real *are real*. Then I wonder how much of that is Frank and how much of it is you. Is Jack, I mean. And, Jesus Christ, Frank, I can't even keep this straight in my own head."

"Megan, it doesn't matter what my name is. I changed it once to help me hide from something, to start a new life, *this* life. That's all that matters. All of those things that you loved about me are *me*."

"I don't even know who you are," she said. "I don't know if I want to. Those people, Reginald LeGrande, I can't imagine that anyone that I would want to be with would know anyone like that. But more than that, you lied to me about who you were, and all I keep thinking about is...what else about you isn't true."

"I'll admit," Jack said, looking around the empty tasting room, "I'm not sure I know who I am anymore, and I can't answer some of those questions."

"Can't or won't?"

"Does it make a difference?"

"I suppose not," she said softly. Jack knew in his heart that's what sealed it for him.

"Goodbye, Frank."

"Megan, wait," he said hastily, trying to pull it all back but knowing that it was hopeless. "My real name is Jack Burdette."

"Then I guess this is goodbye, Jack."

Megan hung up.

That night at his house, Jack had told her that no one knew his real name because it was too risky to know. He was afraid that any accidental disclosure would endanger his family, or at least bring them a lot of unnecessary pain. It was the most powerful secret Jack had, and he told her now because he thought that would be the thing to make a difference.

Megan just used it to say goodbye.

He stood in silence for long moments and felt a crushing weight on his shoulders.

A week ago, Jack had pulled off the largest jewelry heist in history, not to mention one of its greatest cons. He'd won, only to find he'd lost one of the things he'd done that to protect.

Jack refilled the wineglass and set to work, closing the place down. He had a jazz playlist going over the tasting room speakers.

Jack alternated between rubbing a bar rag on the polished granite surface and absently sipping his wine. He looked up into the dark room and felt both tense and at peace. It was a feeling for which there were no words. Jack had the money to keep his winery afloat. They decided to go forward with the acquisition of the Sine Metu plot because they were amazing, nearly legendary grapes, and they would be able to sell the entire harvest. Coughlin was quietly putting the word out to some winemakers that Kingfisher may need some help after the crush, so at least they wouldn't be completely adrift without a winemaker if Megan decided not to return. Which, it appeared, she would not.

Jack was contemplating survival when Special Agent Katrina Danzig walked through the tasting room door.

Jack stared at her with a blank expression for a matter of moments while she stood somewhat awkwardly in the threshold. He was stripped bare. The woman he loved, the one he'd risked everything in order to have a future with, had just said goodbye, and now this...cop was showing up at his doorstep to give him a hard time. Jack stared hard at her for a few long moments. When she didn't say anything, Jack gingerly set his bar rag on the counter and picked up his wineglass. "There's a line about gin joints that seems applicable here."

Danzig wore an expression that suggested the Bureau had not issued her a sense of humor.

"You'd better have a really compelling reason for me to not call my lawyer."

"I just wanted a word."

"Hugh tells me that the Bureau dropped the investigation into me when they realized it was all bullshit that LeGrande fellow made up. So, unless you came here for a couple cases of wine, I have to say," Jack paused, "this feels a lot like harassment."

"I don't drink," she said.

"So, it's the other thing, then."

"I just wanted to ask you a question."

"I thought Hugh was pretty clear that if you wanted to talk to me again, you needed to go through him. Let's find out for sure." Jack reached into his front pocket and made to pull out his phone.

Danzig's hand went to her hip.

"Easy," Jack said with a voice that was equal measures lost patience and simmering anger. "It's a phone."

"Put the phone down, Jack."

Jack flashed angry eyes at Danzig but thumbed the phone open and said, "Hey, Siri. Dial Hugh Coughlin's mobile." The phone informed him that it was dialing his attorney.

"This isn't necessary."

"Like hell it isn't. You took your swing and you missed, and now you're harassing me at my place of business," Jack said as he waited for Hugh to pick up. He tapped the speaker function so she could hear but grimaced when it went to voicemail. Jack looked up to find a haughty smirk on the agent's face. "Hey, Hugh, so I know you said that if the FBI had any more questions for me, they needed to go through you, but Special Agent Danzig seems to have forgotten that because she's here at the winery and wants to talk to me. Call me back when you get this. Or come over with a restraining order. Either one." Jack hung up and returned her smug look with a shrug. He turned around, set the phone down, grabbed a glass from the counter, and refilled his glass from the open bottle of Osprey. "Want a glass, since this is obviously an informal chat?"

"I'm fine."

"Suit yourself," he said and took a sip, leaning against the back of the bar. Now he was stalling for time until Hugh called him back, so he decided to indulge her. "You wanted to ask a question, so go ahead and ask."

"The morning after LeGrande's house burned down, we showed up at your house to arrest you, but you were nowhere to be found. Where were you?"

"This seems highly irregular."

"You were adamant the first time we spoke that someone was trying to frame you and that you weren't really Jack Burdette. If that's true, it seems like it would be in your best interests to convince me of it."

"Is this all off the record?"

"I'm not a reporter, Mr. Fischer, I'm a federal agent. Anything you say to me is on the record. But you're also not under arrest. Call it a curiosity."

Jack had no experience with her side of the law, but all this still felt very off to him.

"I had dinner with a friend in downtown Sonoma, and then we had a couple bottles of wine. I crashed in his spare bedroom." Jack had landed at Sonoma County Airport just before ten and met Hugh for a drink and a late supper. He made sure to pay the check with his credit card so his name appeared next to a timestamp. Then he and Hugh went back to Coughlin's and got proper drunk. Jack teetered on telling Coughlin everything but didn't.

"Lucky you," was all Danzig said.

Less luck and more Rusty burning through several favors to learn that they'd gotten a warrant and were coming for him.

"My neighbor called me and said there were a bunch of police at my door that morning. I had to tell him that you people got the address wrong. I hope you can appreciate how embarrassing that was."

Danzig was launching into her rejoinder when Jack cut her off. "I told Highway Patrol all of this when they interviewed me about Paul Sharpe. You know all of this, so what are you doing here?"

Danzig was opening her mouth to respond when the door opened and a man walked through.

Coughlin could not have gotten there that quickly, and this man was much, much larger.

"I'm sorry, we're closed," Jack said as the man stepped through the doorway.

Danzig half twisted to face him.

"I'm not here for wine," came the reply. His English was good, but there was no mistaking the Eastern European varnish on the words. Mostly the emphasis on the *r* that was almost like gravity sculpted the sound. The man took exactly four long strides, putting him in the center of the room, a pistol already in his hand.

"I'm a federal age—"

"I don't care," the man said, cutting her off. He fired.

Agent Danzig was between Jack and the stranger, so he couldn't see where the gunshot hit her. But the agent folded with the impact and fell to the floor with little more than a light but forceful "uh" escaping her lips.

"Put your hands behind your head, Burdette."

The face was familiar, but Jack didn't know from where. Was this someone he'd done business with?

"Who are you?" Jack asked when his hands were laced at the base of his skull.

"I think you know."

"I think I don't," Jack replied sarcastically.

"Milan Radić. I believe you knew my protégé, Ozren Stolar."

"Oh, you've got to be fucking kidding me," Jack said aloud, simply losing all composure. Then, loud enough for Radić to hear, "How are you not dead?" Of which, Jack was genuinely curious. He'd seen Rusty put three shots right in Radić's chest, and then Jack had checked his pulse. Which, admittedly, he'd only ever seen done on television and now realized he'd probably felt the wrong part of the Serb's neck.

"I was awake, barely conscious, as you and your friends discussed things by the porch. I know all about Hassar. That's how I found you here."

"But Rusty's people," Jack asked, flicking his eyes down to Danzig's crumpled form on the ground. She was lying in a kind of fetal position, and he could see blood pooling on the floor. He had no idea what that meant, though, since he was obviously a poor interpreter of the thin line between life and death.

"They're Italian," Radić said, by way of an answer. He lifted his shoulders as if to add, *What do you expect?* This could mean he bribed his way out, overpowered and killed them, or simply walked off while they were having a smoke break. Whatever the truth was, Radić wasn't sharing. Somehow, that word didn't make it back to Rusty. "So, you'll give me the money that Hassar paid you, and I will leave you to whatever your policeman friend has in store."

"What an asshole," Jack said, again under his breath.

"The money, Burdette."

"What, from the register?" When Radić didn't react, Jack added, "I obviously don't have it here."

"Of course not. You will transfer it."

"No," he said, shaking his head. "I will not."

"Excuse me?"

"You heard me. I gotta tell you, you guys are a swell lot of thieves. You and Ozren both just roll in and expect me to hand everything over because you have an accent and a gun."

"Enough of this. The money, now," Radić said again, pulling the hammer back on his pistol to emphasize the point.

Jack's phone rang, and Radić's eyes moved on instinct to the sound. Without thinking, Jack grabbed the Osprey bottle on the counter and hurled it at Radić. The bottle sailed through the air, spraying wine, and flew right past the side of the Serb's face, smacking into the wall behind him with a wet crash. Radić flinched and turned his head from the flying bottle and subsequent impact. Jack saw a dark flash of motion on the ground as Danzig rolled onto her back, pistol out and tightly gripped in both hands, followed by three precise, clipped shots. A trio of fire-bright flashes burst from the muzzle of Danzig's small pistol, and the tasting room filled with the acrid smell of gunpowder. The first shot hit Radić just above the sternum, the second a few inches higher just below the neck, and the third just below the chin. His head snapped back and exploded as the bullet exited the back of his brain. Radić crumpled to the floor, and this time there was no confusing his fate.

Danzig, still on her back, kept the pistol leveled, though Jack could see from the strained expression on her face that it was causing her considerable pain. He could see now that Radić's bullet struck her in the right shoulder. Taking that hit at such close range would've been enough to send her to the ground, but Danzig had the sense to play dead so that if the opportunity presented itself, she could do exactly as she did.

Danzig was on her feet by the time Jack made his way back around the counter, a clean bar rag in his hand.

She walked over to Radić's body and slid his pistol out of reach with her right foot.

"Stay over there, Jack," she said and moved around Radić's body. She knelt without taking her eyes off Burdette and felt for a pulse. Satisfied that the Serb was indeed dead this time, she walked over to where she'd kicked Radić's gun and picked it up with a pen, careful not to touch it with her hand. Danzig walked over to the bar and set the gun on the counter. She turned to Burdette.

"Sure you don't want that glass of wine now?" Jack asked.

"Who was that?"

"His name is Milan Radić. He's a Serbian thief, one of the Pink Panthers."

"What was he doing here?" There was the faraway look in her eyes that people got when they were concentrating on something besides the conversation in progress.

"I'm starting to think I've got an idea, but maybe why don't you tell me what you're *really* doing here, Agent Danzig, because you didn't show up here to ask me a couple questions. And I just now noticed that you're not here with your partner."

"I got an anonymous tip that said if I showed up here tonight, I'd catch you making the exchange of the Carlton jewels to someone matching his description." She thumbed at Radić.

"That anonymous tip was Reginald LeGrande."

"Of course it was," she snapped, apparently annoyed at him connecting an obvious dot.

"So, LeGrande tips you to be here tonight, and then he

dimes me to Radić, telling him to wait until you're inside and then take us both out. That effectively kills the investigation, right?"

Danzig shook a negative. "Not really, but I can see where he'd think that. We're after him for forgery, and that's a different division than me, but LeGrande wouldn't know that. His lawyer is working on immunity because he was a CHP informant for so long, but I don't think that'll fly. Even if it does, that's just for the state crimes. We're still going to nail him for the forgery. I can see, though, from his line of thinking how he'd conclude that killing me would kill the investigation. He's probably assuming that with you and me dead, the blame goes to Radić, and he's cleared of any involvement."

Jack didn't say anything in response.

"What's Radić's angle here?" Danzig asked.

"Reginald probably promised him a share of the jewels."

"But," she said in a quizzical tone, "he mentioned money."

There was a bitter and hilarious irony here, Jack thought. Reginald tried to set up Jack and Danzig to get killed by a Serbian gangster so that he could walk free, and it never would have mattered because he didn't plan to kill the right cop. Reginald also didn't know that Radić overheard the discussion about the arrangement with Hassar, so when the Serb showed up here, he planned to just cut out Reginald entirely.

A knot formed in Jack's stomach, and it was a heavy, cold thing. Selling him out to the police was one thing, but Jack would never have thought Reginald would set him up to be murdered. There was just no honor among assholes anymore.

"Just so we're clear," Danzig said in a flat tone, "I don't want you to think that this is one of those 'moral dilemma' situations where I let you go because you distracted him."

"What are you talking about?"

Her face soured with annoyance that she was actually going to have to go through the effort of explaining it to him. Danzig motioned to Radić's body with her free hand. "Your friend there basically confirmed everything I've been saying. I can't let you walk."

"Seems like the thing to do in this situation, saving your life and all."

"You're a criminal," Danzig said, as though she were explaining something to a child after a string of "but whys."

"Am I?"

"Semantics," she said through a grunt of pain. "You're wanted for over twenty jewelry thefts in Europe, not to mention the Carlton InterContinental."

"Am I?" Jack asked, and she shot him an incredulous look in response. "No crime was committed, Agent Danzig." A smirk broke across his mouth. "What's the short form of that? Agent, Special Agent, what?"

"Special Agent Danzig is fine."

"Jesus, no wonder you people never get anywhere."

"This is over. I'm arresting you for the Carlton InterContinental heist. I'll have the Sonoma County Sheriff remand you into custody until I can have you transported to San Francisco."

"Like I said, no crime was committed," Jack said matter-of-factly.

"What are you talking about?"

"I was paid to do it."

"Oh, I don't doubt that."

"By the owner," he said slowly. "That's what Radić was talking about."

Danzig formed a response but stopped before the words left her mouth. Jack's three words clearly short-circuited her synapses.

"So far as I know, all I did was relocate those jewels at a time and place as determined by their rightful owner. He got wind that someone was going to steal them"—Jack let his words hang in the air—"so he hired me to get them first."

"That's ludicrous," she shot back. "He'd have just hired more security guards."

"Have you seen how these guys operate? The Panthers?" Jack asked, incredulous. "They smash Audis into storefronts and then wave MP-5s at people. You really think a couple extra unarmed French rent-a-cops are going to stop that? I was an insurance plan, nothing more."

"You really expect me to believe that?"

"Would I admit it if it wasn't? Ari Hassar wasn't going to trust his collection to a couple extra French guards, so when he thought he didn't have any other options, he called me. He wasn't going to lose face by cancelling the show, and I suspect he probably wanted the publicity. Or the notoriety. In those circles, I'm not even sure there's a difference."

"How did he know he was going to get robbed?"

"Ask him," Jack said, shrugging. "But consider that most of his security staff are ex-Mossad. You do the math."

"Even if what you say is true, you're still aiding in a conspiracy to commit insurance fraud on a pretty massive scale."

Jack only shrugged again. "Whatever he did after I gave them back is entirely up to him, and I'm not party to it. Besides, if that's true, you're talking about dollar values equivalent to the economies of some countries. Neither Hassar nor his insurers are going to publicly admit what happened, and you don't have the jurisdiction to make the inquiry. As for your friends at Europol, something tells me Hassar probably has that covered." Jack let that sink in. "The insurer is going to go along with something that might look a little 'gray area' but is, essentially, not illegal. They're more worried about the perception that they're honoring their obligations, and they know that no gem business that operates at that level is entirely clean. You know what's happening to Hassar's business right now? It's skyrocketing because of the notoriety. People love to be a part of something they think is almost shady. Hassar is probably making arrangements with his insurers to pay that money back very quietly as we speak." That part was entirely fiction, but Danzig was too stunned to pick up on it.

"What about all of the jobs LeGrande said you pulled?" she asked.

"Who pulled?"

"Don't get cute, Jack."

"You ever see a James Bond movie?"

"Of course," she said, sounding irritated.

"So they've been making these movies for, what, fifty-sixty years now? About every ten years or so there's a new 007, but the films," Jack wagged a finger knowingly, "never acknowledge this. So, there's this theory going around for the last couple years that James Bond isn't one guy. It's actually a code name for a bunch of different spies. See, that's how they explain away the fact that someone named James Bond has been assassinating the enemies of the Crown since the sixties." Jack paused a moment. "You're trying to tell me that a thief named Jack Burdette had this long and storied career and is wanted in connection with twenty-some odd heists in Europe or elsewhere, and you make it sound like this is just the tip of some great criminal iceberg. You know what that makes me think?"

"I can only imagine," Danzig said flatly, her voice oozing annoyance.

"Maybe Jack Burdette is just a name that thieves use to confuse the shit out of people like you."

Danzig had no response, whether out of spite, confusion, or simply to not acknowledge the point, Jack didn't know.

After the fire, there was no credible evidence beyond LeGrande's testimony that Frank Fischer was actually Jack Burdette. Danzig showed up there on a last, desperate hope that she could find something to connect him, but any possibility of that had bled out on the floor.

"How does Paul Sharpe fit into all this?"

"If I had to guess? Reginald probably told him that Kingfisher would be an easy mark. It might even have been a grander scheme on his part to increase his share and spread his risk around. Sharpe found out you guys were after LeGrande and went after him to cover his tracks. You guys will have a fun time untying that knot."

Danzig shot him a look that was a slow, acid burn but said nothing. Then she holstered her pistol and pulled out her phone. Jack didn't know who she dialed, but he assumed it was the Sonoma County Sheriff. Danzig identified herself as a federal agent and said one suspect was down and another was in custody, that she'd need local law enforcement and a paramedic.

Jack picked up his own phone and hit the button to redial Coughlin's missed call.

"What are you doing?"

"I'm calling my attorney."

"Why?"

"Because I don't trust you."

Coughlin picked up on the second ring, and Jack told him Danzig was here, contrary to their understanding with the FBI, and to get over to the winery immediately. Best to let the lawyer's blood get to a solid boil on the way over.

They could hear the sirens approaching in the distance.

"Are you listening to me?" Danzig said, and Jack was suddenly aware that she'd been talking. His mind was on what he was going to say when Hugh walked through the door—the sheriffs as well.

"No," Jack admitted. Jack shot her a sideways look. "Shouldn't you be conserving your strength? You just got shot."

"I'm aware. Asshole." Danzig grimaced as a bolt of pain crashed over her face, contorting the lines into awkward angles. She held a bar cloth against the bullet wound. "I just told you I'm going to catch you someday."

"Not a Cabernet fan?"

Danzig closed her eyes and sighed heavily. "Your friend, Scott Donners? He's good, but he hasn't covered all of his tracks. Not as well as he thinks he has, at least. It's a matter of time. When I get him, I'll have you."

"Scott Donners?" Jack asked, suddenly uneasy. "What the hell are you talking about? I don't know anyone by that name."

"Robert Scott Donners?" Danzig said again. "Oh, that's right," she said with a knowing, haughty tone. "I forgot. He goes by Rusty now."

30

Danzig didn't travel back to New York. She was summoned as soon as she was healthy enough to fly.

Immediately. And in no uncertain terms.

Showing up at Burdette's winery turned out to be ill-advised in the Bureau's eyes. Even though she'd saved his life and also connected him with one of the Pink Panthers, she'd still been ordered to cease and desist by a Special Agent in Charge and promptly disobeyed it. That situation promptly turned into a clusterfuck of its own. Lattimore already had his hands full with CHP and the strain this operation had put on that relationship. He now had a fatal use of force incident in his jurisdiction by an agent that didn't belong to him and the Sonoma County Sheriff was involved.

She'd gotten into a good bit of trouble for going to Fischer's place to begin with, but what really sent Lattimore over the edge was the fingerprints. Danzig had Fischer taken to the Sonoma County Sheriff's Department while the paramedics were working on her gunshot wound and had him fingerprinted in order to run a reference check in the National Criminal Information Database. When she entered his name and prints, she attached "Gentleman Jack Burdette" as a known alias. The database came back negative, but he was in there now and she took some slight consolation in that.

The fallout was righteous and severe and fast.

The Bureau could move quickly when it wanted to.

It was bad enough that a special agent had pushed a search warrant on what was not being termed as "spurious and circumstantial evidence," which resulted in damage to a civilian's home, but for that same special agent to then harass the citizen at his place of business after she'd been ordered to stand down was beyond the standards for professional conduct. The blowback against the Bureau for hounding Frank Fischer was already mounting, and it was clear to Danzig that Lattimore was throwing her to the wolves to protect the Bureau, his office, and himself.

Lattimore called Darren Givens, her supervisor and boss of the Gem and Jewelry Program, and said she was now harassing a legitimate businessman and prominent member of the Sonoma community. He said Givens needed to get her the hell out of Lattimore's jurisdiction before he took it any farther up the chain. He said Danzig was lucky to have her career after the last few days. Danzig knew that what she'd done had risked Lattimore's career and what he was out for was blood, her blood.

Givens said as much when she got back to New York.

Not that it much mattered.

Givens told her that he agreed with some of what Lattimore said. She'd absolutely exceeded her authority there, and without Ozren Stolar to identify Burdette, Givens didn't think they had enough to pursue Burdette. Right now. "Your initial instinct was right," he said. "If you'd just have goddamn *waited*, we could get LeGrande once he was in prison—just like you said. We're not beat cops, Kate, we don't make busts in a couple days."

Danzig hated the diminutive form of her name and never used it. Now was not the time to call attention to it, however.

"I think this Fischer guy is probably Burdette, but we can't touch him now. Not until he steals something else." Darren paused and looked across his desk at her for a long, quiet time. "Unfortunately, that will be our problem from now on."

"What do you mean, 'our'?"

"You're getting reassigned."

"I'm what? You can't be serious," Danzig said, exasperated. She was so at a loss for words she couldn't think of anything but asking if Darren was serious, which of course, he would be. It had to be Lattimore. Jesus Christ, that guy cast a long, vindictive shadow.

"I am serious, and you know better than to ask that," Darren said. "I don't know where yet, the Bureau doesn't move that fast, but you're off the task force immediately. And you're done in Gem and Jewelry." Darren shrugged and held up his hands, as if to show her the invisible shackles of bureaucratic efficiency that so completely tied them, there was just nothing he could do.

The formal use of force review hadn't begun yet, but she had some initial interviews with an agent assigned to that task in San Francisco. The initial determination was that if it wasn't for her, Frank Fischer would have been murdered. Kurt told her that was probably the only reason she still had her badge. She'd spend the next few days tied up with the use of force review, and when that was done, Darren explained, there would be some administrative leave. After that, she'd be given some bullshit job until her transfer was processed.

Kurt Sinclair called her that night.

"I heard they took you off Gem and Jewelry. I'm sorry for that."

"I could give a shit about the program. I'm pissed that they took me off the task force. There isn't anyone else that knows Burdette like—"

"Katrina, I'm saying this as a friend. You really need to learn when to keep your mouth shut."

Danzig was quiet for a long time after that.

They awkwardly listened to each other breathe for a bit.

"Kurt, I'm sorry if you were caught in the blast radius here. I hope you know that I was just trying to do my job. I really think this is the guy."

"It's fine," he said somberly.

But it wasn't. A few weeks later, about the time that she learned about her new assignment, she learned that Kurt Sinclair paid the price for vouching for her, for giving her operational control of the case. Had they been successful, Lattimore would have praised Kurt for his decisive thinking in bringing in a subject matter expert to lead the hunt for one of the world's most elusive thieves. But they weren't, and Kurt paid the price. Most likely, his career was capped. He could get another assignment if he wanted it, but it would be at best a lateral move.

It wasn't enough that she'd just sidelined her own career, she'd cost her mentor his as well.

Cases fell apart all the time. That wasn't the issue. The cardinal sin of the FBI was fucking up in public and bringing discredit upon the Bureau. You do that, and hell hath no fury...

31

Jack arrived in Italy in late October. He was traveling under the Frank Fischer name but also had an American passport and driver's license under the name Edward Ryan. Edward Ryan was a businessman, international real estate development, and had a corporate card registered to a company called Global Development Services, Ltd. Edward Ryan had expensive tastes and hired a midnight blue Ferrari 458 Spider from a luxury car rental that catered to the world's traveling elite. He drove to Tuscany wearing a gray suit and blue-and-white check shirt.

He'd purchased two international first-class tickets and waited in Rome for a few days before admitting to himself that only one of them would be used.

Megan had returned to the winery for harvest in September and crush the following month, but her presence there was tense and all business. She didn't want time alone with Jack and didn't want to talk to him about what happened between them. Jack thought that it was Milan Radić that sealed it for him. Though he didn't tell her what he'd done in that tense conversation on his deck, Megan knew he was hiding something and suspected it was criminal. An FBI agent shooting and killing a known criminal in the tasting room confirmed that. Megan confronted him about the incident, and it was their one and only conversation on the subject.

She wanted to know who this guy was and why he was at the winery. Jack told her that Milan Radić was part of a network of thieves operating in Europe called the Pink Panthers. They were mostly soldiers from the former Yugoslavian countries, and now they stole jewels.

"What'd he want with you," Megan asked in a way that said she didn't want to hear the answer any more than Jack wanted to say it. If it went unsaid, that thing always had a chance, however small, of not being true.

"He thought I had something he wanted. A very wealthy man paid me a lot of money to steal some very valuable things because he knew people like Milan Radić were going to come for them. He wanted the world to think they were stolen."

"Why not just go to the police?" she asked.

"You have to realize that a lot of people in the world don't trust the police. But this man, this businessman, he wasn't a citizen of the country where his things would be stolen and didn't think that those authorities, the French, were very good."

"So he hired you to take them before anyone else could get them?"

"That's right."

"Is that why you're always traveling? Because you're stealing things?"

"I'd say about three quarters of the time. Sometimes I legitimately am talking with other winemakers. I'm trying to learn this, trying to be better at it. I know I have a lot to learn. I'm trying to get away from doing the other thing."

"From being a thief," Megan said again.

"If it wasn't for this thing, Kingfisher would have gone under. The money this businessman paid me to...to protect his property is what kept us afloat after Paul." And probably still would after it, Jack knew. The State of California assured Frank Fischer that they were doing everything they could to recover that money and that Paul Sharpe would be prosecuted to the fullest extent of the law (the State's Attorney particularly emphasized that phrase), but they said they needed to prepare Fischer for the reality that they would likely not recover very much of the money Sharpe stole.

If Jack hadn't done the Carlton job, Kingfisher would have been wiped out. But Megan didn't see it that way. She saw only that if he hadn't done that thing, whatever it was (though Jack suspected she'd been able to put it together), Milan Radić wouldn't have shown up at the winery and tried to kill him. What would happen next time when there wasn't an FBI agent present?

Jack being a thief was a proxy, he knew, for Jack having lied about who he was. Megan told him as much. Jack knew he shouldn't have lost his temper, and it was one of the few times he had, but the logic was so infuriating he couldn't help himself. Should he have told her on their first date that he was a thief, that he changed his name so the Chicago mob wouldn't hurt his family? At what point would it have made sense to tell her, other than the exact moment he did?

Megan said she didn't know the answer to that question, and Jack knew there wasn't one. But she'd made up her mind, and that was that.

Megan stayed through harvest because she loved the winery, loved the people there, and Jack secretly believed that she was trying to find a way, in her mind, to make it work. She announced to the team that she was leaving shortly after crush, which was when they juiced the harvested grapes and began the fermentation process. She said she needed to take some time off and think about what she wanted to do next. Everybody at the winery knew about their relationship even though Jack and Megan had tried to keep it a secret. They assumed there was a kind of falling-out and that's why she was leaving.

Jack was forced to admit to Hugh much of what he'd said to Megan. Hugh was Frank Fischer's mentor in the business, his guide and his very good friend. As Jack was now forced to admit to himself that there was no such thing as separate lives, he told Hugh. The old lawyer's reaction was very different than Megan's had been.

Hugh laughed and said only that he'd been doing land deals in wine country for thirty years and it wouldn't surprise him if they found out Hugh's past was more checkered than Jack's. He agreed to keep Jack's identity a secret and understood his need to hide. He did say that Jack needed to decide who and what he wanted to be. Hugh wouldn't cover for him and wouldn't lie for him, wouldn't help him be a thief. Jack said he understood. What Jack didn't say then was that he was very nearly broke after having used everything he made from the Carlton job to save the winery. If he hadn't needed to pay Enzo and Rusty to help him get away with it, Jack would have walked away with a lot of money, but that's not the way the cards broke. Jack promised Hugh he'd never ask the lawyer to cover for him, but Jack stopped short of saying he was done being a thief.

Jack and Hugh kept the details of Milan Radić and the shooting from Kingfisher's employees, saying only that Frank was helping the FBI with an investigation and that it was related to Paul Sharpe's embezzlement. Sonoma was a pretty small community, however, and word quickly spread that a man had been shot and killed.

Reginald and Sharpe were both in custody awaiting trial. Sharpe's was an archetypal embezzlement case, with some felony arson for good measure (which he and his attorney still emphatically denied), and there wasn't much fear he was going to get off. Reginald's was the more complicated. There was the matter of his being an informant to the California Highway Patrol for nearly a decade. The cases he helped them close and the criminals he served up would be offset somewhat by the fact that he was giving them the competition and still running crews on the side. The passport fraud and the money laundering were federal, and that's what Jack was worried about. This, as much as genuine friendship, was the reason Jack came forward to Hugh about being a thief.

They hired a legal team under the guise that they expected this LeGrande fellow, a career criminal, to make wild accusations about Frank Fischer, a legitimate businessman, in order to save himself during his trial. Once Jack told Hugh his story, the lawyer very much understood Jack's desire to keep his identity a secret. This would be difficult to navigate, and their strategy relied on Frank Fischer never taking the stand to be asked by Reginald's defense attorney if he was actually Jack Burdette. However, Hugh knew from conversations with the US Attorney and the subsequent internal fallout from Special Agent Danzig's actions that the government was (ironically) trying to protect Mr. Frank Fischer. Normally, a case like this would garner a lot of attention, but the government was trying hard to keep it quiet.

While one might expect that a high-profile criminal defense attorney would jump at the chance to represent a client like Reginald LeGrande in a trial like this for the publicity alone, he actually had a hard time retaining what one might consider quality representation. First, there was the matter of payment. The government seized all of his assets, and he obviously wouldn't be getting the insurance money for the house that burned down since it was purchased illegally and while he was on parole (there was a separate insurance fraud investigation underway now). No one much wanted to touch him. Hugh assured Jack that any attempt Reginald made to out him at the trial would be futile.

There was always the possibility that Reginald would disclose Jack's identity somehow, during the trial, before or after. There was no way to truly prevent it. Jack could only put steps in place to stack the probabilities in his favor and minimize the fallout if it happened. It would have been easier to kill him, but even after everything Reginald had done, Jack didn't think he could take a life.

Not even one as worthless as Reginald LeGrande's.

So, it seemed that Frank Fischer was, for a time anyway, safe. Jack thought it was damned fine time to get out of town for a while.

Jack took a few casual steps forward, gravel crunching under his feet and kicking up little clouds of yellow dust around his loafers. A warm Tuscan sun beat down on him, illuminating the valley he looked across with a shade of yellow-gold that only existed here. Jack fell in love with Italy during his time in Turin, in those heady days when he and Enzo worked tirelessly, job upon job, to perfect their craft. Since then, Italy had always been special to him.

Jack's eyes tracked across the valley to an estate atop the ridge on the other side, surrounded by cypress trees and a beautiful vineyard that rolled up and over the hill. It looked like heaven. "That," said the woman who stood slightly behind him, "is one of the oldest vineyards in the Chianti region. Villa Cafaggio."

"Good neighbors," was all Jack said, but he knew exactly who they were. He'd had their wine. In fact, that was one of the reasons this property was so enticing to him, though he chose to play up his ignorance to his *agente immobiliare* knowing what she probably thought of bon vivant Americans. He turned to face the woman. She was in her mid-thirties, tall, and looked like a model. She wore a white blouse and red skirt that was just professional enough and hid her eyes behind large, round sunglasses. Her English was excellent, and she had a slight British accent. Jack assumed she was the one her firm sent to negotiate with the rich foreigners buying property here. She cradled a leather portfolio in one of her arms as one would a baby.

"Well, Mr. Ryan, what do you think?" The property she'd shown him was incredible and exactly what he was looking for. The villa itself was in a state of disrepair and would need major remodeling, but it had enormous potential. The vineyard itself was equally in a state of disrepair and would need several years of solid care, luck, and grueling work before it would yield sellable fruit.

Maybe that was what he needed.

Jack wouldn't make this his home, certainly. He loved Kingfisher and that was his place, but maybe a little side project was what he needed to put some space between himself and what had happened. Between himself and Reginald, himself and Sharpe, himself and Special Agent Danzig. Danzig might not have been able to arrest him, but Jack Burdette was finally in the system now. Jack's fingerprints and his picture were now in a federal database, and the name "Jack Burdette" was listed as a known alias of "Frank Fischer."

No one really got the story right, just that someone tried to extort Frank Fischer and it ended badly because Frank was friends with an FBI agent who just happened to be there. As Jack had told Danzig that day, people wanted a piece of something that was just a little south of shady to make them feel dangerous, and these words proved prophetic. Business at the winery surged after the shooting, particularly when it was clear that the owner, who was well known and better liked, wasn't implicated in anything. A little notoriety is exceptional marketing.

"I think it's perfect," Jack said, turning his head slightly to look at the neglected villa that would soon be his new home. At least for the time being. He couldn't stay here long, a few weeks maybe. He needed to get back to Kingfisher and oversee the hiring of a new winemaker. Hugh knew some people that could step in to help, but Jack learned the hard way that this was a partnership that relied on personal chemistry as much as actual chemistry and whomever he hired had much to live up to.

"Wonderful," she said, her voice lilting in a way that he knew was expertly practiced. Tradecraft was tradecraft, Jack mused. "Shall we discuss the terms?"

The global real estate market was still down from the economic collapse five years prior, and Jack was getting this place at an absolute steal. *Maybe use a different phrase when talking about it*, he told himself. Between the purchase and what it would take to revitalize this place, the rest of his Carlton money would be drained, but Jack thought that was okay. He'd hire a local vineyard manager to tend the grapes for him, and it would be a few years before these could be pressed. If he got usable fruit, Jack might make a few cases for himself, or he could always just sell the harvest to another winery. It'd be a while before he even knew what he had.

Jack came upon the idea for buying this place as a kind of

fresh start for him and Megan. Before he left, Jack told her what he was doing. He said maybe that's what they needed. Honestly, he hadn't expected her to show at the airport, nor in Rome for the few days he waited. His heart was still heavy when she didn't. But it was an open-ended ticket, and maybe she'd take him up on the offer.

"Of course," he responded, and she led him back up the gravel path to the villa.

They were halfway to the old house when the agent paused and turned, regarding the vineyard on the property. "When we met yesterday, Mr. Ryan, you said that you were retiring here."

"That's right," Jack said, unsure of where exactly she was going with this.

"It's no business of mine, of course, but I am curious. Why a vineyard?"

Jack placed his hands inside the pockets of his gray pants and turned back to the valley, showing the agent his profile. "I don't know. I've spent my entire life working for someone else. I thought it would be nice to work for myself for a change, and I love wine."

"So you intend to make wine, then?"

"Well, we'll see. I need to figure out what shape those grapes are in first. Why do you ask?"

"It's just that many Americans such as yourself come over here with this romantic notion of making wine but don't know the first thing about it. The Tuscan hills are dotted with empty villas purchased by businessmen who've let their vines go to hell. That's what happened here." She extended a slender arm toward the rows of distended vines. "It would be a shame if it continued."

"Oh, I agree," he said seriously.

"So, tell me, Mr. Ryan, do you know anything about

making wine?"

Jack considered the real estate agent for a time. Then a sly smile broke his lips. Jack pulled the phone out of his pocket and dialed.

"No," he answered, "but I know someone who does."

AUTHOR'S NOTE

A Legitimate Businessman is based on an actual theft that took place at the Carlton InterContinental Hotel in Cannes on July 28th, 2013. I have attempted to replicate the details of the actual crime as closely as possible in the book. The escape of suspected members of the "Pink Panther" gang from the prison in Orbe, Switzerland, just days prior to the heist also occurred, though I condensed the timing to better fit the story.

As of this writing, the Carlton heist remains unsolved.

THE SCHOOL OF TURIN
Gentleman Jack Burdette #2

He's playing a dangerous game, living two lives. But he only has one to lose...

Jack Burdette wants a normal life but cannot give up his criminal past. Though he works to build a legit business as a wine-maker, the infamous jewel thief can't resist the thrill of a heist.

But when his latest job goes sour, he has no choice but to make a devil's bargain to avoid arrest.

Under the thumb of a Serbian gangster, Jack is forced to commit a series of high stakes crimes he wants no part of. With the authorities closing in and an old friend pushing him to settle a long-forgotten score, he fears this caper could well be his last.

Can Jack bottle up his past and still escape with his skin?

JOIN THE READER LIST

Never miss a new release!

Sign up to receive exclusive updates from author Dale M. Nelson.

SevernRiverPublishing.com/Dale-M-Nelson

As a thank you for signing up, you'll receive a free copy of *The Robber*, a Gentleman Jack Burdette short story.

YOU MIGHT ALSO ENJOY...

The Gentleman Jack Burdette Series

A Legitimate Businessman

The School of Turin

Once a Thief

Proper Villains

The Bad Shepherd

Never miss a new release!

Sign up to receive exclusive updates from author Dale M. Nelson.

SevernRiverPublishing.com/Dale-M-Nelson

As a thank you for signing up, you'll receive a free copy of *The Robber,*
a Gentleman Jack Burdette short story.

ACKNOWLEDGMENTS

This book is dedicated to my parents, Maynard and Noreen Nelson. Thank you for always encouraging me to write from the time I could pick up a pen, to find my voice and to never give up. I love you both and am very grateful I got to be your son. Thank you, too, for introducing me to the family hobby, wine. Cheers.

Special thanks to Jonjie Lockman for your expert knowledge of the wine industry, the Napa and Sonoma regions and, most importantly, the financial aspects of the business. Your suggestions were invaluable. Any factual errors are mine.

ABOUT THE AUTHOR

Dale M. Nelson grew up outside of Tampa, Florida. He graduated from the University of Florida's College of Journalism
and Communications and went on to serve as an officer in the
United States Air Force. Following his military service, Dale
worked in the defense, technology and telecommunications
sectors before starting his writing career. He currently lives in
Washington D.C. with his wife and daughters.

For more on Dale Nelson's writing, visit him on the web at
severnriverpublishing.com/dale-m-nelson/

Made in the USA
Las Vegas, NV
12 February 2022

43798294R00215